DEVILS WITH WINGS

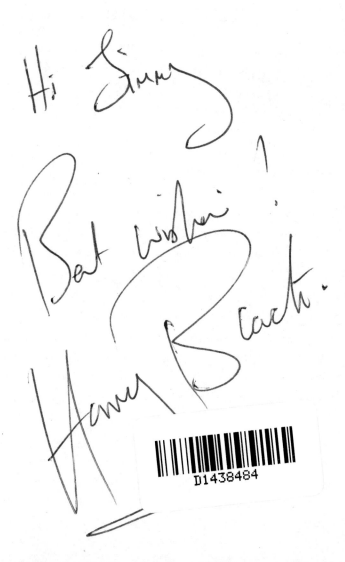

Hi Jimmy

Best wishes !

Harry Beach.

Praise for Harvey Black

"I loved it, I read this great book from cover to cover and whole-heartedly recommend this book. A great debut book, a talented author." – D G Torrens

"Harvey Black is on to a winner here. A well researched first book with a gradual build up of confidence in the prose which bodes well for the future." – Paul C

"The story is well paced and very well researched. The authors own military background comes though in his writing." – Nick Britten

"An excellent first book, full of historical facts and clearly written by someone who has a passion and deep knowledge for his subject. An author to watch out for in my opinion." – Melanie Tollis

"The amazing writing ability of Harvey would be missed, the atmosphere, the daring the drama, all are brought out on a tale well woven and well paced and so well written." – Parmenion Books

Amazon book reviews

A qualified parachutist, Harvey Black served with British Army Intelligence for over ten years. His experience ranges from covert surveillance in Northern Ireland to operating in Communist East Berlin during the Cold War where he feared for his life after being dragged from his car by KGB soldiers. Since then he has lived a more sedate life in the private sector as a director for an international company and now enjoys the pleasures of writing. Harvey is married with four children. For more from Harvey, visit his website at www.harveyblackauthor.com. For more about the *Devils with Wings* series, photos and maps visit www.harveyblackauthor.org.

Also by Harvey Black:

Devils with Wings Book 2
Silk Drop
The airborne invasion of Crete

Devils with Wings Book 3
Frozen Sun

HARVEY BLACK
BLACK
DEVILS
WITH WINGS

SilverWood

Published in 2012 by SilverWood Books
30 Queen Charlotte Street, Bristol, BS1 4HJ
www.silverwoodbooks.co.uk

Copyright © Harvey Black 2012
Cover image © Bundesarchiv, Bild 101I-569-1579-14A/Photo: Dr Stocker

ISBN 978-1-78132-068-6
Also available as an ebook

British Library Cataloguing in Publication Data
A CIP catalogue record for this book is available from the British Library

Set in Bembo by SilverWood Books
Printed in the UK by The Short Run Press
on paper certified as being from responsible sources

To my wife Melanie, for her patience

Chapter One

The Oberleutnant signalled for the two MG 34, general-purpose machine guns to be set up on the right flank on hill 172. The grassy hilltop, four kilometres to the east of the village Wola-Gulowska, north-east of the city of Pulawy, in Poland, overlooked the deciduous woods below where the rest of the First Battalion, the First Fallschirmjager Regiment was moving into position. Its task: to flush out and assault a Polish artillery regiment that was believed to be positioned in and around the woods.

The hilltop provided an ideal vantage point with good fields of fire. The Oberleutnant, from second company, the First Battalion, had also set up two additional troops of Fallschirmjager on the left flank to provide supplementary cover for the companies that would assault the woods below.

Although he was yet to see combat, his four years serving in the German army prior to joining the Fallschirmjager had given Oberleutnant Bier the confidence he needed to complete his task. And, more importantly, he had the confidence of his men. The twenty-five year-old officer, tall and dark-haired, favouring the Fuhrer's hairstyle and moustache that many emulated, appraised the cover available to him and his men. There wasn't a great deal of cover. The short carpet of grass and few shrubs were not sufficient for Bier and his men to lose themselves in, and the few boulders that were scattered along the stretch ahead were too conspicuous, not to mention lethal.

The Third Battalion had recently lost a paratrooper, not from direct fire, but from flying particles of rock fragmented from boulders such as these, executed by an exploding grenade. Bier lingered on the memory of the injury the soldier had succumbed to: a deep open gash on the neck. He would ensure that the lesson had been learnt and the same fate would not befall his platoon. Because of this lack of cover and the additional risk of being silhouetted against the backdrop of the sky behind them, Oberleutnant Bier had ordered the men to dig shell scrapes, those shallow depressions that would provide them with some cover. They couldn't dig any deeper, as only less than a metre below the surface it was pure rock. Although he had told the paratroopers to dig the shell scrapes, it had not been necessary. These were Fallschirmjager, paratroopers from the elite 7th Flieger Division, 'The Green Devils'.

It was ten in the morning, on the 24th of September 1939 and, as part of the continuing subjugation of Poland, a battalion, overlooked by the hill, was due to start its assault on the woods below. They would enter the woods from three sides, the Oberleutnant's platoon providing them cover from the hilltop.

As the Oberleutnant moved forward to check the positions of his troops, ensuring they had interlocking fields of fire and knew the entry point for each element of the battalion assaulting the woods, his Feldwebel, who seemed agitated, approached him.

"Sir, look, over there!"

Feldwebel Manke was pointing at what appeared to be a Polish soldier walking towards them.

The Oberleutnant looked up to see a Polish soldier, sporting a brown 'rogatywka' field cap. With a brown officer's field jacket, tight breeches and shiny black boots with spurs, everything about his appearance suggested he was a Polish officer, and a cavalry officer at that. In addition, he carried a dark brown field bag and leather pistol holster, further supporting the premise that he was an officer. His behaviour appeared most odd. He continued to walk up the slope of the hill but seemed fidgety and kept looking behind him.

"Feldwebel, bring him over here," commanded the Oberleutnant.

Manke grabbed hold of two troopers, ordering them to secure the Polish officer and bring him to the Oberleutnant at the double.

The two soldiers picked up their weapons and ran towards the approaching man. He continued to walk towards the German position, paying little attention to the two German paratroopers. Just before they were able to get a hold of him, the Polish officer suddenly started punching his right arm up and down in the air, looking back over his shoulder.

Feldwebel Manke looked at his officer. "I don't like the look of this, sir. What's he up to?"

Before Oberleutnant Bier could respond, the first rounds came in from the north-east, one hitting the shoulder of one of the troopers who had gone to secure the Polish officer. The second trooper was hit twice in the leg, the shock clearly on his face as he went down, his legs lifeless and unresponding. He wasn't even able to feel the blood radiating from the entry point of the bullet, blooming like a darkened rose, soaking his combat trousers. His last thoughts were of his fiancée as the light seemed to fade and all that was left was darkness.

The Polish soldiers had been lying in a dip, unseen, about two hundred metres below the crest and had been well hidden. They must have been on their way up to secure the hilltop, to cover their assembling troops below, when the German paratroopers had beaten them to it coming up the other side.

"Gun group, give covering fire," shouted Oberleutnant Bier.

"Where's the enemy?" screamed Feldwebel Manke.

The Troop Commander on the far right called out, "Two hundred metres, lone boulder, LMG!"

"Number one and two gun group, target that LMG!" ordered Bier. "Get their bloody heads down!"

The MG 34s opened up immediately, a swathe of shots finding its way to the advancing Polish soldiers. Both Bier and Manke threw themselves to the ground before they too became a target for the Polish gunners.

The Polish officer could no longer be seen; he had obviously retired quickly once the firing started. His role as a distraction for the German soldiers had been successful. While they had been focusing their attention on this single soldier, the Polish unit had been getting into position to assault the hilltop.

The two gun groups were now returning heavy fire on the enemy soldiers. Both rifle troops, although being on the left flank where it was difficult for them to clearly see a target or the enemy, also returned fire. Although the rifle troops' fire may have been ineffective, it added to the clamour of sound, hopefully disrupting the Polish advance. But the Polish troops had the upper hand; as their patrol had ambushed the paratroopers and taken them completely by surprise, they were now the hunters. The paratroopers had been caught on the hop. The majority of the Fallschirmjager Division had not yet seen any action and their inexperience had been shown up today.

Two more troopers went down from the hail of bullets that the Polish attack force was still able to dispense, despite suppression fire from the Germans. These elite soldiers had been bounced by the supposed less experienced and less professional Polish army. Fire now started to come in from both flanks. It appeared there was more than one point of assault and the initial unit in front of the gun groups was not alone.

"Feldwebel, we need to pull back and try and counter-attack their flank," Bier shouted above the surging sound. "If we stay here, we'll be overrun. Stay with the gun groups and I'll pull one of the rifle troops out of line."

"Get going, sir, we'll hold here," yelled Manke above the tumultuous sound of the gunfire coming towards them and the additional noise of the paratroopers returning fire.

The Polish force, numbering some one hundred men, had split into two assault teams, outnumbering Bier's men by some three to one. They were currently skirmishing up the north face of the hill.

One Polish platoon, presently pinned down by the quick reaction of the two German gun groups throwing out twelve hundred rounds per minute between them, could not make any headway. But the second Polish platoon, numbering over sixty men, was trying to outflank the paratroopers' position by attacking the left flank where the two rifle troops were situated.

If he was to recover the situation, Bier had no option but to counter the Polish attack by getting around their flanks and attacking them from the side and from behind. If his men were forced to retreat, it would not only put them at a disadvantage, particularly as they would have to pull back down the reverse slope but, more importantly, they would be failing their comrades currently moving into assault positions down below. Should the Polish soldiers secure the hilltop, they would then be able to pour a devastating fusillade of fire down on the Fallschirmjager preparing to assault their Polish comrades below and also act as spotters to bring down a barrage of artillery fire.

Once Manke's two gun groups were returning effective fire and giving covering fire to Bier's men, Bier ordered one of the two remaining rifle troops to pull back.

"Feinberg, pull your troop back!" he bellowed. "Get them below the crest of the hill quickly!"

Bier's eyes were darting left and right, trying to absorb all that was happening and to counter with an expedient response. The troop pulled back in good order, but the men were nervously looking over their shoulders checking that the enemy was not in hot pursuit behind them. The remaining troop was holding its own, but for how long? thought Bier. Would he have time to outflank the enemy?

On the outside, he appeared calm and composed to his men but, on the inside, his stomach churned and his mind raced with inner doubt.

"Feinberg," called Bier to the Unteroffizier in charge of the rifle troop pulling back. He continued to rapidly make his way around the hill, talking to the Unteroffizier as they ran. "Once we can see the enemy," he said breathlessly, "I want you to take four men forward about five metres, hit the deck and keep the Poles busy. Keep their heads down! I'll take the remaining men around and behind them. Keep your eyes peeled for us though." Bier was shouting, trying to ensure everyone heard what he had just said. The last thing he wanted was his own men firing on him. His heart was pounding, throbbing in his ears, his mind racing, constantly questioning his actions. But he kept any doubts under control; he needed to keep it together, keep his troop together and get his platoon out of this with minimum casualties.

They continued to skirt round the hill. The firing from their comrades rattling on the hilltop, although still incessant, was diminishing in sound, and the resonance of the firing from the Polish soldiers assaulting the hill was increasing. The gun groups could hold their own for a while, but ammunition was not limitless and barrel changes would be needed soon.

But the rifle troop of twelve men would be under considerable pressure and, if the Poles were able to bring a light machine gun to bear down on them, they may well buckle. If the rifle troop gave way to their Polish attackers, the enemy would be able to roll up the rest of the platoon's flanks with relative ease.

"Sir," hissed a paratrooper directly at Bier's side. "There they are." He pointed to Polish soldiers advancing on the *kameraden* they had left behind on top of the hill.

"Right, Feinberg," he instructed, "take your men forward and give them hell. The rest of you with me."

"Right, sir, and good luck."

Feinberg took his men forward onto the right flank of the attacking Polish platoon, and Bier took the remaining eight paratroopers with him, moving slightly lower down the hill to continue around and come up behind the enemy. He heard Feinberg and his men open fire and, smiling, thought of the horror on the faces of the Polish platoon suddenly finding paratroopers firing at their flank. In a few seconds, they would get a second surprise as he and his men came at them from the rear. Suddenly they were there: the Polish troops right in front of them.

"Spread out in a line," hissed Bier to his men.

He prayed to God that Feinberg would see his *kameraden* approaching the enemy's tail end; otherwise it could all rebound on them and the advantage gained could very well turn into a catastrophe. Suddenly, there was a Polish korporal in front of him. The look of astonishment on the soldier's face and the look of shock in his eyes as he twisted round to look at his attacker said it all for Bier. They had caught the Polish completely by surprise.

They had believed themselves close to taking out the impudent paratroopers on the hill, and the last thing they expected were more paratroopers coming at them from the side and from behind. Their commander could not have been in combat before, or was not well trained; otherwise he would have sent part of his force to do exactly what Bier was doing now.

When the Erma machine pistol reverberated in Bier's hands, and the rounds exited the short, blue gunmetal barrel, the surprise on the soldier's face turned to complete terror as the bullets took the korporal in the side knocking him down. Bier stepped over the stricken soldier. He didn't stop to check whether or not he was dead; he didn't have time. He was now in the thick of it and had to concentrate on the other enemy soldiers appearing in front of him, track the position of his soldiers around him and keep alert for his men still firing down from the hilltop.

The paratroopers had the advantage and the Polish platoon was in chaos. Out of the eight paratroopers with Bier, two had machine pistols. Although rifles were effective at long-range, the machine pistols came into their own in close combat. They were proving to be murderous at this close range, scything through the Polish ranks less than ten paces away from them. The Polish panicked, falling back, confused at the events that were unfolding, trying to escape the onslaught that was being unleashed upon them.

"Keep pushing them back," screamed Bier to his men. "We mustn't lose the momentum."

Bier held back, letting his men continue to rout the Polish

troops. He sought out Feinberg, seeing him further up the hill to his right. He saw him stand up, look straight at him, then turn and call down to his men to cease fire. If Feinberg's men continued to fire at the retreating Polish troops, they would soon be in danger of hitting their own men. If they fired even further to the right, there was the prospect of them hitting the paratroopers manning the MG 34s.

Feinberg yelled to his men to remain in position while he ran to warn the rest of the platoon what was happening. Bier saw Feinberg running east and guessed he was going to warn the gun groups and the rifle troop of the current position of Bier's troop. Bier continued to move his men forward, mopping up the Polish soldiers. The Polish soldiers were completely demoralised. As if being attacked from three sides wasn't enough, to then collide with their other platoon, the one assaulting the German machine gun position, it just got worse. Both platoons wrere now exposed to Bier's men on their flank and there was chaos caused by the retreating soldiers crashing into their ranks. Crippling fire from the MG 34s, was just too much. This was the last straw, and the remnants of the two Polish platoons, in complete disarray and pursued by the firepower of the German MG 34s, retreated down the hill they had earlier advanced up in confidence.

"Cease fire! Cease fire!" Bier shouted.

There was too much confusion now and the current victory could quickly turn into a tragedy if a paratrooper was killed by one of his own men. The firing ceased and there was a sudden unmistakable silence, apart from a ringing in the ears as a result of the close combat conditions. The smell of cordite was almost tangible; it invaded the nostrils and left a bitter taste in the mouth.

Bier looked about him; Polish soldiers were lying scattered around, many dead and even more wounded. What must have been seen as a certain victory to the Polish force was now a defeat of the worst kind. Looking higher up the hill, his gaze met with Feldwebel Manke, the shocked look on Manke's face reflecting how Bier himself felt about the carnage that lay before them. Bier dreaded to think what the casualty count was on both sides, but was even more concerned for his own men. Had this attack not been repulsed, had he not acted quickly and counter-attacked the Polish unit before they gained a real advantage then it could have been he and his men retreating, he and his men lying scattered around dead and wounded, and he would have failed his comrades below.

Bier instructed the troop under his command to check the Polish dead and wounded, and went immediately to seek out Feldwebel Manke. It was over, they had won. They had held their position and were still able to provide cover for the operation being conducted below, but it wasn't without cost. At least three paratroopers were dead and eight wounded; some of the wounded would not make it through the night. Had the Polish troops got to the hilltop sooner, prior to the paratroopers, then the entire operation would have been in jeopardy. It was a close call, but they had triumphed.

Feldwebel Manke reported to Oberleutnant Bier that the wounded were being treated and the platoon had rearmed and were in position to again provide cover for the units below. Just as he had finished, they heard gunfire from the east of the woods. The action below had clearly started.

Chapter Two

The German Polish attack plan was 'Fall Weiss', where two army groups, North and South, would conduct a pincer movement cutting western Poland off at a point east of Warsaw.

The Treaty of Versailles had created Poland, in order that areas that had once belonged to the losers, specifically Germany, Russia, Austria and Hungary, could be reunited. France and Britain had an expectation to form a strong Allied country on the eastern borders of Germany, in effect exposing Germany to two fronts. Previously this had proven to be Germany's Achilles' heel.

Poland felt herself to be a strong country in her own right. With an army of over a million men, supported by over four hundred aircraft, eight hundred tanks and four thousand artillery pieces, Poland was a force to be reckoned with andwith Britain's and France's vow to come to her aid in the event of war, Poland even felt unconquerable.

Hitler, though, wanted the old Provinces of Silesia and Poznan back, along with the establishment of a corridor to Danzig. Britain and France did nothing to assist the Poles, although they could have attacked Germany from the west while the main German army was tied up fighting the war against Poland, but it failed to do so. Although militarily stronger than the German army, neither France nor Britain relished an all-out war with Germany.

At precisely 4.45am, on the 1st of September 1939, German tanks thundered across the Polish border. Less than four hours later, Britain and France presented Hitler with a final demand to withdraw from Poland without delay or they would declare themselves at war with Germany. Sixteen days after the initial invasion of Poland by Germany, on the seventeenth of September, the Soviet Union invaded Poland from the east, as per the non-aggression pact between Germany and the Soviet Union and the signing of the Molotov-Ribbentrop agreement. This secret protocol divided Northern and Eastern Europe into German and Soviet Spheres of Influence, part of that being the division of Poland between Germany and the Soviet Union.

Army Group South, led by Generaloberst Gerd Von Rundstedt attacked from Silesia and Monrovia and quickly swept all Polish opposition aside. On the sixth of September they took Krakow and were closing in on Warsaw. By the ninth, elements of Army Group South had reached the River Vistula, near the City of Pulawy. The Germans were making rapid progress and, three weeks later, the First Battalion of the First Fallschirmjager Regiment was about to cut its teeth on the Polish army.

Paul, Erich and Helmut, three officers with the Fallschirmjager, were delighted at the news that they were at war with Britain. Hotheaded young men that they were now, they would soon come to realise the full consequences of what Hitler had started. On the twenty-first, during another unexpected dry autumn day, their battalion was dispatched to secure Ulez airfield where a large Polish force was said to be heading. The three Platoon Commanders of the First Company, commanded by Oberleutnant Volkman, were standing around a Steiner Jeep contemplating what this latest deployment had in store for them.

"Another bloody hot, dry day," moaned Helmut to his fellow officers.

"I thought it was meant to be the wet season," added Erich.

"Stop complaining, the both of you," interrupted Paul. "If it was pissing down with rain and we were up to our backsides in mud, you'd be the first to wish for the heat again!"

"You're right as always." Erich laughed.

"And what is the forecast for next week then, mister weatherman?" added Helmut, punching him playfully on his arm.

Paul recognised that they were ganging up on him, as they often did, and turned it back on them.

"For you, Erich," he said, pointing at his friend, "just more dust. Come on, let's go."

They dug in around the airfield only to move again two days later. They moved north-east of the airfield, along the railway line, then east to the village of Urszulin. They were getting impatient for action and weary of the trudging around, trying to get to grips with the illusive enemy.

On the afternoon of the twenty-third, a German living in the local area presented himself to a German sentry, claiming he had important information on the whereabouts of the Polish army. Although the sentry had his doubts that this little man knew anything, he thought it best to take him to HQ, just in case. He was escorted to the battalion command post and put in front of the Battalion Commander Major Gruber, who, irritated by the continuing failure to get to grips with the enemy, was not best pleased to be interrupted by a local civilian.

The sentry escorting the civilian came stiffly to attention. "I beg to report, sir, this civilian claims to be German and that he has information as to the whereabouts of the enemy."

Before the Major could respond, the civilian blurted out, "There are Polish soldiers in the woods, Herr Major. I've seen them!"

The man was a balding, small individual with a nervous twitch. His naturally anxious disposition was exacerbated by the staring eyes of the Battalion Commander and his Adjutant, Hauptman Niemeyer.

"Where did you see them and how do you know they were Polish soldiers?" asked Gruber in a clipped voice, showing his obvious annoyance at being disturbed.

"I saw them in the woods next to the village of Wola-Gulowska," the civilian responded quickly, eager to please and change the oppressive atmosphere that he sensed in the tent.

Gruber turned to Niemeyer and pointed at the map. "This would place them about eight kilometres from here, north-east of Wola-Gulowska." He turned sharply towards the civilian. "What business had you in those woods, Herr?"

"Onken, sir, my name is Onken. I live in the village of Wola-Gulowska and was out walking my dogs in the wood when I heard horses." Onken wrung his hands constantly as if he was trying to wash something away.

"Horses, you say?" asked Gruber leaning forward, starting to take some interest in what this irritating little man was telling them.

"Yes, sir, and guns, big guns, artillery pieces," replied Onken. He was keen to maintain the positive two-way conversation.

"How many men and guns?" Gruber questioned him urgently now, recognising that the wait to get to grips with the enemy could perhaps be over.

"I only saw half a dozen guns. I didn't want to hang around. I wanted to get away as quickly as possible before I was seen." His eyes flicked from Gruber to Niemeyer and back, beads of sweat trickling down his face, looking for any doubts they may have about his story.

"How do you know that they were Polish soldiers?" challenged Niemeyer.

The civilian straightened up to his full five feet, three inches and, puffing out his chest, replied proudly, "I was in the army during the First World War." He hesitated before adding, "I was a cook." Then he snapped the heels of his tattered workboots together.

"How many did you see?"

"Hundreds, yes, hundreds." He spoke frantically, knowing that he'd left the woods so fast that he didn't really see how many there were.

"Jager, take our guest to the Feldgendarmerie and I will send someone to question him further."

"Yes, sir," responded the sentry, thinking about how he was going to retell the story when he went off-duty. He grabbed the civilian and pulled him to the opening of the tent, leading him out.

"Where are you taking me?" the civilian spluttered at the two German officers. "I've been very helpful to you. I'm a loyal German." Fear was obvious in his eyes. He had expected to pass on his information, be thanked, and even given a small reward for his services to the German army; not to be arrested.

The last the Battalion Commander and the Adjutant heard, as he was escorted forcefully out of the HQ, were his mutterings that he was a loyal German and a request for some sort of reward for his services.

Gruber moved to the six-foot table, the centrepiece of the battalion command tent. Sitting on its edge, he studied the map spread across the table. The numerous crease marks in this well used map sometimes made it difficult to read the detail. He beckoned Niemeyer over and pointed to the map, his finger circling the woods by Wola-Gulowska. "It will be a full battalion effort, two companies acting as blocking forces and one company flushing them out."

"Volkman's our man for that, sir."

The Commander looked up, a slight twinkle in his eyes. "He sometimes scares me more than the enemy." They both laughed.

The sentry, now back outside, was nonplussed by his senior officers' behaviour. He would never understand what made them tick.

Gruber turned to Niemeyer. "Get the company commanders together. If he's right, we could see some action for the battalion at last."

They both grinned conspiratorially. Although mature Luftwaffe officers, the excitement they felt at finally tracking down the enemy was palpable. Finally, the battalion was to get to see some action.

Erich ran up behind Paul, calling to him. "Paul, Paul, the alarm's gone off! We're to report to Volkman for a briefing at Company HQ."

"Any idea what it's about?" responded Paul as Erich came alongside him.

"I don't know what the flap is, but we've got to get our platoons ready to move out at one hour's notice."

"Packed rucksacks and make ready the weapons' containers," said Paul, quoting the Fallschirmjager mantra."Something at last, eh, Erich? Let's go and get the teams ready then."

"I saw Unterfeldwebel Grun and forewarned him. I told him I would get hold of you while he gets our platoons together. We'll meet him back at the lines."

"Well, what are we waiting for then? Let's go."

Leutnant Paul Otto Brand was a tall, athletic twenty-one year-old Fallschirmjager officer, Commander of the First Platoon of First Company, the First Battalion, the First Fallschirmjager Regiment, and proud of it.

He was born in Brandenburg an der Havel, a town in the state of Brandenburg, west of Berlin, located on the banks of the Havel, with a population of some eighty thousand people. After leaving school, his first job was working in an aircraft manufacturing company, Arado Flugzeugwerke, where, as an apprentice, he learnt the trade of aircraft building.

In 1937, he volunteered for service with the RAD, the Reichsarbeitsdienst, the Reich Labour Service, and spent nine months with an Arbeitsgruppen where he was encouraged to join the army. It was while serving in the army that his desire was born to serve in the Fallschirmtruppe, and he was subsequently sent to Fallschirmjager Regiment 1 in Stendal.

He had only been serving with the paratroopers for twelve months, but felt at home with this unit. The thought of finally experiencing action with this elite regiment was the last tick in the box. This was his first command and he was keen to do right by his country, right by his unit and right by his men.

Leutnant Erich Fleck, also twenty-one years old but two inches shorter than Paul's six foot two, commanded the second platoon of one company. He and Paul had gone through the intense paratrooper training together at Stendal-Borstal.

They came across the two paraded platoons, and Paul left Erich to go and join number one platoon and his Senior Non-Commissioned Officer, SNCO, Unterfeldwebel Max Grun.

Unterfeldwebel Max Grun, Platoon Sergeant for First Platoon, quickly came to attention on seeing his platoon commander approaching and saluted. "Platoon paraded and ready for inspection, sir."

Paul returned the Feldwebel's parade-ground salute.

"Thank you, Max. Stand them at ease and call the troop commanders over."

"Leeb, Kienitz and Fischer, front and centre now!" bellowed Max.

Max, the SNCO for the platoon, was the disciplinarian, the enforcer of military discipline for the unit. Although still a key position in the paratroopers, the role differed slightly in that in the Fallschirmjager: self-discipline was paramount. These were elite soldiers, proud of their regiment, proud that they were paratroopers: 'The Green Devils'.

Max, born on the 16th of May, 1911, a couple of years before the Great War, was the son of a docker in Hamburg. He himself had followed in his father's footsteps, leaving school at sixteen and going to work as a docker on the famous Hamburg docks. Midway through his twenty-second year, he lost interest in his father's profession, but he also had a hankering for something different, something more exciting, so he joined the German army. It was also said, although no one would actually say it straight to the tough docker's face, that there was a possible paternity suit in the offing; hence the desire for the army and foreign shores.

Max excelled in his newly chosen profession and quickly moved up through the ranks to become the Unterfeldwebel he was now. He had earned the respect of not only his subordinates but also his superiors. Always looking for a challenge, wanting to take ever greater risks, at the age of twenty-six he volunteered for the newly formed Fallschirmjager. He successfully completed his training at Stendal and was now happily the platoon Feldwebel for First Platoon.

If this was Paul's first command, then the heavily built, ex-Hamburg docker, with over five years' army service behind him, did not take advantage of it. In fact, they had a rapport from their very first meeting. When, at their first encounter, Max had pointed out that the Leutnant should take his lead and allow Max to run the platoon, Paul's response had been simple: "But who will lead you, Unterfeldwebel Grun, and keep you out of the Hamburg bars and brothels and out of trouble?"

The Leutnant had clearly read Max's personnel file and was aware of his escapades when last on leave. Members of the Heer, the Wehrmacht, had been taking the piss out of the Luftwaffe soldiers, not realising they were Fallschirmjager and, after Max's response, clearly wished they had left the Luftwaffe soldiers alone. Subsequently though, Max was arrested by the Hamburg police. Fortunately for him, one of the police officers knew him and knew he was a Fallschirmjager, and so he got off lightly. Max couldn't suppress a smile at the Leutnant's response. Leadership was established, a rapport had been fostered and the relationship between the stocky ex-docker and the tall athletic officer was sound. To Max, Paul was not like many of the other officers. There was strength but without arrogance; there was knowledge, but he was not afraid to ask his NCO's advice if he was unsure of something; and he was loyal to his men.

The three troop commanders, Unteroffiziers, gathered around their officer and senior NCO, pulling up canvas chairs at Paul's direction.

"Gentlemen," said Paul, "the Oberleutnant has called all senior officers for a briefing. I don't know what it concerns as yet, but we've been ordered to prepare our equipment for an operation. So, just go through the basics, make sure all of the men's equipment is present and functional."

"And check with the quartermaster," interjected Max. "See if they've been given any indications of ammunition and food requirements. It might give us advance warning of how long we'll be away."

"Are all the men fit and well?" questioned Paul.

They all nodded.

"Good, also make sure your men get their letters finished and lodged with the Feld Post. We don't want to think the worst, but we don't know how long we'll be away on operations."

"Make sure they stay in touch with their loved ones," added Max, smiling.

"Don't let me down. I'm looking to you to ensure that the men are ready." Paul looked at each one in turn. "We may need to move with as little as one hour's notice, so keep on your toes."

The Unteroffiziers shifted in their seats, looked at each other and at Paul and Max expectantly. They were picking up on the obvious suppressed excitement within their officer commanding. They were equally keen to see some action and prove themselves because many, like Paul, had not yet seen combat. In fact, Max was the only one to have seen any action, and that was in Czechoslovakia.

"Right, dismissed."

The Uffzs saluted and returned to their units to get them ready for the impending operation.

"Max, a quick word. I want you to check and double-check the platoon's readiness. I want them ready for any contingency. Once I know what's expected of us, we can finalise our equipment. Keep the troops on their toes and be ready to move out at a moment's notice."

"They will be," Max assured as he saluted.

Paul returned the salute and left them to it. He headed off to look for Erich and Helmut, his two fellow platoon commanders, leaving his troop commanders and Max to prepare for their upcoming operation. He had every confidence in them. He could see Erich — he too had just finished briefing his men — and made his way over to join him. They were camped at a large Polish farm about forty kilometres from the town of Pulawy, a town in Eastern Poland in the Lublin Province. The farm consisted of a number of large barns which First Company was using as its billet. Erich's platoon was paraded in front of one of those barns which was also their eating and sleeping quarters. Paul's and Helmut's platoons were similarly accommodated in a much larger barn, much to the farmer's displeasure, on the other side of the farm.

"Have you heard anything yet?" enquired Erich as he saw Paul approaching.

"No." Paul took advantage of the bale of straw and sat himself down. "I was hoping you might have picked something up."

"What do you think it's all about, Paul? Do you think it's another wild goose chase? We've been running around after these Poles for days now. They're like ghosts. My troopers are starting to get pissed off with it, but then so am I."

"You and me both," responded Paul. "Let's hope it's something real this time, eh?"

Before Erich could add something else, their fellow officer, Leutnant Janke, called to them. "Hey, you two, come on! We've been summoned by the Raven," relayed Helmut as he approached his two brother officers. "If we hurry, all will be revealed at last." He laughed.

The two officers joined in with his laughter, noticing that Helmut, ever the pessimist, was in good humour today.

"What's that you're eating?" enquired Erich.

. "I persuaded that miserable farmer to part with some Polish sausages, and he proceeded to pull out half a dozen kabanos wrapped up in what looked like a newspaper. I got you guys some as well." He held out the wrapper offering them the smoked sausages. "There's two each. I need the extra one because I'm a growing lad."

They grabbed two each, stuffing one in their tunic pocket and one in their mouth, while Helmut rewrapped his last two and put them away.

Mumbling through a mouthful of sausage, Erich reminded them, "We'd better get to Company HQ, or the Raven will be making sausage meat out of us."

Suddenly dawning on them that they had been called to an operational briefing, they hurried off.

Max looked across at the group of officers talking and laughing. All can't be too bad with the world, he thought, if Leutnant Brand and his fellow officers were in such high spirits. With a lighter heart, he returned to the kit inspection he was conducting. Not too light that he couldn't bollock one of the troopers if they had the audacity to present him with inadequate kit.

Paul, Erich and Helmut headed off to the briefing with their Company Commander, Oberleutnant Gunther 'The Raven' Volkman. They found the Oberleutnant ensconced by a Stower 40, a light cross-country vehicle, with his company sergeant Feldwebel Braun.

The Raven was looking at a map that had been displayed on

what looked very much like a school blackboard easel. It seemed quite pertinant; sometimes with the Oberleutnant you felt you were back at school.

"Paul, Erich, Helmut, pull up a seat. We finally have a task for the battalion," Volkman said sharply. He was smiling as he said it though and was almost jovial, which was very unusual for this tough company commander who often seemed to have little sense of humour. He was not known for his bedside manner, although he was a good soldier and a good officer, highly respected by his subordinates and his commanders. But he was not known for small talk.

Oberleutnant Gunther, the 'Raven' Volkman, was a true Prussian aristocrat, born in Fischausen, East Prussia, on the 15th of January, 1913. His dark hair, his deep-set, hooded dark eyes and prominent, almost Roman-like nose had quickly earned him the nickname 'The Raven'. Even the senior officers, out of Volkman's earshot, referred to him by his nickname. He had been a platoon commander during the occupation of the Sudeten and the later scuffles in Czechoslovakia where he had earned an Iron Cross Second Class, his combat badge and wound badge. He had quickly appreciated that the Fallschirmjager, the elite 7th Flieger Division, was destined for great things. He believed they would have an active role in any forthcoming military action that the German forces would be involved in and this would be the best route to recognition, promotion and the possibility of further medals.

Joining the rest of the company headquarters staff, they pulled up a canvas chair each and made themselves comfortable.

"Bachmeier!" shouted Volkman. "Coffee for these gentlemen. I assume you won't refuse a cup of coffee?"

They all nodded fiercely, none of them having had a chance to get a coffee before being called to their commander's briefing.

Volkman pointed to the map with his swagger stick, a throwback to his Prussian roots. He was very much the aristocrat. "Here," he pointed to a village on the map, "eight kilometres from the battalion's current position, we have reason to believe there are over five hundred Polish troops with horse-drawn artillery. We believe them to be around the wooded area here." He tapped the map. "Next to the village Wola-Gulowska, north-east of the town of Pulawy."

He paused while his orderly Bachmeier handed out coffees to the three platoon commanders and the company staff present, the company sergeant major and two clerical assistants.

Paul cupped the mug of coffee in his hands, savouring the warmth and the smell, waiting for it to cool further so he could also enjoy its taste.

"When you're ready, gentlemen," Volkman instructed impatiently. "The Second Company will assign a platoon on Hill 172, to the east of Wola-Gulowska, to cover the woods here. They will consist of two MG 34 sections and two rifle troops. The rest of Second Company will cover the woods to the south, a front of about two thousand yards. Third Company will cover the north and west, and we will cover the east. You'll be pleased to hear, Brand, that we will be using your platoon as our advanced patrol, supported by Second Platoon. Janke, your platoon will act as the company reserve."

Helmut looked at his colleagues, his disappointment obvious, their pleasure equally so.

"Your platoon, Brand, will form up here," Volkman continued, pointing to a position on the map east of some woods. "Second Platoon will be on your right flank, slightly back from your line. You are to advance in a shallow 'V' formation and will be the first unit to hit the treeline tomorrow. Leutnant Fleck, your platoon will give Brand a fifty-metre head start and, should they come into immediate contact with the enemy, you'll be in a position to either cover their retreat or hit the enemy on the flank. Everyone understand so far?"

They all nodded their assent.

Paul placed his coffee cup down on the dry earth beneath his seat, and stared intently at the map. "I have a question though, sir. When will the rest of the battalion make their move and, if we do come into contact, what are their orders?"

"Good question, Brand," responded Volkman, leaving the map and walking back to his canvas seat, indicating to his orderly to refill their cups with coffee. "Drink up, we never know when supplies may dry up, so we might as well make the most of it. To answer your question, Leutnant Brand, we are the beaters and the rest of the battalion are the hunters. They will remain in position just outside the edge of the wood line. So, when you do come into contact with the enemy, which you will, you must force them west. Whatever direction they take after that, the rest of the battalion will be waiting for them. If you don't make contact initially then move further into the woods and flush them out. Once the action starts, Brand, make all of the noise you can; make them think that there's a full battalion coming towards them. That goes for you too, Leutnant Fleck."

"What about my platoon?" chimed in Helmut, concerned that his men didn't have a role to play.

Volkman waited until Bachmeier had finished refreshing their cups from a fresh pot of coffee before he answered the obvious concerns of the platoon commander. He could sense that they were all keen to get a piece of the upcoming action. But the experienced Oberleutnant knew that, even though a good percentage of his force would be needed for face to face combat with the enemy, a well positioned and effective reserve could turn a possible defeat into a victory.

"Your platoon will be the company reserve. Your role is just as key to the success of the operation as the other two platoons. If we're taken by surprise, or the Poles decide to push back at Brand and go east, it will be your platoon that will plug the gaps and back up the rest of the company. Also, if any Polish troops filter back through one and two platoons' lines, it will be up to you to deal with them.

"We move out at eight tomorrow. There will be a final briefing at one today but, in the meantime, make sure you get your men prepared. That's all, gentlemen. Dismissed."

The platoon commanders returned to their respective platoons to brief their men and ensure they were prepared and ready for the next day's operation. Paul and Erich empathised with Helmut but both were glad that their particular platoons would be at the forefront of the advance and would likely be the first in action.

They chatted energetically together as they made their way back, discussing ideas and options for the task ahead tomorrow whilst slapping Helmut on the back in condolence.

Chapter Three

The 1pm briefing went ahead on the previous day as planned, and each platoon knew what their role was in the impending action. It was now 6am, on the 24th of September, and all three platoons were preparing to march out, as ordered, at eight o'clock.

Autumn was usually Poland's most popular season: refreshing, cooling weather after a hot, dry summer. Typically, during September and October, revitalising rains would saturate the dried countryside, turning the poor quality road network into a quagmire of thick, viscous mud, along with swollen and raging rivers. But, this year, the fall had remained dry so far, making it ideal for military-type operations, allowing tanks and other vehicles to move easily over the dry, dusty ground.

Paul had gathered his platoon together to give them their final briefing, a summary of the main one they'd had earlier. "Gather round," he directed.

The thirty men of his platoon gathered round in a semi-circle.

"We'll be moving out at eight. There will be one truck per troop."

"No Tante Ju, sir?" asked one of the troopers, Auntie June being the pet name for the Junkers-52 troop carrier they would normally parachute from.

"You'll have to get your feet dirty for a change, Petzel. Now button it!" retorted Max.

Although a sharp retort, it was said with some humour, causing the assembled troopers to relax slightly; Petzel receiving guffaws and pats on his back from his fellow paratroopers.

"We'll be taking the north-eastern road for about two kilometres," continued Paul, smiling at the camaraderie that he felt for these tough men he had the privilege to lead. "Swinging east to the village of Wola-Gulowska, through Konorzatka then north for two kilometres to be dropped off at our final drop zone." Although not parachuting in, Fallschirmjager terminology was always used.

All picked up on the suppressed excitement in their commander's voice and on his face. But Max knew that the rush behind Paul's eyes hid deep anxieties he felt about leading his men into battle for the first time, doing the right thing and ensuring his men survived.

Paul continued. "Unteroffizier Leeb, your troop will take the lead in the line of march. I want a good man on point. We don't want to get caught napping. We'll stay in line of march until we reach the drop zone. Once there, we'll form our usual 'V' formation for crossing open country."

"Yes, sir," acknowledged Leeb.

"Unteroffizier Kienitz, your troop will follow first troop."

"Understood, sir," replied Kienitz.

"Unteroffizier Fischer, your troop will be third in line and will be the platoon rearguard in line of march and the platoon reserve. I know you and your men will be disappointed but you must still keep alert and on your toes. We don't know how this is going to pan out and, if your troop is needed, you must be ready."

Fischer acknowledged the task set for him. "We'll be ready if called upon, sir."

"We'll leave the drop zone and your troop will break away once we get to the start point. I will give you your coordinates and your troop will move forward at the allotted time of nine thirty. You'll be on the platoon's left flank two hundred metres back. Should the platoon get into any difficulty and need to pull back, you will be in a position to cover our withdrawal or counter-attack the enemy's right flank. Are you clear on that, Fischer?"

"Yes, sir," answered Fischer, shoulders back and head held high at the potential importance of his troop's role.

"Should we get into deep shit, it will be your troop's responsibility to help get us out of it. Any questions?" Paul opened it up to the entire group.

"Is the estimate of enemy troops still the same, sir?" Max asked.

"Yes, about five hundred Polish troops."

"Do we know the quality of the troops we'll be up against, sir?" piped up Leeb, commander of one troop.

"We believe them to be artillery troops, so they're not front line infantry. But, there are still five hundred rifles out there. Any one of them has the capability to kill you. So, be confident, gentlemen, but not over confident.

"Unterfeldwebel, anything you want to add?"

"Just this, sir, remember the tenth commandment. Keep your eyes wide open. Tune yourself to the utmost pitch. Be nimble as a greyhound, tough as leather, hard as Krupp steel. You shall be the German warrior incarnate."

The troopers' pride was obvious in their faces; this was one of the Ten Commandments they had to learn during their training at Stendal. In their minds, it set them apart from all other soldiers. They were the elite.

"And finally," continued Max, "once in the woods, keep your troops' spacing tight, not too tight that they make a good target for a Polish grenade, but it will be easy for troopers to get separated if the woods become dense with masses of undergrowth. Understood?"

"Yes, Unterfeldwebel," responded the troop commanders.

"Understood?" repeated Max louder.

"Yes, Unterfeldwebel," roared the troop commanders at the tops of their voices.

Paul was just about to release the commanders to go to their respective troops when Oberleutnant Volkman joined them.

They all snapped to attention.

"At ease, gentlemen. Is your platoon ready, Leutnant Brand?"

"Yes, sir." Brand saluted. "They have been briefed and are ready for the job ahead, Herr Oberleutnant."

"I'm depending on you, Leutnant Brand. I don't want any fuck-ups. One Company is leading the entire battalion and One Company is being led by your platoon. Fleck will be on your right flank and Leutnant Janke will be three hundred metres behind you in reserve."

"Fischer's troop will be roughly in line with them, sir, on our left flank, acting as our platoon reserve," Paul informed him.

"Good, good, Brand, you seem to have everything covered. Gentlemen, I shall leave you to it. Good luck."

They all saluted their Company Commander and he left to join second platoon where he would have his company command post.

"Right, get your men together," commanded Paul. "We move out in ten minutes. Max, I want you with three troop. Should we get into a situation, it may well be three troop that gets us out of it."

"Right, sir."

"Max?"

"Yes, sir?"

"This could be a straightforward operation, but equally it

could go belly up. Keep the men on their toes. We can't afford any loss of concentration. As ever, I and the rest of the platoon will be looking to you, Max."

"I understand, sir."

The stocky Unterfeldwebel moved off to round up the platoon, thinking, it's you we'll be looking to, sir, if anything goes wrong. The fair-haired, sturdy sergeant had only been with Paul for six months and, although they were officer and NCO, a mutual bond of trust and respect was forming between them. The six foot two, lanky but athletic Leutnant and the five foot ten, stocky, muscled NCO were like chalk and cheese: Paul, an intelligent, articulate and natural tactician and Max the solid Rottweiler. To this day, no one knows how Max got into the Fallschirmjager, ten kilos over the accepted weight for a paratrooper.

All three of the Unteroffiziers and their troops looked up to Paul and Max. They were both leaders of men, albeit in slightly different ways, who obviously took an interest in the well-being of the platoon not only as a whole but also in them as individuals. They often walked in awe of the tough Unterfeldwebel who would brook no nonsense and was extremely protective and supportive of his young platoon commander.

A paratrooper came running over to Paul and gave him a quick salute. It was Obergefrieter Konrad from Two Troop.

"No saluting now, Konrad, we are on ops. You don't want the enemy to single me out, do you?"

"Of course not, sir, sorry, sir. Just reporting, with Unteroffizier Kienitz's compliments, the troop is ready to move out."

"Thank you. Tell Unteroffizier Kienitz we'll move out in five minutes."

Konrad just managed to stop the reflex action of saluting again and jogged back to his troop. Three Troop also reported their readiness to move.

Paul called over to Unteroffizier Leeb, Commander of One Troop, "We move in five."

"Right, sir." Leeb started to gather his troop together ready to move forward.

Fifty metres to the right, Paul could see Max and Kienitz doing the same with the second troop. He also knew that Fischer would be following suit with Three Troop. He trusted them; they were good troop commanders and good soldiers, and would do right today.

Five minutes later, they moved out and assembled by the trucks waiting to transport them to their drop-off zone.

There were three two and a half tonne Krupp Kfz 81s waiting for them, one per troop. The Kfz 81, or Krupp Boxer as it was known, was one of the workhorses of the German forces. Paul stood by the lead Boxer, watching his platoon assemble by their appropriate vehicle. Although they are not Tante Jus, he thought, at least they had the best vehicles available. Examining the ground they had to cover, they would need the all-round, independent suspension to get them across some of the terrain they would encounter. He was glad of their elite status, giving them a priority over other units for these prized vehicles. He looked up at the sky. Although today was grey and overcast, the ground was still dry and the dust still invaded every cavity it encountered. Perhaps Erich and Helmut will get the rain they so desired sooner rather than later, he mused.

He looked about him and saw that the platoon had fully formed up and was awaiting his command to go. He caught Max's eye and nodded.

Max then barked, "Mount up, vacation time is over. Time to earn your excessive pay."

This was the signal they had all been waiting for, and they climbed onboard, one troop per truck. Paul took his place next to the driver in the lead vehicle. He gave the word for them to turn their engines over which started straightaway as the drivers had warmed them previously, ensuring that they would start immediately when required. Also, they were in fear of Oberleutnant Volkman's wrath, should one or more of the vehicles let the Fallschirmjager Company down.

"Pass the word, *laden und sichern*," commanded Paul. "Lock and load."

Once Paul was given the go-ahead by Oberleutnant Volkman, he ordered his platoon to move out, leading first company, followed by the rest of the battalion, to their drop-off point.

The first two kilometres of the route headed north-east then, turning east, followed a route just south of the woods, believed to be occupied by a Polish artillery unit. The route was more of a dirt track than a road, but the vehicles they were in were more than capable of transiting along it. Paul was sitting in the cab of the lead vehicle and, looking behind, noticed they were leaving a fairly heavy trail of dust, so ordered the driver to reduce speed.

Although German vehicles were continuously active in the local area, he didn't want to attract special attention to this particular convoy. At the seven-kilometre mark, not far from Hill 173 where a platoon of Fallschirmjager, led by Oberleutnant Bier, another friend of Paul's from Second Company, should be moving into position, they turned north-east.

After two kilometres, they turned north for the final leg. Now they drove over very flat, grassy, open-plan fields or pastures, through the occasional gate which they quickly opened to pass through, until they reached the drop-off point. The vehicles came to a halt. They were half a kilometre east of the edge of the woods they had come to conquer. The Boxers debarked their human cargo and returned back to the camp via a different route so they didn't get in the way of the rest of the company that was slowly catching up behind them. Paul gathered his platoon together and they quickly moved off, leaving the drop zone clear for the rest of the company that was probably no more than five minutes behind them.

They advanced, in line of march, to their start point. Fischer's troop had already left them earlier to move into position some two hundred metres behind them on their left flank, in line with Third Platoon acting as the company reserve. Let's hope they weren't needed to get them out of trouble, thought Paul.

"It's time, sir," informed Leeb, interrupting his commanders thoughts.

Paul nodded in acknowledgment and ordered the men to get into formation. The two troops were in line, in a shallow 'V' formation, spread across about one hundred metres. The base of the 'V' at the front and in the centre. Once in position, they awaited the command to move forward. Paul had one gun group on the left flank and a second gun group on the right flank, ensuring that they were well protected on both flanks with heavy firepower.

The gun group of a troop consisted of an MG 34, a machine gun first issued in 1934, hence the name, but considered to be the first modern general-purpose machine gun. Manned by a three-man team, it provided the troop with a high volume of sustained firepower, designed to keep the heads of any enemy well and truly down. At in excess of 600 rounds per minute, this machine gun gave the troop, and the platoon, exceptional firepower but did not sacrifice the unit's speed of movement or its tactical freedom.

Paul scanned the wood in front of them for the third time with his binoculars, straining to see into the foliage and seek out any potential ambush. At this distance, he could make out the edge of the wood but could not distinguish individual trees deep inside. He could wait no longer and had to put his doubts aside. Besides, if he waited too long, he would have the Raven breathing down his neck. He wasn't quite sure what he feared most: the enemy or his Company Commander. He smiled at that thought.

Unteroffizier Leeb also smiled. His Platoon Commander seemed quite relaxed, so it should go smoothly and they could soon be back at camp for a well-earned schnapps.

They were just less than half a kilometre from the woods, giving them the opportunity to form up without the enemy easily bouncing them.

"Let's go, Ernst."

The troop got up from their crouching position in the ankle-high grass and started to move forward in a line towards the wood in front of them, some three hundred metres away. Second Platoon, led by Erich, was on their far right flank with Third Platoon in reserve. On Paul's left flank, some two hundred metres behind, was his own third troop. If the enemy were waiting for them and Paul and his men walked into an ambush, the Polish soldiers would probably wait until they got closer; in all likelihood, when they could make out and target individual soldiers, or even when they could see the whites of the paratrooper's eyes. Close enough that they would make easier targets and Paul and his men would find it difficult to extricate themselves, but not so close that they were in easy grenade range.

At such close range, it would be very difficult for Paul and his men to disengage without taking heavy casualties, and they would very much need the help of the rest of the platoon and the company mortar troop. Even then, the consequences would be dire. Think positive, thought Paul. It was a very large wooded area and the odds that a Polish unit would be waiting at this exact spot were slim.

They continued to move forward. Paul could now distinguish the odd, large tree standing out from the background. He scanned left and right to check that his two troops were holding the line and looked back over his left shoulder to confirm that Unteroffizier Fischer and his troop were keeping pace with them. Two hundred paces to go and the edge of the wood was becoming more defined.

Paul could distinguish the odd oak tree on the extremities of the wood, where the teeline was much thinmner, an ideal hiding place for a trap. One hundred paces and Paul started to feel edgy. If they were going to be hit, it would be anytime now.

The wood was old, made up of mainly deciduous trees, turning brown due to the onset of autumn. The trees had large trunks with outspread branches, interspersed with brambles and thorn bushes and smaller saplings struggling to survive in the limited space between the larger trees and undergrowth. The oak tree in front of Paul as an oak; reminding him of the one he used to climb as a boy back home.

Fifty paces. If they were ambushed now, they would have no option but to charge straight at them and fight their way through. As they entered the wood, the foliage and canopy closed in around them, shutting out what little light there was on this dull, grey, overcast day. It smelt musty; the damp, stale smell of mould pervaded his nostrils.

Paul then fully appreciated Max's warning to the troop commanders at the briefing. They would have to keep a close eye on their men to ensure none got seperatedf. Equally important: ensuring that they didn't get too far ahead and get mistaken for the enemy or get shot by friendly fire should any action with the enemy occur.

The ground underfoot was treacherous. Fallen and broken branches, slippery autumn leaves and hidden hollows, all ready to trip up an unsuspecting paratrooper. The woods were quiet with only the occasional drone of a bee or the flapping wings of birds flying from tree to tree. Being autumn, the leaves had started to fall to the ground creating brown mulch in places underfoot. The decaying, damp smell of rotten vegetation reminded Jager Fessman of his poaching days.

They were well into the wood now. Initially, some eight hundred plus men assaulting the wood seemed like overkill. But now, being completely enclosed by trees and undergrowth, it felt like the entire battalion would be swallowed up by its enormity. They continued forward slowly, the odd snap of a branch or twig a paratrooper trod on, hidden beneath the carpet of leaves and decay. Occasionally, a grunt could be heard as a paratrooper missed his footing and stepped into a hole or burrow left by some small animal of the wood.

Paul looked back and could barely see the outer edge where they had just entered. He checked his compass to confirm they were headed in the right direction. The last thing Paul wanted was to suddenly find themselves back out of the wood again having walked in a circle. They were going slightly too far to the right and Paul had word passed along to the two troop commanders to follow his lead as he turned slightly left. He also warned them about making too much noise. They all knew this, but it had to be said. The right of the line speeded up slightly and the left of the line slowed down until they matched Paul's directions and then continued on. They were well inside the wood now and, with instincts sharper than most, Fessman sensed danger. His warning to the platoon commander was timely. Had it not been so, the platoon may well have blundered straight into the Polish troops and the element of surprise would have been lost.

"Down," hissed Fessman. "Ahead, sir, you can just see a clearing through the gap in the trees there. I think I can see a sentry at the edge of the clearing."

The platoon took to the ground, hugging it closely, trying to become a part of the foliage that was beneath them and around them.

"You must have eyes like a hawk, Fessman. Well done." Paul turned to Leeb who had moved closer to his side. "Send a runner to Unterfeldwebel Grun, and tell him and Unteroffizier Kienitz to get over here now."

"Right, sir. Shall I get Fischer as well sir?"

"Yes, but whoever you send tell them to go carefully. Fischer's men will have itchy trigger fingers."

Leeb dispatched two troopers for the task and, within ten minutes, there was a platoon leader conference.

"Right, Max, Fischer, what's the situation to your front?"

"We've spotted the clearing too, sir, but there are no sentries to our front."

"I sent a scout forward, sir," Kienitz informed Paul. "He's reported back saying there's a battery of guns in the clearing."

"Are they unlimbered?" asked Paul.

"No, sir. They look as if they've either just got here or are about to leave."

"How many men?"

"About sixty, sir, typical for an artillery battery, I would've thought."

"Was there any activity?"

"They seem pretty relaxed. They only have a few sentries and we can only see two in front of our platoon line."

"OK, listen in," commanded Paul. "We can't move forward and the rest of the battalion should now have finished manoeuvring into position on the edges of the wood. They'll be expecting us to kick things off and panic the enemy into withdrawing directly into the blocking force. This is what we're going to do." Paul briefed the troop commanders and informed Company Headquarters of the action he was taking. He had also decided to bring the reserve troop forward for the attack on the Polish troops. Just as Paul had finished briefing his platoon commanders, they heard gunfire off to the west. First the sound of a light machine gun, clearly not a German weapon so likely to be Polish, followed by Polish small arms fire. Then they heard the response from an MG 34: the distinctive, unmistakable buzz saw sound. The sounds came from the west, from Hill 172, the location of the platoon from Second Company, tasked with securing the hill and acting as high cover for the battalion. Bier obviously had his hands full; soon it would be Paul's turn.

"Keep the men moving, Leeb," hissed Paul.

Now that the action had well and truly started, the men became even more alert than they were before the firefight on hill 172 had started. The tension was self-evident. They were all hyped and ready to go. The first thing that needed to be done, to effect Paul's plan, was to take out the sentries. With them still in place, Paul wouldn't be able to get his platoon close enough to catch the enemy unawares without being discovered.

Two paratroopers crept forward quietly; their target: the two sentries spotted to the platoon's front on the edge of the clearing. Fessman, with a knife in his right hand, leopard-crawled to within twenty paces of the Polish sentry. He had removed his Fallschirmhelme, his jump helmet, and left his rifle and ammunition bandoliers and his stick grenades behind. All he had was his model S84/98 bayonet and his 7.65mm sauer model 38 pistol. He would shortly be using his bayonet in anger, for the first time. The sentry was looking towards the west, away from the direction of First Platoon, obviously focusing on the firefight that was in progress on hill 172. It sounded as if Second Company was in the thick of it. Soon it would be First Platoon, First Company's turn.

Fessman crept closer and closer to the sentry, now fifteen metres away. The sweat was starting to soak his uniform making him shiver as it cooled on his body. Ten metres. He could now see the distinctive features of the sentry's face. He looked quite young, no older than eighteen or nineteen, probably a conscript soldier. He remembered his platoon commander's comment: they may not be infantry soldiers but they can still shoot and kill. Five metres. He was directly behind the sentry now. The sentry was short in height, five foot eight inches, no more than that, not a problem for Fessman's five eleven.

He leopard-crawled the last stretch without making a sound. The scrape of his boot against a fallen branch or the snap of a twig on the ground would alert the sentry. Then he would have no option but to get up quickly and run at the sentry, killing him before he had time to sound the alarm. That would be a tall order. These last few moments were crucial. He made it without disturbing the sentry's attention which was still firmly transfixed by the firefight in the west. Fessman could almost reach out and touch him. He could hear him clearing his throat, fumbling in his pocket for what turned out to be a packet of cigarettes. He would wait until the sentry had lit it and taken his first drag. He didn't want the soldier's arms in the way.

Rising up behind the sentry, and breathing in the man's strong body odour, he quickly placed his hand around the sentry's mouth, the knife placed beneath the man's chin. In one swift movement, Fessman clamped the sentry's mouth tightly shut to smother any sound, thrust the blade up and into the underside of the lower jaw, through the upper oesophagus and into the brain. At the same time, he pulled them both to the ground with the Polish soldier's body on top of him, wrapping his legs round the Polish soldier's legs, clamping them, preventing him from thrashing around. The left hand remained fixed around the man's mouth pulling his head back, Fessman's right holding the bayonet, scrambling the blade around inside the skull until all that was left was a minor tremble as the force of life was extinguished from the unknown soldier. Fessman felt the trickle of urine being absorbed into his own uniform and smelt feaces as the sentry evacuated his bladder and bowels during those moments of death.

Over to the right, a second sentry met the same fate at the hands of the equally proficient Stumme. Fessman stood up, holding his bayonet up in the air thrusting it up and down twice, signalling success to the platoon. Paul gave the signal and the platoon of paratroopers moved forward. Fischer's troop on the left flank moved up to the clearing. Now reinforced by a gun group from First and Second Troop, they were to give covering fire. His troop also assigned its rifle squad to support First Troop in the assault. That meant that Paul would have twenty men to conduct the assault on the enemy unit.

All three troops were on the treeline, unseen by the unwary Polish soldiers. Thirty-two men now overlooked the unsuspecting Polish artillery battery, going about their business, oblivious to the incubus that lay biding their time, waiting for the right moment.

Max was amazed that the enemy had allowed them to get this close, and the consequences for the artillerymen would be plain for all to see once the firing started.

"Well done, Fessman, Stumme. Good job carried out on those sentries." Paul patted them both on the back. "Remind me to never meet you two on a dark night!"

"You sounded like a herd of elephants," retorted Max, not wanting the troopers' success to go completely to their heads. But they all knew that the Unterfeldwebel was pleased with their work. Had they messed it up and given the game away, the platoon would be in a very different situation now.

"If the rest are as incompetent as those sentries, sir, then we don't have a lot to fear from them," suggested Max.

Paul turned towards him. "We still have sixty Polish rifles pointing our way though, Max, don't forget that."

Max nodded, bowing to his commander's common sense

Paul looked to the left; Third Troop was in position, MG 34s set up and ready. Two hundred and fifty-round belts in each gun, the number twos already lining up the next two hundred and fifty-round belts for when they were needed. He looked about him and, to his right, First and Second Troop would assault with small arms and grenades while Fischer's men covered them with the three MG 34s. They were dependent on Fischer knowing when to cease fire, or the three MGs would cut Paul's men down like corn if his timing was wrong. If successful, the Polish artillery men would face a swathe of steel that would cut down the unsuspecting soldiers and keep the heads down of those lucky enough to get to ground quickly enough.

Paul looked at his watch, it was time. He gave the signal and the two troops rose up. He looked across to Second Troop, seeking out Max, catching his eye. The slight nod between them reinforced Paul's determination and boosted his confidence in leading his men in this attack. This would be his first time under fire; in fact, for all of them except Max who had been involved in the German army's operation in Czechoslovakia.

They started to move forward just as Fischer's troop opened fire. The devastating hail of bullets hit their targets; the sudden cacophony of sound startling the paratroopers advancing, even though they had been expecting it. The first barrage of fire took out a young Polish korporal sitting astride an ammunition box smoking his fifth cigarette of the day. Unfortunately it was to be his last as the two heavy-calibre bullets sliced through his body taking him backwards to the ground.

An officer, a matter of feet away from the soldier, was struck in the back of the neck as he was inspecting the limbered gun to ensure it was ready to move out. It didn't matter anymore; he would never finish his task. Two Polish soldiers playing cards on top of one of the limbers were both hit: one had an arm smashed by a heavy bullet; the second soldier was hit in the chest, dead before he hit the ground. His fellow card player, still holding his cards in his right hand, the left hanging useless at his side, scrutinised his comrade's eyes, glazed and watery, staring at him, unblinking.

The battery commander looked about him, shrieking at his men to take cover and return fire, but not taking cover himself. Halfway through his final set of commands, a slug from a German rifle sliced through his lower jaw, severing the lower part of his face, his mind continuing to command his men, his hands clutching what was left of his face in horror.

A further eight soldiers were hit by the weighty bullets from the MGs and small arms fire coming from the Fischer troop. Considering Fischer's initial concerns about being left out of the action, it was he and his men that were delivering the first blow. Fischer's onslaught continued, incessantly, two hundred and fifty rounds had already been fired by the machine guns and the number two gunners were already feeding in fresh belts. The Polish soldiers, who up until now had been focusing on, and hiding from, the gunfire from the machine guns on their right, now saw the rest of Paul's men advancing on them from their left. This second group of soldiers opened fire on them and it seemed as if hell was suddenly on the earth. The ones that weren't firing back were dead, wounded or too fearful to raise their heads above whatever shelter they had found.

Paul saw a Polish soldier rise up in front of him, about two metres away, his rifle, although shaking, aimed directly at his chest. His eyes were staring, displaying hatred or fear, Paul could not tell. He had heard it said that, at the time of death, your past flashes before your eyes. This did not happen for Paul, but he did feel a deep dread in the pit of his stomach and, for a split second, he imagined that his life was about to be ended. He didn't hear the shots that took the young Polish soldier's life; half a dozen rounds from a machine pistol striking the soldier in the chest and abdomen. He didn't hear the soldier's scream; all was drowned out by the discordant noise around him. But he did see the soldier flung back by the force of the bullets; he saw the rifle drop from his grip and he saw the man's eyes widen even further in horror and disbelief, his mouth gaping wide in a silent scream before he died.

What seemed like minutes later, but in fact was less than a couple of seconds, Paul was back in the real world of a continuing battle and, looking to his left, he saw Max with a smoking machine pistol and an assured Hamburg smile that said it all.

The moment had passed. Both he and Max were moving forward to continue the action.

He came across a young artilleryman cowering on the ground, his rifle held out in front acting as a shield. Paul knew that he should dispatch the enemy soldier, take away the threat of an armed combatant left in the rear, but his finger resting on the trigger of his MP40 failed to respond. However, common sense prevailed and, as he was about to extinguish the vulnerable soldier's life, a paratrooper running past put two rounds into him without even a second thought and then continued to pursue the retreating enemy.

The Polish lines were in chaos: officers and NCOs calling to their men in an attempt to rally them, but to no avail. Although the onslaught from the machines guns suddenly ceased, Paul's two remaining troops were amongst them causing further casualties, and the Polish troop's courage was waning. For the first time, Paul could hear the crying horses. They were trapped in the harnesses, tethered to the limbered artillery pieces. The horses' heads were held high, and they were exhaling through their extended, flaring nostrils, their eyes wide with trepidation, squealing in fear.

The Polish artillerymen were pulling back, seeking shelter and protection in amongst the trees, leaving their artillery guns and horses behind, little knowing that the Fallschirmjager of Second Company were waiting for them, to sweep up any stragglers that had escaped First Platoon's onslaught. The savage crack of a German grenade, thrown at the fleeing Polish soldiers by Herzog from One Troop, was immediately followed by the heavier detonation of a Polish grenade. Although fleeing from the paratroopers, some of the Polish soldiers were doing their best to cover their comrades' withdrawal. A sergeant could be seen rallying some of his men behind a limbered artillery piece, using it for cover. He had managed to get half a dozen young soldiers together, pulling them into position, thrusting their rifles forwards in an effort to get them firing at the paratroopers coming their way.

A few of them started to get some rounds off, but they were so badly shaken that they probably wouldn't have hit a German soldier even if he had been directly in front of them. But the sergeant's efforts weren't totally in vain as it gave the rest of the Polish force a few extra seconds to extricate themselves and flee deep into the woods. They had held the Fallschirmjager up for a matter of seconds before grenades thrown by Jager's Geyer, Lanz and Renisch exploded amongst them, killing the sergeant and two of the gunners, injuring one, the remaining two discarding their rifles, raising their hands in the air and throwing themselves at the mercy of the Green Devils.

Fianally, there was a lull in the fighting, giving Paul the opportunity to assess the situation. Three Troop was still in position on the edge of the clearing covering the rest of the platoon. Two Troop on Paul's right had reached the far side of the clearing and were firing on the fleeing soldiers. One Troop on Paul's left were mopping up the last of the enemy. A body suddenly landed next to Paul, the huge bulk proving to be Unterfeldwebel Grun. "I think it's all over, sir." He beamed, his face splitting into a wide grin. "They've had enough."

"Thank God, Max."

Max looked at his commander's face, the strain on it plain for all to see. "Are you OK, sir?" he asked anxiously.

"I'm fine, Max, and I'm glad that we've won. But this was just slaughter; they didn't stand a chance."

Max grabbed Paul's shoulders, sensing the deep remorse that he obviously felt at the killing that had just occurred.

"If the boot had been on the other foot, sir, they would have done exactly the same. By catching them with their pants down, some of our soldiers will live to fight another day now."

"As ever, Max, you're right. Let's get this finished. Have Two Troop secure the east, west and north perimeter of the clearing; Three Troop to remain where they are; and One Troop to gather up the prisoners and check all of the dead and wounded Polish bodies. Oh, and inform Company HQ that there are some fleeing soldiers heading in Two Company's direction."

"Will do, sir." Max pushed himself up off the ground with his powerful arms and sprinted away to carry out his officer's orders.

The silence was palpable. The fighting on hill 172 had long since ceased; the Polish soldiers in the clearing were either dead, wounded or prisoners of war. Even the horses had settled down. All that could be heard were occasional moans from some of the wounded, both German and Poles alike. Paul could smell the sweet scent of blood, almost tasting its metallic tang on his tongue. He felt tired, exhausted even. The adrenalin rush had all but dissipated, leaving him aching and breathless. But he had a platoon to command and could not leave all the work to Max. There was also the potential for a Polish counter-attack, although he doubted it, but he would still need to check on the position of his men. He too pushed himself up off the musty ground to search out his troop commanders and check that his orders were being carried out, but also to provide encouragement to his men who would, although elated by their victory, be feeling the strain of the last few hours as well.

Chapter Four

Paul looked around, feeling slightly removed from the activity going on about him, not in a dream state but nevertheless as if he was on the outside looking in. He sat on the limber of one of the Polish one hundred and five-millimetre artillery pieces, left behind by the Polish artillery battery. In fact, all six of the battery's guns had been left abandoned as they fled from the attack pressed by Paul's men. Over sixty men had been overcome and defeated by his thirty-two paratroopers who suffered only two minor casualties. It was their first battle and their first victory. Someone had been looking down on them today.

The limber that Paul sat on shuddered as the six horses still harnessed to it were skittish even now, even though the firing in the immediate vicinity had ceased. A Polish soldier was talking to the horses in his local tongue, stroking their muzzles and calming them down. It had been Max's idea to use the Polish prisoners to take care of the mounts until a local German supply unit, with horse-drawn wagons, could send over some of their men experienced in handling horses. The fight had been knocked out of the Polish force; they would not cause any further problems for the platoon. In fact, they seemed to welcome the opportunity to get close to their animals again. There was clearly some form of a bond between these horses and their keepers. It appeared that the benefit to the horses of having a soothing, recognisable voice calming them was reciprocal, as it had an equally calming influence on the Polish soldiers.

Paul looked across at his men where they were attending to the Polish wounded and gathering the remaining Polish prisoners together; those that had not retreated and run off into the woods to be later captured and imprisoned by the other Fallschirmjager units involved in this operation. It was eleven forty-five. They had been in a raging battle for a little over fifteen minutes, yet it felt like they had been fighting for a full day. He was proud of his men in their first operation, their first time under fire. They had not let him down; they had not succumbed to the fear that grips your stomach so tightly, like a vice, that can make your legs jelly-like, losing their strength, and the dry mouth that makes your tongue feel outsized and misshapen.

His thoughts were interrupted as Max came running over to him, bringing him back to reality, back in control, back to being a platoon commander.

"Right, Unterfeldwebel, report."

Max immediately stood to attention in front of his platoon commander to formally present his report in true German military fashion. There was a time for the informality that often existed between the two comrades-in-arms who held a mutual respect for each other and there was a time for the formal disciplined approach as required by the German military machine.

"Herr Leutnant, I beg to report that we have taken twenty prisoners, found nineteen dead and seven wounded."

"What about the platoon's casualties?" Paul was immediately concerned about the welfare of his own men.

"We have two casualties, sir, two minor wounds. Jager Geyer has a shrapnel wound in the buttocks. The rest of the platoon have found this to be a cause for humour and their entertainment for the day."

Paul smiled in return, the informality they were used to slowly returning. "We'll have to find him some cushions for the return trip. Who is the other one?"

"Jager Kempf from Second Troop. A round clipped his wing, but he'll be back on strength within the month."

"And the horses?"

"Well," grimaced Max, "out of the thirty-six, eight have either been killed or injured. The two injured ones have been put out of their misery. The Polish soldiers begged us to shoot the horses. In fact, we gave them a weapon and allowed them to do it themselves. I don't think any of the platoon were up for it, to be honest. Shooting a soldier who is shooting back at you is one thing; shooting a defenceless animal is another matter."

"It's strange, Max. I almost feel more for the horses than I do for the soldiers we've killed," reflected Paul.

"I understand where you're coming from, sir," Max empathised. "They've been brought here at man's bidding, not of their own choosing."

"It was a good idea to let the Poles look after the remaining horses. I'm not sure what we would have done with them otherwise."

"Again, they asked to be allowed to take care of them. The ones still alive are even now traumatised by today's events, much like their keepers. Just as well. Our troopers may be good at soothing a good woman, but a horse? Never!" Max grinned.

"Thank you, Max. Have the platoon assemble and gather the prisoners together. We'll be returning to our transport."

"What about the Polish wounded?"

"Leave them. Another company will be here shortly to take control of the local area. They can take care of them."

"What about the rest of the battalion?"

Small arms fire could now be heard in the wood to the north.

"I've just been informed by Oberleutnant Volkman that the remnants of the artillery regiment have surrendered and some three hundred prisoners have been taken. Over fifty Polish dead counted so far and God knows how many wounded."

"What about our casualties, sir?"

"We've got off fairly lightly, Max. The battalion has only eight killed and thirteen wounded. The Oberleutnant was particularly pleased with the platoon. It's put the company in good standing as a whole and the Battalion Commander is well pleased. If he's pleased then our lord and master is also pleased, it seems."

"They performed well, sir, for their first action and so did you. The platoon was well trained, well led and the action well executed, and our casualties low as a result of that."

"Thank you, Max," responded Paul, slightly embarrassed by the sudden tribute from his senior NCO who he himself had mutual respect for. "The success of their training lies very much in your court." Looking around the battlefield, he reflected on the differing fortunes of the enemy, glad that it was not he and his platoon suffering defeat and all that went with it. "Not so good for the Polish, eh, Max. They'll not be heading back to barracks for a celebratory drink today. Gather the men, let's get out of here."

Max came to attention. "*Jawohl*, Herr Leutnant."

The infantry company turned up, along with some farriers from the supply regiment, to take control of the prisoners, the Polish wounded and, of course, the horses. The farriers actually looked quite pleased. To quote one of them: "They are good horse flesh," and would quickly be integrated into the supply unit pulling the wagons that kept the German army fed and watered. An artillery officer also turned up. It seemed that the surviving guns left by the Polish artillery regiment were also going to find service in the German army.

The platoon collected its gear, assembled by the edge of the clearing and headed back the way they had come. The trek through the wood seemed very different this time and somehow faster. Once they had cleared the outer edge and back out into daylight, they found the Boxers waiting for them. It seemed that Paul's platoon had been given precedence over all other units. The paratroopers climbed wearily onboard; the fatigue of the last few hours had clearly taken its toll. The earlier banter and swapping of stories on the way to the woods had gone. Post-battle, the journey was completed in silence. All the Fallschirmjager, the Green Devils, wanted now was to get back to their camp and sleep. For some, it would probably be a fitful sleep.

In the cab of the lead vehicle, Max watched as his platoon commander's head slowly slid down the window of the Boxer, sleep overcoming all. The noise of the trucks, the inane chatter of the driver seeking information about the battle, the insecure thoughts as to whether he had acted correctly throughout the action, drifted away. You sleep, thought Max. You deserve it. We came through today and survived. We owe that to you.

Chapter Five

By the 27th of September, the battalion had set up a new camp just east of Pulawy, Poland. They were on the outskirts of a small village called Zagrody, in the administrative district of Gmina Zyrzyn situated in eastern Poland, forty-one kilometres north-west of Lublin. The village was quite small, the population no more than a few hundred. The battalion had moved there to rest and refit after their action in the woods outside of Wola-Gulowska and to await further orders.

Earlier that month, on Sunday the seventeenth of September, Lublin had finally surrendered to the German army. On that very same day, as per the Ribbentrop-Molotov pact, the Soviet Union invaded Poland from the east. The Red Army's invasion had made the Polish defence plan defunct as they now had to fight on a second front, so the overall battle was clearly lost. The invasion by the Soviets had come as a surprise to Paul and his fellow officers, but they welcomed the possibility that it would bring the war to a close sooner than expected. Saying that, the invasion of Poland had progressed very quickly and the unit in its entirety believed that the Poles would have succumbed to the superior German forces very quickly anyway.

The Company HQ staff, plus Paul, Erich and Helmut, along with the senior NCOs, moved to a complex close to a working mill which sat next to a small brook running off the Kuraowka River. Max had made good friends with a pretty young woman who worked at the mill and just happened to be the miller's daughter. Max, with his ludicrous Polish, attempted to speak to her as often as possible, much to the disgust of her father. The daughter, Magdalena, was a tall, dark-haired beauty, with high cheekbones and a slightly pinched face, typical of Polish women in that area.

One morning, the furious miller approached Paul, berating him and waving his arms about with gestures of indignation. Paul, after calling over one of the battalion clerks, who spoke Polish, to translate for him, was informed that the 'blond beast' was bedding his daughter and that he expected Paul to put a stop to it immediately. He partially placated the angry father by telling him that, although it was not his responsibility to manage the love affairs of his daughter, he would investigate the matter and speak to his NCO. This did not please the miller entirely but he left with the knowledge that Paul had promised to look into the matter further.

"Max," called Paul next time he saw the big, fair-haired, ex-Hamburg docker, "I believe you have a sudden passion for freshly baked bread?" He grinned.

"I don't know what you're on about, sir," replied the disgruntled Unterfeldwebel. "I'm just making sure the men get their rations of fresh bread. We don't know when we'll have the opportunity again."

"Are you sure it's not your rations that get priority, Max." Paul continued to bait him. "Make sure you don't put any buns in the oven."

At this point, Max, red-faced, realised that his platoon leutnant was making fun of him and a grin slowly spread across his face. "I'll make sure that the oven door is kept firmly shut, sir."

"See you do, Max," replied Paul, patting him on his solid shoulder. "We don't want any broken hearts and trouble with the natives, do we."

Magdalena had clearly developed a deep attachment for her *olbrzym blondyn,* giant blonde, man and was distraught when the unit pulled out later that day. She was no longer going to see the love of her life.

Paul could be found lying on his bed, still weary after the recent battle in the Wola-Gulowska woods. The entire battalion was now accommodated in and around a small rural village situated about ten kilometres from Pulawy. The First Company's officers Paul, Erich and Helmut had been given some well-earned days on leave. They spent some of that time relaxing by visiting the seventeenth-century town of Pulawy, as had the rest of the battalion's officers at some point during the last few days. Situated on the Wisla and Kuraowka Rivers, the town had a population of over twenty thousand souls. During the mid-1800s, it had been known as Nowa Aleksandria, the name changing a few years after the failure of the 1831 uprising. Close by was a charming medieval village with a small market square where they had stopped for a Polish beer on the way to Pulawy. The weather was still warm and pleasant, but not as dry and dusty as it had been these past few weeks. The three comrades talked about how surreal it was. One day they were fighting and killing the enemy then, a few days later, they were drinking beer in one of their village squares. A number of ancient houses, shops and churches, and even a synagogue surrounded the small square. Paul and his fellow officers found it quite relaxing after the pressures of battle. Even the local Polish population were being polite, although perhaps for the wrong reasons, partly in fear of the occupying army.

Little did they know that later, in what would turn out to be a World War 2, three German concentration camps would be built and operated around the town of Pulawy. The town's Jewish population of over three thousand, initially confined to a ghetto, would later be murdered at Sobibor camp. Paul also learnt that, in the 1920s, Pulawy was the scene of a huge battle between the Polish army and the Soviet Red Army, when a Polish force, directed from Pulawy, circled and defeated a strong force of some 170,000 men. This drove the Soviets from Poland giving them twenty years of stability until, reflected Paul, the recent German invasion.

While in Pulawy, the three young men visited some notable buildings, feeling more like tourists than Fallschirmjager officers. They paid a visit to the temple of Sibyl and planned to go to the Marynka's Palace, once the home of Princess Isabelle Czartoryski, but now the home of one of the German Wehrmacht Division's Headquarters. They quickly skirted that tourist spot, not wanting to be seen by any senior officers!

Returning from their excursion, they felt relaxed and rested; ready to face whatever the military would throw at them. They had been allocated a small cottage to bunk down in until the unit received its next set of orders from the Regimental HQ. The cottage was typical of many in Poland, being a one-storey bungalow with a small kitchen, a wood burning stove, which also provided the cottage's heating, a lounge, that also served as their eating and bathing area, and two bedrooms, one of which Paul shared with Erich, much to his annoyance. Although Paul could sleep almost anywhere under almost any circumstances, Erich's snoring well and truly put that to the test. The cottage also had an outside toilet, which was a luxury under the circumstances.

The Poles clearly resented having to give up their homes to the occupying German soldiers, understandably so, but were careful not to communicate that too forcefully. After all, the war had not gone well for Poland and the current occupying troops were likely to be here on a more permanent basis.

A Military Police unit had attached itself to the battalion headquarters to ensure the good behaviour of the soldiers in the area. But, it also had a responsibility to monitor and control the activities of the local population. In this particular role, they seemed to take great delight in making life difficult for the inhabitants of the village. Paul had already clashed with one of the Military Police, also known as 'Kettenhunde' or 'Chain Dogs', a name given to them as a result of the chain and gorget they wore around their necks. They often worked in close cooperation with the Secret Field Police, Geheime Feldpolizei.

Paul had been returning from checking on the accommodation for his platoon, their welfare very much at the forefront of his thoughts, when he walked into an incident between a group of villagers and the Feldgendarmerie, the Military Police. A Military Police Feldwebel was wearing in what appeared to be a milk-soaked uniform. A Polish peasant was cringing on the ground in front of another Military Police NCO who was beating the man about the head with the butt of his machine pistol. Other villagers cowered nearby.

Paul intervened directly. "Cease that immediately!"

The NCO stood up straight, no longer bending over the Polish victim on the floor. "Keep out of it, soldier, if you know what's good for you. It's none of your business."

If the Feldgendarmerie thought that his military police uniform and large physique would intimidate this boy of an officer, he was about to find out differently.

Paul stretched to his full height of six feet two inches, a good four inches taller than the thickset policeman, and leant in towards him, looking down on him and commanding, "Front and centre and stand to attention when you address an officer!"

The policeman suddenly noticed the jump smock and boots and the parachutist's jump badge. His eyes also flickered to and settled on Paul's officer tabs. If he had any doubts, seeing the Fallschirmjager helmet aided his realisation that this was no ordinary officer and no ordinary soldier. He quickly brought himself to attention and gave Paul the Nazi salute.

"*Jawohl*, Herr Leutnant, this scum spilt milk all down the front of his uniform." He pointed to the other Feldgendarmerie.

"That's as well, maybe," responded Paul, "but it doesn't warrant a beating with the butt of your gun. See I don't catch you treating the local population like this again, Feldwebel."

"Look at them," said the Feldgendarmerie, pointing in the direction of the villagers, all frozen to the spot; in fear of staying and getting embroiled in the dispute between the two German soldiers but also in fear of walking away, drawing attention and bringing down the wrath of the policemen on themselves. "They're just cowardly scum that need a firm hand if they're to be brought under the control of the Third Reich."

"The ones I fought yesterday were not cowardly, Feldwebel," threw in Paul, getting angrier by the second. "They may have been inexperienced and not as professional as our soldiers, but they were far from cowardly. But then you wouldn't know much about that, would you, from the safety of your billet in the village?"

"We still have an important job to do, Herr Leutnant," the Feldwebel spluttered back. But he was clearly embarrassed and his companion chose to look away, not wanting to see the shame being heaped upon his colleague. First, because the officer was right – they had both been in the rear-area while the fighting was in progress and, secondly, he didn't want this paratroop officer switching his attention to him and having the embarrassment of being berated by him in front of the very peasants he despised.

The first military policeman, though, needed to save face here and, slowly regaining his composure, replied, "The control of the rear-area is our affair, Herr Leutnant. We come under the control of the District Commander, not the Fallschirmjager. I will report this incident, of your interference in military police affairs, to my commander."

"As you please, Feldwebel, but if I see you beating the locals again, I may well show you a taste of it. You are dismissed."

The two Feldgendarmerie saluted and, disgruntled, left the area. Paul noticed that the Polish victim had scampered away as had the rest of the villagers that were here only a few moments ago. He thought nothing more of the incident and headed back to the cottage where he was billeted.

Again lying on his bed, he was reflecting on his performance at the recent battle and that of his men. He had been told that the mission overall had been a success and that his platoon and, as a result of that, his company were held in high regard. The downside was the number of dead and injured. His platoon got off lightly with only two injured. Jager Kempf from Second Troop with an injured right arm and Jager Geyer with a shrapnel wound to the buttocks. A painful, non-life-threatening injury, but providing great amusement for the platoon. No doubt this event would be replayed over and over again in the future. The most popular joke being that at least Geyer had got rid of his constipation problem. Both would be back with the unit within the next four weeks.

The rest of the battalion was not so lucky, losing eight killed and thirteen wounded. Fortunately all of the wounded paratroopers would recover. For the Polish unit, things had been very different. Fifty Polish artillerymen had lost their lives, leaving behind mothers, fathers, sons, daughters and wives. Many more had been wounded. Although they fought bravely, they were no match for the Fallschirmjager. Their training and military skills were no match for the aggressive, tough, professional paratroopers that made up the 1st Fallschirmjager Battalion. Paul was staring up at the low, wood-beamed ceiling when he was disturbed by the sound of clattering boots.

Erich burst into the bedroom. "Paul, you're wanted at HQ. The Raven is screaming for you!" he exclaimed excitedly.

"What's it about?" Paul asked as he quickly scrambled off his bed, frantically searching for his jump boots which he found had been kicked under the bed. They badly needed a polish but they would have to do for now. It would not do to keep Oberleutnant 'The Raven' Volkman waiting.

"He's probably got some extra duties lined up for you."

I wonder, thought Paul. Were they going to get orders for another mission? But, if that were the case, then all of the officers of the company would be called for, including Erich. Oberleutnant Volkman was asking for Paul specifically. He quickly pulled on his side-laced FJ jump boots with their cleated soles, only worn by paratroopers. Erich helped Paul get ready as best he could, passing him items that he would need to wear or take with him, in particular, his pistol holster and Walther P38. Although Paul carried a P38, many preferred the Sig Sauer.

"Right," said Paul. "I'll have to do." It was a dilemma: spend more time getting ready and face the wrath of the Raven for being late, or hurry to his appointment and risk being rebuked for his turnout.

As they were still operational, Paul would have to wear his combat uniform which included his M1938 paratroop helmet. The cut-down appearance of the standard coalscuttle helmet was safer for paratroopers when landing.

Erich handed Paul his MP40 machine pistol saying, "You'd better jump off now, Paul. The Raven was looking really agitated when I saw him."

"I'll be off then. If I don't come back, send out a search party for my body." He was smiling as he said it, but it was an uneasy smile. Meeting Oberleutnant Volkman was not always pleasurable; in fact, was it ever pleasurable? Paul asked himself. Maybe he was being unfair and it was just a simple administrative matter. He left the cottage through its only door and turned right down the track that went through the middle of the village to the headquarters.

"Good luck, Paul," Erich shouted after him, but Paul didn't hear him. His mind was too occupied running through likely reasons for this sudden demand to see the Company Commander.

I hope nothing has happened to the platoon's wounded, or maybe something has happened to my parents, thought Paul. He was racking his brains mercilessly for a potential reason. At least then he could have some answers ready to any likely questions in the hope of satisfying the Oberleutnant.

As he marched quickly down the track, the villagers cleared out of his way and, when he looked in their direction, they averted their eyes. After ten minutes on the track that led him through the centre of the village, a small community of no more than thirty cottages similar to the one Paul was billeted in, he arrived at the HQ.

The HQ was a two-storey affair; still a wooden building, but it was more like a palace compared to the other village dwellings around it. He was not surprised by the Raven's choice. Volkman never seemed to be uncomfortable, no matter where they were. Even on exercise or out in the field, he seemed to ensure that he had his creature comforts. This though did not detract from him being a good soldier, well respected by his officers and men. As he approached the door, a Fallschirmjager came to attention and saluted the young officer. He was obviously on sentry duty and Paul recognised him as an Obergefrieter in Helmut's troop.

Paul returned the salute. The sentry informed him, "The Oberleutnant is waiting for you, sir, and said you were to go straight in."

"Thank you, Keller," said Paul, suddenly remembering the paratrooper's name.

The soldier was impressed that Paul knew his name, but it did not surprise him: Leutnant Brand had a good reputation amongst the paratroopers as being a fine officer.

The soldier obviously suspected that all was not well and that Leutnant Brand was probably in for a hard time from their Company Commander. The thought was without malice. Paul was a popular officer within the company. They also knew that he was not to be trifled with or taken advantage of.

Paul entered the building, walking straight into the living room and rather than a wood burner there was an open log fire. The crackling, spitting log fire was a nice welcome after the dreary cottage, with its wood burner that gave out more smoke than it did heat. There were a few oil lamps scattered around the headquarters. Clearly the generators had not been set up yet. In the dimly lit quarters, barely sixteen metres square, the fire cast flickering shadows over the room and its two occupants. Either side of the fireplace, angled so that they faced towards the warmth of the fire, sat two officers. The half-light and the shimmering effect of the fire made their faces seem artificially long and drawn. It was warm too. Paul could already feel the sweat trickling down his back, a result of his earlier rush to get ready, his fast walking pace to get to the HQ promptly, then entering a fire-baked room. Wearing his combat uniform plus steel helmet only added to his discomfort. On the left of the fireplace was Oberleutnant Volkman and, on the right, an officer he did not recognise. But he did recognise the Feldgendarmerie uniform and he felt his stomach knot as he realised what this might be about. He quickly came to attention and saluted the two officers. "Leutnant Brand reporting as ordered, sir."

"At last, Leutnant Brand," rebuked Volkman, the hooked nose profile making him even more raven-like as he turned towards Paul. "I requested your attendance some time ago," he said in a clipped, impatient voice.

"I apologise, Herr Oberleutnant. I came as soon as I was notified."

"Well, you're here now, Leutnant Brand. Stand easy." Volkman gestured with a flick of his wrist and the swagger stick he always carried with him.

Paul relaxed slightly into a stand easy position, his MP40

pointing downwards, although he felt far from comfortable in the two officers' presence. His eyes flicked to the window directly behind Volkman, distracted by a troop of paratroopers marching by.

"This," Volkman pointed to the other officer, "is Major Eichel, of the Feldgendarmerie Troop Twelve, who has come to see me about a most disturbing matter."

Paul's mind raced. What could it be? he thought.

The Major stood up. His uniform was immaculate, almost as impeccable as Volkman's. Clearly, there were aristocratic roots in the Feldgendarmerie as well. He was quite a short man and probably some forty-five years old which seemed quite old for the rank of Major, particularly with his aristocratic links. With grey, thinning hair that was swept back and a round face, he looked almost paternal. He was a good six inches shorter than Paul and, although not stout, he noticeably had an appetite for good food. The father-like impression was to soon dissipate, however.

He walked across to the window behind Volkman and looked out, leaning on the window sill. "Are you a crusader, Leutnant Brand?" he asked without turning around to look at Paul.

"I'm not quite sure what you mean, sir." Paul looked and sounded slightly bewildered.

"Oh, I think you do know. Your love of the Polish peasant is evident in your behaviour," mused the Major.

It suddenly dawned on Paul what this was all about and he felt his stomach knot as he thought back to the incident with the Feldgendarmerie patrol yesterday.

"It has been brought to my attention that you came to the aid of one of the Polish peasants yesterday," the Major said, still not looking round from the window. In fact, he appeared to be examining the structure of the window framework, his face suggesting contempt for its poor fabrication. "Just look at the construction of this building and compare it to one constructed in the Reich. It's almost medieval."

"I stopped a German NCO from beating one of the local population, sir. That's all," defended Paul.

At that point the Major swung round to look directly at Paul. "What my NCOs do in their line of duty is none of your damn business, Leutnant Brand. We are still at war with Poland. We need to keep a tight rein on these peasants who may well be potential partisans, fifth columnists or even saboteurs. They must be kept in check if we are to ensure the security of the rear. Your battalion will not always be here, Leutnant Brand."

"But, sir," interjected Paul, "the locals were just going about their daily chores."

"That is your opinion, Leutnant Brand!" The tirade continued. "Not the opinion of my NCO who is a military policeman carrying out his duties, which you chose, in your wisdom, to interfere with."

"But, sir—" Paul was not allowed to finish.

"If we're to have *lebensraum*, living space, we must have the occupied countries and the populace under control as quickly as possible. We do not need the services of a highly trained Fallschirmjager officer siding with and aiding the locals." The lecture continued. "It will not be tolerated, Brand, do you hear?"

At this point the Major's face was bright red and flushed; his neck muscles were attempting to bulge out of the collar of his white uniform shirt.

"As I pointed out to you earlier, Herr Major," interrupted Volkman, "Leutnant Brand has just come back from a very taxing but successful mission against the very Polish enemy you speak of. I'm sure it was a lapse on his part as a result of the physical and mental fatigue he has experienced, this being his first time in action. I am sure he wishes to apologise and assure you that this momentary lapse will not reoccur."

"You're correct, Oberleutnant. You did make me aware of this fact and, as a result of your intervention, I shall not be taking any action against this young officer." Eichel turned to Paul. "I accept your apology, Leutnant Brand, and your assurance that there will not be a reoccurrence. I hope you have learnt something from this meeting today."

Yes, I have, thought Paul, it has just been reaffirmed to me that the Feldgendarmerie are a bunch of jumped-up, arrogant autocrats. But he brought his feet together in a parade-style click, his arms straight by his sides, and, looking over the right shoulder of Major Eichel and in his best parade-ground voice, said, "*Jawohl*, Herr Major, it will not be repeated, sir."

Major Eichel walked back to his seat and reached for his cap that had been placed on the small table by the side of the chair.

"You are dismissed, Leutnant Brand. Make sure that we don't meet under these circumstances again."

Paul saluted and was about to march out when Volkman

commanded, "Stay where you are, Brand. I also want a word with you."

Volkman stood up and saluted his superior who smiled, probably anticipating that Paul was going to get a further reprimand from his commanding officer.

Eichel placed his cap on his head, returned Volkman's and Paul's salutes and allowed himself to be escorted from the building.

"Right, sit down, Brand," commanded Volkman. "You can remove your helmet."

Paul moved across the room, removing his helmet as he did so, relieved to get rid of the hot, sweaty piece of heavily padded metal. He took the seat just vacated by the Feldgendarmerie Major.

"That was a stupid thing you did, Paul," Volkman reprimanded him. "You don't give these Chain Dogs any opportunity to get their claws into you. Once they have their hooks in you, they will keep you there and it can only hinder your career, not help it. Major Eichel has assured me that this will not be held on record and that the matter is forgotten."

"But, sir," defended Paul, "we can't just go about beating up the locals because they spill milk on an NCO's uniform."

"We're in a new world, Brand." Volkman spoke softly, almost unheard of. "All of us must tread carefully. We are soldiers, no, more than soldiers, we are Fallschirmjager. Our job is to fight our country's enemies and we have proven today that we do it well. We must leave the civilian administration and politics to others. We have not had this conversation, Brand. Right, now to other matters. You and your platoon excelled itself in the action against the Polish artillery unit. This has been a credit to your platoon and, as a result, a credit to your company. For our first action as a Fallschirmjager unit, we have come out of it with flying colours. You are to be commended and I have recommended you for an Iron Cross which has been accepted. This is one of the reasons why the Herr Major was so easily swayed from taking any further action against you. It wouldn't look well to charge a true Fallschirmjager hero, now would it." Volkman grinned.

Paul was in disbelief. Five minutes ago, a Feldgendarmerie Major was tearing a strip off him, potentially putting a blot on his career for the rest of his Luftwaffe service, and now he was being told that he was being awarded an Iron Cross.

"Thank you, sir, I'm honoured," he stuttered, still unable to believe the sudden turnaround.

"The Regimental Commander will be presenting the award to you personally, along with the other recipients. I am pleased to say that I will also be presented with an Iron Cross First Class."

Oberleutnant Volkman was already an Iron Cross Second Class holder, having fought bravely in Czechoslovakia as a platoon leutnant. Paul thought it was funny to think that Volkman had been just a platoon commander like himself and that, one day, Paul too would reach the dizzy heights of commanding his own company.

"So, Brand, you'll need to get your best uniform sorted out. You will be in front of the entire battalion along with the other recipients of their medals. Your platoon was very much in the thick of the fighting and I have been able to allocate your men with some additional awards. That, in itself, is recognition for you and your platoon. Out of the twenty awards for the battalion, four go to you and your men."

Paul was shocked and amazed. What seemed to him as merely carrying out his duty and doing what was expected of him, leading his men into battle and defeating the enemy, was clearly viewed by others as excelling in his obligations.

"Have you anyone in mind, Leutnant Brand?" queried Volkman.

"Yes, I do, sir: Jager Fessman and Jager Stumme. Their expertise and courage in taking out two sentries, without raising the alarm, enabled the platoon to successfully surprise the artillery unit and defeat them. Had they not been successful, the outcome could have been very different."

"That's two. The third?"

Paul had no hesitation in identifying the third recipient: someone who displayed strong leadership, had brought additional experience to the platoon with an insightful training approach, and, last but not least, had saved his platoon commander's life. He thought back to that moment with a shiver: the enemy soldier rising up in front of him, the rifle aimed directly at his chest and Max's intervention, killing the enemy soldier and saving Paul's life.

Volkman waited patiently; he knew the thought processes Brand was going through. He too had experienced the tatses and smells of combat. The names of men killed, incidents that resurrected deep thoughts bringing them to the forefront of your mind.

"Unterfeldwebel Grun, sir. Although all fought well, without exception, these three stand out the most."

"Very well then," said Volkman, "those three it is. I want your written recommendations on my desk by last light. The parade will be held tomorrow at two, so make sure your platoon get their kit sorted out. I feel sure Unterfeldwebel Grun would, be fairly intolerant of any Fallschirmjager letting the platoon down. Also, make sure yours is immaculate. Don't let me down," warned the Oberleutnant. "The Fallschirmjager are the elite. We must excel at whatever we do."

Chapter Six

"Bachmeier!" called Volkman. "A glass of schnapps to celebrate, Brand, yes?"

"That would be very welcome, sir."

"None of that peasant vodka sweepings though; it's only fit for subjugating the peasants and keeping them happy and in line. Bachmeier, where are you, damn you?" Volkman called again impatiently.

The bespectacled orderly rushed into the room and stood to attention at the side of Volkman who was not a man who suffered unnecessary delays.

"Sorry, sir, I was organising lunch for our next visitor."

"Well, you're here now. A schnapps for the good Leutnant and myself please."

The orderly rushed off to fulfil his officer's wishes. Being an orderly for the Oberleutnant must be a real challenge, thought Paul.

"While he gets our drinks, I'd like to discuss another matter with you – two actually." Volkman uncrossed his highly polished boots and leant forward towards Paul. Paul automatically did the same, almost feeling compelled to imitate his commanding officer's actions.

Volkman lowered his voice. "The first is that I shall be leaving the Company, but not the battalion. I'm finally getting my captaincy and will be taking up a position as the Adjutant at Battalion Headquarters."

Paul's response could not be hidden, as his eyebrows involuntarily raised in surprise. Although it was not really a surprise. Not only was the Raven ambitious but he was also a first-class officer and soldier. "Congratulations, sir. When do you take up your post?"

"In a few days, Brand, so you're not getting rid of me just yet." The Raven smiled as he observed Paul's reaction to the news. "Not a word of this to anyone, Leutnant Brand, is that clear?"

"Of course not, sir," responded Paul, but thinking, wait till I tell Erich and Helmut about this. Hauptman Volkman, he thought. The Raven was moving up the ladder, promotion to Hauptman and Adjutant was no small step. He would effectively be the battalion second in command. Promotion and an Iron Cross First Class – Volkman was doing very well for himself. Paul's ambition at the moment was to reach the dizzy heights of Oberleutnant and command a company of his own. He would worry about the step beyond that at a later date.

"Who will be taking over command of the Company, sir?" Paul enquired.

"Your new Company Commander will be Oberleutnant Faust. You will hear more about him later. The second subject I wish to discuss with you concerns a new undertaking for you and your platoon. We have a special job for you and your men. You will appear be an airfield construction unit, but there is more to it than that. We'll be joined shortly by Oberst Baum."

Baum was the Regimental Commander, so it must be something important, thought Paul. But he couldn't imagine why Baum would want to talk to a mere junior Leutnant like himself. Maybe it was to congratulate him. Paul mulled itover; maybe his incident with the Feldgendarmerie had escalated to higher authority. But Volkman would have surely said something about that, he thought.

"He'll tell you more about it," continued Volkman, Paul realising that the Oberleutnant was still talking to him, "when he arrives."

At that moment, the orderly returned with the schnapps. He placed the tray, holding a crystal decanter and glasses, no doubt from Volkman's personal store, on the table between the two Fallschirmjager officers and proceeded to pour each of them a drink. Volkman sat back, clearly waiting for the orderly to finish before he continued his discussion with his junior officer. The honey-coloured drink, along with the crystal glasses, glinted, reflecting the dancing fire. The crackling of the logs brought back memories of Paul's last Christmas at home in Berlin. He had sat in front of a fire, not dissimilar to this one, with his family, sharing a drink and a joke. But reality was opposite him now in the form of his Company Commander.

"Don't be too miserly with it, Bachmeier!" snapped Volkman.

"It's not every day that we get to drink to the success of two of our Fuhrer's heroes." Volkman was clearly in one of his rare good moods. Promotion and a second Iron Cross naturally contributed to the Raven's high spirits.

The orderly placed a glass on Volkman's side table and a second glass for Paul on the bigger coffee table in between the two officers, and then left the room. He probably tucked himself away in the kitchen or, judging by the size of the cottage, a second room in the back. Volkman picked up his glass, sniffed the aroma, a distinctive but pleasant smell that was already filling the room, adding to the smell of the wood smoke given off by the log fire. He held his glass up towards Paul, Paul following suit.

"Here's to the success of our battalion, to the success of the Fallschirmjager and to the success of our beloved Third Reich. And, of course, to you, Leutnant Brand. You show promise and I shall be watching your progress closely. No more cock-ups like yesterday though."

"To success, sir," joined in Paul.

"Is there a spare glass for me, before you two drink it all?" boomed a voice.

They had been so immersed in the discussion and the following toast that they hadn't noticed the officer who stood facing them with the sentry standing behind him.

"I'm sorry, sir, but the Oberst insisted on walking straight in," announced the unfortunate sentry, looking flustered. But what was he to do, just a private? He could hardly stop the Regimental Commander from entering the Company Headquarters.

"That's all, Keller, thank you," said Volkman, standing up to welcome his Regimental Commander.

The sentry saluted and hurried back outside to continue his watch, worried that this might be seen as a lapse in his duties and could reflect on him badly. But the two senior officers, who had more important things to consider, had already forgotten him. Paul pushed back his chair and also stood up. Both he and Volkman saluted smartly, the Oberst returning the salute with a flick of his gloved right hand to his cap. Paul offered the Oberst his chair, but it was refused.

"You stay there, Leutnant Brand. I'm sure the Oberleutnant can conjure up another chair, and a schnapps, of course," he said, smiling.

"Thank you, sir." Paul remained standing by his recently vacated seat.

Volkman called for the orderly again and a chair and a glass of schnapps was quickly brought in for the Oberst, who now sat adjacent to Paul and Volkman, facing the fire. Oberst Baum, Paul instantly recognised, was the Commander of the First Fallschirmjager Regiment, FJR1. Volkman's Company, part of the First Battalion, came under the command of Baum along with the Second and Third Battalions and fourteen *Panzerabwehrkompanie*.

Oberst Bruno Baum was a Fallschirmjager from Willmaischorf, Prussian Silesia, a Prussian like Oberleutnant Volkman. He had joined the army cadets at the young age of twenty-two where he started his military career, receiving the Iron Cross First and Second Class while serving in a West Prussian Infantry Regiment in World War 1. On joining the Reichswehr, he took command of the First Battalion, General Goring Regiment, the first German unit to become an operational airborne contingent.

In 1936, at the not so young age of fifty-three, he was the first German paratrooper to jump from an airplane. He became Commander of the 1st Fallschirmjager Regiment, FJR1, in 1938.

Although Paul had seen him before, he had never been this close to his Regimental Commander and was surprised how short he was.

"Well, Oberleutnant, what have you told this young aspiring general so far?" Baum smiled as he looked at Volkman.

"I have informed Leutnant Brand of his and his platoon's awards and that he has been selected to join a trials battalion that is being assembled in Hildesheim. He will, I'm sure, not want to move out of an operational unit."

Baum pulled out a gold case and took out a cigarette before offering the case and its contents to the two officers who both refused. Paul didn't smoke and Volkman only smoked cigars from Cuba. Baum lit the cigarette, taking a deep draw before expelling a blue cloud of smoke which was drawn upwards by the thermals from the fire. Volkman slid an ashtray across the coffee table for his superior to use.

"Disgusting habit, young Brand, you remain a non-smoker. You still smoking those disgusting cigars, Gunther?" It was a rhetorical question. The Oberst brushed cigarette ash off his tunic trousers and drew again on his cigarette, adding to the blue cloud hovering above their heads. Then he looked at Paul. "You are to be congratulated, Leutnant Brand. I will get a great deal of pleasure presenting you, and the other recipients, with the awards tomorrow. When I was charged with creating the first Fallschirmjager Battalion, it was probably one of the most difficult tasks ever given to me, but it was also my proudest moment. At that moment in my life, I had never flown before, never parachute jumped out of an aircraft and wasn't even sure what the concept of a paratroop unit was." He took another draw on his cigarette. "When we first asked for volunteers, surprisingly there were up to some sixty men who came forward from each company and enrolled. Very soon, I had a full battalion. It has grown since then, naturally, to what it is now." He looked straight at Paul as he said, "It's men like you, Leutnant Brand, and your Company Commander that have helped fulfil the dream of an elite force. A force that operates outside of the normal military boundaries. Anyway, enough of my chatter, let's get down to business."

Oberleutnant Volkman had heard all of this before, but he never tired of hearing it. He too shared the dream of an elite paratroop unit that he hoped one day would grow in size and be a key tool used by the military to meet its objectives.

"You too, Oberleutnant, the Iron Cross First Class is a great honour and your promotion is well deserved. I take it that you've made Leutnant Brand aware of the change in your circumstances?" Baum looked at Volkman enquiringly.

"Yes, sir, but he will keep it confidential until it's officially announced tomorrow."

"Well, Leutnant Brand," Baum continued. "I have a new assignment for you and your platoon."

Before continuing, he stood up and walked around the back of Paul, until he was standing in front of the fire, rubbing his hands together. Turning round, his back now to the fire, his hands clasped behind him absorbing its warmth, he continued. "You are to join Hauptman Kaufmann and Oberleutnant Faust as part of a trials unit to be based in Hildesheim. You will take your platoon with you, to be integrated with Oberleutnant Faust's engineers." He held up his hand to counter any protests Paul might raise. "I understand your concerns about leaving an operational unit, Brand," he continued, recognising Paul's flickering eyelids, which were probably intimating a mild objection. He reached down to the coffee table, picking up his glass of schnapps, taking a nip. "Excellent, Oberleutnant, no doubt from your personal cellar?"

The Raven nodded.

Baum continued. "Poland is all but beaten, and it's unlikely that there will be any further major fighting, the Russians have seen to that, and the likelihood of specialist parachute operations is very doubtful. Enjoy the break, young Brand. Believe me, you'll have ample opportunity to get into the thick of it in the very near future. The unit you're being attached to will be training in utmost secrecy and, once you leave this room, you are not to breathe a word to anyone. Do I make myself clear?"

"Yes, Herr Oberst," responded Paul promptly, now all ears and very attentive.

"Oberleutnant Faust and Hauptman Kaufmann will brief you further, I'm sure. But, you will have to deal with the disappointment from your platoon. You will only be at liberty to tell them that they will be partaking in an experimental training school. And absolutely nothing to your cronies, Janke and Fleck. They will be kept equally busy elsewhere."

The Oberst was clearly well informed, thought Paul, smiling to himself.

"Right, Hauptman Volkman," the Oberst referred to the Oberleutnant's new rank, "I shall leave you to your duties and let Leutnant Brand get his platoon ready for departure, which will be immediately after the presentations are over."

He placed his now empty glass on the table and made his way back round to the other side. How he could stand in front of the fire in that heat for so long, Paul couldn't imagine.

"What about lunch?" asked Volkman.

"I am sorry, Gunther, but I have much to do."

Baum was handed his cap by the orderly and his two subordinates quickly stood up, saluting their Regimental Commander. He returned their salutes and left as quickly and as quietly as he had arrived.

The snap of the sentry coming to attention could be heard clearly outside, probably caught unawares again by his illusive Regimental Commander. The Raven remained standing and Paul followed suit. Clearly the meeting was over and he was being dismissed.

"The presentations are tomorrow. Immediately after that, and

I mean immediately, your platoon will be transported to Pulawy railway station and taken by train to Hildesheim."

The meeting over, Paul saluted, turned sharply to the right and left the HQ. On his return to the cottage, his thoughts were a maelstrom and he was oblivious to all around him. The village, the villagers and the saluting soldiers passing him were not even seen or heard and he was surprised to find himself suddenly outside his billet.

He was sitting on a bench under an old oak tree, a five-minute walk from the village confines, overlooking a small pasture. He was watching a local Polish farmer tending his cattle and his smallholding. Back in Germany, his uncle would have put his cattle in the barn by now, keeping them under cover during the winter months, feeding them fodder saved during the summer months. When he stayed there during holidays, his uncle used to pay his nephew pocket money for helping him feed them and muck them out. It was likely that this local farmer did not have a barn, but maybe a coral somewhere where he could feed and keep watch over them during the winter solstice.

Paul wondered if the farmer's life was simple, without the worries of command, without the many intricacies of military life, not having to comply with the day-to-day demands of the German military machine. But, he knew deep down, he would never want to trade places. This farmer's life was probably spent surviving. Breeding his animals and growing enough food to feed his family, and maybe a little left over to sell for a few luxuries. Paul cogitated about his meeting with Erich and Helmut after his audience with his Company and Regimental Commanders. It had not gone well. The conversation with his friends had been quite difficult. They both knew that he had been to see the Raven, and it soon became common knowledge that Oberst Baum, the Regimental Commander, had also been in attendance. When he had explained that his platoon would be attached to an experimental training unit in Hildesheim, for them it didn't quite hang true. Erich in particular was struggling to match Paul's story with the urgency of the meeting earlier that day. For the first time since they had known each other, since meeting up at the Stendal training camp, they felt uncomfortable in each other's presence: Erich because of Paul's evasiveness, and Paul because he was not being open and truthful with his friend. There wasn't a rift between them, but there was certainly an estrangement. Helmut was also put out by the Paul's secrecy.

Paul heard the rustle of grass behind him and turned to see Max approaching, powerfully striding through the field, his gait recognisable at any distance. His brooding time was over. It was time to leave the farmer and return to his military existence.

"Leutnant, the platoon will be assembled in the hour as you requested, sir," reported Max, saluting as he did so.

"Thank you, Max. Come and sit down. Rest your weary limbs for a few minutes."

Max joined his platoon commander on the bench. "Is all well with you, sir?" he enquired, clearly concerned over what he perceived was a mood of despondency.

"Would you be a farmer, Max?" Paul said, pointing to the farmer toiling in the field.

"Not a chance, sir, plodding around in all weathers, mucking out cattle. I haven't seen a single milkmaid since we've been in this godforsaken country."

Paul laughed; Max's outlook on life never failed to raise his spirits. "I have some good news for you." He was still keen to avoid Max's original question. "You are to be awarded the Iron Cross Second Class along with Fessman and Stumme. I too will receive an award."

"Well deserved too, sir." Max beamed, jumping up and grabbing Paul's hand to shake it. "But why me?"

Paul flexed his hand, trying to get some feeling back into it, and pulled Max back down onto the bench. "Because, Unterfeldwebel Grun, the success we had the other day was due to you, and soldiers like Fessman and Stumme. In fact, I'd like to give the entire platoon a medal. They fought well. You also saved my life, Max, that can't be forgotten."

"Hmm."

Paul looked at Max's serious face. "What is it?"

"The girls in Hamburg would be quite taken by a returning hero bearing medals." Max grinned.

"You're a rogue, Unterfeldwebel!" Paul's mood was lifted. "We have a new posting: the platoon is being sent to an experimental training unit in Hildesheim."

Max stood up suddenly, disappointment clearly on his face.

"But, sir, why are they sending us back to a training unit? We're needed here at the front, surely. How are the rest of the Company, and the battalion for that matter, meant to manage without us?"

"I understand your disappointment, Max, but bear with it. The platoon has been highly commended. They won't waste our expertise for nothing."

"But what sort of training?"

"That's all I can say for now, Max."

"But, sir."

"I'm ordering you not to question it further, Max, understood?"

Max looked down at his commander, his confusion obvious. They had just proven their worth. Surely their place was at the front, and not training spotty-faced recruits. But his trust in Paul was implicit. "*Jawohl*, Herr Leutnant."

"Good. Let's go and talk to the platoon."

"One other thing I need to discuss before we go, sir."

"Yes?"

"The mail has finally caught up with the Company."

It was one of the Reich's true achievements that the mail could get through to the troops under any circumstances.

"Is all well?"

"Unfortunately Jager Roon had been notified that all was not well with his mother. His last letter informed him that her doctor could no longer treat her illness and she had to go into hospital."

"How is he?"

"He's naturally upset, sir. Unfortunately a later letter from his father told him that his fifty-eight year-old mother has died. Due to the late arrival of the letter he's been unable to attend his mother's funeral. I've said that I'll speak to you about getting him home on leave."

"Of course, Max, he must go. I'll clear it with the Oberleutnant."

"I told him I thought you'd try, sir, but he insists on staying with the unit. He thinks his father will be fine. He's written to him. With the unit being operational, he's insisting on staying with his *kameraden*."

"I understand that but I'll speak to him anyway."

Paul got up off the bench and rested his hand on Max's rock-hard shoulder. "Let's go and brief the platoon, eh, Max. We have a parade to prepare for!"

The two *kameraden*, the officer and the NCO, walked back to the village; the solid stalwart, loyalty to his Commander unspoken, and the tall, rangy leader, as dependent on Max as Max was on him.

The railway station was busy. Surprisingly so, due to Poland still being in a state of war and now an occupied country. Though some residents were still travelling on the Polish railways, Paul was bemused as to what pursuits could possibly entice them to use the trains during a time of war. The majority of the trains though, stopping over and passing through Pulawy, were troop trains. The steam trains passed through the station at high speed, engulfing the platform and its occupants in a billowing cloud of oily smoke and steam. People disappeared in its swirling mass, appearing later like wraiths suddenly returning from the dead.

The platoon had been secured a carriage to take them directly to Warsaw, changing trains there for their onward journey. In Warsaw, they were again promised a priority carriage that would transport them west to Berlin, via a stopover at Poznan.

Finally, back in their home country, they would be transferred to Braunschweig and ultimately shuttled to Hildesheim by military transport. The priority given to Paul's unit intrigued him, as it did the rest of the platoon. Clearly they were heading for an important task, and the reservations of leaving the front and their battalion were slowly dissipating, replaced by a soldier's natural curiosity.

The platoon were drinking coffee from a field kitchen, set up on the station to service the passing German soldiers and airmen. They were watched over by the inevitable Chain Dogs, willing the boisterous paratroopers to step out of line. But the medals that some of the troopers sported made them a little wary, so for the moment they would let them be.

The platoon did what soldiers do well: eyed up the local talent. They all had a particular eye for one of the German female volunteers serving them. Max was worried that if they continued to drink coffee at the current high rate they would explode. Two hours later they boarded their train, the carriage being surprisingly comfortable and very soon the majority of the platoon were asleep. Paul joined them, slowly slipping into a deep sleep, his last thoughts being about the experimental training unit, but he also turned over in his mind his training days at Stendal.

The mesmeric click, click, click of the carriage's wheels over the track soon had their effect, closing Paul's eyes and shutting down his spinning thoughts.

Chapter Seven

Paul arrived at Stendal station, the home of General Kurt Student's slowly growing 7 Flieger Division. At this time, the Division was only two battalions strong. Paul got off the Deutches Reichsbahn train with his single kitbag, holding his personal effects and other elements of his Luftwaffe uniform, and looked for the assembly point.

The local band were happily playing the *Kadetten Marsch*, the Cadets March, obviously welcoming them to their temporary new home. There was doubtless more than a hundred young men milling around the station, wearing a variety of uniforms, mostly air force, but also including a sprinkling of uniforms from the army and some even in civilian clothes. Many looked equally as lost as he felt. Some looked even younger than Paul's twenty years of age. It was obvious they were all heading for the same place as him: Stendal-Borstal, the home of the parachute training depot, the home of the Fallschirmjager, the home of the 'Green Devils'.

He had seen a pamphlet: the air force wanted volunteers for parachute training. It sounded like a good idea at the time, but perhaps also a good way to commit suicide. The Luftwaffe eagle on the cover of the brochure struck an immediate chord with Paul. The more he thought about it, the more it whetted his appetite. Although the thought of flying into battle rather than slogging through the countryside on foot allured him, there was a twinge of doubt at the thought of jumping out of an aircraft, his life depending on a circular piece of silk!

At eighteen years old, Paul joined the Reichswehr where, as a Junior Leutnant, he spent nine months with a Wehrmacht infantry regiment. Within a week of approaching his Company Commander for a transfer, Paul found himself on the train to Stendal, ninety kilometres west of Berlin. And here he was.

There were various signs indicating where they should form up in groups prior to the arrival of their reception committee. Paul walked over to the appointed collection point, joining the rest of the milling throng, all waiting expectantly, all with some trace of anxiety on their faces as to what the future held for them. As he got closer to the collection point, he found he was walking alongside a youth of a similar age to himself, not so tall, probably two inches shorter than Paul's six foot two, but slightly bigger built than Paul. They looked at each other.

Paul made the first move to speak. "Are you," with a slight shake in his voice, "are you joining the Fallschirmjager?"

His newfound, short-term companion smiled back. Erich was six foot with a similar athletic build to Paul, but more filled out, more bulk. His oval face lit up as he responded to Paul's question. His blonde hair and deep-set blue eyes gave him a look of confidence, a look of self-assuredness that belied his age of nineteen.

"Yes, I am. The name's Erich, and yours?"

"Paul, Paul Otto Brand." They shook hands.

"Well, something's going to happen soon, Paul. There must be well over a hundred of us here by now, and still more arriving. And I'm starving; I've not eaten since early this morning. My parents packed me a lunch, but I'd eaten that by mid-morning."

"I know how you feel," agreed Paul. "I could eat a horse at the moment."

"That's probably what they'll feed us on." Erich laughed. They both laughed, clearly more at ease now that they had found a fellow adventurer and they both seemed to get on quite naturally. They chatted about their hopes and fears for the future, and hit it off extremely well. They had both been in the RAD where, together, they had demonstrated the necessary attentiveness and instant obedience to orders; qualities that were recognised as prerequisites for the German Officer Corps and, in particular, the Fallschirmjager.

Just as they were about to continue their conversation, they heard the loud roar of heavy goods vehicles arriving at the station. Four vehicles ground to a halt alongside the station building as the locals looked on.

The Feldwebels and Unteroffiziers who were going to take care of their future training leapt out of the army vehicle cabs. There was also a Steiner Jeep which an officer, an Oberleutnant, exited from.

Whistles were blown, they were shouted at, screamed at, pushed, shoved and dragged into some semblance of order along the collection point outside the front of the station. Civilians looked on, not sure whether to smile or turn away, seeing it with a mixture of amusement, yet a slight feeling of anxiety for these young men, at the thought of the harsh training these youngsters were about to experience. Some veterans thought back to their youth when they had gone through this day at perhaps another military camp. Some were just civilians out with their families for the day, on a day trip or just out shopping.

It was becoming a more familiar sight these days: young men going off to various barracks throughout Germany to train to become future soldiers of the new Third Reich. Was it a good thing or a bad thing? Most kept their thoughts to themselves, but all had to agree that Germany was regaining its pride and its prosperity.

The recruits were arranged together in groups of about forty, Erich and Paul managing to stay together. They had already made the commitment to keep together that day and, if possible, throughout the gruelling training that was ahead of them. Although they had an inkling of how tough it was going to be, they really had no idea what was in store for them. They would need each other's mutual support throughout the gruelling eight weeks of training. The groups were each allocated to a troop carrier, a heavy goods vehicle with a canvas top. They scrambled up on the tailgate and climbed in; there was barely enough room for forty, but the alternative was to walk or, even worse, face the wrath of one of their instructors. Erich and Paul ended up crushed in towards the front of the truck, about a two-thirds of the way along from the back, and there were still young recruits climbing on board. When all were onboard, some were left sitting astride the tailgate, hanging on precariously as the truck drivers restarted their vehicles for the journey to the barracks.

The cab doors slammed shut as all of the training staff boarded the trucks and, with a roar of engines and belches of smoke that drifted into the back of the vehicles making some of the recruits gag from the smell and choking fumes, they moved off.

They had only been driving for about thirty minutes when, unexpectedly, the four trucks pulled over to the side of the road, coming to a sudden halt with a screech of brakes and a cloud of dust threatening to choke the occupants in the back a second time. The trucks stopped so suddenly that those sitting astride the tailgates were nearly thrown off and had to hang on as if their lives depended on it.

"Are they out to finish us off before we've even started our training?" joked Erich.

"We'll soon find out," replied Paul with a grin. But it was a grin that held unknown expectation behind it.

The cab doors opened and the whistles, shouts and screaming started again. Orders were bellowed at them and they were told to jump down from the vehicles. Once they had all climbed down, they were yet again pushed, shoved, cajoled, dragged and organised into files of four by the Feldwebel and four Unteroffiziers (Uffz). An Uffz was assigned to the group of forty that Paul and Erich were attached to.

They were ordered to face the front. Eyeballing them was the Feldwebel in charge, along with the four Uffzs. The officer, his duty done for now, had obviously continued on to the camp in the Steiner Jeep.

The Feldwebel stared at them. In his thirties, with a wide, sturdy jaw, full lips and a rounded nose, he looked lean and fit and would probably put all of the younger recruits to shame in any fitness test.

"Well, you rabble, I'm sure you all thought your day of leisure, and your taxi ride, was going to continue. Well, I'm sorry to disappoint you. You are recruits of the Fallschirmjager now and your training starts today. You have had a restful journey, eaten your mother's sandwiches, so now it's time to work some of that off. Some of you look as if all you have done these last six months is eat. The camp is ten kilometres away and shortly you will make your way there on foot. This should give you an appetite for your dinner, should there be any left by the time you get there. I don't want any slacking, anyone lagging behind. You stay together at all costs, you stay with your group, and anyone who leaves the group will be punished as will the remainder of the group. Make sure you arrive together. Do I make myself clear?"

"*Ja*," they shouted.

"The response should be *Ja, Feldwebel!*"

"*Ja, Feldwebel!*" they all cried out again.

"I can hardly hear you. You had better start putting more effort into your response than that, otherwise we'll keep you here until you get it right. Is that understood?"

They all screamed at the top of their voices, "*Ja, Feldwebel!*" not sure if they were more afraid of the Feldwebel, staying out in the hot dust of this June afternoon, missing dinner or the ten-kilometre march ahead of them.

Three factors were pivotal in the shaping of a Fallschirmjager: a sense of comradeship, an extremely high level of fitness and chivalry. The paratroopers were encouraged to believe in themselves and, although pushed to their limits in training, would always be reminded that what was being asked of them was well within their capabilities. Although camaraderie was important in any military unit, it was especially significant in the Fallschirmjager. For the Fallschirmjager, it was fostered right from the start, at squad level, platoon level, right through to their parent regiment. As a squad, they would be dependent on each other and it was essential, particularly behind enemy lines, in an uncompromising position, kilometres and possibly days away from being relieved, that this spirit was engendered.

"Attention! Le-e-eft turn, by the double, march."

The Feld and the Uffzs started off at a steady jog, all in time with each other, and the Uffzs attached themselves to their appropriate groups. The groups were a shambles, they were all over the place, and no one was in step. But, eventually, they settled down to a steady, rhythmic pace, staying in a group, faintly resembling a military formation of sorts. It was four in the afternoon and a temperature of about twenty-four degrees centigrade. Not too hot if you were sat out on the patio enjoying a bratwurst and beer, but not when double-marching along a hot, dusty road with tens of complete strangers. And with five instructors screaming at you incessantly.

After thirty minutes, some wished they had stayed at home or been left back at the station. After five kilometres and over an hour of double-marching, it was beginning to tell on the new recruits, and some of the less fit members of the group started to drift backwards. One of their newly agreed comrades, running alongside Paul and Erich, started to slowly fall back, clearly struggling with the pace they were being asked to maintain. Each, although weary themselves, grabbed a piece of his clothing at the shoulder or by his waist to keep him going. They discovered his name was Helmut. They too were now getting tired and feeling the pace. A further hour, and at the eight-kilometre point, they were all shattered. Hot, sweating, thirsty, hungry, their legs buckling beneath them. Constantly being harangued by their instructors, falling down, and literally being picked up by the screams of their tormentors. Many of their comrades had fallen by the wayside. When members of a group had fallen too far back, the rest of their group was also stopped in order for the laggers to catch up. But this did not mean the group could stop and rest; they were immediately thrown onto the floor to complete press-ups, jump ups, squats and other exercises designed to further test their endurance.

The recruits were from a mixed background. Some, like Paul and Erich, were from the Wehrmacht having transferred to the Luftwaffe to join the Fallschirmjager. Others were like their newfound comrade, Helmut, who was already in the Luftwaffe and was transferring to the Fallschirmjager. Some had even come straight from civilian life, but had proven themselves in the Hitler Jugend and other such organisations where they had distinguished themselves.

They eventually marched in through the camp gates totally exhausted, almost disbelieving how every muscle, every bone and every joint in their body seemed to cry out in pain and throb throughout their entire body. The accommodation was not quite what they expected: they were just plain wooden huts. But then again, they weren't there for a holiday. But still they were not allowed to finish. They were lined up, pushed and cajoled into formation and instructed how to stand to attention the Fallschirmjager way, the Wehrmacht and Luftwaffe soldiers helping their less experienced, more exhausted *kameraden*.

A Fallschirmjager Uffz positioned himself at the head of each of these four groups, and standing at the head of the four groups was the Feldwebel that had accompanied them on their march to the barracks. He stood at ease, facing away from the four groups, waiting expectantly. Then an Oberfeldwebel, the senior sergeant of the barracks, marched towards them followed by two other figures.

The first figure was the Oberleutnant who had met them at the station earlier. Another officer they had not seen before accompanied him. As they marched smartly towards the recruits, the Feldwebel gave them a warning and then brought them to attention. This in itself was a shambles as they pulled themselves to attention in one form or another. The Uffzs shouted at them from the corners of their mouths warning them to remain quiet and still.

The Feldwebel, Feld, and the Uffzs were dressed in first-pattern jump smocks, the *knochensnack*, boneshaker, and boots.

The Uffzs had two eagle wings on each arm while the Feld had three. All wore the Fallschirmjager helmet, painted Luftwaffe blue-grey with a single silver-grey Luftwaffe eagle on the left and the national tricolour decal on the other side. All three Luftwaffe soldiers approached and talked to the Feldwebel who was smartly stood at attention. The Feld then did a smart about-turn and faced the four groups, ordering them to stand at ease. They did, again with more of a shuffle than the smartness that would be expected of them in the weeks to come. The senior officer, a Major, the Camp Commandant, looked at each group, sometimes making eye contact with members of the group, but none could hold his searching gaze for long and look him square in the eye.

The day was still very hot and the Major took off his cap, wiping his brow with a white handkerchief he'd pulled from his pocket. He spoke to them, his brow wrinkling beneath his brown but balding pate. But he too looked fit, and clearly didn't limit his activities to just being behind a desk. Both he and the Oberleutnant wore similar dress to the NCOs, except they wore a shirt and tie, typically worn on parade. He replaced his cap.

"Welcome recruits to the Luftwaffe, to the barracks and the training cadre of the First Fallschirmjager Regiment. You are about to attempt to join one of the elite formations of the German forces. Not all of you will pass. Some of you will fail and be gone in a matter of days; some will get halfway through the four weeks training and still fail and go home. The best of you will stay the course and see it through to the end and become members of this unique organisation. This will be more of a privilege for you than for the unit. Once you have completed your first four weeks, you will then go to Wittstock, to complete your second four weeks on the parachute-training course. Only on completion of that will you become true Fallschirmjager. But, that is a long way off. You have got to survive these next four weeks first."

He started to walk up and down in front of the assembled cadre as he continued to inform them of their status. "You are number twenty-seven training company and each of the groups you are in currently is a platoon within that company. Each of your platoons are led by a Feldwebel and an Uffz, with Oberleutnant Nagel and Oberfeldwebel Schubart in overall charge. I will also take an active interest in the progress of your training. I will be here to congratulate all who pass but, in addition, I will be here to dismiss those who fail and cannot make the grade. There is no room for failure, gentlemen, on this course, at this barracks and with this unit. One thing that is critical, one thing you must always remember. Although you have your own individual tests to pass to complete this course, if you wish to become part of this elite unit, you must remember that you are a part of a team. Teamwork is equally important. You not only have a duty to yourselves, but to your platoon, your company, your regiment and to your comrades."

He scanned their faces, willing his words to sink in. Camaraderie was crucial in the Fallschirmjager, particularly so at squad level where it was vital to each and every Fallschirmjager because of their potential isolation in battle. They knew that after most drops they would be out on a limb, kilometres and hours and even days away from support, and so would be totally reliant on each other during that time.

"That is part of the selection process. It is not just about you passing; it is about all of you passing. A failure of one on an exercise is a failure by all of you. I will now leave you in the capable hands of your instructors. Some of you I will see leave during the next eight weeks; some of you I will see at the passing-out parade. They are all yours, Oberleutnant."

The Oberleutnant stood to attention, as did the Oberfeld and the other NCOs. The company was also brought back to the position of attention. The Oberleutnant saluted and the Major flicked the peak of his cap with the glove held in his hand and returned to his office.

The Oberleutnant then took a stance in front of the company. He was in his late twenties, with high cheekbones, almost Slavic in appearance, and a jutting chin that seemed to point at you accusingly when he looked in your direction.

"Right, that was the nice bit, gentlemen. Now it is my and my instructors' turn. While in the barracks, you will double march everywhere. Every time you move about the camp, every time you go to eat in the canteen, every time you go to an exercise or training session, you will double. Any man I, or your instructors, catch walking will be punished, and the platoon they belong to will also be punished. And, believe me, doubling around the camp is far more preferable to any punishment you might receive. You will refer to all of your instructors as *Spieß*, Pike, except for the Oberfeldwebel and any officer who you will call sir. You will be stood to attention whenever you talk to one of your instructors. I will leave you now in their capable hands, but I will be involved in all aspects of your training on a daily basis. I will be watching you every day. I will be watching your progress and I will be watching your failures. Be in no doubt, gentlemen, this is going be the hardest eight weeks of your life and I expect more than one hundred per cent from each of you. Carry on."

The Oberleutnant left and three other Feldwebels joined the Oberfeld, now making four in total, one stood in front of each platoon. Feld Geyer stood in front of Paul, Erich and Helmut's platoon.

"Right number one platoon, listen to me. This is what is going to happen to you the rest of today. You will attend the medical centre for a check-up and to be weighed. If any of you weigh more than eighty-five kilograms, because that is the maximum safe lifting capacity of the RZ1 parachute, you had better lose that weight quickly. Believe me, on this course we will be more than willing to help you do that," he said unsmilingly. "You will then be taken to the quartermaster's where you will be issued with your uniform and equipment. This equipment is your responsibility and, god help any one of you that loses any of their kit! Take your gear to your barrack room which will be pointed out to you; then I want you back outside on the parade ground, in training gear, stood at ease in your platoon formation along with the rest of the company. Your Uffzs will show you the way to the quartermaster's, but remember you double everywhere."

"Platoon, platoon shun! Platoon will turn to the left in file, left turn!"

Another shambles.

"Platoon to the quartermaster's, at the double, double march."

The Uffz led number one platoon to the stores, closely followed by the remaining units. The volume of uniform they were issued with overwhelmed Paul and Erich. Side-laced boots with thick rubber soles, only issued to the Fallschirmjager, an extra-thick upholstered helmet, a jackknife, useful for cutting the parachute harness if it got caught up while landing, and a jump smock and trousers, and a whole list of other clothing and equipment they would need. The jump smock was also specific to the Fallschirmjager, affectionately known as the *knochensack*, boneshaker. Laden down, barely able to see over the top of their loads, they took their kit to the barrack room. Paul, Erich, Helmut and Curt had been allocated a room in the barracks. Paul and Erich had dragged Helmut along on the march to the barracks and Curt had been with them. As officers, they seemed an obvious grouping to share the four-man room. They changed into their training gear and went back outside for what was likely to be another beasting.

Chapter Eight

In the early hours of the morning on day two, loud whistles and shouts sharply awoke the recruits, Paul, Erich, Curt and Helmut, ensconced in their four-man room. They scrambled out of their bunks, sleep still dragging at their eyes and weary limbs, struggling to quickly pull on their full combat gear. They were constantly being reminded by the instructors that they were already late for assembly on the parade ground outside.

All Paul could remember from yesterday was fatigue. He had trained in the Wehrmacht as an officer, but could not remember experiencing such exhaustion and there were still nearly eight weeks to go. He had fallen asleep with the first Fallschirmjager Commandment's voice ringing in his ears: 'You are the chosen ones of the German army. You will seek combat and train yourselves to endure any manner of test. To you, the battle shall be fulfilment.'

But their first real day was about to start, *Harte und Aus Dauer,* toughness and endurance.

Paul grunted to Helmut as he bent over to lace up his boots. "I wonder what delights they have planned for us today?"

"I'm sure it will start off with a nice cooked breakfast served personally by our good-natured instructors," replied Erich, pulling on his jump smock.

"More like a five-kilometre run," laughed Curt, joining in the revelry.

"More to the point, when will we get fed?" Helmut interjected with a pained smile. "I'm starving."

"Yes, we know, Helmut, you're always starving. You're hungry ten minutes after you've eaten," joined in Curt, the fourth Leutnant sharing their room.

"By the time I have finished with you four, food will be the last thing on your mind, Janke," hollered Feldwebel Geyer who had magically appeared in their room.

They all leapt to attention and shouted at the tops of their voices, "*Speiß*."

"If you lot aren't outside in one minute, I will ensure that it will be a long time before you get the chance to eat again. You now have fifty-five seconds."

Feldwebel Geyer left the room to inflict fear in the other recruits struggling to meet the tight timescale set for them to prepare.

The recruits wrestled with their kit to get ready to join the other innocents they could already hear forming up outside in readiness to be inspected and, probably, to receive the wrath of the Feldwebel yet again. When ready, the four rushed outside to join the rest of their comrades forming up on the parade ground.

They all shuffled awkwardly as they attempted to get into some form of order that would satisfy the instructors prowling on the sidelines, propelling, coaxing, bullying the one hundred and sixty men of training company twenty-seven.

The Non-Commissioned Officers, NCOs, continued to scream at the recruits, berating them for their slackness, the poor state of their uniforms and then informing them that this was just a practice and they were to return to their bunks.

Paul, Erich, Curt and Helmut dragged their tired bodies back to their room to disrobe and fall back into bed and, hopefully, get some sleep. It was only two o'clock in the morning.

They were to be disappointed. At three o'clock it started all over again. A second parade was required because they had been so bad at the previous practice. The instructors' sense of humour was very much their own. By three thirty, they were again back in their beds, desperate for sleep. But, at five o'clock in the morning, they were dragged out of their beds for the real start of the day: a five-kilometre run before breakfast.

The cross-country run put a huge strain on their already tired legs. As a result of overnight rain, the going was soft and slippery and, with a shorter stride length to compensate, it put a greater demand on their leg muscles. It was an important part of their training, and a valuable toughening-up exercise.

Forty minutes later, they were back in the barracks, waiting to be released so they could get a quick shower before breakfast; should there be any hot water left, thought Paul. In the weeks to come, they would not care about the temperature of the water. In fact, they wouldn't even know they had been in the shower; they would be so bone tired. After a hearty breakfast, when they finally did get the chance to eat, the food was good and plentiful – even Helmut couldn't complain – they felt better. The rest of the day involved weapons-handling, square bashing on the parade ground, unarmed combat, bayonet practice and various lectures. The lectures were the hardest; they spent most of the sessions desperately trying to keep their eyes open. The training staff had the ideal cure for sleepy paratroopers: press-ups, press-ups and press-ups.

All around them, men were coming and going, vehicles were leaving and arriving, and Junkers aircraft could be heard droning overhead. Troops who had already passed out marched by, heads held high, smartly dressed in their Luftwaffe blue service dress with their recently issued parachutist's badge. Another company, halfway through their training, marched past, looking like ghosts. Their eyes were sunk deep into their heads, their uniforms were encrusted in dirt and dust, and, although marching, they could barely pick their feet up off the ground.

Paul looked at Erich; he could see what he could see and was probably thinking what he was thinking. "They look like they've been to hell and back. That will be us in four weeks."

"It looks like there are only about thirty in each platoon," responded Erich.

Helmut chipped in, "That's a twenty-five per cent dropout rate and they're only halfway through!"

"It just seems so far away," added Curt, rather despondently.

"Look at them, they don't look as if they've been fed for a month," piped up Helmut.

"Food again!" the three comrades uttered in unison.

All four burst into laughter. Even Helmut saw the funny side of his statement. Food was the least of their worries.

"I can see that you four are enjoying yourselves too much. Well, we shall have to make things a little more interesting for you," threw in Feldwebel Geyer who had suddenly come up behind them. "Get in line, now!" he yelled.

They all groaned, their moment of respite over.

Their first full day was the start of several days of tests; part of a test programme to establish their suitability as potential paratroopers. An exhausting mental and physical syllabus started the eight-week training course. This included an air experience flight in an ageing twin-engine Dornier. Many of them, including Paul and Erich, had not flown before. It was an exhilarating first-time experience. The serious aspect of it was to identify those that became dizzy or sick. Those recruits were quickly failed as the resulting dehydration from this effect would impact on the paratrooper's fitness. They needed to be totally fit and alert when they landed, particularly in enemy territory.

By the end of the day, the four comrades and the rest of the training company were beginning to realise what physical exhaustion really meant.

Chapter Nine

They were now in their second week. The fifteen-kilogram pack weighed heavily on Paul's shoulders. His platoon had just finished a five-kilometre run – to warm them up for the assault course, they were told. It now stood in front of them as their instructors Feld Geyer and Uffz Kienitz shouted out instructions. It looked fearful, to say the least.

"This is going to kill us," whispered Erich out of the side of his mouth.

"We're still here," replied Paul. "Stick with it, and you and I will see this through."

"You sound far more confident than I feel." Erich grimaced.

Helmut stuck his head between them. "Come on, you two, we can walk this thing. Stop worrying."

"Only if we drag you over it," responded Paul, pulling on Helmut's pack straps, Helmut almost tumbling forward.

The Uffz shouted for them to drop their packs as they were going to have it easy first time round. Lining up in front of the first obstacle, in two columns, they started the assault course in pairs. When it was Paul and Erich's turn, they ran towards the first obstacle, a one-metre high horizontal post. They looked at each other and grinned, triumphant, not yet knowing that this optimism was to change as the day wore on. They both attacked this first barrier with confidence, overcoming it easily despite the wet and slippery wood.

The second obstacle was not so easy, a one and a half-metre high horizontal post, again wet and slippery and difficult to grip to pull yourself over. They achieved this with some straining and grunting, their fellow recruits close on their heels. Next was the two-metre wall. Here they had to help each other over, completing it but with grazed hands from the brickwork. So far they were coping, but breathing heavily.

"I'm knackered already," said Erich, panting.

"I know how you feel," replied Paul, gasping for air. "Keep moving, Geyer's watching us like a hawk."

They now faced the four-metre wall, twice the height of a man. It looked daunting, to say the least. They had been taught how to climb a wall this high, but now it was time to put it into practice.

Two recruits had crouched down against the four-metre wall facing Paul and Erich, holding their clasped hands in front of their bodies at just below waist height.

Paul took a run at the wall first, his breathing heavy and his heart pounding as he placed his right boot in the cupped hands of the recruit crouched to the right, launching himself up and placing his left boot in the clasped hands of the second recruit on his left. The two recruits then, at the same time, raised themselves up, twisting round to face the wall, forcing Paul up into the air, allowing him, as he lay his body flat against the wall, his raised hands at the same time, to reach and grip the top of the wall. A fourth recruit, sitting astride the top of the wall, leant down, grabbed hold of Paul's uniform and helped yank him up and onto the top. There Paul remained, to help Erich up while the fourth recruit, who had helped Paul, dropped down on the far side of the wall and continued on to the next phase of the assault course.

Erich joined him commenting, "What's wrong with using a bloody ladder?"

"When we do our parachute jumps, I'll make sure there's room on the plane for a four-metre ladder, with its own parachute, of course," responded Paul, having the last laugh as he lowered himself down the other side of the wall, dropping the last two metres with a sickening thud.

If anything was going to get them through the course, it had to be their sense of humour, although the instructors' exasperation at that might be their undoing.

Erich thudded down by Paul's side, grunting as the wind was knocked from his body. They both headed off for the next obstacle; they would have to crawl under this one. It was down in the prone position, keeping their heads and buttocks down in the mud, or they would catch their helmets or backsides on the vicious, sharp barbed wire strands, criss-crossed above them. They were forced on by the efforts of their instructors, admonishing them for taking their time. The exertion required to move forward with short, sharp movements of the arms and legs along the ten-metre distance was starting to tell on them, their uniform and helmet constantly being tugged at by the sharp, rusting barbs above them. Their initial confidence and cockiness was slowly draining away, as was their strength.

They also had to run along tree trunks raised above the ground, maintaining their balance or falling into a quagmire either side, and ditches to jump at the far end. Climbing a thick rope net that tried to wrench their arms from their sockets, hand over hand on a suspended rope above another mud bath and swinging by rope across a wide stream, the course seemed endless. Reaching the end of the assault course, they were shattered but, if they had any thoughts of a brief respite to catch their breath, they were surely disappointed. Their instructors seemed to be everywhere, tormenting them and urging them on faster and faster. Sweat was pouring down inside their uniforms. Their arms and legs ached, feeling like lead weights, thinking they would never be able to pick up their limbs again, let alone continue on any further. But they did; a mixture of their own determination and their ever present instructors pushing them on made sure of that.

The hurdle the next day was to instil even greater fear into the weary recruits. It was one they would have to complete if they were to be successful in becoming a Fallschirmjager in this elite unit. They ran up numerous narrow ramps until they were some twenty metres above the ground, the height of a six-storey house.

Facing them was a narrow plank, supported by a frame that was one metre away and one metre below them. Had it been two metres off the ground, it would have been simple and tackled with ease but, twenty metres above the ground, it was daunting. This was the test they must pass, otherwise their training would stop here and now and they would be transferred back to a Wehrmacht infantry or Luftwaffe unit the very next day.

Paul did not want that. He had been conscripted into the Wehrmacht as a junior Leutnant, through the RAD, and he had now made the decision to join the parachute division. He was determined to see it through. He had no intention of failing this.

Paul, like Helmut and Erich, had served twelve months in the RAD which was originally a labour scheme for the many unemployed in the early 1930s. He had been proud to contribute to the rebuilding of his country's infrastructure but, on completion of his obligatory twelve months, he had little desire to go back to the factory and continue his apprenticeship. It was not an easy life, though. The days were long, often starting at five in the morning and sometimes finishing as late as seven in the evening. But Paul had excelled and was quickly spotted as potential officer material for the army.

He had been invited to join the Heer by a visiting army officer, which he gladly accepted, and here he was now, working his way towards becoming a paratrooper.

Paul reached the twenty-metre high platform and moved out to the edge of the plank where, one metre below him, the other board sat that he would have to leap to if he was to continue on this path to become a paratrooper. He had never feared heights, but then he had never been this exhausted; never had so much resting on this one jump, the anxiety of it all making him sweat even more than the assault course. He was surprised he had any moisture left in his body after the hard training he had been through. His mouth was dry and his tongue felt swollen in his mouth; he was dehydrated and near to collapse.

He gritted his teeth, pushed his left foot forward and out and pushed off with his right leg and hit the plank below before he had even registered the leap. He suspected that his eyes might even have been closed. The relief was palpable and he could feel his limbs trembling as he continued on the rest of the trapeze seeing the grinning Erich and Helmut waiting for him at the bottom. Even the instructors gave him a reluctant "Well done." He had passed this test; he was one step closer to his precious eagle's wings.

It was day fifteen. Today they had gone through the second 'fear of heights' test for new recruits. Each recruit had to jump into a tank of water from a fifteen-metre high tower. All passed; generally the case if they had successfully completed the trapeze course the previous day.

The next day was spent on a long cross-country run followed by the obstacle course again. They were tested against the clock and against each other, again and again. Platoon competitions were fierce and extracted their innate aggression to the full.

Up until now, Paul and Erich had only received training in using hand grenades and the Wehrmacht's standard Mauser Gew 98 rifle and the Kar 98 carbine, both typical bolt-action rifles with a five-round box magazine. Their knowledge of weapons had to be extensive and intuitive. Behind enemy lines, isolated, they would come to depend on this knowledge. Now they were to learn a whole new range of weapons, such as pistols, machine guns such as the MG 34, sub-machine guns, mortars and mines.

Day after day, all they had to look forward to was arduous physical training, morning, noon and night, a toughening process tailored to the light infantry role that the Fallschirmjager were to fulfil. Physical exercise and drill on the square occupied much of the day during the early weeks. Bayonet practice, unarmed combat sessions, weapons instruction; the training and testing were relentless.

Other tests were to follow; some designed to test leadership qualities, looking for inherent initiative and imagination. Manual skills such as field stripping and reassembling weapons again and again, as ever against the clock and sometimes blindfolded. The worst of the training was the written and oral tests, and exams on subjects as various as military law and national socialist history and doctrine.

Their training programme progressed from squad level tactics through to platoon and company level exercises. As officers, Paul, Erich, Curt and Helmut were pushed and tested even harder than the rest. Everything they did, had to be better and faster than the rest of the platoon. This added a new dimension to the pressure they were already under. Eventually they would tackle such obstacles as replica fortifications with lashings of real barbed wire and dummy minefields. The real test, the test that they all feared the most, more so even than the dreaded obstacle course, the one that caused most of the recruits to be RTUd (Returned to Unit), was the interview with the Commandant whom they first saw on day one. His probing questions were designed to tease out the reasons for a recruit wanting to join the Fallschirmjager and test their suitability to be part of this talented unit.

Finally, back in their barrack room, lying exhausted on their beds, three of them swapped stories of the painful day they had experienced. Erich had caught his combat trousers on the barbs while doing the leopard crawl, and was now making repairs. Helmut came into their room, throwing himself down onto his bed completely burnt out. He had just completed, for the fourth day in a row, a punishment for talking in the ranks. The latest one was for grumbling about his hunger pangs, again. For half an hour, he had been running on the spot with his rifle held above his head, which was excruciatingly painful after only a few minutes. Then he had to run a few yards, again with his rifle held aloft, dropping to the floor in the prone position, back up again and continue to run on the spot.

Curt was just staring into space, his mind elsewhere.

Paul rolled over in his bunk and looked at him. "Are you OK, Curt?"

"My needle's broken, damn it," cursed Erich from across the other side of the room. "Can you throw me your sewing kit, Paul?"

Paul sat up and rummaged through his kitbag and, finding his 'housewife', tossed it over to Erich who continued at his attempt to make a repair.

"Just tired," responded Curt.

"We're all tired."

"I know but, seriously, I can hardly move. How am I going to get out of my bunk tomorrow?"

"A good night's rest and you'll feel like a new man tomorrow," Paul said encouragingly.

"That's if they allow us a full night," responded Curt despondently.

The last four nights they had been pulled from their beds to parade in front of Oberleutnant Nagel. They looked dog-tired and dishevelled compared to the immaculate turn-out of the Oberleutnant. He had participated in all of their activities, completing some of the tasks twice over, due to him having to run backwards and forwards, encouraging the recruits to achieve their best endeavours. He seemed tireless to Paul and his friends.

"It will be OK, Curt old buddy," joined in Erich. "Just do what I do. Pretend you're sleepwalking, go through the motions and, when you return, you'll be asleep as soon as your head hits the pillow."

"I'll give it a try," Curt replied tentatively, not sure of the validity of the advice.

Helmut, as usual, was describing the last Wiener Schnitzel he had eaten back home, at the same time scoffing a biscuit he had acquired from somewhere; constantly being told to shut up by the others whose stomachs were also growling with hunger. All of them were probably too fatigued to get off their beds to eat though.

"As if the training wasn't harsh enough," exclaimed Helmut, still panting on the bed. That was the last they heard from him that night; he was asleep before he had taken a breath.

At that point, the lights were switched off.

"*Scheisse!*" exclaimed Erich. "I've just stabbed my bloody finger. I'll just have to make do and hope it doesn't fall to pieces tomorrow," he said disgustedly, throwing his trousers over the end of the bed. He looked around. No one was listening; they were all asleep, grabbing their three hours a night. Seconds later Erich was in the same state of slumber as his comrades.

Chapter Ten

The tank was a Panzer Mark III. It was loud, big and spewed out smoke and fumes as the driver revved the engine.

"This," shouted the Feldwebel, "is a Panzer light tank. It weighs over twenty tons, carries a thirty-seven millimetre gun and can hit a top speed of forty kilometres an hour. Today, you're going to learn how not to fear it. You will learn to conquer your fear."

The Feld indicated to the tank commander situated in the turret, his upper body in clear view. The tank commander looked down into the confines of the tank and spoke to the unseen driver. The armoured vehicle's engine roared, its steel tracks scraping on the road, ripping up the tarmac as they turned the armoured vehicle around a full one hundred and eighty degrees. The tank moved away from them, stopping at a distance of about three hundred metres.

It swung back round to face them, the engine roaring even louder as the monster jerked forward, slowly gathering speed. Its tracks clanked on the hardened ground, the sound getting louder as it gained speed and got closer to the watching trainee paratroopers. The tank jerked in kangaroo fashion as the driver took the armoured vehicle through its gears, pushing it to go ever faster. By the time it reached the recruits, it had reached a speed of over thirty kilometres an hour and shot passed them, covering them in a film of dust. The tank came to a halt some one hundred metres further along, its glacis dipping and its back end rearing up on its suspension as the driver expertly brought it to a halt.

"Right, gentlemen, it's now your turn to perform. I want you, in troops of five, to lie down head to toe in a line over there." The Feldwebel pointed to the narrow track in front of them. "Make sure you keep your legs together and your arms by your side."

Erich and Paul were in the first group of five soldiers to lie down. Paul lay with his head by Erich's feet and his feet touching the head of Franz, another recruit he had come to know well. He squeezed his legs together so tightly that he almost lost feeling in them and his arms became a part of his body. The revving of the tank's engine could be heard as it lumbered slowly towards the first soldier in line. Paul could hear it getting closer and closer, and sweat started to drip down the side of his face and a pool formed on his chest as his racing heart attempted to cope with the fear that was welling up inside. The adrenalin added to the fear, pushing his body to fight or flight, wanting him to get up and run for his life. But that he could not and would not do. He was in this for the long run.

The tank was just starting to move over the first recruit, next to Erich. There was a scream, fear obvious in the cry, but the recruit remained where he was, frozen to the spot, the fear of getting up in front of the moving monster and then facing his *kameraden* and instructors would be the worst of the two evils.

"I don't like this!" shouted Erich, making contact with Paul to help him overcome his fear.

The tank inched slowly over Erich, the huge mass covering him completely, and Paul could sense the shadow of the tank's glacis approaching him. Now it was his turn, the ground vibrating beneath him, shaking him and making his hair stand on end from fear. A dim shadow was cast over his face and a dark, blue-tinted cloud of diesel fumes washed over him, evading every part of his nostrils, mouth and lungs. The tang of the diesel fumes was bitter on his tongue. The light disappeared and he was in complete darkness. The noise was deafening, the roar of the engine and the clatter of the bogey wheels and tracks either side of his face. His face seemed to nearly touch the dark grey underside of this twenty-ton killing machine. The very tracks that were within centimetres of him now had probably crushed an enemy as they were driven under and aside, as it relentlessly pushed its way forward to victory. Just by raising his hand in front of his face, he could touch its black underbelly. The rear of the tank moved slowly past him, billowing dust trailing behind, choking Paul even more than the smoke and fumes. The tank completed its run, and Paul and the rest of the troop were ordered up and back into formation to watch the next victims. They were shaking, their limbs trembled and they all chattered nervously until silenced by their instructors. This was something none of them would forget for a very long time.

Their arduous training continued into week three with a twenty-five kilometre forced march, with full packs and equipment that stretched them all. Many of them afterwards had blisters that had to be treated with iodine and powder. That experience was almost as excruciating as the pain of walking on burst blisters and skinned feet. Binding them tightly after the treatment was the only way to ensure that they could get through the next day, and the day after that. Their last session of the day was to prepare for their first night-time exercise; after that they were free to eat. Every day, after a full day's training, they fell into their bunks exhausted.

Day twenty-two was a full day on the range and, although hard work, it gave them a much needed break from runs and forced marches – although they had had to march three kilometres to the range. But it was a breeze after what they had been through. Weapons training was their favourite activity. It helped make them feel like real soldiers, not just cannon fodder for the crippling assault course. At one hundred metres, Paul and Helmut consistently scored over thirty-six hits out of a possible score of forty. Erich struggled to get over thirty-five, but excelled with the heavy machine gun. They were frequently reminded of their fifth Fallschirmjager commandment: 'The most precious thing in the presence of the foe is ammunition. He who shoots uselessly, merely to comfort himself, is a man of straw who merits not the title of parachutist.' At the end of the session on the ranges, they were tired and had bruised shoulders from a full day's firing, the recoil of the weapons unforgiving, but they felt satisfied. They had an hour practising throwing hand grenades, and then it was back to barracks for weapons cleaning. Normally an onerous task, but today it was another opportunity to gain some respite and re-energise their depleted reserves. And, for once, Helmut wasn't down for any punishments, yet.

Chapter Eleven

Today they had all reached the end of their reserves, both physically and mentally drained. Erich was all for giving up. Lying face down on his bunk in full kit, he moaned, "I can't take much more of this, Paul. They're weeding us out every day." He looked across at Curt's empty bunk. "Curt's gone. Who's next?"

"Look, Erich," answered Paul, who was also lying face down on his bunk in full kit, "we've got this far. We're not giving up now."

"But we started with forty in our platoon and one hundred and sixty in the company. We're down to just over half of that."

"We can make it. We've just one more week to go until our parachute training, and we're nearly there." Paul looked across to Helmut for support.

"Paul, I can hardly stand, let alone do another forced march."

"Bugger off, Erich, get your arse in gear. Let's get out of here and get the show on the road. The sooner we get through this, the sooner you can buy me a pint in Berlin."

Erich smiled; Helmut certainly had a way with words. He crawled off his bed just as one of the Uffzs came barging into the room.

"Right, you three out," shouted Uffz Blacher. "You have five minutes to get ready for the night manoeuvres."

The Uffz moved off to pass on the glad tidings to the remaining members of the company.

Paul was the first to stir. "Come on then, Erich," he said, grabbing his webbing and pulling him up. "If I'm going out into this pitch-dark then you're damn well coming with me."

Helmut grabbed the other side of Erich and they both yanked him up off his bed.

"If you insist. If we're going to see this through then we'd better get on with it. Otherwise there'll be another empty bunk in this room."

All three looked across at the empty bunk, only recently occupied by their fellow recruit Curt. Curt had been unfortunate in badly straining a leg muscle, but was told he could try again once he was fit enough. The three friends were not so sure. Curt was at the end of his tether and the injury was perhaps a lucky break for him. They didn't believe he would be back. Many others, unfortunately, also hadn't made the grade, repeatedly failing on the exercises they were put through.

"I'll see you two shortly," Helmut said as he left the room. He had to leave to be briefed, as he was to be platoon commander for this night's manoeuvres. Paul, Erich and Helmut had to take it in turns to lead the platoon, at the behest of the instructors, testing their leadership further.

Paul's and Erich's determination had got them through so far. When one was in despair of continuing the course, the other found the strength to rally them both and keep them both on track. They had become close friends since meeting at the railway station on their very first day. Had they known what they were letting themselves in for, would they have turned round at the station and headed back home? At this moment in time, neither could truthfully answer that question. The prize of the parachutist's badge was a great incentive and the only thing that was making them drag themselves to the parade ground every time they were called.

It was three in the morning, two days to go before they moved onto their parachute training phase. Out of the original forty recruits in their platoon at the start, there were only twenty-two left. Their platoon, one of three, was to assault the fourth platoon defending a pseudo-ammunition dump, protected by trenches, barbed wire and a minefield. Paul, Erich and Helmut had each been given a troop to lead. They had to force an entry into the complex, as agreed at the planning stage the previous day, allowing Second Platoon to pass through them and secure the complex. The Third Platoon would feign an attack on the defenders elsewhere, acting as a diversion, hopefully distracting the defenders where the real attack was coming from. Paul and his two friends cleared the wire and the minefield and bridged the trench, after killing two sentries, much to their disgust at having been caught napping. Second Platoon passed through the secured entry point and, by 6 am, it was all over.

They returned to barracks. Although physically and mentally drained, all the energy sapped from their bodies, they couldn't help but feel euphoric and were grinning like wild men. The instructors remained stern, but there was a lightening of their attitude towards the recruits. They knew that the surviving eighty-seven soldiers in front of them had proven their worth. The recruits too knew that they had crossed a line and that they had made the grade. Provided they passed through parachute training, they would pass out as Fallschirmjager. Two more days to get through.

Chapter Twelve

This was the last day of the physical element of their Fallschirmjager training. Today, Paul and his companions were told they would be completing a thirty-kilometre march, with full packs, weighing twenty kilograms, plus their weapons and filled water canteens. The eighty-seven recruits started their march at six in the morning. Had they rested for a few days prior to the march, they would have found it relatively easy as their fitness had improved considerably since they had started their training. After one and a half hours and ten kilometres of marching, the company was well into the swing of it. Paul, Erich, Helmut, Franz and Wilhelm had grouped themselves together, committed to ensuring that they all made it through to the end of the march, giving mutual support throughout.

By ten o'clock and twenty-three kilometres later, they were starting to feel it. Blisters that had recently healed were becoming raw again. Tendons were swelling and rubbing against their boots, but it was bearable. Generally they were in good spirits; they knew that this thirty-kilometre slog was the last hurdle, the last big push before they finished this stage and moved on to the parachute training.

By midday, and having nearly completed the march, although physically drained their morale was high, the end was in sight. The column was halted and told to take a five-minute break. Paul and his group immediately held a conference.

"We must have finished the march by now, surely," Helmut kicked off. "But where the hell are we?"

"I don't recognise this place," added Erich.

"It sort of looks familiar," concluded Paul. "But if I'm right then the camp is a good ten clicks from here!"

"Don't be stupid. The march is only for thirty Ks and we've done that," uttered Franz.

"Perhaps we are being trucked back," suggested Wilhelm, hopefully.

"Something isn't quite right," thought Paul out loud.

His foresight, unfortunately, was proven to be correct as the instructors roused the group, informing them that they still had another ten clicks to go.

This time, their positivity left them and their aches and pains that had earlier been subdued by their euphoria of the march nearly being over returned. The blisters that were sore, the pain that had been blocked out earlier, were back with a vengeance and any hurt they had felt before paled into insignificance, compared to the agony they were experiencing now. Their heavy packs bit into their shoulders, chafing their backs, and seemed to have suddenly increased in weight. Just when they were brooding on the prospect of not being able to take any more, they caught sight of the barracks. Smiles started to return to some faces and even conversations were struck up between a few of the soldiers. This was it, a kilometre to go, it was all but over. They marched up to the camp gates; relief clearly on their faces as it was now all over. That last hill climb had been unendurable and had nearly done them all in. Even the tough Helmut was looking wasted. They formed up as if on parade and were then stood at ease, only to be told that, once they had finished a five-minute break and refilled their water bottles, they had another ten kilometres to go. The gasp from the Company was audible; the look on their faces one of disbelief. One recruit was heard to say, "I can't go on, I can't do this anymore," and to that end he sat down and did not move from the spot. He had got this far, but the course was incomplete. He would be failed. The instructors had thrown down the Fallschirmjager gauntlet and he had not picked it up.

"*Scheisse, scheisse, scheisse,*" Erich sounded off. "I can't march another step. I'm not doing it, sod them!"

Both Paul and Helmut strode up to him, watched by their other two friends, and Paul grabbed him by his shoulders. Paul shook him. "It doesn't matter, we march till we drop and, if one of us drops, then we pick him up!"

"None of us are going to fail this now, having got so far," pleaded Helmut.

Paul looked around at his fellow marchers, including those outside of his circle of friends. "We march till we drop, agreed?"

They all looked at Paul and at each other and nodded, as one, in agreement. The Felds and the Uffzs pushed the recruits back into their ranks and drove them on again. Kilometre after kilometre, it seemed to go on to eternity. The last three kilometres were more of a ragged stagger than a march. When anyone looked like they were wavering, those of the Company close by rallied around them coaxing them on, sometimes resorting to dragging them by their uniform, even though they were exhausted themselves. This is what a Fallschirmjager would do.

Their previously tight formation was now spread over some four hundred metres. Some were walking through their injuries and were in pure agony, but all sensed that this was truly the last stretch. The camp was in sight again; they were nearly through. The training staff slowed the front runners down, pulling the platoons and the Company back into formation, encouraging them to look up, straighten up their gear, instilling some pride back into twenty-seven training company, arriving back at the camp as potential paratroopers, not a rabble.

On arriving back at the camp, they were finally dismissed, the majority just collapsing on the spot. Even the mighty Helmut crumpled to the ground. Many were still there some thirty minutes later. The fifty-kilometre march over soft, then hard, then muddy and hilly ground, in full battle order, had burnt them out. But at least they had finally completed the physical element of their training. Only the four weeks of parachute training was left to get through.

Muscles ached, tendons were stretched to their limits, feet were raw with burst and ragged blisters, skin ripped off exposing the soft, tender flesh beneath. This was all part of testing the recruits to ensure that they were worthy of being paratroopers. Just when you thought you had done enough, you had to dig deep and find those extra reserves that lay unseen deep down inside. They had to draw on that inner, still untapped reserve of energy, find that mental can-do attitude, lift their left leg and march. Eventually they all managed to stagger painfully from the drill square to their bunks. The thought of a shower and hot food was not enough of an incentive to drag their tortured bodies to the canteen though – with the exception of Helmut.

It was somewhere around 6 pm and the evening meal was being served. He dragged his body off the bed, muttering as he left, "Food is food, and you never know where the next meal is coming from." He looked back at his two friends. Paul was lying on his side on his bunk, resting his drawn face on his hand, looking tired, dirty. Erich looked even worse, lying flat on his back, eyes closed, mouth open, still gasping for the oxygen his body desperately needed. "We've done the hard bit, you two," he said through dry and cracked lips, smiling.

Erich turned his face and opened his eyes, looking at Helmut, some three kilograms lighter than when they started the course, and smiled. Paul too looked at his now close friend and comrade and smiled. Their smiles broadened; it was true, they had broken the back of the course.

Chapter Thirteen

At last the day had arrived. They were to find out what being a parachutist was all about: the four-week parachute course. The week started with ground exercises, consisting of ground rolls forwards and backwards, jumping out of an aircraft hatch onto straw matting with further roll practices until they became nauseous. Previously they had done some initial preparation training during their first four weeks. Jumping onto a small trampoline then completing yet another forward roll, but this time from a greater height. Somersaulting in the air over a couple of other recruits hunkering down side by side on the ground, the line eventually extending to six.

The weeks continued with lectures on parachute packing, aircraft drill, parachute flight control, if that was what you could call it, shaking your legs about to assist in steering. Practising the rapid removal of the parachute harness, but under stress conditions. Paul and his comrades found that fun: wearing a parachute on the ground, being blown along by the wind from a powerful aircraft engine, known as the 'Wind Donkey', dragged across the rough ground until they were able to untangle themselves from the harness. Much to the instructors' amusement, Helmut consistently struggled to get through this exercise. He failed to get up quickly enough to grab the lines of his chute and extract himself from his harness so many times that, by the end of the day, he was black and blue. When he finally succeeded, he received applause from the instructors and the entire platoon.

The week prior to the first jump consisted of rain and strong winds. All were cocncerend that the first training jump would be cancelled. Although they were all anxious about their first jump, they were equally keen to see it through, to get past this final hurdle and qualify as a Fallschirmjager, a Green Devil. The bulk of their training was finally complete and they were given the all-clear to jump the very next day. Now they were preparing their parachutes. Meticulous care and attention was taken whilst carrying out the task of preparing and packing the *Ruckenfallschirm mit Zwangsauslosung 1*, or RZ 1, silk parachute. They were all taught to pack their own chutes and worked in teams of two, ensuring they checked each other's work. They worked in the aircraft hangars, the chutes laid out on very long parachute packing tables.

"Well, if the chute doesn't open, Paul, then we can always take it back and exchange it for a new one," joked Helmut.

"That's what I like about you, Helmut, your original jokes," Paul ribbed.

Erich, on another parachute packing line, joined in. "I hope you've packed an extra chute, Helmut?"

"A spare is always useful," he replied, bemused by Erich's statement.

"It isn't for a spare. It's to carry your lunch pack," chortled Erich.

"Give me a table and I can eat on the way down," joined in Helmut, used to the ribbing he got about his eating habits.

This started off a wave of laughter that quickly spread to the other recruits in the process of packing their parachutes who learned of the joke just played on Helmut. He was a very popular soldier, and it was well known that Helmut had the appetite of a wolf.

"If you make a mistake packing your chutes," cautioned the instructor close by, "you will end up looking like Janke's squashed lunch when you hit the deck."

The laughter died down and they refocused on the task in hand, but still smiling. Although the instructors were still very much in charge and often on their case, now that the cadre had completed the physical aspect of their training and they had proven their mettle, they had lightened up a little. The chutes they were packing were an automatically deployable parachute, by means of a static line attached to a wire cable running down the inside centre of the transport aircraft. The *RZ1* had a half globe canopy made from white silk, with twenty-eight sections and was some eight and a half metres in diameter. Paul packed the apex of the chute into the deployment bag first, which was then placed into the outer cover with the apex nearest the top. This was where the static line would be attached. The shroud lines were then packed vertically on top of the deployment bag. The four flaps of the outside cover were then fixed with a securing pin which was also attached to the static line. There were many checks done during the course of the packing procedure to ensure the safety of the paratroopers.

The day had finally arrived. At last they were going to be truly tested, jumping out of an aircraft. Paul had already donned the bulky knee pads designed to prevent knee injury on landing, strapped on his parachute and boarded the aircraft. Although up until that point they had been chattering like a flock of birds, now that they were all embarked, there was nothing but silence. The jokes and banter ceased the minute the aircraft door was shut and the pilot taxied for take-off. The Junkers gradually increased speed, leaving the runway behind and the pilot steadily gained height for the drop. Their thoughts turned inwards now, pondering on the next steps they would have to take, leading eventually to free fall. Questioning whether or not they would have the guts to make the leap, not wanting to be the one person to refuse to go, their stomachs knotted at the thought of climbing out through the door.

Paul clenched the end of the static line between his teeth, leaving his hands free in case the aircraft ran into turbulence or, should they ever parachute into battle, the aircraft came under anti-aircraft fire. The dispatcher gave the order to the paratroopers to stand and hook their static lines on to the cable running down the centre of the Junkers' fuselage. Erich and Helmut stood behind Paul, and another recruit, Ackerman, stood in front. Ackerman shuffled towards the open door, the wind blasting through the opening.

Paul looked over his shoulder. "Good luck."

"You too," his friends replied, very much focusing on the open door where they would soon have to pass through into an unknown world of height, wind and fear.

Ackerman, the first man in the stick, was at the open door, the wind starting to tear at his clothing. He stood apprehensively, making eye contact with the dispatcher who nodded encouragingly. The instructors had all been through this first jump during their recruitment days and knew that the adrenaline would be pumping and hearts would be beating twice as fast as normal. Ackerman braced himself in the doorway, as he had been taught, in preparation for launching himself from the aircraft.

The dispatcher yelled, "*Gehen sie! Geh! Geh!* Go! Go!"

It made Paul jump, even though he had been expecting it.

Ackerman launched himself into the waiting expanse, the static line trailing behind him until the distinctive crack as the chute exited the bag and the gut-wrenching jolt as the chute successfully deployed.

Paul shuffled forwards; taking up his position at the door of the aircraft, his first jump and his heart was in his mouth. He could feel the veins in his neck throbbing as his accelerated heartbeat pulsed blood around his body. He looked down, seeing the fields and houses below him through watery eyes, the wind making him blink rapidly to keep them clear. The wind buffeted his face violently, distorting it, an uncontrolled grimace. He grabbed the two handles, one either side of the door, and, in a crucifix position, launched himself horizontally, spreadeagled, out of the aircraft. This reduced the swinging of the canopy, which the RZ1 was renowned for, particularly in high winds, and would help prevent him from becoming entangled in the shroud lines. He had learnt the appropriate posture by being suspended from the roof of an aircraft hangar having his position corrected by an experienced instructor.

The nine-metre static line, attached to the cable in the aircraft, paid out. Suddenly, it became taut, pulling the canopy bag from the chute pack. The bag, torn from the folded canopy, remained behind attached to the aircraft cable, the static line flapping behind the airplane. Paul was in a state of free fall as he descended through the open skies. After a forty-metre fall, the canopy had fully developed and Paul experienced the tremendous jerking effect as he was, as it felt to him, pulled back up towards the aircraft, but with the rest of his body wanting to continue its downward descent. Paul looked up to check his chute; it looked fine. The biggest fear of any paratrooper was the Roman candle, the shoot failing to open, fluttering above trapped in the shrouds, the parachutist plummeting to his death.

He then looked around him. He could see the patchwork of fields and villages below. The view was stunning and Paul felt like he was on top of the world. The time he had spent dreaming of this day had not been wasted. All the pain and suffering he had experienced during his training had culminated in this first jump. It had been worth it. Five more jumps and he would be a fully qualified Fallschirmjager, a Green Devil. His chute swung him around and he could see Ackerman on the ground below him. He suddenly snapped out of his dream state, realising that he was about to land. Terra firma was getting increasingly closer and a feeling of panic set in. As the ground rushed towards him, he heard his parachute instructor shouting orders to him through a megaphone. Abruptly it dawned on him that he should be bringing his feet together and bracing his legs for when he hit the ground. Suddenly, the ground was there. He hit it hard, attempting to bend his knees so he would hit the ground feet first, then his knees protected by the bulky knee pads, and finally his gloved hands absorbing the last of the fall. But, he failed and he landed awkwardly, landed on his coccyx, the pain shooting up his back as he then fell backwards striking his head, his para helmet saving him from any serious injury. His back hurt and he struggled to get up.

"You stupid bastard, Brand," shouted the trainer. "You're supposed to bend your bloody knees and lean forward like I've been bloody teaching you all week. Get your chute gathered and get back to the hut. You'll be going back up within the hour."

He gathered his chute, the euphoria of completing his first jump numbing the pain in his lower back, and headed back, ready for jump number two. Paul would have to complete a total of six drops before he was entitled to wear the coveted Fallschirmschutzenabzeichen, parachutist badge. The first two jumps were individual jumps from a height of two hundred and fifty metres. The third, he would jump with a full stick of ten to twelve men, from a height of one hundred and twenty metres. Considering the static line was nine metres long, it did not leave much room for error. The fourth was a full stick jump at dawn or dusk, the fifth another stick jump at a similar time of the day. The final jump was a tactical jump by the full Company, now barely two platoons. Once that jump had been completed successfully, Paul, Erich and Helmut would finally gain their coveted parachutist badge.

All drops completed successfully, Paul, Helmut and Erich were awarded the silver and gilt qualifying badge. Instructors, who had recently berated, taunted and pushed these recruits hard, now shook their hands. They were recruits no longer: they were now part of a single elite club, the Fallschirmjager.

Once the passing-out parade through the streets of Stendal was complete, basic training was finally over. They would next head off to a *Fallschirm Ersatz und Ausbildungs Regiment*, FEAR 1, for further training before joining their units. There, the newly qualified Fallschirmjager would learn how to handle all types of small arms, learn how to drive a car, a motorcycle, a truck, half-track, tank and even a steam locomotive. They needed to be able to fight in any conditions or any type of terrain, in whatever surroundings they found themselves in, use any available weapon and drive any vehicle they came across.

They were also encouraged to ask frank questions of their officers and expect to get frank answers back. It was an institution, with a sense of kinship that was driven by a common set of ideals. This was the hidden ingredient behind the extraordinary fighting zeal of the Fallschirmjager.

They were Paul's family now.

Chapter Fourteen

Kurt Student, Generalleutnant, Commanding General of the 7 Flieger Division, was sitting at his desk completing some routine administration prior to leaving his office for a meeting with his senior staff. Although the unit had seen some action in Poland, he was disappointed that they hadn't played a key role in the invasion. Even though they had prepared to parachute in to assault some key locations, such as airfields, the invasion moved so quickly that events overtook the planning, and Wehrmacht units secured the targets before the Fallschirmjager even boarded their aircraft.

It was midday, on 27th of October, when his Chief of Operations for the 7th Flieger Division, Major Heinrich 'Heinz' Trettner, disturbed him.

"What is it, Heinz?" he said impatiently, irritated at being interuppted. "You know I have a meeting I must go to now."

"I know, sir, but this has greater importance. Field Marshall Goring is on the phone and wants to speak to you quite urgently."

"OK, I suppose this is one call I must take. You'd better put it through."

Trettner picked up the phone situated on the corner of Student's meticulously organised desk and asked the operator to put the call through before handing the telephone to his Commander.

"Herr Field Marshall, what can I do for you?"

"Kurt," replied the tinny voice at the other end of the line, "I need you to come to a meeting at the Reichskanzlei—Reich Chancellery—at once."

"The purpose of the meeting, sir?"

"I can't discuss that with you now, Kurt. Just get yourself over here as quickly as possible and all will be revealed. I don't even know what it's about myself. When can you be here for?"

"I can get to Tempelhof by about one, sir. Can someone collect me from there?"

"I'll organise it. See you this afternoon."

Goring put the phone down and General Student immediately ordered a Feisler Storch, a small reconnaissance aircraft, to be warmed up. He would fly himself to the meeting in Berlin, ensuring he was there by the early afternoon. He cleared his desk, picked up his leather briefcase and, grabbing his hat and coat, left. He headed down to the vehicle he knew would be there to take him to his waiting aircraft.

The plane was ready, engine warm, and, strapping himself in, he turned the plane towards the runway, his mind contemplating the purpose for his summons, and flew to Berlin.

He landed at Berlin's airport, Tempelhof, just after one thirty and was collected by limousine and taken directly to the Chancellery where the Commander of the Luftwaffe, Field Marshall Herman Goring, welcomed him. Student saluted and they shook hands.

"Good timing, Kurt. Come, I'll take you straight through to the map room. The Fuhrer is keen to meet with you."

"Have you any idea what it's about, sir?"

"Even I've not been taken into the Fuhrer's confidence on this occasion, Kurt. You know as much as I do. How is the Division shaping up after Poland?"

"They are disappointed that they didn't get to see more action. Why weren't they given more to do?" The frustration was clear in the General's voice.

"The Fuhrer gave explicit instructions for your Fallschirmjager to be involved in only limited operations. Anyway, Wola-Gulowska was a success, wasn't it?"

"Yes, sir, they did well. Particularly Hauptman Volkman and a young Leutnant Brand."

"Yes, Oberst Baum made me personally aware, and the Fuhrer himself authorised the awards for that action."

They had arrived at the map room where the secretary led Student inside, requesting the Field Marshall to remain outside. Student followed her in through the large door. He had been here before and never ceased to be impressed by the magnificence of the walnut-panelled room. Hitler was stood with both hands leaning on a large table that was strewn with various maps. He looked up when Student was escorted in and the General saluted, but didn't move from his current position.

"I have a job for you, General Student, and I want to know if you can complete it. This Belgian fort here," said Hitler pointing to the map, "do you know it?"

Student walked over to the map and looked at the area where the Fuhrer was indicating. "Yes, my Fuhrer, I know it well. It's a very formidable emplacement."

Hitler pointed to various aspects of the fort, highlighting structures, gun emplacements and the canal that ran alongside it. He pondered over the map for a few moments before saying, "I have an idea – I think you could land assault gliders on top of Fort Eben Emael and storm the fortress for me." He looked Student straight in the eye. "Is that possible, General Student?"

The Fuhrer's statement and his question stunned the General. The idea was both audacious and yet quite simple in its concept.

"I will need some time to think this through, my Fuhrer. It would certainly be difficult to drop a stick of paratroops onto such a small target and the slow, noisy Junker 52s would give ample warning of any attack." Student ticked the points off in his head. "Jumping from the minimum height of ninety metres," he mused, "they would be spread over a two hundred-metre area. Then they would have to swiftly get to their weapons' canisters before they could start the assault. There would also be some weighty explosives to carry to their targets. The gliders' stealthy approach, on the other hand, would certainly be preferable. Yes, gliders would be a sensible option."

"Well, General Student, let me have your full thoughts by tomorrow. We will meet first thing and I'll share with you a few other surprises I have up my sleeve." Hitler called for his secretary and Student was led out of the map room.

On his way out, passing through the opulence of the Reich Chancellery, newly designed and built by Speer, he gave consideration to the conversation he had just had with Germany's great leader. What possible reason could the Fuhrer have for attacking a Belgium fort? Does he want Belgium next, he thought. Was it part of something bigger? Surely not; they had only just finished a war with Poland and, prior to that, they had reoccupied the Rhineland, instigated the annexation of Austria and occupied the Sudetenland. Britain and France surely would strongly object to any further expansionist plans and act accordingly, with force.

After sleeping on it, Student called in to the Imperial Chancellery the next day, to give Hitler his reaction to the potential operation, although it seemed that the Fuhrer had already made up his mind. Hitler was already convinced that the glider operation was the correct one and the undertaking would succeed.

Student was again taken to the map room. This time, Hitler seemed anxious and clearly not in a mood for a protracted conversation, hence Student quickly came to the point of the meeting: his affirmation that his paratroopers could indeed assault Eben Emael from the air.

"Well, can it be done?" questioned Hitler.

"Yes, my Fuhrer, it can be done, but there is a prerequisite if we are to have any chance of success," pointed out Student.

"And that is?"

"The landings must be made in daylight. If not, at least during the twilight hours."

"Excellent!" Hitler nodded. "Then start making your plans."

"Yes, my Fuhrer. Will your orders be issued immediately?"

Hitler did not seem to hear the question and motioned Student to take a seat next to him as he proceeded to tell the General a story about World War 1. The aim of the story was to impart information regarding the development of a new type of explosive, a hollow charge weapon.

"It can penetrate any structure." Hitler conveyed, "whether it is steel or concrete."

"If true, my Fuhrer, it will take great pressure off the glider force which would otherwise have to carry an excessive amount of high explosives. The paratroopers would also have to manhandle those explosives to the targets."

"Oh, it is true, General Student, don't doubt me."

"I never doubt you, my Fuhrer. Do I have your order to take the fort?"

"Yes, yes, General Student, you have. Take that fort for me! But, this plan must be devised and prepared for in utmost secrecy," Hitler whispered softly, pressing both hands face down on the table, emphasising his point. "I also want you to plan for the securing of the bridges at Canne, Vroenhoven and Veldwezelt."

"What is the purpose of these assaults, my Fuhrer?"

"The Albert Canal equips Belgium with an intimidating barrier blocking any invasion from Germany," pointed out Hitler. "We need to overcome that barrier if we are to be successful in a Blitzkrieg attack on the West."

"An attack on the West?" Student responded in surprise. "Is the army ready to fight such a battle so soon, my Fuhrer?"

"You let me worry about that, Generalleutnant Student," said Hitler dismissively. "I will show you."

Hitler and Student pored over a number of photographs of the bridges crossing the canal and of the Fort Eben Emael. He had evidently studied all aspects of the strengths and weaknesses of the targets. "If we are to successfully transit Belgium, in order to get to France, these bridges across the canal and the Eben Emael Fort must be secured and held," Hitler reiterated.

Hitler and Student discussed the involvement of the Fallschirmjager in the Norwegian and Polish campaigns. Although they hadn't necessarily distinguished themselves, primarily as they had not had the opportunity as they had not been heavily committed, Hitler was still pleased with what they had done. They had only been involved in small-scale actions, so it was very difficult for the paratroopers, a new organisation and a new concept, to make its mark. The unit had, in fact, only completed one operation that involved a parachute drop, this being a small action to secure an airfield to enable reinforcements to be flown in by more conventional means.

Hitler assured Student, after he had made Hitler aware of the disappointment the Fallschirmjager felt at not being more extensively used in the Polish campaign, that they would certainly see some action in the West. Hitler was a clear advocate of airborne troops and their use in future operations, particularly in his substantial plan for invading the West. Hitler made it clear to Student that the airborne and paratroopers were a new untested force that was very much a German secret weapon. He turned back to his maps, pondering his next moves. Student was clearly dismissed and he left the map room quietly.

The following day a courier arrived at Student's headquarters with an important dispatch for the Generalleutnant. Trettner knocked on Student's door and entered his office.

"There's an SS courier here to see you, sir. He is insisting that he hand delivers the dispatch to you."

"You'd better show him in then, Heinz."

"He is from the Reich Chancellery, General. Is there something I should know?"

"All in good time, Major, all in good time. Now please escort the courier to my office."

Trettner left the room and the courier entered the office minutes later. Taking the dispatch from his highly polished leather pouch, he handed it to Student who in turn signed for it, and the SS courier left. He quickly opened the orders and scanned through them. Flieger Division and 22nd Infantry Division, under Student's command, would take the Belgium Reduit Nationale, in the area of Ghent, from the air and hold this important line of fortifications until the arrival of the army. A detachment was to be tasked to destroy the fortress of Eben Emael and further detachments should secure the bridges over the Albert Canal, allowing the Sixth Army to cross the Maas and Albert Canal.

He tapped the document with his finger. "Granite, so the code name for the assault on Fort Eben Emael is 'Granite'."

Although a quiet, modest man, when given the task of forming the Fallschirmjager Division, he had taken it up with gusto. He would apply a similar approach to the Fuhrer's latest orders. Now he had his orders from Hitler, Student wasted no time in preparing his plan to carry out the mission he had been assigned. He sat at his desk, considering who best to lead this daring attack on the Belgian fort. He would also need someone in overall command as the Fuhrer had ordered him to secure three bridge crossing points over the Albert Canal. The people he would need for these four tasks would need to be special, very special. He had discussed it with Oberst Baum, Commander of the First Fallschirmjager Regiment, FJR1, the previous day and it was agreed that a special assault force would be assembled, and Hauptman Wilhelm Kaufmann, the Commander of a Company in FJR1, would assume command immediately. Yes, he had decided, it would be the young career officer, Hauptman Kaufmann. He was both a qualified pilot and a born leader of men. Student had been tracking his career for some time. He was just the person to see this bold stratagem through. Who could he give him as his number two? Someone to back him up, mused Student; he will need a strong team around him. His decision finally rested on Oberleutnant Joachim Faust, currently the Commander of the only engineer platoon in the Fallschirmjager. He knew him to be self-reliant and a competent officer, another potential rising star. He called for Major Trettner.

"Heinz, I have decided on Kaufmann and Faust to lead the

assaults." Student had briefed Trettner earlier in the day on the possible choices and the Chief of Operations had pulled the files on all of the key officers of the Fallschirmjager for Student's perusal.

"The perfect choice, sir," agreed Trettner. "Could I also suggest you incorporate some of Oberleutnant Volkman's Company? He's about to be bumped up to Adjutant, so they will be looking for a new company commander."

"Excellent idea. Leutnant Brand, in particular, proved himself during the action in Poland."

Student pushed the personnel files aside and got up from his desk, walking round to the front and perching himself on the edge. Thinking deeply, his right elbow supported by his left arm, stroking his chin with his right hand. He looked at Trettner. "We could use Brand's platoon and incorporate it into Faust's engineer platoon, putting Faust in overall command. What do you think?"

"That would work, sir. Perhaps we could use other troopers from the Company? Have you considered who might command the glider force?"

"Krause, Heinz, Wilhelm Krause. I talked to General Kesselring yesterday and we are both in agreement that he is the right man for the job."

Kesselring the new Chief of Staff of the Air Corps was aware of Krause's skills as a glider pilot and recommended him without hesitation.

"Where are they now?"

"Still in Poland, sir."

"Are they on any operations at the moment?"

"They're in the process of packing up, sir. I was about to get you to sign the orders for their recall."

Student returned to his desk, looked up at his ops officer and ordered, "See it's done, Heinz, but make sure they're well aware of the secrecy of this assignment. They are to be told nothing, other than they are to be attached to a trials battalion. I want all reference to Fallschirmjager and their military ranks removed from their uniforms. Understood?"

"I will see to it right away, sir." Trettner turned and left Student to his thoughts.

Student deliberated on the task he had been set by Hitler. The entire Western offensive could be dependent on the success of the mission entrusted to him, which he was now going to entrust to more junior officers. He sat back in his chair, lacing his clasped hands behind his head, contemplating the outcome of this bold plan. Germany, it appeared, was to go to war again. This time, his Fallschirmjager would have a key role to play, but what about the bigger picture, he pondered. Germany had just finished a war with Poland. Britain and France were still sabre rattling. Where would a war with the West lead them? The decision had been made – he couldn't influence the outcome now; only ensure that his paratroopers played their part and played it well. He pulled across a sheet of paper and started to draft the high-level plans for this daring operation, born from the mind of their great leader Adolf Hitler.

Chapter Fifteen

Paul, Max and the rest of the platoon had been recognised for their success in the recent action in Poland and had been seconded to a trials battalion. They didn't quite understand what this meant and were initially disappointed that they were being pulled out from an operational unit and sent to a camp in Hildesheim. Their new Company Commander Oberleutnant Faust, Oberleutnant Volkman having moved to Battalion HQ as the Adjutant, assured them that they would not be disappointed.

Hildesheim, a city in Lower Saxony, Germany, is located in the district of Hildesheim, about thirty kilometres south-east of Hanover on the banks of the Innerste River which is a small tributary of the Leine River. The Hildesheim camp, located in the foothills of the Harz mountains started off as a sports airfield primarily used by gliders, prior to being utilised as a long-range reconnaissance school in 1939.

At the guardroom, their identification was thoroughly checked before they were allowed through the gates. Security was extremely strict and, once in, nobody was allowed to leave the barracks without the appropriate authorisation.

Prior to their arrival at Hildesheim, the seriousness of the mission was impressed upon them and they were ordered to sign a declaration stating, 'I am aware that I shall risk sentence of death should I, by intent or carelessness, make known to another person by spoken word or illustration anything concerning the base at which I am serving.' They had been ordered to discard their paratrooper uniforms prior to arriving at the training camp. Equally, no signs of rank were to be worn. The enemy was not to be aware of the paratrooper specific operations training at Hildesheim, and certainly not the prospect of using gliders to land on a target. They reported to the airbase administration and were allocated their quarters.

On the way to their accommodation, they saw a strange engineless aircraft. This was the first time Paul and his platoon had seen a DFS-230, a ten-seat glider. They had known nothing of their existence until then.

"I don't know about you, Max, but I certainly wouldn't want to pilot one of those, or be a passenger for that matter."

"Perhaps they're for dropping supplies, sir. Not much use for anything else."

"Maybe they're still waiting for engines to be fitted," said Leeb suddenly, not wanting to consider the potential alternatives.

Little did they know that, in six months, they would be dropped out of the sky in those very same gliders onto one of Belgium's strongest forts.

"Bloody airfield construction platoon!" moaned Max. "How do I explain that to the females in the bars of Hildesheim, sir?"

"Max, neither you nor I will be going to any bars for some time. You know the orders," cautioned Paul, although he knew that Max was just playing the jester for the benefit of the platoon, trying to raise the spirits of the unit.

Although he was also disappointed, Paul suspected they would be doing something out of the ordinary. As yet though, he couldn't foresee anything preferable to remaining in an operational unit and being with their comrades in Poland.

"I'm sure you would manage to come up with some cock and bull story that made you out to be a hero of the Fatherland."

"That's not fair, sir." Max smiled.

"You just want to flash that tin of yours around."

"No point in having it, sir, if you don't get the benefits."

Looking at Max's grin, which spread from one side of his face to the other, Paul knew exactly what he meant. "You are incorrigible, Unterfeldwebel!"

The rest of the platoon were also smiling now. They were used to the banter that flowed between their two seniors.

They arrived at a brick-built, three-storey barracks and were allocated accommodation. Paul and Max had a room each while the rest of the platoon bunked down in rooms of eight. They acquainted themselves with their new home, followed by an evening meal in the cookhouse. How long it was to be their new home was any one's guess. A good night's sleep and they would then be briefed the following morning on the purpose behind their stay at the salubrious Luftwaffe hotel.

★

It was 8am on a cold winter's morning and Paul and his platoon, along with other soldiers, pilots and civilian staff were assembled in one of the wooden training huts in the Hildesheim army camp. Situated in the foothills of the Harz Mountains, it attracted the cold weather like a magnet. The temperature was barely reaching two degrees during the day and dropped to well below freezing point during the night. The black wood-burning stove, dominating the centre of the room, gave out just enough heat to make the temperature in the hut comfortable, although those at the extremities of the building often felt a slight chill.

The surrounding area was used by the German army for training and manoeuvres and was well suited to the type of training the assault force would need to facilitate.

The training hut, barely lit by the four low-watt bulbs suspended from its low ceiling, slowly filled up until just under five hundred officers, men and pilots were in attendance. Paul and his platoon felt quite inconspicuous in the mass that was assembled there.

There was a buzz of conversation as some paratroopers were reacquainted with old friends or colleagues and swapped stories, catching up on old news. There was also, naturally, a good deal of discussion about the purpose behind such an assembly of soldiers and airmen.

The door at the far end of the hut opened again letting in, briefly, a cold blast of air, making the stove flicker as a result of the draught caused. In walked Hauptman Kaufmann, followed by Oberleutnant Faust and Leutnant Krause, who made their way through the assembly to a small raised platform at the far end of the hut. The three of them mounted the platform and stood behind the chairs and small table that had been placed there for their use.

"Gentlemen," boomed Kaufmann's voice, "please find yourselves a seat, or at least somewhere to perch for the next twenty minutes."

The assembled men found what seats or benches they could, or sat on tables or desks, or even just propped themselves up against the hut's wooden wall. Most tried to get as close as possible to the only source of heat in the hut.

Once they had all settled down, Kaufmann continued. "I'm sure you're all keen to know why you've been brought here," he resumed, loud enough for all to hear. "To this dismal place, and plucked away from your parent units."

Hauptman Kaufmann was a tall, handsome officer, born in

Bonn Germany in 1910. In 1938, he was promoted to Hauptman and actually trained as a pilot, but was quickly brought back to his unit to form Sturmabteilung Kaufmann, which consisted of the individuals now sitting listening to him.

"I'm afraid I can't reveal all to you just yet, but I can tell you the basics, and that we are to train for a number of key operations to be conducted sometime in the future. This group of soldiers and airman, the training that you'll be conducting, is highly secret. You have all signed the secrecy pledge. Be in no doubt, gentlemen, if the purpose of our group and its activities were to get out, it would not only jeopardise our country's interests but could put our future operations, and our lives, at risk."

He looked around the room, attempting to make eye contact with as many soldiers and pilots in the room as possible, to emphasise his point. "Any breach by any of you in this room will have dire consequences for that individual or individuals; one of those consequences being the firing squad."

He remained quiet for a few seconds, allowing the gravity of his announcement to sink in. "Right, enough of that, now to the purpose of our mission. We have to secure four targets. The targets will not be revealed to you at this stage. In order to secure those targets, I will be forming four groups. Sturmgruppe Beton will be commanded by myself. Sturmgruppe Stahl will be commanded by Oberleutnant Adler, his second in command being Leutnant Fleck."

Paul looked at Max and, like Paul, Max's look was one of disbelief. Erich too had been dragged into this escapade. He hadn't noticed him, but he would certainly try and see his friend as soon as the meeting was concluded.

Kaufmann continued. "Sturmgruppe Eisen will be commanded by Leutnant Schiffer with Leutnant Janke as his number two."

Again, Max and Paul looked at each other in amazement. Elements of the First Company they thought they had left behind in Poland must be in the room with them somewhere. Paul and Max immediately started to look around the crowded room and, at once, started to pick out troopers that looked vaguely familiar as being from Second and Third Platoons, comrades who had fought alongside them in Poland.

"And finally," Kaufmann was still speaking, "Sturmgruppe Granite, commanded by Oberleutnant Faust with Leutnant Brand as his second in command."

Now it was Max's turn to stare at Paul in astonishment. He was sure that, in this tightly packed room, Leutnant's Fleck and Janke would be experiencing the same level of incredulity.

"I know you will have lots of burning questions, but please hold them back for the moment. Once this meeting has broken up, your respective group commanders will brief you. Thank you, gentlemen. We will see each other frequently over the next few months."

The trio gave instructions as to where the particular groups were to meet their respective commanders before leaving the stage and exiting the training hut. The soldiers and airmen in the hut slowly moved towards the single exit point, making their way to the next meeting point. Paul's group was to go to a hut similar to this one, but towards the end of the camp. Before they left, Paul and Max frantically searched for their comrades.

Paul spotted Erich first. He looked less skinny than the last time they had been together; clearly being back on decent rations was doing him good. Paul clawed his way through the throng, grabbing Erich's right hand, shaking it hard and gripping his shoulder with his left.

"God, it's good to see you, Erich!"

Erich grabbed Paul's shoulder and the fallout they had recently had over the secrecy of Paul's deployment was now forgotten. Both were ecstatic at being together once again, although it was to be short-lived. "It's great to see you, Paul. You too, Unterfeldwebel."

Erich shook Max's hand, genuinely pleased to see the stocky sergeant. Paul suddenly shot forward as a huge hand clapped him on the back, making him lose his balance. It could only be one person who would consider greeting Paul in this way and Paul turned to see Helmut with a beaming grin across his face.

"One day," said Paul, "you're going to do that to the wrong person, you know." But it was said without malice; it was just Helmut's way, larger than life. He also shook Paul's and Max's hand then threw his arms around Paul, giving a huge bear hug.

"Has he been behaving himself, Unterfeldwebel?" questioned Helmut.

"I couldn't possibly say, sir," responded the diplomatic Max. "If you officers will excuse me, I'd like to track down some real soldiers," and he went off in search of the other platoon Felds to catch up on the news.

The three looked at each other, a trio that had gone through training together; through their first combat experience together and here they were again.

"So, Paul," interjected Erich, "are you airfield construction, experimental tactics or toilet cleaning?"

All three of them laughed.

There was a moment of silence as the three *kameraden* stood in a circle, hands placed on each other's shoulders, genuinely pleased to be together again.

All of a sudden, they felt embarrassed at this show of affection and, after a few awkward coughs, they let their arms drop to their sides.

"So, what happened after I left?" Paul asked, curious as to what had happened when he left Poland.

Helmut answered first. "Well, the very next day I was dragged into the Raven's HQ."

"Battalion HQ now, you know he's been promoted Adjutant, don't you, Paul?" butted in Erich.

"Who's telling this story?" rebuked Helmet.

"Yes, I do know," replied Paul. "That will shake the battalion up."

"He'll be battalion commander before you know it," added Erich.

"Hauptman Volkman. Scary, isn't it."

"Anyway," continued Helmut, looking perturbed at the interruptions. "I was called in to the Adjutant's office and was told by the Raven we'd been selected for special duties."

"Yeah, latrine digging." Paul laughed.

"My first thoughts exactly," replied Helmut, "knowing the Raven's sense of humour."

"Get on with it," said Erich impatiently, noticing that the hut was slowly emptying and they would have to follow the others to their next briefing.

"OK, OK, I just want to get all of the facts right."

"Get on with it," supported Paul, punching him softly on the shoulder.

"He said my platoon was being sent to Hildesheim for duties unknown. We had to discard our badges of rank and put on this bog standard Luftwaffe uniform. You know the rest."

"And you, Erich?"

"Same as Helmut. The day after you'd gone, I got the same speech and here I am. I'm just pleased that we're all together again. Hopefully, we'll be involved in something together."

"Sir," resonated Max's voice. "We need to get a shift on."

"You scared the shit out of me then, Max!" complained Helmut jokingly. "You're like a bloody panther creeping up, and then you open your mouth and scare the bloody living daylights out of everyone."

"Sorry, sir, I didn't realise you were still of a delicate disposition."

Only Max could get away with it, being the most experienced soldier in the Company. He was highly respected by the three young officers.

"Right, come on then, Max," ordered Paul. "Before you get yourself court-martialled for your insubordination." He turned back towards his friends. "I don't know what happens next, but best of luck to you two. We'll try and get together sometime soon, yes?"

They all agreed and started to move towards the exit door, the hut emptying at a faster rate now. The three officers were some of the last to leave. Paul and Max joined the platoon that had been waiting for them outside. The other two platoons were also there; it was almost like a big family reunion. The group broke up, comrades promising to keep in touch, and Paul's platoon walked down the tarmac road to their destination: hut twelve.

The hut was the same size and configuration as the training one, along with the wood-burning stove. By the time Paul's platoon had entered, along with the engineers already there, there numbered fewer than one hundred people. The layout was similar: desks, tables and chairs strewn around the room which they quickly organised at one end of the hut. On this occasion, there was much more room available, as they were just a fifth of the numbers attending the initial briefing. They made themselves comfortable, taking advantage of the tea and coffee that had been laid on for them. Biscuits too. Paul could imagine Helmut's delight and smiled to himself.

Max saw him smiling and smiled back, glad to see his platoon officer back on form again. He knew that Paul had been troubled by their departure from Poland, and suspected that all was not well between him and his two friends. But all was tranquil again. He threw some more logs on the fire, the sizzling and spitting clearly heard as the wet logs impacted with the hot core, and settled back to wait patiently for the next briefing. One lesson he had learned during his time in the Luftwaffe: patience was obligatory.

Chapter Sixteen

The door to the hut opened, and Oberfeldwebel Kanitz, the company senior sergeant, brought the room to attention as Oberleutnant Faust made his entrance.

"At ease, gentlemen."

He made his way over to where Paul was standing and shook his hand. "Leutnant Brand, I get to meet you at last. You're gaining quite a reputation for yourself."

"Thank you, sir, your reputation precedes you as well," Paul reciprocated.

Oberleutnant Rudolph Faust was born in Gelsenkirchen in 1916. At the youthful age of nineteen, he began his military career as an officer cadet in the army's pioneer Battalion 16. He remained with the engineers for only ten months before he was enticed into the new voluntary service, the paratroopers, the Fallschirmjager. By this time, he was commissioned as a Leutnant. He was promoted to Oberleutnant in 1939, and now here he was in command of the pioneer platoon and Paul's platoon that now formed Assault Group Granite.

"I shall give a general briefing to the men now; then you and I and the senior NCOs can go through some of the elements in more detail before opening it up to the group."

"That makes sense, sir," agreed Paul.

"Right, let's make a start then." Faust made his way to an area of the hut that had been set up with a six-foot table, a map board and an easel. There were also various empty noticeboards attached to the walls close by. "We have been allocated an extremely difficult mission," he began. "Just a little over five months to prepare for it. So, be prepared for the long haul." He looked around at the expectant faces of the group. "Our task is to assault a major facility which, unfortunately, I cannot divulge to you at this time. I can't even tell you where it is, what it is, or show you any pictures, for the moment anyway."

The group members looked at each other, all probably thinking the same: how do we prepare to attack a target we know nothing about?

"I will again reiterate Hauptman Kaufmann's security brief. Who we are, what we are doing here, and the purpose of our long-term goal must be treated with utmost secrecy. To the extent that no one will be allowed to leave the barracks unless specifically authorised and there will be no mail or phone calls, in or out. Do I make myself clear?"

The assembled men all nodded their heads and murmured their agreement. Military secrecy was not new to them.

"Do I make myself clear?!"

"Yes, Herr Oberleutnant," they all shouted.

"We will assault this target from the air, not by parachute, gentlemen, but by glider. It is my intention that we put the assault force directly on top of the target."

He waited a few moments for that to sink in, the fact that they would be landing by glider, something none of them had done before, and to allow the murmuring to die down.

Max turned to look at Paul. "So, those papier-mâché gliders are not for dropping supplies after all. They're for dropping us."

"So it would seem, Max, so it would seem," replied Paul calmly, becoming more and more intrigued by this operation and the innovative approach that was being taken. His interest was well and truly captured. They were not going to help construct airfields after all, although, deep down, he had never believed that that would be the case.

"We have nine specific targets to assault, secure and destroy, by landing on them directly. The group will be spilt accordingly, but I shall cover that in more detail at a later date." Faust turned to the easel behind him and pinned up a picture of the DFS Glider. "This will be our taxi," he said, pointing to the glider. "It can carry ten men, with their equipment, or over a thousand kilograms in weight. We will need to get used to it. Sitting in it, getting in and out of it, securing any equipment or explosives we'll need to take with us. We will also need to train extensively in the use of explosives."

Faust made eye contact with the engineers that he had brought with him from his engineer platoon. "I'm sure the sappers amongst us will be more than willing to demonstrate their skills at blowing things up," he said, smiling. "You will practise with explosives until it becomes second nature to you. As we won't initially have any plans of the target, for security reasons, we'll have to recreate a pseudo-target, on the ground, that matches the dimensions of the actual objective. We've been allocated a section of the training area, specifically for our use. We also have this hut as our base and our company headquarters. Most of our internal training will be completed here. Tomorrow we start work, gentlemen."

This was clearly a big undertaking, thought Paul. It was going to require all of their skills, wits and stamina and would undoubtedly test them to the limit. Paul looked at the Oberleutnant whom he knew by reputation to be a strict disciplinarian and a meticulous planner, so Paul had no doubt that the months ahead would be tough and the pressure would truly be on. Faust also believed in realistic training, so it would be intense and not without risk. Like Paul, Faust held his men and NCOs in high regard and gave them the opportunity to contribute to the planning, enabling them to help mould the plan specific to their element of the operation.

"Right, I've talked enough, I think. Are there any questions?"

Paul was the first to ask a question, probably one that was on the minds of most of the soldiers and pilots there. "Oberleutnant, are you able to tell us about the bigger picture? What will the impact of our operation have on the wider context? Besides us, what are the three other groups tasked with?"

"They are valid questions, Leutnant Brand, but I'm afraid, for the moment, both questions will have to remain unanswered. We have explicit instructions, as regards the dissemination of information, to work on a need to know basis. The Fuhrer himself has instructed all military units to operate on that basis, regardless of what activity they are involved in, but particularly where sensitive information is concerned."

Paul had known the answer even before he had asked it, but the question had to be posed so that all present knew where the information line was drawn.

"But I assure you," Faust continued, "when I can release available information to you, I will share it with the group immediately. I understand the need for security, but equally I don't expect my men to operate in the dark when it's not necessary. Thank you, gentlemen. Except for Leutnant Brand and the Senior NCOs, you are dismissed for the day. But, we start in earnest at o eight hundred tomorrow, meeting here. Leutnant Brand, if you will please remain here. Oberfeldwebel, take the senior NCOs to the canteen, get yourselves a drink and meet back here in one hour. Thank you, that's all."

The group started to disperse and Paul made his way over to Faust.

"Right, Paul." Faust pulled up a chair and sat astride it, its back facing towards Paul. "Let's go over my plans and see what you think."

Paul grabbed a chair and joined the Oberleutnant at the table.

"I wanted to go over them with you first, before we share them with the rest of the group. If you have any concerns, ideas or changes you think should be made, then speak up, OK?"

"Understood, sir," replied Paul, suppressing his excitement at the prospect of this clearly important operation they were being entrusted with.

Faust pulled out a rolled-up schematic and unrolled it on the table. Placing weights on the four corners to hold it down, he then smoothed it out. To Paul, it appeared to be a plan of some sort of complex alongside a river or canal. It actually looked like a large fort, with various bunkers and turrets, of a type he had not seen before.

"This," Faust said, pointing at the outline of the structure on the western side of a waterway, "is Fort Eben Emael, which is situated just inside the Belgian border. The actual site for this new fort was determined by the course of the Albert Canal which runs through a channel carved out of a massive feature known as Mount St Peter, some forty metres high. This feature known as the Caster Cutting runs some three hundred metres in length starting from the Lanaye rocks on the Meuse River. Its high, sheer sides are a natural defensive position that is an integral part of Eben Emael's strength. Construction for this fort began in April, 1932, and was completed after three years under the supervision of Commandant Jean Mercier of the Corps of Engineers."

"And its purpose, sir?"

"This cutting here, which goes from south to north and is over one thousand metres long, links the Albert Canal and the Meuse. The cutting and the sheer embankment created by it act as its eastern barrier. The fort overlooks the Albert Canal and its purpose is to protect those bridges that are within its range and prevent an enemy from crossing."

"It's pretty big, sir."

"And well armed, Paul. To the south," he pointed to the chart, "this block is a two-storey structure armed with two sixty-millimetre anti-tank guns and three machine guns. Here is a four-metre gap to cross, impassable by men and machines without the retractable wooden bridge or other crossing equipment. This position itself is covered by an additional machine gun emplacement and the ability to drop grenades from special slots onto the attackers attempting to scale this four-metre gap."

"They've certainly gone to town on their defence," concluded Paul.

"I'm far from finished. On the western flank of the fort is block two; similarly armed to block one, with two anti-tank guns and three machine guns. But, it also has a sally port to enable the defenders to counter-attack any assaulting force. Protecting its eastern flank is block four and five. Block four is the weaker of the two armed emplacements, with two sixty-millimetre anti-tank guns and two machine guns."

He tapped the plans on the table. "Although block five only has one anti-tank gun and two machine guns, sat on top of it is Cupola Sud. It has a retractable cupola with twin seventy-five millimetre guns. These can quite easily target the bridges over the canal, the very bridges that we need to secure. It has a sister turret, Cupola Nord, also with twin seventy-five millimetre guns."

"I take it that these will be some of our targets?"

"Yes, and there are many more. We can't share this with the group yet. It's like a ring of steel and is going to be a tough nut to crack. I can understand the need for secrecy, but it won't make our training easy."

"What about the Dutch?"

Faust tapped the map again, making a sweeping gesture across the border of Belgium and Holland. "The peninsular that juts out here, east of Maastricht, creates a barrier between Germany and Belgium. It's very narrow. So, it's unlikely that the Dutch could hold an enemy up for long."

"Creating a problem for the Belgians, I guess," added Paul.

"Yes, the Belgians hope that the Dutch will hold back any attacking force long enough for them to blow the canal bridges situated here, here and here." Faust had pulled the map across in front of Paul and pointed out the three main bridges across the canal: the Canne, Vroenhoven and the Veldwezelt.

"Will we have to take out the guns they've got to protect the bridges with?" probed Paul further, his searching mind coming to the fore.

Faust took a liking to this young officer, although not much younger than himself. He was inquisitive and clearly had a sharp mind. They would get on well, he thought. "They have one hundred and twenty-millimetre artillery pieces to cover the bridges and various armaments to protect themselves from attack. That's what we have to deal with."

"Are the bridges the targets of the other groups?"

Yes, a sharp mind, thought Joachim. "Right on the button, Paul, that's exactly where they will be dropped."

"Are we invading Belgium and Holland?"

"Those are questions that even I don't have the answers to, Leutnant Brand. Unfortunately I'm not party to the bigger picture, so they're questions we should probably not pursue," rebuked Faust, but only mildly, he was probably just as frustrated at not knowing the greater scheme of things. "So, let's just focus on our task, eh? We'll have enough on our plate, believe me. No one else in the group knows, or is to be told what our target is, or its location, OK?"

"Hence the need to map out a representative target on the ground with tape," mused Paul out loud.

Faust pulled the schematic of the fort forward again. "There are nine key objectives, consisting of cupolas housing six one hundred and twenty-millimetre guns, casemates with seventy-five-millimetre guns and a number of sixty-millimetre, and machine gun posts. I have grouped them into the nine objectives, an assault glider to be assigned to each one. That leaves two gliders in reserve."

"How many troopers are you assuming for each glider?"

"Eight, including the pilot. We have quite a high weight of explosives to carry, the consequence being a reduction in capacity for the number of soldiers that can be carried."

"So, we focus the training on a specific target for a specific glider and its troop?"

"Yes," agreed Faust, "but we'll have to allow for some cross training, in case a glider fails to make the objective. Each troop will have a primary and a secondary objective."

"How will you compile the teams, sir?"

"Good question, Paul, and one that I have deliberated on for some time. Initially, I was going to mix the group, have your men interspersed with my engineers. But your platoon has worked and fought together, so they know each other's strengths and weaknesses and have confidence in each other. The same for my engineers, except they haven't seen any combat, unlike your troopers. So, we learn from each other during training, but for combat they remain the cohesive team they are used to being part of."

"So, my platoon would make up four glider troops?"

"Yes, and any troopers that are spare will be allocated to one of the reserve gliders."

"That selection is not going to be easy," thought Paul out loud, sharing his concerns with his new company commander.

"Don't dwell on it for too long. I suspect we'll all be in the thick of it."

"What else, sir?"

"I have an outline of the training schedule."

"That will help to get everyone focused quickly, sir."

"That's what I intend. They're certainly not here for a holiday." Faust grinned. Turning to the easel and board behind him, he pinned up a chart he had just pulled from his leather briefcase. It was a training schedule. He had clearly been busy while Paul and the rest of the group had been making their way here.

"There are four key training requirements. First, we must become familiar with the gliders. We must learn how to pack them and how to move about them quickly. We don't want some clodhopper putting his boot or his assault ladder through the skin of the glider."

"Particularly not in flight," added Paul.

"Exactly, they need to move about the glider as if it was their second home."

"What about how it handles in flight?"

"Good point. I had considered that and have discussed it with Leutnant Krause. He is just as concerned about the lack of experience amongst his pilots of flying these gliders. So, he has an extensive training programme for them. First, we shall get the pilots to fly the gliders empty, giving them a chance to get familiar with the flight characteristics; also good practice for our Tante Ju drivers," said Faust, referring to the Junkers' pilots. "Once they are familiar with the handling of the empty gliders, we will gradually increase the weight until we are ready to add a human cargo: us."

"I can picture their faces," ventured Paul. "They're used to making their own way down to the ground. They won't relish losing that control."

"It's certainly going to be an eye-opener, Paul, and that goes for all of us," Faust concluded. "They need to get the feel of the glider in flight, how best to secure themselves, and how to brace effectively for landing. More importantly, once landed, how to get the hell out of there quickly."

"Once they're on the ground, they're a fixed target," added Paul. "They'll have to get out bloody fast if they don't want to be target practice for the Belgian soldiers. How many exit points are there?"

"Either through the middle exit door or out through the pilot's canopy."

"So the pilot could be one of the first out?"

"Yes, so they have to be as equally well trained in close-quarter combat as us. They will be our security until the rest of the troop exit the glider. The second key training aim is in the use of explosives and how to destroy, or at least damage, the armaments. Not forgetting the use of heavy machine guns and flame-throwers."

"What will we have available?"

"We will naturally have conventional explosives, but we will also have the new *Hohlladung*, a hollow-charge weapon."

Faust pinned up a picture of what looked like an inverted cone. "This is a hollow-charge explosive. It is a specially configured explosive that can penetrate most known steel and concrete structures that we are likely to come up against. I won't be revealing this to the troops just yet and, even when I do, they will not be allowed to use it in the way it is designed. We'll need to find a way around that somehow, to ensure realism. I won't be introducing the group to those until later in the training programme. They are highly classified, so I want to leave their use until the last possible moment."

"Another secret." Paul grinned.

"Afraid so," retorted Faust, smiling back. "My engineers can take the lead on that in due course. They'll be in their element blowing things up. They can then pass on the rudiments necessary to ensure the rest of the group are able to use the explosives effectively. Thirdly, the actual assault on the target objectives: where we go once the glider lands, the route to get there, what action we take on the way and what we take with us. Basically, what we do when we get there."

"Can my troop take the lead on that?"

"That's exactly what I had in mind. Your men will respect my engineers for their knowledge in explosives, but equally my engineers will respect your troopers because they have been in combat. And, finally, fitness. I know you're thinking that your men, and my engineers for that matter, are fit enough, but we have to be sure. We have to be able to hit the targets hard and fast. Destroy the targets while the defenders are off balance, before they gather their senses and hit back. Also, they will be carrying excessive amounts of equipment. Apart from their own supplies of ammunition and grenades, there will be flame-throwers, heavy explosives and assault ladders. You get my gist, Paul?"

"How long will we be on our own, sir?"

"The plan is for six hours, but you and I both know that's the best case scenario. Should our relief get held up, we could be on our own some time. Then sleep and rest will be a luxury we will have to do without. So, fitness training will be a key criterion in the programme. The NCOs will be here shortly, so I think we should conclude our discussion for now. Any questions, Paul?"

"Not for the moment, sir. I'm sure lots will crop up once we start the Chinese Parliament with the NCOs."

The NCOs, including Max, joined the two officers and they thrashed out the basics of the plan to assault the target, obviously not disclosed to them, and the training schedule that would ensure they were well prepared for it. The debate with the NCOs was lively. A Chinese Parliament was a term widely used by the military community, whereby the unit as a whole was given the opportunity to influence how the operation was conducted. This was a key criteria for the Fallschirmjager.

Chapter Seventeen

Max poured himself and his platoon commander a piping hot coffee, placing it on the table next to Paul who was deeply engrossed in the document in front of him. He was studying the schematic of Fort Eben Emael; not the real schematic but an outline that gave little away about the actual target. It worried him that they were training for such an operation with so little information at the beginning. He knew what the target was, he knew the enormity of what they were up against, but did not share it with his men.

He pushed the schematic aside, exposing the cup stains and graffiti that now scarred the well used oak table. Max pushed the cup in front of Paul, encouraging him to break out of his musing. Sometimes he worried too much, thought Max, and it was usually for others and not himself. They had spent the morning preparing their section of the hut, getting it ready as base for their platoon, somewhere they could use to display their maps and diagrams. They were to conduct a background briefing for the platoon. Today was the day that they would inform the platoon about their troop composition and the objectives they would have to secure. Behind them, the rest of the unit milled around.

"Shall I gather the lads round, sir?"

"Yes, Max, do that. Let's get this thing kicked off."

"Right, you lot," Max called. "Gather round. Time to get some work out of you."

"Pull up some chairs and get yourselves another drink," instructed Paul. "There may be some biscuits left if the Unterfeldwebel hasn't eaten them all."

The platoon laughed and Max growled, "You'd better leave some of the ginger snaps!"

The splashing of mugs being filled and chairs being scraped across the wooden boarded floor ceased and the platoon of twenty-six men, some were missing, settled down, waiting patiently for the start of their commander's briefing. This brief was more personal than the ones given by Kaufmann and Faust. This time it was their leader and the actions that came out of this would be carried out by them on the battlefield.

"You have all been told the basics of the operation that we're to be involved in," confirmed Paul. "Now the Unterfeldwebel and I will appoint your troop line up and designate the targets specific to those teams."

The platoon glanced sideways at each other; they now felt that the move from Poland had been worth it after all. In fact, the rest of the battalion had returned to Germany and were now kicking their heels in their barracks. Both Paul and Max could sense the suppressed excitement of the platoon.

"We have been assigned four targets and will be allocated four gliders. Each glider will carry one pilot and seven troopers."

"Doing the sums, sir," piped up Leeb, the Commander of Number One Troop, "that will require twenty-eight men and, including yourself and the Unterfeldwebel, we have thirty-two."

"On the ball today, Leeb, I didn't know maths was your strong point," noted Max.

"You are quite correct, Uffz Leeb, four of the platoon will be attached to another troop, hence the four that are not here with us. But, that doesn't mean they won't see any action. On the contrary, I have been assured that we will all have an equal opportunity to get to grips with the enemy. Max, can you read out the team lists."

"Troop one will be yours, Leeb. You'll have Geister, Beiler, Fessman, Petzel, Stumme and Jordan. That adds up to seven, just in case you couldn't work it out." The corner of Max's mouth turned up in an amused expression. "The eighth will be your pilot. Once the pilots have completed their initial flight training, they will be joining us."

"Will they play an active role once we've landed?" questioned Leeb.

"Once we've landed, they will play a full role in the assault and, beforehand, they will train with us, not alongside us. Is that clear?"

The platoon all nodded, taking the Unterfeldwebel's point onboard.

He continued. "Troop two will be commanded by Leutnant Brand. With him will be Kienitz, Forster, Straube, Kempf, Weyer and Konrad." They all nodded in acknowledgment.

"Troop three, Fischer, is yours along with Lanz, Halm, Braemer, Roon, Sesson and Wagner.

"And finally troop four. You've drawn the short straw as the remainder of you will get the pleasure of working with me."

There was a good-natured groan from the troopers that were left: Waldau, Renisch, Geyer, Rammelt, Geib and Pelz.

They knew that they could expect no quarter from the Unterfeldwebel as he got his team ready for the task ahead, but equally he would ensure that the entire platoon was pushed hard and were at their peak, well able to carry out what was being asked of them. They all knew that this tough NCO's leadership and military skills would enhance their chances of success, and survival. Saying that, the other troop commanders would be equally persistent in bringing their teams up to speed for the forthcoming action.

"Now you know your troop line-up," announced Paul. "We'll now go through your targets. It will only be at a high level at this stage but, as we build up our intelligence on the target, we will add it to our pool of knowledge."

"Troop one, Uffz Leeb, will have a cupola to secure and destroy. It has two seventy-five-millimetre guns, and there will no doubt be a machine-gun post providing cover as well. Troop two, my troop, has to secure and destroy a casemate, which is believed to contain three seventy-five-millimetre guns. Again, there will no doubt be supplementary cover. Following this, we have another bunker to tackle, with machine guns that have a two hundred and ninety degree arc of fire.

"Troop three, Uffz Fischer, your target is an anti-aircraft position. Taking that out is crucial to the safety of the gliders that will be following us in. But, you haven't got off that lightly," continued Paul, smiling. "I know you like a challenge, so you have a secondary objective, another cupola, which holds two one hundred and twenty-millimetre guns."

"And last but not least, Unterfeldwebel Grun. Your target is another casemate. This one also has three seventy-five-millimetre artillery pieces, and again probably defended by other emplacements. We will all have additional targets that we'll need to be familiar with, in case a glider fails to arrive, or the troop it was tagged for fails for some other reason."

They all knew what the other reason was: either failure through incompetence, or death.

"Once we've successfully destroyed or secured our targets, we will have other tasks to complete. But, these will be done as a consolidated unit. The four troops will then effectively operate as one."

Paul put his hand up in the air, palm facing outwards, as he'd noticed that the platoon, quite naturally, was on the verge of bombarding him with questions. "I know you have a lot of questions and queries floating around in your heads, but at the moment the information I have and the information that I can release to you is minimal. If I were to speculate, or provide you with inaccurate information, it could be detrimental to the operation."

"How are we to train then, sir, if we don't know what we're training for?" challenged Leeb, always the most outspoken of the Uffzs, but also the strongest leader and a likely replacement for Max one day.

"Shall I take this one, sir?" asked Max, recognising that his platoon leader was being put in a difficult position. He had a duty to his men, to provide them with the information and best tactical solution for their upcoming mission, but equally he had an obligation to keep the main target confidential, to preserve any leaks from getting out and potentially jeopardising the sortie.

Max continued before Paul could respond. "As Hauptman Kaufmann and Oberleutnant Faust have alluded to, we will mark out the representative dimensions of the target on the training area allocated to us. This will enable us to practise our orientation and movement to and from our glider landing points and our respective targets. We can get a better understanding of speed and the difficulties we might come across carrying the equipment we will have taken with us."

"But," interrupted Leeb again, but he wasn't allowed to finish.

"Uffz Leeb, you're not listening to what you're being told," interjected Max abruptly. "We have to do the best we can until the necessary intelligence is made available to us."

Leeb remained quiet, his frustration clear, but he knew better than to cross the line with his platoon sergeant. Both Paul and Max empathised with him but were unable to impart any more information.

Paul joined in. "I understand your frustration, Leeb, as I do for all of you. But, it is what we have been dealt. We have five months to prepare. In the meantime, more and more information or intelligence will be released to us as and when it becomes available."

"So," continued Max, "let's focus on getting to understand the scale and dimensions of our target as a whole, become conversant with the gliders, your first flight being in about two weeks. Familiarise ourselves with the explosives and other equipment we will need, and build up our fitness."

Paul took over again. "We'll be creating a sand model in the hut here, building up a picture board as photos become available, and improving our knowledge of the targets."

The duo continued to pacify the platoon, conveying as much information as they were able, with Max taking a turn again.

"We shall be visiting and examining various complexes that are not dissimilar to our target, so you will acquire some experience, to touch and feel, and appreciate its scale."

Paul finished off by closing the meeting. "The rest of the day, our four troops will be given explosives instruction by our sappers and, by the end of the day, there will be a rough schedule of the training plan on the board in here. Dismissed. Thank you, Unterfeldwebel."

Chapter Eighteen

The first month at the Hildesheim camp was spent building up their level of fitness. Although relatively fit before they arrived at the camp, it was not at a level acceptable to Hauptman Kaufmann or Oberleutnant Faust. Or, for that matter, Leutnant Brand, who recognised not only the importance of the target but also their need to be physically ready for it. All three wanted 'Group Granite' to be honed to perfection; the same for the other groups, not wanting a lack of fitness to hinder any aspect of the operations. This had meant long runs, carrying increasingly heavier weights, almost reminiscent of their recruitment days at the training camp in Stendal.

But today was the day they were going to familiarise themselves with the glider, something none of them had ever seen close up before. They had seen the pilots conducting training flights and had seen the gliders scattered about the camp but, to date, they had not been given the opportunity to touch one or climb inside. The DFS-230, known as a freight-carrying glider, was now being inaugurated into the Fallschirmjager's arsenal as a means of carrying them into battle.

Max looked at the twelve-metre glider with horror. He turned to Paul and whispered, "Sir, they can't possibly be serious about us flying in that thing, surely?"

"It looks like it's a distinct possibility, Max. Just look at those luxurious seats."

At that moment Oberleutnant Faust joined them. "Right, gather round."

The paratroopers gathered around to listen to the commander of 'Group Granite'.

"This is the DFS-230 glider. For this simple operation that we have dreamt up for you, this is going to be your taxi. No jumping out of Tante Ju; we'll be landing in style."

The group laughed, supporting his joke.

"The glider will allow us to approach the target noiselessly and probably undetected until it's too late for the enemy. It will also enable the troop to be inserted directly onto the target as a cohesive unit, with weapons at hand, rather than being dispersed as you would parachuting. And then having to get to the equipment canister for your personal weapons. For this morning, I just want you to familiarise yourself with it. Get used to climbing in and out of the glider, sitting down in it with your weapons, moving around inside and exiting through the two openings at the side and through the cockpit roof. We'll have seven troopers aboard each glider, plus the pilot. You need to be comfortable with this aircraft, even more so than you would with a Junkers. Although it's built of tubular steel construction and has wooden wings, the body itself is fragile. The last thing we want is a jump boot or rifle barrel poking through the sides. It may improve ventilation, but will do the airworthiness of the glider no good whatsoever."

The group laughed again.

"The pilot will probably ask you to leave, isn't that right?" he said to Leutnant Krause, turning to the glider pilot who had just joined the group.

"It might have an impact on its trim," Krause said, smiling.

"Leutnant Krause is in command of the glider flotilla and will answer any questions you may have about his baby. Right, gentlemen, you have the next four hours to familiarise yourselves with your new mode of transport. Carry on."

Paul turned to the other NCOs also in attendance. "There are three gliders so my platoon will take this one, and split the other two between you, OK?"

The two NCOs acknowledged with a nod of the head and called to their men.

"Gather round," Paul called to his contingent. "We'll go over it one troop at a time."

"And take it easy. We don't want any damage. You never know, this may be the one we have to fly in!" added Max cheerfully.

"Unterfeldwebel?" piped up Fessman, the platoon comedian. "They're kidding, aren't they? It looks like it's been built in someone's backyard."

"Maybe we should fill it full of ballast, add you to it, and send it up for a test," responded Max.

"Maybe he wants to be a wing walker, Unterfeldwebel," added another.

"Didn't you know, Fessman, you're the one who has to climb out of the cockpit and release the tow rope," pointed out another paratrooper from the back of the ranks.

Paul looked at Max and nodded, Max understanding that it was time to stop the horse-play and move on and explore the craft in front of them. There was no frustration in Paul's nod or Max's subsequent orders to start to do what they were there for. Both of them welcomed the banter generated by the platoon. It just added to the feeling of camaraderie that there was amongst them and the Fallschirmjager as a whole. Although a little wary, the paratroopers had every faith in the gliders and the pilots who would fly them. These craft were going to deliver them to the point of battle.

Paul turned to Krause to ask a question. "The wheels, are they jettisoned after lift-off?"

"Yes, Leutnant Brand, we'll be dependent on the ski for landing."

"Does it have brakes, sir?" queried Max.

"Unfortunately not, Unterfeldwebel, but we are currently looking at ways to slow it down. Any suggestions would be more than welcome. We are considering barbed wire wrapped around the ski as one potential option."

"What's the landing distance?" continued Paul with the questioning. If he was putting his life in the hands of a frame with wings, he needed to have some comfort that all would be well on landing.

"Its expected landing distance is thirty metres, but we are, as I have said, experimenting with some alternative braking systems."

Paul was the first to step in through the side door. He looked around; it certainly wasn't spacious inside. The seats were in tandem, in a single line, six facing forward and four facing backward. The rear four were removable to allow the carriage of additional equipment or supplies. In fact, for the upcoming mission, three of the rear seats would be removed to allow the paratroopers to store the additional explosives they would need to take with them to tackle the fort's defences. Paul looked left to the pilot's cockpit, if you could call it that. It contained a seat and a few controls. The instruments were phosphorescent, to allow the pilot to see them in the dark, and included an airspeed indicator, altimeter, turn-and-bank indicator and compass; the minimum required to fly the glider effectively. Not so much fly, more control it plummeting to the ground, thought

Paul. He looked up at the top of the canopy and, standing on the pilot's seat, pushed the canopy up and over to the right. He envisaged climbing out through that exit point with weapon in hand. It would be difficult and, should the pilot survive the landing, he would probably be one of the first out. He moved deeper into the glider, the gap either side of the seats being not much more than the width of a man's boot, reaching seat number six facing forwards, where he sat down. He looked to the front of the light aircraft and saw Max's bulk entering the glider, followed by other paratroopers. Paul could already hear the glider creaking in protest as a result of the weight being imposed on it, steadily increasing as more and more troopers climbed onboard. The seat was small and hard, and the space cramped. He was told that they would not be in the air for more than forty minutes, which was just as well. Loaded with the pilot, seven paratroopers and their personal equipment, plus the additional equipment they would need to take in order to complete their mission, any longer and it would get quite uncomfortable and claustrophobic. Just wearing his jump suit, without all of the additional paraphernalia a paratrooper wore, Paul's six foot two frame was very snug indeed, his head touching the roof of the craft. Just a quick calculation of ten seats in a twelve-metre glider allowed only one and a quarter metres of space for the paratrooper's seat, himself and his equipment. That did not take into account the space required for the cockpit and, of course, the tail plane.

Max moved up to where Paul was sitting, trying the straps that would hold them securely when the glider hit the ground. "I'm not sure it's safe for me to sit down, sir." He grinned.

"We'll have to put you on a diet then."

"I'm not getting enough food as it is, sir!"

Max sat down on the seat in front of Paul and, with just the two of them, it appeared as if the entire cabin was full.

Paul slid back to enable the other soldiers of his troop to position themselves astride the long bench that ran down the centre. When all seven were seated, they got the first impression of just how little space there was and how difficult it would be to decamp from the plane. Should the glider be damaged, on its side, or even having somersaulted, they would have to make a fast and furious but difficult exit.

"Right, Max, I'm going to have a look around the outside. Let the rest of the guinea pigs take a look at their palatial mode of transport."

"Where do they serve the coffee and *bratwursts* on this bus?" a paratrooper was heard to sound off.

It was just typical of the soldiers' sense of humour and it hid what they were really thinking. They were going to fly into battle in a fragile box with wings, without an engine, with no armament and limited control of its descent. In fact, the paratroopers had no control at all.

"A flying box," Paul thought out loud.

"It is pretty much what it is, sir," agreed Max, reflecting on what his platoon commander had just said. "Let's go, sir. I'm getting claustrophobic already and I haven't been onboard for more than a few minutes."

Paul and Max moved back towards the central door, practically climbing over the other men, a lesson learnt already: last in, first out; and exited out of the door, ducking down under the wings and into the fresh air. A thump and a groan from Max indicated that he had not ducked low enough. The relief was palpable. The one positive, if there was one, was that at least the paratroopers would be more than ready to get out of the glider when it landed. The other men of Paul's troop also exited the plane, allowing the rest of his assault force to take a turn in the confined space.

"We clearly need to spend some time getting acquainted with that baby," said Max.

"We need to allocate some time to run through loading and unloading," agreed Paul. "We can start off slowly and then practise until we are able to get out in record time."

"Definitely start off slowly, sir. It won't take much to damage the outer skin if we're not careful."

Paul and Max started to walk around the external elements of the glider. Looking at it from front on, they could see just how narrow it was; no wonder it was so cramped inside. Moving further around the side, they could see that the ski, situated in between the jettisonable pair of wheels, ran as far back as the centre of the wings.

Max bent down to look underneath the glider. "We don't yet know what type of ground we'll be landing on, but if it's something like wet grass, this baby is going to take some stopping."

"Let's hope that Oberleutnant Krause and his team come up with some braking solutions, eh, Max? Right, let's go and talk to the troops and get some feedback on their experience and answer the questions they will undoubtedly have."

The officer and the NCO returned to the side of the glider to gather the men together and discuss the advantages, and disadvantages, of their new means of transport.

Chapter Ninteen

It was towards the end of January 1940 and the weather had deteriorated considerably. Although daytime temperatures were starting to climb to a high of minus eight, the night-time temperatures could still drop below minus twenty.

Sturmabteilung Kaufmann had been exercising now for three months and the training was progressing to Hauptman Kaufmann's satisfaction. Group Granite had slowly built up its stamina and general fitness through vigorous physical training, enhanced by carrying extremely heavy weights, mimicking the weights of the explosives they would have to carry for real. They visited fortresses in Czechoslovakia and Poland in order to see how they were constructed, their general layout and, more importantly, what the key issues were in assaulting such formidable structures. It was clear that, although flame-throwers could have a significant impact on taking such heavily fortified bunkers, they couldn't damage them enough to make them inoperable. And, to enable the paratroopers to access the bunkers, they would need to use a significant amount of high explosives to achieve entry, and ultimately, their total destruction. But, they were concerned at the magnitude of explosives needed, to be used across the eleven assault troops, and the subsequent impact on the weight carried by the eleven gliders. They were finally going to be taken into the confidence of Hauptman Kaufmann, Oberleutnant Faust and, ultimately, the German High Command, and told of their Fuhrer's new secret weapon.

Today, they were going to Karlshorst in East Berlin, to the sapper school, where they were to receive a second lesson in fortress construction, the first lesson being prior to a future visit to the Benes line in Czechoslovakia. They had flown up from Hildesheim the previous night, staying overnight at Schonefeld airport. They were also going to get hands-on exposure to explosives' handling. Apart from Oberleutnant Faust and Leutnant Brand, Group Granite was still not party to the true identity of the target they were to attack.

The unit struggled to put their training activities into perspective at times, piecing together the relevance of each activity presented to them. At least today they would be shown one of the army's secrets: the new wonder weapon. A weapon, they were told, that would overcome their concerns about tackling the thick steel doors blocking the entrances to the bunkers, the concrete embrasures, the armoured turrets and observation cupolas.

"Are you ready, Max?" Paul asked.

"Yes, sir," responded Max. "I've always wanted a career in construction. Had I known I was going to be an airfield construction engineer, then train to be a builder, I would have gone straight from the docks to Holzmann's." Philipp Holzmann AG was a German construction company based in Frankfurt.

"You could always put it to good use when you leave the Fallschirmjager, Max," said Paul with a smile.

"A future without the Fallschirmjager, sir?" Max retorted in mock surprise.

"Come on, Unterfeldwebel, let's get moving before you have me in tears."

Max called out to the platoon. "Let's be having you," he commanded. "Troops one and two to truck one, and three and four, you've got truck two."

The paratroopers, stamping their feet and flapping their arms about them to keep warm, started to move towards the trucks. Clouds of frozen respiration hung in the air. They climbed onboard their respective vehicles, huddling together on the benches to benefit from the additional warmth of each other, the driver then securing the rear canvas flaps as per his instructions. Security was still paramount, and the movement of troops in and out of the camp was kept very much under wraps. Paul and Max claimed the passenger seats in the cabs, it was their unwritten right, secretly pleased that they would have the benefit of the cab's heater. But, even that was struggling to maintain a decent temperature inside the cab, it being so cold outside. There was some sympathy for the troopers in the back of the unheated cargo area, but it didn't last for long. Character building, thought Max to himself as he headed for the cab of the second truck.

Paul was soon engulfed in the warmth of the cab, now that both doors were shut, and asked the driver, "How long to Karlshorst?"

The young Luftwaffe driver, quite small and skinny, probably not much older than eighteen and who didn't even look as if he had started shaving yet, turned to Paul, his thick spectacles perched on the end of his nose, one of the arms taped together in an obvious temporary repair. "About an hour, sir."

"Wake me when we are about ten minutes away," instructed Paul.

"Yes, sir," the driver confirmed, snatching peeks at his passenger, wondering who these tough-looking Luftwaffe soldiers were who had suddenly descended on his camp. They certainly didn't look like normal Luftwaffe airmen or soldiers. Especially that mammoth one of an Unterfeldwebel, who made him jump every time he opened his mouth. He thought no more of it. He had specifically been told not to ask any questions. He put the troop carrier into gear, let out the clutch and pulled slowly forward towards the open gate, checking his wing mirrors to confirm that the second vehicle was following.

Suddenly, Paul felt his arm being shaken, and he awoke with the right side of his face cold having been pressed up against the side window of the cab.

He felt stiff and his arm ached where he had slept on it, while using it to support his head. They had arrived at the Karlshorst camp, passing the monolithic, two-storey main building and driving round to the rear of the depot. After showing his pass to the guard, they were quickly driven through the rear camp gates without any further interference, obviously expected.

A major met them as the platoon decamped from their vehicles. Paul followed him into a small stand-alone building, where the proverbial wood-burning stove was throwing out as much heat as it was able. The men made for it eagerly congregating round its heat. It had been a cold journey in the back of the canvas-covered wagons.

The major approached Paul, introducing himself and shaking his hand. "I'm Major Muller." He turned towards two NCOs who had just entered the building, followed by two sappers bringing in an urn of coffee and *kuchen*, cakes, a welcome sight for the frozen Fallschirmjager, who immediately flocked around the perceived feast. "And this is Feldwebel Rhodes and Feldwebel Scholz."

They both saluted the major, but not Paul, his rank not obvious to them.

"This is Leutnant, uh." The major hesitated, not having a

name to give them, "From an airfield construction platoon based in Hildesheim." They then both saluted, Paul returning it.

"It is he and his men who you will be instructing today." He turned back to Paul. "Both Feldwebels are explosives experts and have used most of their talents in anger in Poland. I don't know what you gentlemen are up to, or even who you are, but I have been instructed, from the highest levels, to offer you every assistance, particularly in the handling of explosives."

"Thank you, Herr Major, I appreciate any assistance you can give us."

The major looked at Paul who, like the rest of his platoon, wore no unit insignia or titles or badges of rank. However, he did notice Paul's Iron Cross Second Class and his combat badge; he and some other members of his unit had evidently seen combat. But he had been given specific instructions to give them any assistance they may require, and was not only left in no doubt as to the consequences of not providing them with the necessary support but also the consequences of discussing their presence on the camp with anyone.

He turned to the two Feldwebels. "I shall leave them in your capable hands. Should you need anything then contact me immediately."

The two Feldwebels drew themselves up into a position of attention and saluted the major, as did Paul, and responded, "*Jawohl*, Herr Major."

The major turned on his heel and then left.

Paul and Max walked up to the two NCOs, shook their hands and introduced themselves as Paul and Max. The two Felds had no idea who they truly were, but Paul had the presence of an officer, and the stocky Max certainly carried himself like an NCO.

"We are in your capable hands, gentlemen. How do you propose to conduct the day?"

"We'd like to split your unit into two, sir," replied Feldwebel Scholz. "One section being instructed on conventional explosives and the second section will be shown the *hohlladung*, hollow-charge weapon."

"Right, let's get on with it then. Over to you, Max."

Max split the unit into two groups. The first group headed off with Feldwebel Scholz to look at conventional explosives; the second group went with Rhodes to look at the new weapon that had finally been made available to them.

The first group were given the basics of handling explosives, such as bangalore tubes, blasting caps, pole charges, particularly useful for pushing into an embrasure of a bunker, cluster charges, ball charges and demolition charges. Once given the theory, they put it into practice on the ranges, small explosions sounding round the camp at regular intervals.

At midday, they broke for lunch and were escorted to the canteen. They were seated in the engineers' canteen, but were allocated tables well away from the rest of the occupants. The canteen was generous in size and well lit; the engineers were obviously well catered for.

Max sat down next to Paul, placing a plate of *bratwurst* and *sauerkraut*, along with a pile of potato noodles, on the table. Lowering himself into the well-worn seat and stabbing at a *bratwurst* with his fork, he muttered, "They certainly eat well here, sir. Can we get a transfer?"

Konrad chipped in, "I haven't had gingerbread since I left Germany to go to Poland." He tucked into it and sipped on a glass of fresh apple juice.

"There's coffee and *kuchen* afterwards," added Halm. "They live like kings here."

"Yes," agreed Paul, "but they are not Fallschirmjager."

They all nodded; not one of them would swap places with the engineers, good food or not.

After an excellent lunch, it was back out into the cold for the paratroopers to continue their training. This time, the groups swapped over and it was Paul's group's turn to look at the new super weapon.

"Right, gentlemen, gather round," instructed Feldwebel Rhodes, placing his hand on a large conical device in the middle of the table.

Fortunately for this aspect of the instruction they could remain inside, benefiting from the heat generated by the stove.

"This, gentlemen," he said, patting one of four devices laid out on the table "is a *Hohlladungwaffe*, a hollow-charge weapon. There are three types: this oblong one is a three-kilogram standard demolition charge, the beehive-shaped one, a twelve and a half-kilogram hollow-charged weapon, and the father of them all at fifty kilograms which, as you can see, is split into two parts. Come forward and get a feel for the weight."

The troopers gathered round touching and picking up the devices.

"This is going to take some carrying," said Leeb, struggling to pick up the fifty-kilogram dome.

Rhodes intervened, separating the two parts of the explosive device. "It can be broken down into two, each part weighing approximately half of the total."

"That's better," concluded Leeb, picking up the device again. "But it's still bloody heavy. How long to reassemble, Feldwebel?"

"They can be carried to the target by the web-carrying handle, and once there can be assembled in about twenty seconds, by screwing the two sections together. You then detonate it with a ten-second delay, *sprengskapsel*, a number eight igniter, inserted into the top of the charge."

Max turned to Paul and whispered, "We'll need to find a simple way for the men to carry that thing to the target. They'll need to keep their weapons at hand. We can't afford to have half an assault troop carrying and not able to defend themselves."

"You're right, Max," agreed Paul. "We'll also need to practise assembling the larger charge on top of the target, in double quick time."

"The smaller charge is a single piece?" piped up Fischer.

"Yes," responded Rhodes. "It's ignited in just the same way as its larger brother. One thing I do need to add – the larger of the two has to be handled with care. It is of a delicate make-up and handling it too roughly could have a dampening effect on its potency."

As a group, they got used to the weight of the devices, assembling the larger one and going through the process of setting the fuses.

"Right, enough of looking, let's take it outside and let a few of them off. These are expensive bits of kit to make, so we'll be joining the other group for this demonstration. If someone could bring the small and large hollow-charges?"

Leeb picked the larger device, one in each hand and exclaimed, "God, these are bloody heavy. I hope we don't have to run far with them."

"Stop whinging, Leeb," called Fischer. "Pass one here and get on with it."

They left the building and joined the other group on the ranges to see a live explosion of this new super weapon. By the end of the day, they were fatigued and also slightly deaf from the blasts of the numerous devices they had exploded during the day. This had been a real hands-on session, not just an introduction. If handled correctly, they would add real value to their mission; handled carelessly, they would kill the handler. On completion, they were once again settled in the trucks to take them back to their overnight barracks at the airport. Tomorrow, they would be having a lesson in construction, Max's favourite subject. On the return back to the airport, Paul and Max shared the cab of the first truck, much to the delight of Leeb and Kienitz, who shared the second cab, Fischer having been too slow and losing out. Max leaned towards Paul, who was sitting on the window side of the truck's bench seat, and, so the driver wouldn't be able to overhear, whispered, "It's all well and good seeing those explosives being set off, but they're not much bloody use blowing a dent in the ground!"

Paul was equally perturbed by the demonstration. The instructors had been given explicit orders not to explode the device in the way it was intended, on an armoured cupola or concrete structure. They had in fact exploded it on the ground. Although it made an impressive sound and shook the ground beneath them, leaving only a shallow crater, they didn't actually see it punch through concrete or steel. "I agree, Max. I will speak to Oberleutnant Faust on our return."

They both fell into a silence after that, not wanting to say too much in front of the driver, but also the warmth of the cab, the rhythm of the journey, slowly lulled them both to sleep. All soldiers, the world over, take any opportunity to sleep. In combat, they never know when that luxury will be theirs.

The driver looked across at them: the burly sergeant and rangy officer slept as if they hadn't a care in the world. It's alright for some, he thought, and then returned his gaze to the road to concentrate on the real task of the day: driving his military vehicle on the Reich's business.

Chapter Twenty

Between 1935 and 1939, the Czechoslovakian government built a network of fortifications along its border with Germany and Hungary. The purpose being a defensive countermeasure against a potential threat from the ever rising belligerence of Nazi Germany. The Benes Wall consisted of heavy defensive fortifications such as casemates, bunkers and artillery emplacements, and smaller structures, such as pillboxes, anti-tank ditches and other tank countermeasures. By September 1938, Czechoslovakia had built two hundred and twenty-six heavy fortifications and ten thousand smaller ones. It was the larger of this type of fortification that Hauptman Faust had in mind to use to provide an additional, more realistic training medium for Group Granite. The fact that the French had assisted in the building of the Benes Line would also help to give a better understanding of the construction of Fort Eben Emael.

The group was transported, by Junkers transport aircraft, to an airfield in the town of Pardubice, about ninety kilometres east of Prague. On arrival, they were transported by military trucks to a small village called Babi, just north of Trutnov. There were a number of casemates made available to them for them to practise on and Assault Group Granite was split across three bunkers. The casemate allocated to Paul's platoon was a huge affair, with three embrasures - sporting weapons of various kinds. The front of the highly camouflaged blockhouse had three embrasures: one directly to the front and one splayed either side, off at an angle of about forty-five degrees. Paul, Max and his three troop commanders approached the behemoth, astounded by its size and solidity.

"The best approach," observed Fischer, "is round the back. I hope the gliders land us exactly where we want them to."

"Yes," agreed Leeb. "If they land us in front of it then we are deep in it."

"Listen up," Paul intervened. "I want you to have a good scout around this bunker, inside and out, including the observation cupola on the top and any entrances and exits. Once you've seen enough, we'll set up some scenarios assaulting the casemate to practise, one assault troop at a time. Understood?"

They all nodded.

Paul turned to Uffz Fischer. "I want your assault troop to prepare a direct frontal assault. You have smoke grenades with you?"

"Yes, sir, plenty."

"Good, I'll leave it up to you as to how you want to tackle this, but you'll need to carry the dummy fifty and twelve and a half-kilogram explosives with you. Anything else will be live, understood?"

"OK, sir, we'll get on it right away."

Fischer went to walk away but Paul quickly stopped him. "One more thing: we will do a critique once all four assault troops have had a go. OK, Fischer, carry on."

Fischer left the group, moving to join his troop and pass on Paul's instructions.

Paul then turned to Leeb. "I want you to attack from the rear, again using the dummy explosives."

"On our way, sir." Leeb left to gather his men.

"Max, I want you to attack from the half front, attacking the angled embrasure that is the same side as the entrance point."

"Explosives again, sir?" enquired Max.

"Not your team, Max. Have Geyer and Rammelt completed their full flame-thrower training? Now is an opportunity for them to put it into practice if they have."

"We'd better be last then, sir. It's the last place you would want to enter once Geyer and Rammelt have fried it," said Max with his usual lopsided grin.

"Makes sense," agreed Paul. "See to it, Max."

"I'll go and round up my troop."

Paul walked over to his assault troop and called out their names.

"Obergefrieter Konrad, I want you to take the troop around the bunker. Get a good look at the embrasures and the general layout. When you've done that, I want you to pull together an assault plan for attacking the fort from the left side as we are looking at from the front, understood?"

"Yes, sir," responded Konrad, snapping to attention as he did so. "Right, you lot, get your gear together. We're going sightseeing."

The troop, designated as assault troop two, gathered their gear and followed Konrad to the structure dominating their immediate vicinity. Obergefrieter Konrad was normally the number two of Uffz Fischer's troop, in its conventional organisational structure. Paul believed him to be a very capable soldier and the most promising to one day take over from Fischer as troop leader. This was an ideal opportunity to give him his head and test him while, thought Paul, he hadn't got his troop commander looking over his shoulder.

Paul checked that all the assault troops were making their way to the bunker complex and followed them in. Concrete steps led down to a heavy steel door, pushed back on its hinges by the preceding paratroopers who had left it open. He stepped over the small raised edge of the frame and into the dim interior; the low wattage bulbs, supplemented by the shafts of light passing through the gaps in the embrasures, were barely able to push back the darkness. One light bulb was flickering, making the paratroopers look as though they were participants in a black and white film. The bunker was cold and it made him shiver, the damp smell invading his nostrils; it was dank and depressing.

Paul's eyes slowly accustomed themselves to the gloom and he moved forward to the centre of the casemate, passing Petzel and Stumme who were examining the thirty-millimetre machine gun in the left-hand emplacement. The centre embrasure held a seventy-five-millimetre gun which would have been used to break up any potential assailing infantry before they could strike, or to be used against advancing armour. At the far end of the bunker, opposite the third embrasure, with a second thirty-millimetre machine gun, were a set of steps leading up to a circular armoured cupola. He headed over to it, slowly climbing the damp, slippery steps until he could see through the slits situated on all four sides.

He looked through the front-facing aperture, envisaging what the commander, probably a senior sergeant, would see. The ground in front was clear of any trees or shrubbery, ensuring there was a good field of fire for the bunker's weapons. Paul envisaged that the bunkers on Eben Emael would have similar clear fields of fire. Without this cupola, the bunker would be practically blind. But, it was protected by similar structures either side, with smaller machine-gun armed pillboxes in between. A formidable target, he thought. Hit this cupola, imagined Paul, and their sight would be severely restricted. Their observations would be limited to looking through the gun embrasures. That would be difficult to achieve as they would be pouring out a steady rate of fire if they were to be able to hold an attacker at bay. He stepped down from the observation dome, descended the steps and walked over to Max who was trying to peer through the right-hand embrasure. Max heard him approach and turned in his direction.

"This is going to take some breaching, sir," pointed out Max as he ran his hand over the rough, deep inner concrete skin. "This must be an arm's length thick."

"Perhaps the only way is to blow a hole through the top," proposed Paul.

"I don't think we could carry enough explosives, sir. The gliders wouldn't be able to carry that sort of weight," replied Max gruffly, clearly concerned that maybe they were biting off more than they could chew.

Paul thought back to their explosives training at Karlshorst. "Let's hope those 'super weapons' do the job then, eh Max?"

"I hope to god they do, that cupola up there looks pretty solid to me." Max pointing to where his commander had just descended from.

Paul looked back at the rusty cupola, made of solid steel and probably as thick as a man's fist.

"Dislodging that would not be easy, Max, I agree."

Again Paul thought back to his conversation with Faust, and the picture of the cone-shaped charge he had been shown and the ones they had practised on in Karlshorst. Could it really blow a hole in something like that?

"You wouldn't catch me fighting in a place like this all the same, sir." Max shuddered. "It's a death trap!"

"You've got to get near it first, Max, then breach it."

"I know that, sir. Now I can see the benefit of the gliders. If they could land us behind one of these things, we would give them a nasty surprise," said Max more cheerfully.

"Yes indeed, if we can be on top of them in the dark, before they know what's hit them, it would make a world of difference."

"One of our targets is meant to be very similar to this, except it's got three seventy-five-millimetre guns, and they are all forward-facing."

"Yes, a dry run on this site will definitely be good practice for us. Get the men together, Max, it's time we did some practice runs."

Max headed off to round up the troops and Paul headed

outside. Although it wasn't a bright day, just a normal dull winter's day, the intensity still blinded him when he exited the steel doorway leaving the dark interior behind him. He climbed back up the steps and quickly walked to where the platoon's trucks were parked, along with the equipment they had brought with them. Fischer was already there, with his assault troop gathered around him, probably talking through the approach they were going to take in order to secure the site.

"How long do you need, Fischer?" Paul called over to him.

"Another ten minutes, sir. I just want to quickly go through a dry run."

"OK, you have ten minutes."

The rest of the platoon had drifted back to their makeshift headquarters next to one of the trucks, and Paul went over to his troop to see how Konrad was progressing. Fischer was first up with a frontal assault. Not necessarily the best approach, but if the targets weren't secured either side and they were unable to get beyond the front of the target, it may be their only option. Fischer's men positioned themselves at the ready and Max gave the order to commence. Geister and Beiler were in position with an MG 34 and immediately opened fire on the casemate, spraying the cupola and embrasures to keep the heads down of the fictitious enemy defending. At precisely the time they opened fire, Petzel and Jordan jumped up from the grass throwing two smoke grenades each which, within seconds, produced a billowing cloud obscuring the front of the complex. There was a slight easterly breeze that, had Leeb not anticipated it by having the grenades thrown slightly to the left, would have quickly cleared away the smokescreen, exposing the attackers to the defenders' weapons. As it was, the smokescreen drifted nicely across the front of the bunker, hiding the attackers.

Again, Paul thought about Leeb's future prospects, and, yes, he would make a good platoon Feldwebel. He was swiftly drawn back to the scene unfolding in front of him as Leeb, Fessman and Stumme, carrying a now unfolded ladder, jumped up from the ground and charged towards the bunker, throwing the ladder up against it to the left side of the centre embrasure. The MG 34 had ceased fire, and Petzel and Jordan, having completed their task of throwing the smoke grenades, ran towards the right-hand embrasure to guard against a surprise attack from the defenders, should they leave the safety of their concrete hide to swat these impertinent paratroopers off. They disappeared into the smoke and, as it started to clear, Paul could make out Leeb, closely followed by Stumme, climbing the ladder with enough explosives, they hoped, to destroy the observation cupola, blinding the bunker's guardians. Fessman, in the meantime, had approached the central embrasure, crouching beneath it, and was placing an explosive device, attached on the end of a long pole, through the gaps in between the concrete walls of the stepped embrasure and the seventy-five-millimetre gun. Petzel and Jordan were crouched down between the embrasures covering the backs of their comrades. That done, and Leeb having placed the dummy explosives on the cupola, they all returned to the makeshift HQ. There were no explosions, other than the smoke grenades, as all the explosives used were dummies. The only similarity to the explosives they would use for the real thing was the weight. They would only get to use them in anger when they assaulted their target. The platoon reviewed the action of Leeb's assault troop and all agreed that it went well. Not the best approach to attack from the front but, if they had to, it couldn't have been done any better. How they would have fared, had it been manned, was another story.

The next two assault troops, Paul and Fischer's, carried out their dummy attacks. Again, both were conducted successfully. But, all knew that, against a determined enemy, the outcome had the potential to be very different.

Max's assault troop was now ready to kick off. Again, an MG 34 was the opening gambit, with swathes of steel splattering the face of the bunker, followed by the ubiquitous smoke grenades. But this time, Geyer, who was armed with a flame-thrower, leapt up and opened fire on the right-hand gun position. A stream of ignited flammable liquid shot out towards the casemate, blasting a gap through the smokescreen, exposing the embrasure to its tormentor. The flame engulfed the embrasure, spewing flames through the gaps left to allow the thirty-millimetre gun to swivel from side to side. Had the bunker been occupied, the men inside would have smelled the fuelled flame, felt the scorching heat and, if unlucky, been splattered by the burning fuel, instantly igniting their clothes and, possibly, the ammunition next to them. With the stream of flame bouncing off the armaments, the walls and ceiling, potentially igniting the ammunition stored inside, it was a devastating weapon. The other effect, apart from the sheer psychological impact on the defenders inside, was its hunger for oxygen. If not killing them by fire or explosion then it would suck out the precious oxygen inside the bunker depriving them of life that way. Geyer ceased fire, handing the weapon over to Rammelt, giving him an opportunity to continue with the two-second bursts of death and destruction, expanding his experience of handling this deadly and unforgiving weapon.

They ceased firing, and the rest of Max's assault troop placed dummy explosives on the steel door which, once disabled, allowed them to toss grenades inside, followed by the complete occupation of the bunker complex. The bunker was a blackened mass, some areas of it still on fire, either from the burning gel or as a result of the still searing heat. Max and his team came out of the bunker after only a few moments, their faces blackened.

They all grouped together for a post-exercise review. The exercise had been beneficial. They now knew what they were truly up against, and if their final target was of a similar standing to this one, they were in for a tough time. They had little doubt that an assault for real would be stoutly defended. They packed up their gear, stowed it on the vehicles and headed to a local camp for the night, before returning to their camp back in Hildesheim the next day.

It was a good practice session, but Max and the rest of the platoon were still not aware of the target they would be up against. The supposedly impregnable fortress of Fort Eben Emael.

Chapter Twenty-one

After their initial introduction to the DFS-230 glider, Paul's men spent many hours practising getting on and off the fragile aircraft. They established the best way to position themselves within the glider and found that it was best to straddle the small central seat, one behind the other, facing the front of the aircraft. Their gear would be stored, in the main, beneath their seats, held in place by their jump boots, the remainder hitched to the sides of the glider or to the tubular steel framework. Large items had to be secure. If they broke loose during flight, it could cause mayhem for the paratroopers inside the glider, with their limited space and the restrictions on movement. Or it could impact on the trim of the glider making it difficult for the pilot to control, or even damaging the glider and potentially making it unairworthy. On landing, the sudden deceleration from a speed in the region of one hundred plus kilometres per hour to zero in a matter of seconds meant that any loose item would be a real danger to the craft's occupants.

Leutnant Krause and his glider pilots not only had to learn to fly an unladen glider, but also had to learn to fly the DFS-230s fully laden with equipment and troops. It was one thing to fly an empty glider, but the handling characteristics were very different when fully loaded with troops and their equipment. Equally, it could be quite disconcerting with Fallschirmjager onboard breathing down your neck. Getting used to their banter could be a distraction for a pilot not used to the Fallschirmjager's sense of humour.

Today, it was Paul's platoon's turn for their first flight in one of the gliders. The glider had been loaded the previous day, in the configuration they had finally arrived at after many hours of discussions and trials to get it right. They were particularly concerned about getting quick and easy access to the special weapons. The lead Junkers pilot was given the signal to take off, and the throttles were pushed forward with the engine revolutions increasing until a tumultuous roar, almost in anger, and the tugging at the plane's brakes, told the pilot the Junkers was ready to be released. It was usually a slow, cumbersome aircraft, but then it was never meant to have been a thoroughbred fighter plane. But, this day, it had to act as a tug, hauling a ponderous cargo behind it: a fully laden glider packed with paratroopers and their equipment.

Paul's assault troop were in the first glider, followed by Max, Leeb and Fischer's troops in the remaining flight of the four gliders. Paul looked forward. He was sitting in the number two position, directly behind the pilot. Although the pilot, Hempel, now a key member of Paul's assault troop, didn't appear nervous, he was anxiously checking and double-checking his controls. His own safety was dependent on his skill as a pilot, as well as his passengers. The tow rope grew ever taut as the Tante Ju started to inch forward, but the glider remained where it was.

Paul didn't want to distract the pilot during take-off, but he did need to ask the question: "Is there a problem, Hempel?"

"No, sir, all's well. We're just trying to ensure the tow rope is taut enough before we go for it; otherwise there will be too much of a jerk and it may snap or come away."

Just as the pilot had responded to Paul's troubled question, the tension was suddenly broken and the glider jerked forwards, slowly trailing its attendant aircraft. As the towing aircraft gained speed, with the glider following in its wake, the pilot pulled back on the stick and the Junkers wing wheels gradually left the runway, its parasite still in tow. In spite of the Junkers leaving the runway, the glider pilot kept the stick straight, clearly waiting until he was satisfied that the glider had reached take-off velocity before committing to the rotation. Satisfied, he pulled back on the joystick and the glider too started to leave the runway behind.

Paul watched through the cockpit side window, fascinated as the buildings and vehicles at the side of the runway flashed by faster and faster. Its ungainly undercarriage was finally left behind on the runway and the airfield it had been struggling to leave was suddenly disappearing rapidly beneath them. Paul clasped the pilot on the shoulder and said, "Looking good."

"So far so good, sir," Hempel responded, but his eyes never left the tow plane nor the flight instruments. In fact, his eyes danced over the controls and the Junkers ahead, constantly checking the position of his tow and the trim of the glider.

Both the pilot of the towing aircraft and the glider relaxed slightly; the trickiest element, the take-off, having been completed successfully. All the Junkers pilot had to do now was get into the right position and order the release of the glider. For Hempel though, his job would then in reality truly start. They continued to climb, pushing to attain a ceiling of a thousand metres, hedges and trees below becoming smaller and smaller as they unhurriedly crept to their zenith. The glider pilot leaned back towards Paul. "We'll be released soon, sir. Then I'll bank the glider round to bring her in for a landing."

"Feeling good, Hempel?"

"You're in good hands, sir. It's not just you that I have to get down safely. I want to enjoy a good life too," he countered with a grin.

Paul had every faith in him as a pilot and as a member of his assault troop. Recognising that the pilots were an indispensable member of the assault force, Faust had ordered that they become a part of their relevant troop and train with them in all aspects of the operation. Not only would they be a valuable member of the team, bringing additional firepower and able to carry some of the weighty explosives, they would in fact be one of the first out of the glider when it landed. They would be in a position to provide some immediate security for the rest of the troop while they extracted themselves from the body of the aircraft. Paul passed the word back down the line that the tow rope was about to be released.

"It's gone, sir," shouted the pilot. He gently pulled the stick around and slightly up, compensating for the height he knew they would lose in the turn. The glider tilted and Paul shouted back the command to brace. He could feel the glider losing height, as if it knew that its tormentor could no longer control it and it could now drop back down to the earth. He looked through the cockpit's left side window, watching the ground getting clearer as they lost height. Looking forward, he could see the pilot firmly gripping the joystick, keeping control as the glider bucked, caught by a crosswind throwing it sideways But the pilot was good; he knew his stuff and soon had the glider back on track. Looking over the pilot's shoulder at the altimeter, Paul could see that they were below five hundred metres, confirmed by the ever increasing speed at which the trees and fences were passing by below.

"Standby, standby," shouted the pilot, not looking at Paul on this occasion. He had his hands well and truly full, coaxing this one-ton deadweight to a safe landing on the ground. There was no runway, just a field.

Paul shouted back again to his troop. "Brace! Brace! Brace!"

He could see very little now. The pilot had pulled back on

the stick to gain a little extra lift to slow them down and flatten out the aircraft to prevent it from ploughing into the ground nose first. He wondered what it was like for the men in the back. They were completely blind to what was happening and the glider only had a few, very small, low windows. Then they hit, slowing from a speed of a fast train to one of a slow motor car in a matter of seconds. The paratroopers were immediately thrown forwards, hanging onto their seats, bracing themselves for the impact that wanted to tear them out of their positions, shoving them into the man directly in front of them.

The glider scraped along the ground, a perfect landing; now it was out of the Pilot's hands. The glider's central ski brake, and the barbed wire attached to it, bit into the earth, slowing the glider down. They stopped suddenly. The wing sagged over onto the ground and the pilot unbuckled his harness, stepped up onto his seat, unlatching the cockpit and pushing it up and over, leaping out onto the front and down. Paul followed suit, climbing on the seat as the pilot had done, having to duck more due to his height, and levered himself up with both elbows, careful not to catch his machine pistol as he pulled himself through, and joined the glider pilot on the ground in a defensive position.

Inside the glider, Forster had kicked out the hardboard hatch, to clear the egress from the body of the plane, ducked under the wing and out, running around to the tail of the plane to secure the rear of their position. He was quickly followed by Straube, Kienitz, Kempf, Weyer, Forster and Konrad who formed a circle around the glider, securing their position.

Paul shouted the all-clear and they formed up at the front to share their experiences. They chattered like monkeys, any fear or anxieties they had had about flying in the glider and landing on the ground dissolved. They gathered around their pilot slapping him on the back, laughing and joking. He had just become the eighth member of the troop, having more than earned his place. Paul looked across the field at the other three gliders that had just landed and could see Max, his heavy-set figure unmistakable, talking to his men.

Max looked over, saw his commander surveying the landed gliders, and held his thumbs up for him to see. Giving Paul the message that all the gliders had landed successfully and safely, he knew that the safety of his platoon would be at the forefront of his mind. All they had to do now was land at dusk, over enemy territory and attack a well-armed target.

Chapter Twenty-two

The preparation for the assault on the three bridges crossing the Albert Canal just west of Maastricht was near completion, as were Group Granite's preparations. The assault force was all but ready to conduct the assault on the Belgian fortress, Eben Emael. Training had started immediately they had gathered together at Hildesheim, and now they had been practicing and developing their tactics for over six months and were as close to being ready as they would ever be. Some of the best glider pilots in the country had been conscripted into the experimental transport glider command. It was commanded by Lieutenant Krause who, in November 1939, got his marching orders to immediately move from Gibenat to Hildesheim, leaving the training of glider pilots there to others. They had been training extensively on the DFS-230 glider, starting with flying empty gliders, adding cargo and, ultimately, passengers, the Fallschirmjager, whom they were going to transport into battle.

They had resolved all of the issues that had arisen: from the way the explosives and weapons were lashed to the rear and the sides of the glider, to slowing the glider down on landing. By wrapping barbed wire around the central ski and through using a braking board, they were able to stop relatively close to the target. After a shaky start, the pilots had excelled themselves and were now consistently landing within twenty metres of their chosen target. That was in ideal conditions; they were yet to be tested under fire, over a strange target and under combat conditions.

The paratroopers too had worked hard to prepare for the undertaking ahead of them. Their levels of fitness had been honed to perfection, as both Hauptman Kaufmann and Oberleutnant Faust were firm believers that physical fitness was a key factor in the success of the mission. They had frequently practised carrying their equipment from their pseudo-glider landing place to their target, which included the fifty-kilogram hollow-charged weapon. They practised carrying it in two parts, one in each hand, running with them to their target and assembling them in a matter of seconds. They had to do this at night. They also practised blindfold so it became second nature to them.

Secrecy had been paramount during their training and the build-up to the assault on the fort. Should it become known to the Belgian forces that the German army was to use gliders in an attack or that they had the new hollow-charge weapon that could pierce twenty-five centimetres of steel, it would have seriously jeopardised the mission. In fact, two Fallschirmjager had been sentenced to death as they had inadvertently disclosed who they were to some civilians. This was later reprieved, and they participated in the action.

Faust had a tough task on his hands and was unable to disclose the location to his assault force which made it difficult to plan and train for the operation. To help provide a semi-realistic training programme, Faust superimposed the objective's dimensions on the training ground. This helped them to develop the tactics necessary to secure their kill. At first, they only had plans and documents of their target to view; later, photographs supplemented these. Although initially scarce, towards the end of their training, information and intelligence slowly filtered through to them as they got closer to their jump-off date.

Some photographs had been taken overtly from Lufthansa flights flying over the target area. Picture postcards collected from tourists and visitors to the country were also used to increase their knowledge of the fort and the surrounding areas. As the quality and volume of photographs increased, they underwent stereoscopic analysis to better evaluate the target's depth and associated dead ground, further improving their knowledge. One big advantage they had was that two German companies had been involved as sub-contractors on the construction of Fort Eben Emael. Interviewing these companies gave Faust's team a deeper insight into the construction of the fort.

As a result of this additional intelligence, they were able to build a sandbox, a three-dimensional representation of the target, improving on the plans and photographs. This was added to daily as new reconnaissance photography was updated. Later, they were given a model of the target, made by one of the glider pilots, giving them an even better feel for the layout and complexity of their target.

They had completed a rehearsal in April. Now it was time for a full dress-rehearsal, the final one.

Previously they had been placed at their start locations on foot, where they would be expected to land as if in a glider, and on the sound of a whistle, to signify that they had landed, were then free to sprint to the target, carrying their full range of equipment, and carry out the assault. This final rehearsal would involve a full glider landing, consisting of the full flight of eleven gliders and eighty-eight Fallschirmjager.

Paul was in the hangar with his four assault teams going through the final briefing before commencing the exercise. They had been given the approximate date of their mission which was only a week away. This rehearsal was crucial. It was to be an exhaustive final check of their preparations. If there were any flaws in their strategy or tactics, this would be the last opportunity to iron them out. It was unlikely; they had pursued every likely occurrence that could impact on their mission, and they had trained to counter every conceivable incident.

"Unterfeldwebel Grun, Fischer, Leeb, Kienitz, front and centre," ordered Paul, leaving the rest of the soldiers to continue with their last-minute equipment checks. "The gliders are in situ."

"Are they hooked up to their tows?" asked Leeb.

"Yes, and the pilots are doing their final checks. Max, are you happy with the stowage of your equipment?"

"Yes, sir, checked and double-checked."

"Leeb?"

"I've had Geister check it over independently. All is ready, sir."

"Fischer?"

"As ready as we'll ever be, sir."

"Kienitz and I have both been over ours. It looks like all is shipshape then. We load in twenty minutes. Gather the men together, Max."

Once they had grouped themselves around their platoon commander, he spoke to them quietly, but confidently. "Well, this is the final practice. We've done this before, we know what we're doing, and there's no reason for it not to be a success."

He looked around the group; they were fit, had trained hard in practising their tactics, and handled explosives like it was second nature to them. He caught Fischer's eye who nodded he was ready. Kienitz gave him the thumbs up. Leeb beamed, as confident as ever. And Max? Well, Max never seemed perturbed, his confidence unshakable. Seeing his staunch sergeant banished any brooding thoughts Paul may have had.

"We've been through hundreds of dry runs. Treat this like the real thing, and remember, go in hard, go in fast. Troop two with me, let's go."

The paratroopers picked up their personal weapons, whether it was an MP 40 or Kar 98, and walked out into the coolness of the early morning air. It was still quite chilly, although the temperature would rise to above fifteen degrees during the day. It was three thirty in the morning, still dark; dawn wasn't due for another hour, the time of their landing. The gliders, along with their tugs, were all lined up on the runway and Paul's assault troops made their way to their respective transport.

Paul saw Faust walking over to him, accompanied by Hauptman Kaufmann. They were in combat mode, so no saluting. Instead, they shook hands and wished each other good luck. Paul left them and headed over to his glider, glider number two; his would be the second to land, Leeb's being the first. He popped his head through the door, ducking under the wing, and saw that the pilot was in position, in his cockpit seat, already strapped in and ready to go.

"A fine morning for a flight, sir," said Hempel cheerfully, "but a bit bloody cold."

"A bit of exercise will soon warm you up," shouted Forster from somewhere towards the rear of the plane.

"So, when do we get refreshments?" shouted Kempf.

Then the laughter started, jokes passed to and fro, releasing the tensions that were inherent before the start of any operation of importance. None wanting to fail, none wanting to let their mates down.

"Looks like I have a plane full of comedians, sir," countered Hempel, smiling.

Paul looked to the right. "How are the first-class seats back there?"

Konrad, who would be sitting directly behind Paul during the flight, answered, "The children are a bit lively, sir, but they'll settle down once the airsickness sets in."

Paul felt a tap on his shoulder and extracted himself from the main body of the glider.

"It's time to load and secure, sir," said a Luftwaffe airman who was obviously acting as runner for Oberleutnant Faust.

Before Paul could say thank you, the airman had hurried off to warn the next glider crew to get ready. The excitement was discernible. This was probably the biggest thing to have occurred since the airman's recruit training days. Paul took one last look around, climbed into the glider and helped Konrad secure the kick-out panel. He touched the pilot's shoulder. "How long do you think?"

"A matter of minutes, sir. You can see it's getting lighter already," the pilot said pointing upwards.

Paul looked out of the window and could see the beginnings of dawn. This would only be a short flight to the target; the aim was to practise a full landing and assault on their targets, not to test the pilots' flying abilities. They had already proven themselves to be competent in both take-off, transiting and landing. The aim of this rehearsal was to hone their ground tactics. Their very last opportunity to correct any faults before they enacted the real thing.

"The Junkers is powering up his engines, sir. Not long now."

Paul shouted back to his troop, passing on the pilot's information. He looked round with difficulty as they were so tightly packed. Konrad was leaning sideways so his officer could see better. Although it was starting to lighten up outside, inside was still dark and all he could see were their muddied faces and the whites of their teeth showing through their grins. These were his men, they would not let him down, and he would not let them down.

There was the sudden bright light of a flare, flickering above the cockpit, travelling higher in the sky.

"That's the signal, sir. We're on our way," Hempel informed Paul.

Paul heard Konrad passing the message back. The three engines of the Junkers screamed and the plane was soon pushing forwards, dragging the reluctant glider along with it. The sudden feeling in the pit of Paul's stomach told him that they had left the ground and were climbing up towards their intended ceiling. It seemed only a matter of minutes before the pilot informed Paul that they were releasing the glider. There was no sickening drop; the pilot had full control of his flight. The familiar banking to the left told Paul that they were losing height and that Hempel was positioning the glider and searching out his target.

"Got it, sir," he shouted out excitedly. "We're going down!"

Chapter Twenty-three

It was the morning of 9th of May and they were at a new location: the airfield at Ostheim, near Cologne, some 240 kilometres from Hildesheim. The entire Assault Group Granite had been moved there in some secrecy. The camp was secured by barbed wire, lined with rush matting to block out any prying eyes, and patrolled twenty-four hours a day by military guards.

Some elements of Sturmabteilung Kaufmann had joined them, other elements having been transferred to an alternative airfield close by at Butzweilerhof. The paratroopers had been kicking their heels and, as the days got closer to the launch date for the operation, tension mounted. Their training now complete, all they had left to do was go over their mission again and again. Checking and double-checking that the team members all knew what was expected of them when the day came.

Max was sitting on the ground outside the building designated as their canteen for the short time they would be there. He sat with his back up against the brick wall, his feet stretched out in front of him, a glass of orange juice in his hand, passing the time of day with the three Uffzs.

"Five days to go," said Leeb to no one in particular.

"Getting close now, boys," added Max, keeping the relaxed conversation going.

"Are you nervous, Feld?" asked Fischer, sitting up. Until then he had been lying on the ground with his arm over his eyes as if asleep.

"Not nervous. Just wanting our teams to do well. Not let the rest of Granite down."

"We've got it off pat now though," threw in Kienitz.

"It's never pat," countered Max. "If the gliders are OK, if our pilots land us in the right place, if we land in one piece, if we get to the target and we come back alive, then it's pat. All we can do is put into practice what we have been taught and trained to do."

"I don't think we can do anymore to prepare," added Leeb.

"I don't disagree," supported Max. "You can over train. But we've done enough and I think we're ready."

Before anyone could add to or comment on Max's statement, Kienitz jumped up and pointed to some furniture vans driving into the base. "Is somebody moving in?"

"They've come from a big house," added Fischer. "That's the fifth vehicle that has just pulled up."

"Let's go and take a look," suggested Max, picking himself up off the grass and heading over to the recently built hangars.

The three junior NCOs also leapt up to follow their platoon sergeant to investigate what was going on. The hangar doors were being slid back as they arrived and one of the removal vans reversed into the cavernous space, alongside one that was already in place.

"It's the gliders!" blurted out Leeb.

"They're in bits," added Kienitz

"The crafty buggers," said Max as he ran his hands down the canvas side of one of the glider bodies.

The gliders had been disassembled at Hildesheim and transported in furniture vans, to hide them from curious eyes. Once in the hangars, they were reassembled.

"Oi, you lot," shouted one of the Luftwaffe ground crew, Oberfeld's. "Leave those alone. If you haven't got anything better to do, I'll soon find you a job."

The four comrades laughed and started to walk back to the entrance to make their way back to the canteen, Leeb shouting back over his shoulder, "Make sure you look after our babies."

They continued cracking jokes, their laughter drifting across the camp. The Luftwaffe Senior NCO, in charge of assembling the gliders, watched them go. He didn't know what it was all about, but the gossip said that they were going to fly in these gliders on some strange mission. They were all confined to camp until further notice and not allowed to contact their families. Whatever it was they were planning to do, he didn't envy them and wished them luck. The four comrades returned to the canteen, this time to play cards; anything to pass the time.

Paul had gathered his men together in one of the hangars. It was time to brief them fully on their operation. Everything they had been training for so far had been on a supposed target, their information from photographs, plans and sketches. Now they would finally get to know what it was they were going to assault, where it was located and the reason behind it. The men gathered around their commander, pulling up chairs, whether wooden or canvas, some even sitting on the spare wing of a glider. It seemed pertinent that they were holding the briefing alongside one of the very gliders that, in a matter of days, would be flying them into battle.

"*Kameraden*," Paul said to his men, "the time has come for us to prove our worth. I know we were tested in Poland, but that was just a sideshow. In two days, the results of our efforts will determine the success of the entire operation. We have been training hard; you have been training hard. We must now demonstrate that our training was not wasted, that the confidence our our Fuhrer and superiors and have in us is not unfounded. We go into action tomorrow."

The silent hangar suddenly sprang into life as the thirty-two paratroopers and pilots broke into a buzz of chatter, the suspense finally over. The day had come. They were to go to war again.

"Our gliders are here waiting for us." Paul patted the glider that was situated directly behind him. "Moved here in furniture vans, I believe." Paul smiled, as did the rest of the platoon.

"I'm just glad they didn't treat us as furniture, sir," piped up Max.

"They would have had me to deal with." Paul returned Max's smile.

This typical banter between the Leutnant and the older senior NCO helped to relax the men. They had just gone through six months of intensive training, the strain was starting to show and there was some tension in all of them. But the waiting was over.

"I've called you together for our final operational briefing," continued Paul, now back on track. "As you know, at our initial briefing, we were not the only units of *Sturmabteilung Kaufmann*. Some of you will have seen several of your *kameraden*, who you had served with in Poland, at Hildesheim."

Paul moved closer to his men, who were in a semi-circle around him. His voice echoed as he continued speaking, the enormity of the hangar reflecting his voice around the high four-storey walls. "We're going to be a part of a much bigger operation. *Sturmabteilung Kaufmann* is going to facilitate the passage of General Fedor von Bock's Army Group B and the Fourth Panzer Division crossing the Dutch and Belgium borders east of Maastricht."

A buzz again filled the room, and Paul waited for it to settle down before he continued.

"After his briefing by High Command, Hauptman Kaufmann, based on his mission analysis, concluded there were four critical tasks to complete in order for his assault group to succeed. *Sturmabteilung Kaufmann* has four missions to complete. Groups Steel, Iron and Concrete must seize and prevent the destruction of the Vendwezelt, Vroenhoven and Canne bridges that cross the Albert Canal."

They were finally being given their target, after six months of training, and also the targets of the other three storm groups in *Sturmabteilung Kaufmann*. Their small-scale, seemingly insular preparations to storm a fort in a neignouring country were going to be part of something much bigger. Paul allowed them to get it off their chest, sharing their thoughts with each other, some looking at him in disbelief, at what he had just told them.

"Does that mean we're going to war again, sir. Another Poland?!" enquired Kempf.

The hangar was silent. They all looked at Paul waiting for his answer, wanting to know what it all meant, what the bigger picture was.

"I truly don't know," came back Paul's reply. "We are clearly moving into a foreign nation's territory in force. It can only be seen as an act of war."

"What's our role in all of this, sir?" asked Max, bringing the briefing back on track.

"Ours is the prize: Eben Emael, the supposedly impregnable fortress that protects those crossings over the Albert Canal. The very crossings that the other *Kaufmann* teams will be assaulting. So, not only is Fourth Panzer Division dependent on us, but so are our comrades who will land by glider to secure the three bridges I mentioned earlier."

All the work done in the sandbox at Hildesheim now slotted into place. They were to invade Belgium, their role being the destruction of a key fort in the country's defences. Paul continued to brief them on the sequence of events. Times when they were to eat and sleep and the time when they would be awoken, should any of them be able to sleep. They were like coiled springs, waiting to be unleashed. Part of them didn't want to wait; part of them was excited at the prospect of battle; part of them was nervous, not at the prospect of action or death, but of not wanting to fail their comrades, their country or their Fuhrer.

"As you can see, our task is critical to the success of the operation to cross these bridges. We have three key tasks to accomplish in order to achieve success on taking the fort."

Paul turned to Max and nodded his head, the signal for Max to unroll a large photograph of the fort, the most recent taken. He pinned it up on an easel that was close by, brushing it flat as he did so. Before moving away, Max looked over the photograph, turned to look at Paul then at the Fallschirmjager looking at him. "It looks just like what we've trained on. It won't be a piece of cake, but we can do this."

Max walked away and joined the rest of the troopers, who were again waiting on Paul's next breath.

Paul walked over to the photograph, fresh off the photo interpreter's light table, and pointed to the target. "First, we must destroy the weapons on top of the fort, particularly the anti-aircraft emplacement."

He made eye contact with Fischer, the assault troop leader whose responsibility it was to take out this battery. "Left in action, this battery could impede further glider landings and restrict any additional reinforcement or resupply."

Fischer nodded, accepting the importance of his and his team's role. He looked around at his troop, confident and proud to have the responsibility placed upon them. They were ready.

"Secondly, we must destroy the gun batteries that cover the very three bridges being assaulted by the rest of our *Sturmabteilung*. We must destroy them. Otherwise they'll be able to bring fire down on the vicinity of the bridges and seriously hamper the assaults being conducted by Steel, Concrete and Iron."

"We'll need to be pretty sharp then, sir," rejoined Max. "If the batteries are on the ball, they could bring fire down within minutes of us touching down."

"That's why we've been practising so hard. We've got to put them out of action fast."

"Do we know what their response time is, sir?"

"We believe they'll have skeleton crews, but there will also be a signal system, I'm sure; an alarm to warn the rest of the garrison who may be off-duty and not situated in the fort itself. But you can be sure of one thing: the minute the first glider lands on the fort, bells will be ringing loud and clear. And finally," he continued, "we must attack and destroy the fort's entrance and exit points. We must keep the garrison bottled up. We're not a big enough force to hold off a significant counter-attack and we will also be spread pretty thinly across the top of the fort."

"What's the strength of the force we'll be up against, sir?" Leeb asked concerned.

"Good question, Leeb. You beat me to it. The Belgian defenders are not completely defenceless. The fort holds a garrison of some twelve hundred men, a formidable force to be attacked by our mere eighty-eight paratroopers."

"We're not mere paratroopers, sir, we're the best," jumped in Max.

"How right you are, Unterfeldwebel Grun," Paul replied, smiling. "How remiss of me to forget."

"It happens sometimes, sir." This brought a chuckle from the paratroopers.

"You'll be pleased to hear there are some negatives for the fortress's defenders. Of the twelve hundred men, over two hundred are technicians and support staff; only the remaining one thousand are artillerymen and infantry."

"There you go, sir, odds down to ten to one already."

Max's take on the troop numbers brought a laugh from the men who were all starting to visibly relax. That was the Unterfeldwebel's intention.

"Also, due to a shift system whereby the garrison is split into two, each shift serving for one week-about means that there are only ever five hundred trained men manning the fort at any one time. Reducing the odds further, Unterfeldwebel, to a trifling six to one."

This brought a further laugh from the men, their officer getting one up on the platoon sergeant. What the defenders had to face were eighty-eight determined Fallschirmjager who had trained for six months with nothing else in mind but subjugating the fortress and denying the enemy a chance to prevent the German army from completing its larger goal. The challenge was theirs: the full Granite glider force landing at their appointed places at the right time, attacking and destroying a shocked and poorly trained force, allowing the rest of *Sturmabteilung Kaufmann* to secure the bridges.

"As you all know, we've been divided into eleven troops, one per glider. Each troop is responsible for destroying their target, and also the objective of the section next to them should that section fail to arrive or not succeed in their mission. That is why we have been focusing on a secondary objective for each troop. You know yours; be prepared to switch targets when necessary, or destroy your secondary target as well as your own, if required. We've been training with the new hollow-charge devices and we believe that they will penetrate the concrete casemates or artillery and observation domes. Although you've been given time to practise their assembly and have had a demonstration of how they work, you were only ever allowed to explode them on the ground. It was decided, rightly or wrongly, that the risk of the secret of these devices getting out was too great for you to see them used in anger. These hollow-charges, placed on a casemate or turret, and initiated, will penetrate some four centimetres blowing a hole through it and killing some of the occupants. So you see, gentlemen, we have the toys to do the job."

They spent another half an hour throwing questions and answers to and fro until everybody was satisfied they had extracted all the information that was available. All they could do now was eat, play cards, talk or try to sleep.

Chapter Twenty-four

Paul and Max sat outside the canteen; a table and chairs had been dragged outdoors enabling them to sit and watch the never-ending activity that seemed to have kicked off ever since they had been given the go-ahead. It was eight in the evening, and truckloads of Luftwaffe ground crew had turned up. They were immediately given the task of pulling out the gliders ready to be attached to the Junkers tow planes that had been landing at the airfield since dawn that day.

The entire platoon were now gathered outside the canteen; they had little else to do. They had checked their kit again and again. They had checked each other's kit again and again. They had completed their wills, written letters home, those only being released once their mission was complete. Now they were just chatting, swapping stories about their training during the last six months, talking about family and loved ones back home. Asking questions of their superiors, with Paul, Max and the Uffzs answering what questions they could. There was a cheer from the paratroopers on the periphery of the group, and when questioned what the celebration was about, they proceeded to point to the field kitchen that was drawing up close to one of the hangars.

They all charged across to the hangar, the field kitchen a welcome distraction, and the food, of course. By the time Paul joined them, they were already walking away with steaming plates of sausages and mashed potatoes, heading back to the canteen to eat it before it cooled.

While they were eating, the Luftwaffe ground crews were finally pulling the gliders out of the hangars, doing it in the dark as the floodlights had been turned off to protect the gliders from prying eyes. The Junkers were jockeyed into position, the gliders then secured to the towlines and the release catches checked, and checked again. Paul knew the glider pilots would be over there, making sure no damage was done to their precious craft and that the release gear truly did work.

A Luftwaffe Feldwebel ran up to Paul and saluted. Paul was wearing his Fallschirmjager badges and titles of rank again.

"With Oberleutnant Faust's compliments, sir, but could your troops board the gliders immediately."

With that, he saluted again and went to find the rest of Group Granite to pass on the instructions given to him.

"Max," called Paul, "let's get the men together. We're mounting up."

"Doesn't the Oberleutnant trust that we're ready, sir?"

Max said it with humour. He would probably do the same thing himself if the positions were reversed.

"He just wants to make sure you're not out womanising, Unterfeldwebel Grun. Now, get the men together."

"Right, you lot, in your troops, left to right, come on. We don't want to keep the Oberleutnant waiting."

Once assembled, Paul, Max, Fischer and Leeb led their assault troops to their respective gliders and boarded them, a final assembly called by the Oberleutnant keen to make sure nothing was amiss. The final checks completed, they were dismissed until the operation start time of three thirty in the morning. But, they were instructed to stay within the confines of the hard standing, the hangars or the canteen. This was it; they were getting close to the point of no return. With little else to do, the adrenalin pumping through their veins, they went back to playing cards and writing letters. Some, like Max and Paul, went to find somewhere to get their heads down. They didn't know when they might next get some sleep.

It was two forty-five in the morning. Paul woke with a start, his shoulder being shaken.

"Sir," hissed the orderly, "it's time."

"Time? Right, thank you," responded Paul groggily as he sat up and lifted his legs off the camp bed he'd been sleeping on. He rubbed his eyes, bringing himself round after what had been a surprisingly deep sleep. "Has Unterfeldwebel Grun been roused?"

"He was already awake, sir. He asked me to call you."

"OK, thank you."

Paul heaved himself up off the camp bed and started to pull on his gear. Trust Max, he thought, to be up first. He probably threatened the orderly with a pain worse than death if he didn't wake him up first. Max joined him five minutes later with a steaming hot cup of coffee.

"You never sleep, Max?"

"Someone has to watch over my sleeping beauties, sir, you excluded, of course," he said with a grin.

"Are the men ready?" Paul knew that Max would have the platoon ready and shipshape.

"The gliders are fully loaded. We've been asked by the glider pilots to relocate some items, to ensure the optimum balance. We don't want to overload our flying pack horses, do we."

"This is it, Max, the culmination of all of our training."

"It had to come sooner or later. We couldn't have free food and board forever."

"They couldn't have kept you cooped up here for much longer either."

"That goes for all of us, sir."

"Right then, Max, let's go."

Paul clasped his NCOs' wrist, not moving for a second, but saying, "Thank you, Max, your strength has helped get us through these last six months. As a result we're better prepared."

"Don't you fret, sir. We've got this licked."

They left to join the rest of their men.

The paratroopers went about their preparations quietly and seriously. They were composed because they were confident in their plan, confident in their unit and confident in themselves. At three thirty, Assault Group Granite was formed up in full battle gear, Oberleutnant Faust going over the final checks with his officers and senior NCOs. They made their final preparations. Paul was wearing a stripped down version of the basic load-carrying belt: a leather belt, 'Y' straps, his automatic pistol holster on the left hip, gas mask bag, bread bag for his rations and one canteen for water. He carried an MP40 sub-machine pistol and two sets of triple magazine pouches attached to his belt and 'Y' straps. Many of the force carried the *Karabiner*, Kar 98k. With it came a cloth bandolier they hung around their neck, the ammunition pouches dropping both sides of their chest, fixed in position on the waistline, either side of the belt buckle. The twelve compartments sported one hundred and twenty rounds. This might seem excessive, as they were only meant to be in combat for six hours before being relieved. But, in an intense conflict, ammunition could rapidly be consumed and, should they not be relieved until later, they would be very dependent on a resupply.

Paul checked that his torch was working and that the rest of his command also had their torches available for immediate use. He clipped his to the front of his tunic. He had asked Max to ensure that the soldiers also stowed away some biscuits or chocolate, just in case their relief was delayed or that their resupply failed to appear.

Spread across Paul's teams, they had four MG 34s and all the explosives they would need. Another element of the assault force carried a *Flammenwerfer*, flame-thrower. Group Granite was fortunate to have the new lighter model, the series 40. This deadly weapon could shoot a flame up to thirty metres long for up to ten seconds, although the engineers recommended that they use one- to two-second bursts. Paul knew he would certainly not want to be on the receiving end of that flaming oil.

Max walked over. "All's well, sir. Shall I check your kit now?"

"Yes, go ahead."

Max handed Paul two egg hand grenades and two stick grenades,

"Secure these well, sir. I'm sure they'll come in handy. I've made sure the rest of the troops are well stocked."

"Smoke grenades?"

"Each troop has twelve. Forster, Straube and Kienitz have them in your troop."

Max checked his commander's fighting equipment and Paul did likewise for him. All was well. They gathered the troops together and gave the instruction to start loading the special weapons onboard the craft, waiting silently on the runway with one wing down on the ground, the other pointing into the sky as if indicating it was ready to complete its task. In the gloom of the early morning, they looked like phoenixes waiting to come to life. Max supervised the assembly and the last minute loading of the special explosives. This was completed efficiently and without any problems. Distributed across the eleven gliders, they would carry some two and half thousand kilograms of explosives. A third of the explosives carried by the group would be made up of the new fifty-kilogram and twelve and a half-kilogram *hohlladung*, hollow-charges. The remainder would be made up of more conventional explosives.

Paul's final task was to heavily smear his face and helmet with mud, the purpose being to hide as much of the sheen as possible. He noted that the rest of his force was following suit, complying with a basic rule of camouflage: of hiding the shape and shine of your face and helmet. He ran his hands through his fair hair before placing his helmet on his head and securing the strap. Faust gave the order to load.

Paul and his men made their way out to the gliders, an oil lamp flickering in front of a board by each aircraft identifying which glider was allocated to which troop. Boarding the wrong glider wouldn't be a problem until they landed; finding they had got a glider with the wrong equipment stowed, or they couldn't locate everything, would be a disaster for the assault troop unlucky enough to experience that. Paul was the last one onboard glider two. He could hear his men behind him, shuffling on the central bench attempting to get comfortable for their forty-minute flight.

Hempel too was getting himself comfortable. For the next forty minutes, he was the most important person on board. He was checking his controls, ensuring that the wing flaps and rudder responded to his foot pedals and joystick. The clock was ticking; they would soon be in the air. Hempel leant back and spoke to Paul. "Any minute now sir."

Just as he spoke, a flare soared above them. It was time. No amount of doubt or reflection could stop it now. If Group Granite was to secure this seemingly invincible fort through shock tactics, they had to land all eleven gliders, their assault troops intact, within minutes of each other and within metres of their targets.

Chapter Twenty-five

It was ten past four in the morning on the 10th of May 1940. The troop was part of Assault Group Granite, an extension of the advanced guard of the German airborne assault on the Low Countries. A vanguard operation was aimed at key sectors of the Belgian border, to take control of Fort Eben Emael and the Albert Canal bridges. They were at the forefront of a massive German invasion to take Western Europe. Assault Group Granite, commanded by Hauptman Joachim Faust, was tasked with taking Fort Eben Emael, securing the gateway to the soft underbelly of this vulnerable and unprepared country, about to be caught off guard by a devious and determined enemy.

On this day, three regiments of the Belgian 7th Division were holding the line of the Albert Canal with their right flank anchored by the fortified complex of Eben Emael. This fortress was armed with two one hundred and twenty-millimetre guns and sixteen seventy-five-millimetre guns in armoured turrets and casemates. Eleven gliders would land on top of the fort, secure it and ensure it remained in their hands until relieved by 4th Panzer Division, of XVI Panzer Corps.

The airborne assault was launched in support of this German offensive. The opening attack was to be made by the 7th Flieger, a Luftwaffe unit commanded by General Kurt Student, and 22nd Infantry Division commanded by General Graf von Sponeck. The 22nd Infantry Division was an army airborne formation with troops and equipment suited for transported by air, to complete whatever task was expected of them. On this occasion, the 22nd was tasked to take The Hague and, if possible, obtain the submission and cooperation of the Dutch Crown. The division was also to take the airfields at Valkenburg, YPenburg and Ockenburg, lying to the north, east and south of The Hague respectively.

The rest of 7th Flieger were to occupy Rotterdam and Waalhaven airports, strike at Dordrecht, the Moerdijk bridges across the Maas estuary, clearing a corridor for the German 18th army. One critical role of the 7th Flieger was to take the bridges at Veldwezelt, Vroenhoven and Canne, and take Fort Eben Emael, reputedly the strongest fort of its time in the world, defended by elements of the Belgian 7th Division.

Adolf Hitler himself had taken a personal interest in the planning of the surprise capture of the Albert Canal bridges, despite the scepticism of the OKW, the German High Command. He was a strong supporter of the new parachute force and had suggested that they use gliders as a new mode of attack. Paratroopers would not be able to land directly on the objective by parachute, with precision needed in the first instance. To reduce the warning given to the Belgian defenders, it was decided that gliders would deliver the primary strike.

A special detachment of forty-two gliders had been formed under the command of Hauptman Kaufmann, made up of four hundred and fifty men, including pilots, of the 2nd Parachute Battalion. For six months, the battalion had undergone rigorous training at a secret location, training in the use of explosives, and going through the manoeuvres necessary to take the key gun emplacements and secure strategic bridges. On the left bank of the canal, twenty gliders would land right in the middle of the defences covering the bridges at Veldwezelt and Vroenhoven, the objective being to cut the cables to the bridge demolition charges and the telephone lines. A further detachment was to land at Canne and a detachment of eleven gliders was to land on top of Fort Eben Emael itself. The force was ready to complete its task, and the aircraft were taking off from Ostheim airport as planned.

With her three engines roaring at full boost, the Junkers hauled at the glider behind it, enticing it to finally let go of its link with the ground, ferrying its passengers, eight determined men with their equipment, explosives and courage, to the Belgian coast. The Junkers three BMW radial-piston engines strained, the aircraft struggling to keep itself in the air at its lower speed of two hundred kilometres per hour whilst pulling the heavy, barely airworthy glider, the *Deutsches Forschungsinstitut fur Segelflug*, DFS-230A behind it in tow. Assault Group Granite flew towards Denmark in an arrow formation, in three groups of three planes each, and one group of two.

A chain of three aircraft was called a 'kette'. Normally a Junkers used in a parachute drop would carry up to fourteen paratroopers, but on this occasion they were mere spectators, their silent companions towed behind them in this instance would be taking the Fallschirmjager into battle. They circled, slowly, over Ostheim airfield, gradually gaining height before they flew west to form up with Group Steel. The two glider flights met up and continued with their flight west, the pilots following a marked flight path, leading them to the release point for the attack. Groups *Granit* (Granite), *Eisen* (Iron) and *Beton* (Concrete) took off from Ostheim, and Group *Stahl* (Steel) from Butzweilerhaf.

The Junkers pilot of the lead plane peered out of the cockpit window into the gloom of this early spring morning, a great deal of responsibility resting on his shoulders. He was an experienced pilot, and the lead pilot of the formation with at least five years' experience flying transport aircraft like these. Saying that, until this operation was instigated, he had never towed a glider let alone towed one into battle. He, and his co-pilot were watching out for the markers put into position on their route, to guide them to the target area and the release point for the gliders.

His co-pilot pointed to the first rotating beacon. "There it is. We're bang on line." The beacon was their first marker point and could be seen from their port side.

"There's the searchlight too," indicated the pilot. "Check the timing, will you?"

The glow of the searchlight disappeared and the co-pilot started counting the seconds on his watch. "One, two, three," the chain of aircraft droned on, "…eight, nine, ten. It's back on, ten seconds on the dot."

"Looking good," responded the pilot. "But just check to make sure it stays on for only thirty seconds. I doubt there will be any other searchlights lit, but better to be sure."

"OK, sir, better to be safe than sorry."

"Is there any of that coffee left in the flask?"

"Soon as I've checked the count, I'll pour."

"There, it's out, bang on the button. I'll get that coffee now."

They were leaving the first searchlight behind and could already see the next rotating beacon. The two after that would see them over Buir and Lucherburg, putting them roughly halfway to the target and the release point.

Hempel leant back towards Paul. "I can see the beacon at Lucherburg, sir. That puts us about halfway to the release point."

Paul's stomach knotted. They would be in action soon. He passed the information back down the line to his troop: "Halfway."

184

He could feel the tension rising in the glider cabin. Were they, like him, questioning their ability to complete the mission? He didn't think so; they exuded confidence. On the surface, Paul did the same. He didn't show them the doubts that he sometimes felt as their leader. He wouldn't let them down. Anyway, Max would be there somewhere. Just picturing the burly Unterfeldwebel there to back him up made him feel a little easier. He berated himself knowing that he should snap out of it. He had men to lead into battle; he didn't have time for self-doubt now.

The glider immediately behind Paul's contained Max and his assault troop. The pilot Engels had also informed his assault troop commander of their location and the fact that they were halfway there.

"Looking good," Max commented, completely relaxed. He'd had his jitters as they were boarding the gliders, but now he was ready; now he was unshakeable. They had trained hard and well. Yes, things could go wrong, he thought, but that is life. The fundamentals were all there. The tactics were right, the training had been intensive, and they were well led. Oberleutnant Faust was an exceptional officer, and so was Leutnant Brand. They would get them through this and lead them to victory.

The Junkers pilot sipped his coffee, pulling a face as he did so. "Canteen coffee again?"

"It's the same coffee we have every time, sir," replied the bemused co-pilot.

"I know, and it never gets any better."

"Look." The co-pilot pointed out of the window. "It's the second searchlight sir. I know, count the seconds."

"We don't want to take our paying passengers to the wrong place, do we?"

The co-pilot fumbled with his watch and started his check of the searchlight timings. "Yep, same as the first one. Not far now, sir."

"About twenty kilometres, ten minutes to go then. This tailwind must be stronger than we thought. It puts us ahead of schedule," the pilot said worryingly.

"How far ahead, sir?"

"I'd say about ten minutes. We still need to gain some height as well."

"What will you do?"

"Let's check our height and time once we get to the searchlights at Aachen."

Hempel shouted to Paul, "We're at the release point, sir, but we're not being released." He sounded concerned.

"What could be the problem?"

"We're not at the correct height for one, sir. I think these winds have pushed us too quickly and we haven't been able to climb fast enough."

"Could we make it from here?"

"I doubt it, sir. We need at least another four hundred metres."

"Are we still climbing?"

"Yes, but we're crossing over the Dutch border as we speak. They will be none too pleased."

"When this all kicks off, none of them will be pleased."

Through the wisps of cloud, the keen-eyed co-pilot had spotted the searchlight, showing the location of their next step, the release of the gliders, and the last of the support they would see from the ground.

"What do we do, sir? Do we still need to climb four hundred metres?"

"We'll have to keep going. We've got to get the gliders to the right height for release. If we release them now, they'll never make it to their targets."

"But we're crossing into Dutch airspace, sir." The co-pilot sounded alarmed.

"A bit late to worry about that now. Very soon the entire German army will be crossing into their space. I have no option. We have to gain some more height."

"Flak's coming our way, sir," shouted the co-pilot, his eyes wide with fear.

"*Scheisse!*"

The glider shook as an explosion burst somewhere above them.

"The buggers are firing at us, sir!"

"Are we at the right height yet?" Paul asked.

"Close enough, sir. I hope to God we get the release soon."

Puffs of smoke could be seen above and to their right, the flak clearly aimed at other aircraft in the armada.

"We've got it, sir, the signal to release. Stand by!"

Paul shouted back to his men, who had sensed something was wrong, particularly as they could hear the anti-aircraft fire going on around them. Although they had some very small windows just below the wings, it didn't give them a particularly clear view, and they certainly couldn't see what was happening ahead of them. Crouched together, in a cramped, enclosed space, being fired at with nothing to fire back with. left them with a feeling of helplessness. Another flash, more puffs of smoke in the sky to the front of them. The Junkers dropped sharply to avoid the bursts of fire, and Hempel quickly matched the Junkers path, not wanting to snap the tow line.

"Time to release, sir."

"Let's do it."

At this point in time, they were close to their ideal height. It was now the turn of the glider pilots to prove their worth. Hempel initiated the release. Troop two was ready to descend.

Fischer was also holding onto his bench seat as his pilot, Stadler, guided the glider downwards, following in the wake of Paul's glider in front. They had the unenviable task of flying close to the anti-aircraft battery on top of the fort, their first target.

Max's pilot also dropped the tow line, and now, unfettered from its umbilical cord, it swooped down, seeking out its final destination.

Leeb touched the shoulder of his pilot Menzel. "There go three of the gliders. Are we next?"

"Yes, I'm just giving them a bit of space before I release. With this flak flying around, we may need to jink about a bit."

"Get ready, we'll be dropping shortly," Leeb shouted back to his troop.

"That's it, we're free," declared the pilot.

The glider fell, Leeb's stomach coming up to meet him.

Menzel looked up at the Junkers transports as they pulled up and away from them, increasing speed now they had rid themselves of the gliders. Their task wasn't quite over: they had to drop dummy paratroopers, with firecrackers attached, to try and confuse the enemy, helping to cover the activities of the rest of *Sturmabteilung Kaufmann*. The Dutch and Belgians were now their enemy, thought Menzel. Six months ago, he was flying sport gliders for fun. Now, he was about to go to war with the Dutch and the Belgians.

Chapter Twenty-six

Paul looked towards the front of the glider, through the glazed removable cockpit necessary for the exit of the pilot and himself, the rest leaving by the kick-out panel at the side. Over the shoulder of the pilot, he could clearly see the searchlights stabbing the early morning sky with their beams, searching out the impudent enemy breaching their sovereignty. He shouted a warning to his men that the glider was about to be released.

The Junkers aircraft towing the glider jolted and seemed to rear upwards, this as a result of releasing the dragging weight of the glider that for the last twenty minutes had been threatening to pull it out of the sky with its seeming inability to fly. The one-ton glider took what felt like a sickening dive, now that it had lost its power source and its capability to fly anywhere but down. The glider was not necessarily designed for full flight, but more a controlled descent. The pilot, Hempel, although deemed an expert glider pilot, had only completed twelve hours' flight training, struggled and fought with the controls which appeared to want to tear his arms out of their sockets.

"There's no turning back now, sir," he shouted to Paul. "It's down all the way."

He sounded relaxed, considering he had no engine and that the flak batteries somewhere below were still trying to seek him out and bring him down more quickly than he planned. Hempel actually felt relaxed; he was in control now and, the lower they got, the harder it would be for the flak to get them. He didn't want to wish ill on his colleagues, but it was likely they would be the flak gunner's prey now, rather than the silent gliders.

"How long?" asked Paul.

"I'd say about eight minutes, sir. The tugs released us a bit closer to the target than planned."

"Does that cause us any problems?"

"Crossing the Dutch border under tow hasn't helped. A gaggle of throbbing aircraft crossing into your airspace is hardly difficult to miss."

Paul had to agree; they had lost some of the element of surprise. He could only hope that the fortress garrison believed that an attack, if there was in fact going to be one, would occur elsewhere, their perceived invulnerability clouding their judgement. The glider shook as an explosion burst somewhere off to their right.

"I think that was wide of the mark, sir. I don't think they have us in their sights now, we're probably too low."

"ETA?"

"No more than four minutes."

Paul called back to his men; it was time for them to complete their final checks. There was little they could do in the confined space so it was more about keeping them apprised of events. All they could really do was ensure that their weapon was ready, their magazine was secure, and they could see that the explosives they would need to exit the plane with were close at hand. Some reached beneath their seat touching the equipment stored there, making sure it hadn't moved since the last time they had checked, probably no more than a couple of minutes ago. It was a reflex action, nothing more. Hunched together, some whispered encouragement to each other; others ran through the sequence of events yet again, not wanting to fail their comrades; and others hummed a song to themselves, or just waited in silent anticipation of what was to come. Another flash in the sky above them. The pilot had been correct: the enemy gunners were pursuing the impertinent Junkers pilots, cursing them for their audacity in crossing their borders.

As Assault Group Granite headed towards its target, their comrades in the other assault groups were approaching their assigned objectives. Assault Group Steel in their transport gliders flew through a hail of anti-aircraft fire as they approached the Belgian border and their target bridge at Veldwezelt. Assault Group Concrete and Iron had flown too far over the Dutch border and the enemy had been alerted by the sound of the straining JU 52s. They too were receiving the attention of the Dutch and Belgian defences.

Hempel motioned Paul to lean forward again towards the front of the shaking glider. The pilot proceeded to shout instructions into the officer's ear.

"It's going to get a bit bumpy, sir. I'm getting some crosswinds; everyone has to hold on tight."

Paul reiterated the warning to his men.

"Stand by, stand by," yelled the pilot. "Two minutes!"

The one hundred and one-kilometre flight had taken them only thirty-two minutes. Soon they would be landing; soon they would be on their target; soon they would be in action. The message was passed along the line to each member of the troop, warning them that they were only two minutes away from their objective. The Fallschirmjager each checked their equipment again and, in turn, checked their comrade's. A close-knit, crack unit like this recognised their interdependency on each other.

Paul cast an eye over his troops as best he could, sitting behind each other on the wooden bench down the middle of the tubular steel, linen-covered aircraft. Some of them were obviously feeling airsick, resulting from the glider's well-known instability in the air. Sat in the dark, with a constantly buffeting aircraft played havoc with your senses and they would no doubt be looking forward to the moment when they could exit the aircraft, no matter what that held in store for them. He thought about wishing them good luck, but that would sound downbeat. They didn't need luck; they just needed to do what they had been trained to do and were good at. One minute later, Paul held up his arm indicating they were a minute away from landing. He gave the command to brace, and the other six Fallschirmjager behind him held on as if their lives depended on it, and in some ways it did. The glider curved round as the pilot shouted to Leutnant Brand that the fort was in sight. The glider whistled as it plummeted further and further down, closer to the ground and closer to its target. Ten other gliders containing the remaining members of Assault Group Granite were all streaking towards their respective target points on top of Fort Eben Emael.

"Brace! Brace! Brace!" Paul shouted.

Now there was anxiety in Hempel's eyes as the glider got closer and closer to its target and subsequently closer to the ground. Not anxiety because of the impending action, but apprehension of missing the target or, even worse, crashing the glider and letting his comrades down. Their target was construction twelve, Maastricht one, a complex of three seventy-five-millimetre guns. The pilot could now see his target landing area, between construction eighteen and twelve, and pulled back on the stick at the last minute in an attempt to put the glider into a semi-stall, slowing it down before allowing the front of the skid to strike the ground.

It struck with a nauseating thump that threatened to tear each man apart as they were thrown from side to side in the plane like papier-mâché dolls. The glider screeched and scraped along the ground, the barbed wire around the central skid acting as a brake trying to slow the glider down, the additional brake attached below also adding to the friction and braking effect.

The paratroopers had been flung forward as the glider touched down, and they remained where they were knowing the stopping force would get worse yet. It came to a jarring halt as it swerved around to the right, on itself, tipping over onto its right wing, which shattered under the force, sending splinters of wood and pieces of fabric across the ground. There was almost a second of silence. The scrape of the glider on the roof of the fort had ceased, the wind was no longer whistling past, and the grunts of the paratroopers thrown back and forth and side to side as they came into land had stilled.

But Paul shattered the silence. "Out! Out! Out!" he yelled at the top of his voice, shocking the glider's occupants into action.

The front canopy of the glider was ripped open, pushed upwards and to the side.

"Out quickly!" Paul shouted again.

Speed was essential; they could hear now the shouts of alarm from the guards in the fort, shaken out of their reverie by the sudden attack from the skies. To the south-east, the anti-aircraft battery was in full swing, firing at the descending gliders, hoping to destroy them before they landed, or at least kill as many of the occupants as they could. That was Fischer's target. They couldn't help him; he was on his own.

Hempel was up on his seat, launching himself out of the glider, jumping down from the left, the clear side of the cockpit, immediately taking up a defensive position to cover his comrades while they also exited. Paul also followed suit, seconds behind him, the cockpit was also his best option for a fast exit. He crashed down by the side of the pilot and, seeing Maastricht one in the murky distance, congratulated the pilot on his accurate landing.

"Well done, Hempel, remind me to use you again."

Hempel smiled at the praise, but Paul didn't see it. He was already making his way round to the side of the glider assessing their location on top of the fort as he went to meet the rest of the troop. He had memorised every metre of this fortified stockade. Although the greater part of the forts weapons were placed to defend an attack from outside the fort, they did have some weapons covering the flat, exposed centre. Both MI Nord and Maastricht two posed a significant threat to the landing gliders and were predestined to be targeted early in the operation. Paul hoped they would be successful; if not, it would increase the danger to his team.

Immediately on landing, Konrad had kicked out the side panel attached to the the glider, pushing it aside as he too exited the plane as fast as he could, the rest of two-troop leaping out of the aircraft behind him. The troop quickly moved left, putting some distance between them and the glider that so far had not come under fire, but its large profile could possibly draw the attention of the fort's defenders. They didn't need any orders; they knew exactly what to do. Forster had grabbed the collapsible ladder; Straube and Kienitz each had one half of a fifty-kilogram charge in their hands, weighing them down heavily. Kempf and Weyer had set up the MG 34 to cover the troop as it prepared its equipment ready to move forwards. Konrad had a twelve and a half-kilogram charge on a strap around his neck and shoulder.

Paul turned to his men to check they were all ready. A second glider struck the ground behind them.

"That will be Uffz Fischer," hissed Kienitz, "going for the AA battery."

A third troop glider hit the ground with a sickening crash, striking one of the small machine-gun emplacements killing two Belgian soldiers who had ventured outside to seek the source of the pandemonium occurring outside.

That would be Leeb, thought Paul, taking out Cupola Nord, south-east of them. "Right, let's go," he shouted to his troop.

Paul and Konrad led first as they were the least encumbered by equipment and explosives. Behind them ran Forster, Straube and Kienitz, Kempf and Weyer off to the right, ready to cover them with sustained covering fire if necessary. Another glider landed to their west; probably Max going for Maastricht two, thought Paul

A blinding flash lit up the dawn sky, followed quickly by the explosive sound of a German grenade going off in the distance. The action had well and truly started and Group Granite was in the process of subjugating the enemy fort.

Then all hell broke loose: a Fallschirmjager off to Paul's right went down. It was Weyer, a bullet into the right shoulder exiting out of his lower abdomen, a second bullet from an enemy rifle striking him in the chest, with a third in the leg meant it was unlikely he would survive the day. Kempf dived to the ground, grabbed the MG 34 off the badly wounded Weyer, and, in the prone position, pulled the machine gun into his shoulder ready to fire. Once he could see any telltale flashes of gunfire, he would give them some of their own medicine, he thought.

They would have to leave Weyer to his own devices for the moment. The mission had to take priority; there were other German lives depending on their actions today.

"Hempel, strip Weyer of any MG belts quickly," called Paul. "We need to get out of here. We're too exposed."

Hempel quickly complied, rapidly crawling over to where injured soldier lay and taking the spare ammunition belts for the MG 34 from around Weyer's shoulders. A second Fallschirmjager cried out as two bullets zipped past him. Paul dived for cover and returned fire along with the other members of the troop. The other troops of the assault force were also experiencing fire as the enemy recovered from their initial shock.

Although Kempf was on his own now, with the MG 34 he quickly put down covering fire which seemed to do the trick and the enemy went to ground.

They were again up on their feet; they had just fifty paces to get to their target which was now clearly visible. Skirmishing forward, the ankle-high grass swishing as it was brushed and trampled by the para jump boots, they headed for the target. Every time Paul hit the deck, the air was forced from his lungs and, no matter how much training you had done, no matter how fit you were, under intense combat conditions your breathing was always laboured. They were twenty paces from their target and could see the three embrasures angled away from them, the home of the three seventy-five-millimetre guns. The sky lit up to their right; obviously one of the other troops had been successful in their attack, or at least were attempting to take out a target.

Paul's troop now faced west and were situated south-east of the target casemate now in front of them. Having approached it from its front left side, they were invisible from the embrasures, but not necessarily the observation cupola on the top. Paul shouted instructions to his men. The instructions were brief, they had practised this so many times, and, apart from Weyer being badly wounded, it seemed little different from their last rehearsal. They all knew their respective roles and were in complete control.

"Kempf, set up the MG around the front to cover us. Hempel, you're his number two."

Kempf picked up the MG 34 again and, followed by his new number two Hempel, scooted to the front corner of the casemate to cover his comrades from an attack in that direction.

"Konrad, rear side cover. I'll join you shortly."

Konrad didn't reply, just made his way into position. They were now completely covered from a surprise attack. Paul didn't need to say anything to the rest. They were already in action.

Forster had assembled the portable ladder, placed it up against the casemate and was then covering the southern arc while Straube and Kienitz heaved their charges up the ladder. Straube peered over the top of the casemate before taking the last step up on the ladder. He lifted the heavy charge and placed it gently on the concrete roof in front of him before heaving himself up on to the top behind it. He crouched down and moved to the side, casting his eyes over the top of the bunker. It was quiet. He moved the charge across so it was now at his side, then provided covering for Kienitz as he joined him on top of the bunker.

They could see the armoured observation dome at the other end of the concrete casemate and headed for it as quickly as they could. Straube, who was in front, felt sure he had seen a pair of eyes glinting at them through the observation slit.

"Better be quick, Uffz, I think we've been seen by the occupants," he hissed back to Kienitz.

"Once they get a taste of this lot, they'll have other things on their minds," retorted Kienitz as he heaved the lower twenty-five-kilogram element of the hollow-charge weapon onto the top of the dome. He could see lights inside the bunker and smelled what seemed like rotten eggs, obviously the consequence of an enclosed space continuously occupied by men. Straube followed suit placed the top half of the device into position and began to assemble it ready for setting the fuse. He could hear the firefights in the distance, but was sure he could also hear a clambering sound beneath the dome and the sound of heavy breathing. Time to go, he thought. Just as he had finished connecting the two parts, a firefight started below them between the Fallschirmjager's MG and some Belgian soldiers who had decided to venture out of their bunker to see what was happening. Straube must have been correct in his thinking that they had been spotted through the dome's slits.

They both heard a clunk as an object bounced off the steel dome and landed at Kienitz's feet. He looked down, his eyes widening in disbelief. "Fucking hell," he screamed, realising it was an enemy grenade. His reactions were swift, dropping his rifle to the roof of the bunker and, in one sweep of his right hand, picking up the grenade and throwing it back down to his unknown attackers. The heavy thump of the detonation was clearly heard as it exploded amongst the Belgian soldiers who had launched it in the hope of sweeping the impudent paratroopers off their fort. It had backfired. That and the devastating fire coming from the troop's machine gun proved too much and they scuttled back into their protective shell.

Straube had completed the assembly of the device now and set the ten-second fuse. "Go, go, go!" he shouted, counting down as he charged towards the other end of the casemate, Kienitz close on his heels.

"Nine…" They had reached the top of the ladder.

"Eight…" Straube swung his rifle on its sling round to his back and lowered his legs onto the ladder and scooted down.

"Seven…" Kienitz followed suit and they both landed with a thump besides Paul.

"Bugger, sir, that was a close one," exclaimed Kienitz.

"Six…"

"Never mind that, Kienitz, it's time we weren't here."

"Five…"

"Let's go," Paul called loudly to his troop. Noise didn't matter now. The local silence was about to be shattered beyond all recognition.

"Four…"

The entire troop, less Weyer, who was still out there somewhere badly wounded, pulled back about twenty paces from the Maastricht one casemate before hitting the deck.

"Three…"

Just as they had gone to earth, one of the seventy-five-millimetre guns fired, the shockwave blasting past Paul and his men. They assumed that it was the hollow-charge, and were surprised that it had not been more ferocious.

But Straube was still counting.

"Two…"

"Keep your heads down, that wasn't the charge," he yelled.

"One…"

The thunderous explosion immediately followed Straube's last count as fifty kilograms of destruction ate into the armoured dome, shaking the very foundations of the bunker. The blast from the detonation of the hollow-charge weapon engulfed Paul's troop in a shock wave. The piercing din numbed their eardrums and, had they not intentionally kept their mouths open, could have done some long-term damage. They kept their faces down. There were still bits of shrapnel shrieking past them, the clang on Konrad's helmet indicating that not all were just passing by.

The eruption above the dome had formed a smoky cloud that now spiralled above it. Below, the devastation was even worse, the blast knocking two of the gunners off their feet and the crust that broke off the inside of the dome as a result of the hollow-charge effect shattering into hundreds of deadly splinters, killing two of the Belgian gunners. The violent expansion of energy transmitted downwards, followed by globules of molten metal, the main force punching a hole through the armoured plate, ripping through their fragile flesh, leaving exposed bone and mangled tissue. There was no one to help the wounded men, not that much could be done for them other than to perhaps comfort them as their lives were slowly extinguished by the extent of their injuries. The rest of the gunners were in shock, concussed by the ferocity of the blast from above them.

Although slightly deaf from the force of the blast, Paul knew that they still had work to do. He shouted to Konrad whom he knew had a twelve and a half-kilogram charge. His voice was louder than he intended, due to the cotton wool effect in his ears from the explosion.

"Konrad, Forster, Straube, with me. The rest of you provide us with cover." Paul jumped up and they followed him back to the bunker.

They flattened themselves against its side, clouds of dust still dropping down around them. They needed to be quick, while the occupants were still stunned from the blast.

"Konrad, I want that charge you have put in the nearest embrasure. Stick it in there under the barrel," he said, pointing to the nearest seventy-fivemillimetre gun protruding out of the casemate, the one that had fired earlier.

Konrad took the charge from around his body and placed it

under the barrel as far into the embrasure as he could reach and set the ten-second fuse while his commander and comrades covered him.

"It's done, sir, let's shift!"

They ran back to the rest of the troop and got their heads down again, waiting for yet another blast. The explosion shook the ground; again, it was worse for the occupants of the bunker. The gun, blown off its mountings, struck the gunner who had been leaning up against it as he was recovering from the earlier attack on the dome. A second gunner took the blast in his face as he was trying to peer into the dawn outside, seeking out his tormentors, angry and wanting to hit back. It killed him instantly. Others in the vicinity, trying to escape from the devastation beneath the dome, and attempting to drag their wounded comrades to safety, were also caught in the blast. But the sacrifice of the two gunners who were killed was not completely in vain: their deaths had sheltered the others from the worst of the effects. As for the gun, it was badly twisted, blown off its mountings and would never be fired again.

Paul was far from finished. "Konrad, Forster. Weyer can only be fifty metres from here. Go and see what you can do for him. If you can get him back here, all well and good. If not, then make him comfortable and get back here quickly."

"We're on our way," responded Konrad, pleased that they could go and help their fallen comrade.

"No more than five minutes," hissed Paul after them.

He couldn't afford to be without a third of his troop for too long.

"Right, Hempel, Kempf, cover us again. Kienitz, Straube, with me, and get your grenades ready. We need to keep them off balance."

They again ran forward, thumping up against the side of the casemate. Paul peered around the corner. Although the furthest two guns could be seen jutting out of their embrasures, the first gun had completely disappeared. He crept up to the damaged embrasure, smoke still spewing from its interior. The weapon slit was no longer four right angles but a jagged hole of shattered concrete with spikes of steel reinforcements jutting out like broken teeth.

"Get ready," instructed Paul. "One grenade each, on the count of three."

They each got a grenade ready and, on Paul's final count of three, ran round to the front of the damaged embrasure and threw in their grenades, this time throwing themselves flat on the ground in front of the bunker. The blast came, most of it projecting inwards into the confines of the gunroom. Having barely recovered from the first two attacks, the senior NCO, who was partially injured himself, was supervising the removal of the many injured, dragging them to the entrance of the steps that led down into the fort's interior. He was leaving the dead, saving his and his soldiers' rapidly depleting energy to pull the injured to a place of safety. Although his efforts were not in vain, as many of the wounded had been dragged to the steps, the violence of the grenades ripped into him, taking him in the back and throwing him over one of the soldiers he was trying to help. He was dead before he hit the ground. Little did Paul know that that had been the last straw for the gunners and they retreated to one of the lower levels to escape the death and destruction that was being meted out to them.

"They'll not bother us any more. Let's get a marker panel on top of the bunker," instructed Paul. "We don't want those trigger-happy Stuka pilots lobbing bombs down on top of us. Check out the dome as well."

Kienitz and Straube picked up the ladder that had been blown away by the first blast and skipped up the steps, much quicker this time without the excessive weight of the hollow-charges and ran over to the dome. There was a hole big enough to put your fist through, but they couldn't see into the smoke-filled room. They extracted the panels from the bag and made the shape of a swastika. This was the recognition sign for the Luftwaffe, informing them that this target had been secured. Job done, they hastened back to the ladder, keen to rejoin their comrades.

Paul looked at the bunker, the three-gun casemate. Its weapons that had been aimed north towards the bridges of the Albert Canal were in Fallschirmjager hands. A shiver ran down his spine. He knew enough about the destructive force of the explosives and grenades they had used to know that had the occupants been anywhere near the points of attack then inside would be complete mayhem, sustaining injuries he didn't even want to contemplate. He snapped out of his dark thoughts. There was no time to dwell on it and no time to rest; they had another task to fulfil. It was four thirty-five in the morning; they had been on the ground for no more than fifteen minutes, yet it seemed like hours. They were already exhausted and had an unquenchable thirst that hadn't been satiated by the water they carried with them, but they still had work to do. They heard a rustling sound to their east. It was either the two paratroopers returning from helping their wounded comrades or the Belgian gunners had got round behind them and were counter-attacking. Paul and his men were alert, weapons ready. They heard the password hissed at them. It sounded like the guttural tones of Forster, his voice normally quite deep and booming. His throat was probably dry, like the rest of them.

"Show yourself," Paul hissed. He was still wary, just in case the paratrooper had been coerced into getting the troop to expose itself. But, deep down, he knew that the tough paratrooper would rather give his life than help entrap his fellow soldiers.

Forster came forwards, bent at the waist carrying one end of a collapsible ladder they had turned into a stretcher. At the other end was Konrad, equally bowed by the weight of the hefty Weyer strapped to the centre part of the makeshift stretcher.They placed him gently on the ground.

"He's unconscious, sir," Forster informed Paul, "but alive. We've strapped up his wounds as best we can, but we need to get him to an aid station whenever possible."

Paul looked down at him. Weyer's face was a sickly white. He had clearly lost a lot of blood and needed treatment soon if he was to live. "OK. We'll take him as far as the approach to MiSud, dropping him off before we make the attack. Then we can pick him up on our way to the HQ bunker."

Chapter Twenty-seven

Paul sent two men to collect a second fifty-kilogram charge from the glider. They would need it for their next target. They returned five minutes later, breathing heavily, handing the two charges to other colleagues.

"OK, let's get going."

They were to join up with the rest of Paul's assault force at MiNord, to be the assault group's command post. There, they would also meet up with their Group Commander Oberleutnant Faust. MiNord was a machine-gun bunker which could cause considerable risk to the other troops carrying out their specific tasks that morning. All being well, this bunker should have already been destroyed. But, on their way there, they had a second objective to take out: MiSud. Like Fischer's troop, they also had two targets.

Paul gathered his assault troop together and they headed northeast to MiSud. He hoped the others had been successful in capturing MiNord as its three machine guns covered the flat top of the fortress in a two hundred and ninety degree arc and, if they saw his troop crossing, the paratroopers would make a perfect target. MiSud was about three hundred paces to their north-east, but they knew that MiSud had a machine gun covering the bunker's south-west arc. So, Paul led his team east to come in around the back of the bunker, even though it took them directly into the firing line of MiNord. An explosion lit up the sky in the vicinity of MiNord, easing Paul's fears slightly. This meant that not only would the occupants of the bunker be distracted, due to their focus on their own safety, but it would also give the combatants in MiSud something to occupy their minds.

Paul could hear the two men carrying the wounded Weyer grunting behind him; Hempel and Kienitz had taken over carrying the make-do stretcher. He raised his hand to stop them and crouched down; everyone followed suit. They were approaching directly behind the casemate now. He turned to the two stretcher-bearers.

"This is it. Leave Weyer here and we'll move forwards another ten metres. Let's go."

They advanced closer to the target and positioned themselves into a line where they could observe the bunker for a few seconds, confirming there were no troops waiting for them on the outside. Once he was satisfied that all was quiet, he gave the order: "Go."

Forster ran straight for the bunker, jinking from side to side like a hare being chased by a fox, finally turning right to run up the path at the side taking him to the top. As he got to the top, he could see the bunker had a periscope hole. He quickly pulled a one-kilogram charge from his pack, hastily igniting the fuse, and, after a two-second count, threw it into the periscope hole. He dropped flat onto the roof, covering his ears as, two seconds later, the conventional charge exploded.

Feet could be heard running away from the charge when it was thrown but, after the explosion and its sound effects had died down, there was silence. Forster then stayed where he was, providing cover for the rest of the troop. This distraction gave Paul the opportunity to carry out his next attack on this perceived indestructible target. Once the explosion initiated by Forster had occurred, Kempf and Konrad ran forward to the southern-facing embrasure that contained one of the machine guns. Kempf quickly placed a six-kilogram pole charge into the stepped gun slit and set the fuses.

"Fire," he shouted as he sped round to the rear of the casemate and joined Konrad. They both flattened themselves against the bunker's outer wall.

Above them, hearing the word 'Fire', Forster fell prostrate on the roof.

No sooner had the words left Kempf's mouth than the charge in the gun slit exploded.

Kempf and Konrad returned to the troop's position, passed on their way by Straube and Kienitz carrying the last fifty-kilogram hollow-charge between them.

Placing the lower half against the wall quickly followed by Straube's contribution, the apparatus was assembled. This time, no one was hanging around. They had already seen its power on top of Maastricht one. They wanted to get as far away as possible. Even Forster wasn't chancing it and joined them as they sped east to join the other paratroopers. They slid to a halt in between Paul and Hempel, wriggling down into the slight hollow they had discovered earlier.

"It's done, sir," Kienitz informed Paul. "Pray to God it does the trick."

They all buried themselves as deep into the trough as was humanly possible, hugging the ground as if it were a lover. But the air was still wrenched from their lungs and the force of the discharge tried to tear their hands away from their ears. A hot blast passed over the tops of their heads and they would have surely burnt but for the protection of their para helmets. Black turned to white as multiple flashes of the detonation lit up the area. Kienitz's arm seemed to jerk in the flashing lights as he moved it, in a strobe-like effect, as if in a black and white film. He moved his arm to his side touching the place where he had felt something glance against his leg. As he pulled his arm back, his hand was wet and he could smell the warm scent of blood on it.

"I think I've been hit, sir," he said calmly.

"We'll check it soon," responded Paul.

Inside the complex, soldiers were blown back against the walls of the bunker. Some of them were burnt terribly but still alive, running, screaming through the corridors past their comrades, trying to seek relief from the terrible searing pain. Now the sound of the explosion had subsided, Paul and his men could hear the screaming agony of the wounded soldiers deep down in the bunker, recently their home, but now, for some, it would prove to be their coffin and final resting place. Although he and his men felt for them, as they were soldiers too, it was brief as they still had a task to complete and now was not the time for self-indulgence.

The troopers were alert now as the area suddenly became quiet, apart from the occasional staccato of machine-gun fire in the distance. Movements could be heard to their left; German voices shouted recognition codes, identifying them as Max's troop returning to the fold after effectively destroying their target, Maastricht two, the bunker complex with three seventy-five millimetre guns.

Max's bulk suddenly appeared at his platoon commander's side as he was examining Kienitz's injury. Kienitz was lucky; it was minor, caused by a piece of metal or concrete from the last explosion slicing through his combat trousers and taking a two-centimetre chunk of flesh with it. Paul tore at the trouser leg and Max placed a field dressing over the wound.

"I guessed it was you, sir, causing all of this racket. And what do you call this, Kienitz? It's just a bloody scratch," Max said, smiling.

"And you've the platoon commander acting as your bloody nurse."

"It's good to see you too, Unterfeldwebel," responded Kienitz, returning the smile, but wincing as the bandage was pressed down on his wound. "I'm glad to see that your concern over your men's well being is at the forefront as usual."

Max picked up Kienitz's hand and placed it on the bandage, telling him to press down on it and hold it there while he bound it to his leg. "You'll be up and about in a few minutes," he scoffed.

"It's good to see you, Max. I take it all went well?" Paul asked him.

"A piece of cake, sir. I see you have things sewn up here."

"Unfortunately, Weyer has been badly hit and we've still to check out this bunker. Could you get your troop to set up an all-round defence and see to Weyer while we finish this off? Weyer's about ten metres behind us."

"Consider it done, sir." Max started to get up to carry out his orders.

"And, Max," the Unterfeldwebel stopped and turned around to face Paul, "it's good that you made it."

"You too, sir, I told you we'd get this done." With that, Max got up and left to organise his men.

Now that Paul's troop had some local cover from Max's men, they all moved forward to look at the extent of the damage. A hole had been blasted right through the concrete. The shockwave that had been propagated, followed by the hot, explosive gases mixed with vaporised steel and concrete, had torn into the men stationed inside, turning some into blackened and blistered corpses in front of their fellow soldiers. It had done its job and the hole was large enough for the paratroopers to get through. The troop would need to climb through the sixty-centimetre hole but, before that, two grenades were thrown in for good measure. Once the force of the blast had dissipated, they climbed through.

Forster and Straube gently eased their way in. They knew they had a few minutes' grace as the enemy would still be recovering from the exploding grenades, but that didn't stop them from tossing one back if they knew that enemy soldiers had entered their gun room. When they climbed inside, it was very dark and full of smoke caused by the various explosions. They waited for the smoke to disperse, not knowing what they would walk in to, but it didn't and they couldn't see a hand in front of their face. The smoke and fumes were also making them gag and choke. Coughing would give them and their position away. Reluctantly they put on their gas masks and eased their way further into the casemate, the bunker. There were no lights, so they hurriedly found their torches, glad that their platoon commander had insisted that they should be ready at hand. It was a risk, but they had no option but to use them. They scanned the inside of the bunker and saw three dead soldiers lying there along with two severely wounded. More could be seen further in. It was carnage! Both the wounded were in a bad way, suffering from severe concussion. The paratroopers went to look at them, but there wasn't much they could do. They needed to look to their security first. They moved deeper into the bunker and saw a second Belgian gun crew that had fallen by the northern machine-gun post. All were dead.

The trooper felt his way further and further into the room, hearing Straube's breathing rasping through the gas mask as he followed close behind. Somewhere to his front and to the right, a telephone suddenly rang. The paratrooper visibly jumped.

"It's just a telephone," Straube said. "Aren't you going to answer it?"

"OK then," replied Forster, slightly bemused by this event.

He felt his way along the wall getting closer to the field telephone and picked it up. *"Was ist eine Angelegenheit, dies ist nun ein Deutsch Festung?"* What is the matter, this is now a German fortress?

There was a scramble of voices on the other end of the phone and Forster put it down. He and Straube both suppressed a laugh. Had they not been wearing gas masks, their grins would easily have been seen by torchlight. When they reached the far end, they slowly made their way down some steps but, at the bottom, steel doors barred their way so they had to return to the top.

The Belgian troops, probably demoralised by the sheer destructive force of the explosions, had retreated from the casemate and pulled back down the tunnels into the interior of the fort, leaving their dead and wounded behind.

The troopers returned to the Belgian wounded. They were both in a bad way, but they had to leave them for now as the fort was still not completely in their hands. They switched off their torches and headed for the light now showing through the gaping hole in the side of the bunker, climbing back out to report their findings to their officer. On getting out, they peeled off their gas masks, breathing in deeply, sucking the fresh air into their lungs, their skin smoke black where the mask had not covered their faces.

Paul handed them his canteen. He could imagine what their throats must feel like. "Well, report." Paul needed to know. He had decisions to make about whether to move his entire force to the HQ, or leave an element here.

Forster started. "It's a bloodbath in there, sir. The machine guns are finished. They won't be using them again in a hurry."

"What about soldiers?" probed Paul, needing a full assessment.

"There are at least five dead that we could see, sir, and two wounded."

"How badly?"

"One won't make it through the night, but the other could survive if treated soon."

"What else?" asked Paul quickly.

"We followed the steps to the bottom, but the steel doors were well and truly shut. I think they know that there's nothing to come up here for. It's finished as a defensive point."

Paul called Konrad over to join them. "Forster will update you, but I want you, these two and Hempel to remain here. Get a recognition signal on top and see what you can do for the Belgian wounded."

"Will do, sir," responded Konrad. "Where will the rest of the troop be?"

"I'll take them with me to our HQ which is hopefully MiNord by now. I need an update. Once I know the current status, I'll get word to you. Keep your wits about you. This isn't over yet."

"I agree, sir," said Max as he joined in the conversation. "They haven't counter-attacked yet, but it's bound to happen soon."

"You heard the Unterfeldwebel. Stay alert."

"We need to move out, sir," Max reminded him. "There may still be plenty to do and we need to touch base with the main group."

The remainder of Paul's troop rapidly moved away from the emplacement, followed by Unterfeldwebel Grun and his men. They had again picked up Weyer who was still unconscious, although they had managed to staunch the blood loss. However, he needed to remain in one place, not to be jigged around every five or ten minutes. Once at headquarters, he could get more attentive treatment. They headed north-east towards MiNord and, after a matter of minutes, were challenged by German paratroopers from the other glider parties that had landed to secure MiNord, Eben two, an observation cupola, and two further cupolas that were found to be dummies.

MiNord had been secured, and Paul could see the effects of a fifty-kilogram weapon against the side of the casemate where a hole big enough to climb through had been blown. Oberfeldwebel Waechter, whose troop had attacked this bunker successfully, met him.

"Good see you're OK, sir. How are your men doing?"

Paul updated him, making him aware that MiSud, and Maastricht-one and Maastricht-two had been secured or destroyed.

"The others, sir?"

"I'm waiting for Uffz Fischer and Uffz Leeb to meet us here, but I'll send a couple of runners out to look for them."

"Good. I can get that reported back to Hauptman Kaufmann pronto."

"Where is Oberleutnant Faust?"

"He's on his way, sir. He had a mishap on the way. He's had to get another glider and tow. We also have a second glider missing, so we're down by sixteen men now. You're in command until the Oberleutnant joins us, sir."

Chapter Twenty-eight

Earlier that morning, Max's troop had their task to complete. Max leant forward. He was sitting directly behind the glider pilot. The pilot had circled twice, scanning the ground below, attempting to get his bearings and discern his landing point.

"How's it looking?" Max enquired.

The pilot, Stadler, looked about him before responding. "There's the junction of the canal and the Meuse River, but I can't see the bloody target. Where the hell is it?"

"What's that there?" said Max, pointing to what he thought was a glider coming in to land below them.

"Yes, there it is, there's the target," Stadler said excitedly. "Damn it, I'll have to go round again."

"Have you enough height?"

"Just, we're coming in from the east, and I'm tracking round to the north-west now." The right wing dipped down as the glider tilted over to the right. "We're about four hundred metres from the target." After taking the glider round on a circuit, he levelled off and pushed the stick forward slightly as he lost more height in readiness to hit the ground.

"There, Max, there!" shouted Unterfeldwebel Stadler, pointing to the casemate that could be seen out of the port side of the Perspex cockpit.

Max, sitting with the rest of his troop in the cramped glider, could just make out his target. It looked to him as if they would land slightly behind it and to the right. Perfect, he thought, the guns are targeted with an arc covering from the north-west to the north. They would be approaching the casemate from the south, as planned, from its blind side. The glider pilot was now coaxing his plane, which was rapidly losing height, to the ground and onto its target. He tipped it round slightly to the right, coming on a line directly north. If he'd got it right, he would come to a stop just behind and to the right of the target. He was dead straight now and very low, passing Cupola-Sud on his right as he dropped the glider for the last time to bring it in to land. Max's troop had to destroy Maastricht-two, the sister casemate to Maastricht-one, the target of his platoon commander.

"This is it, Max, I'm committed now," Stadler said with a grin. "There's no turning back now."

Max leant back, shouting at the top of his voice, "Brace! Brace! Brace! We're going in."

Just as Max had finished shouting the warning, the glider's ski connected with the ground. Neither the pilot, Max nor the rest of the troop need have worried. It was a textbook landing. The glider slewed to a halt, coming to a standstill with the exit hatch of the glider facing their target a mere thirty paces away.

"You're a bloody marvel," praised Max. "Now let's get out of here."

The pilot quickly pushed at the Perspex cockpit; it easily moved up and out of the way allowing Stadler, with Max hot on his heels, to make a quick and clean exit. A bright flash to the east indicated that Group Granite was starting to make itself felt. Max heard the side panel being booted out, and was quickly joined by the rest of his troop. He sent Pelz and Renisch to scout ahead while he waited for Geyer and Rammelt to grab the heavy hollow-charges. They both came out clutching one half of the heavyweight charge each, quickly followed by Geib and Waldau.

Two further gliders hit the ground, both containing other troops of Group Granite. One of the gliders struck the top of the fortress at too steep an angle, nose first, the front of the glider digging into earth, somersaulting over onto its back. Still sliding along, the wings were ripped from the main body and shattered as they hit the uneven ground. Amazingly, the troop onboard, although dazed, still deplaned as they were trained to do, seeking immediate cover and moving towards their objective.

Max looked round, as did the other members of the troop, as a huge explosion erupted to their front, coming from the direction of Maastricht-one.

"Leutnant Brand has started the party then," concluded Geib.

"It's one nil so far then," added Rammelt.

Max looked confused; clearly he was not party to the bets being wagered that his troop would be the last one to complete their task. He promptly forgot about it and refocused on the matter in hand. The target was now to their front and they swiftly hard targeted towards the casemate, darting left and right, where they met their companions who had been sent on ahead.

"Its all clear. They're quiet as mice," said Pelz.

"They must be bloody deaf," added Renisch. "We've scouted the front and sides. There's no one to be seen."

"They're probably wondering what the hell is going on to their front," suggested Max. "That can only be good news for us."

Their target was now directly in front of Max's troop. Approaching it from the rear, on its left side, its blind spot, they were invisible from the embrasures.

"Let's get it done," ordered Max.

They implemented their well-rehearsed plan. Geib set up the MG just around the side of the casemate to cover their right flank to the north and east, while the others assaulted the bunker, Stadler acting as his number two. Renisch covered their left flank. Max placed the ladder up against the rear bunker wall and held it steady as Geyer and Rammelt struggled up it with their heavy loads. Once on the top, they both headed for the armoured observation cupola on the upper surface of the concrete casemate as briskly as they could, bearing in mind the heavy loads they were carrying. Geyer, who was leading the way, quickly heaved up the heavy lower part of the device onto the dome.

Rammelt joined him and he too hefted up his section of the device, marrying it up with its partner. As separate items, they were a normal explosive charge. Still deadly. But, when married together as one, it was lethal.

"It's done, I'm setting the fuse now," warned Geyer. "Headache time it is."

And with that he dashed off to the ladder, scuttling down it as fast as he could, with Rammelt close behind him practically landing on top of him in his haste to get away. They flattened themselves against the wall, waiting for the thunderous explosion they knew would come.

I'm getting too old for this, thought Max, but his notions were driven from his mind as the shattering explosion above rocked them all with its crippling blast, fatal to the soldiers directly below, cowering in fear of what was transpiring above them. They had seen an attack occur on their sister casemate, Maastricht one, and their command centre had warned them that they were under general attack. They were in the process of getting the guns ready to fire when they heard thumps and clangs coming from the dome above them and could see boots blocking the visors. Their curiosity was quickly answered; the overwhelming shock wave from the detonation of the hollow-charge above shattered their ear drums with its violence. Then, as if still not satisfied, it rained hot molten metal and shards of concrete and steel down on them. Pelting them with its violence, slicing, gashing, piercing and burning their soft bodies, extinguishing their lives and snatching the victory they had imagined they would achieve through a last heroic defence.

Although protected from the blast, Max's troop still felt the effects of the pressure wave as it first wrenched the air from their lungs, tugging at their uniforms, before the vacuum created by it sucked the air and dust back to swamp them in its blanket of earth and fine dust.

They were far from finished. Their task was to put the gun emplacement completely out of action. At that moment in time, they could not be sure of what permanent damage had been done.

Pelz and Waldau sprinted round to the front of the casemate, placing a twelve and a half-kilogram charge beneath one of the seventy-five millimetre guns.

"If Egon and Stefan haven't given them a big enough headache then this ought to."

They scampered round to the back of the bunker, quickly followed by the MG team, throwing themselves to the ground, all tucking their heads beneath their arms, elbows covering their ears, waiting for the explosion they knew would come.

The flames and debris shot out of the front of the bevelled wall, the rest of the force of the blast rupturing the gun and blowing a hole in the embrasure. Belgian soldiers were crouched behind the mechanics of their guns, waiting for the enemy soldiers to attack and finish the job. Many of their comrades were lying dead beneath the observation dome, some just wounded but screaming in agony, begging for water, for help and even their loved ones. Although scared, they held their rifles out in front, in readiness to make one last stand. They had agreed to go down fighting. The explosion burst amongst them, their stand finished, the fight literally knocked out of them. They extracted themselves from the carnage, taking what wounded they could carry or drag with them.

The paratroopers felt the power of the blast as it was transmitted through the walls of the casemate to where they were taking cover. Pelz and Waldau, recovering quickly from the calamitous noise, made their way back round to the front. The explosive had done its job. They approached the still smoking embrasure that was now just a jagged hole. The gun could no longer be seen; they assumed it had been blown back inside. Pelz tried to climb through the gap but the smoke was still billowing out, choking him, so his attempt to enter the bunker was stalled. Too much time had been lost since the explosion. They knew they would have to throw grenades in before they made another attempt at entering the bunker. They tossed three grenades in, one after the other. Once theses exploded, there was no hesitation: they entered immediately. Waldau covered while Pelz cautiously entered the casemate, desperately holding back a grating cough caused by the smoke and dust surging around him, filling his nostrils, gritty on his teeth. Whether he breathed through his mouth or his nose, the effect was the same. His throat already dry, the dust just aggravated it, but to cough and clear his throat would only announce his presence and give away his position attracting possible enemy fire.

Holding his breath, taking his helmet off, Pelz quickly donned his gas mask. Pulling the straps of his mask over his head, settling the rubber surface snug into his face and replacing the helmet, he breathed out heavily to clear the toxic air. It had taken precious time and he was annoyed that he hadn't thought of it sooner. He groped his way forward, the grey dawn light offering little illumination inside the enclosed bunker, resorting to his torch to find his way around. He was surrounded by death and destruction, the smell of the acrid, toxic gases still invading his sense of smell through his mask. He pulled two stick grenades from his belt. Priming both, he tossed them down what appeared to be an ammunition elevator. He remembered seeing something similar during his training on forts in Czechoslovakia and Poland.

A Belgian gunner rapidly clambered along the tunnel, dragging his comrade away from the casemate. The grenades exploded above them, damaging the ammunition elevator that fed the three guns, and the metal staircase which was the only access to the guns. The explosion also impaired some of the electrics. The Belgian artillerymen who had sought shelter down the steps to the level below the gunroom were flung back from their positions as the grenades did their work. Smoke filled their lungs and blinded their eyes in the already darkened space and they moved back further down the tunnel seeking safety.

Unterfeldwebel Grun's assault troop had completed their task. The casemate, known as Maastricht-two, was no longer capable of taking part in any further action, its role of defending the Albert bridges had just ended. Its two remaining guns, although still aiming north in the direction of the bridges they were to cover, were powerless to intervene in the advance being undertaken by the German army below them. With the three guns from Maastricht-one also out of action, Fort Eben Emael had lost the use of a third of its main artillery. With a further two guns lost at Cupola Nord-1, things were looking dire for the Belgian defence.

Max called his troop together. "Well done, lads, but we need to get moving and join up with Leutnant Brand and the rest of the group. We'll head for MiNord, but go via Maastricht-one, just in case the Leutnant is still there."

They were all crouched down, listening to Max's instructions, daylight starting to peek through. "We have no idea what the score is, so we're going to move tactically. I will take a half section forward first with Geyer, Rammelt and Geib. Stadler," Max turned to the pilot, also a sergeant like Max, "you follow up with Waldau, Renisch and Pelz. Everybody clear?"

They all acknowledged Max's orders.

"Let's go then."

The half section led by Max moved off and to the left, quickly running forward for about twenty paces then hitting the deck, covering a one hundred and eighty degree arc in front of them, weapons ready. The remaining section then thundered past them on the right. Once twenty paces in front, they too hit the ground and took over covering the troop. The roles were reversed every twenty to thirty paces. Speed was of the essence; the faster they moved, the more difficult it would be for an enemy to latch on to them and, whilst they were running, their comrades would cover them.

After about a hundred and fifty paces they could see Maastricht one but couldn't detect movement. Max called a halt, brought the troop together and sent Geyer ahead to scout the area. Geyer quickly arrived at the bunker, but there was no Troop Two to be seen. He noticed the damaged embrasure and peered through. He could discern nothing but a mangled mess. He returned to inform Max.

"There's no one there, Unterfeldwebel."

"What's the state of the bunker?"

"A bit of a mess. They've blown up at least one of the guns."

"Any sign of the enemy?"

"Not a soul."

"Right, listen in. We're heading north-east to MiSud. Same formation and we continue to hard target. I'll lead, let's go."

A few minutes later, they hit the deck again. They could see MiSud, but also some activity around it. Max hoped to God it was a Group Granite team. He was hoping it would be the Leutnant's men and not a Belgian force waiting in ambush for them. He again sent Geyer forward to investigate. Geyer quickly returned, informing the troop that all was well.

Max led them forward and saw that the bunker had been taken, smoke still floating around in the air, a strong smell of cordite. He scouted round looking for his platoon commander. He spotted Paul leaning over another paratrooper who appeared to be wounded. It looked like Kienitz. He hoped the injury was just a minor one.

Chapter Twenty-nine

Fischer, commander of the third assault troop, also sat immediately behind the glider pilot, giving him a feel for the progress of the flight, and immediate egress, following the pilot out of the cockpit canopy once they had landed. His platoon Commander had given him two tasks: first, to take out the anti-aircraft position situated between Cupola Nord-1 and Cupola Sud-1, and then Cupola-120, two, one hundred and twenty-millimetre guns encased in a revolving armoured turret.

Their parent aircraft had released the glider, and the pilot was now scanning the area in front of him, seeking out the target. It consisted of four thirty-millimetre anti-aircraft guns. To say that the pilot was uneasy about landing close to an AA battery was an understatement. He was deliberately piloting his plane, and his passengers, straight for the very thing that was designed to knock them out of the sky. He was praying that they wouldn't be discovered until the very last minute, when the angle was so low it would be impossible for the Belgians to bring their guns to bear.

"I can see them, Karl, down there," shouted the pilot, Uffz Engels.

The glider was sweeping around from the east and then banking right to fly north and land alongside their first target. Fischer looked out of the cockpit and could see the guns below. Only three were firing, but away from Fischer's position, aiming at a glider elsewhere. Then, having spotted this other attacker sneaking up on them from the east, they swung their guns round to meet it. The bright, radiant rounds coming towards them almost seemed leisurely, yet the standard configuration of one tracer round for every four standard rounds meant that between each illuminated round there were four deadly bullets. Fischer looked at the display, mesmerised by the show that was playing out in front of him until common sense prevailed and he remembered that they were attempting to shoot him out of the sky and kill him and all of his men.

"They've stopped firing!" Engels pointed out.

Fischer leaned forward and looked down. It was true; not a single gun was firing. The Belgian gunners were having severe problems. One of the guns had failed to fire from the start and all three of the others had jammed at some point during their firing cycle. The fort's anti-air defences had fallen almost without a shot being fired.

But Fischer and his men were not aware of that and still had to destroy their first target. The Belgian soldiers could resolve the issues with the anti-aircraft guns at any minute. They were also a force that could operate in Group Granite's rear area. They had to be neutralised.

Fischer shouted back to his troop, "Lock and load."

He also cocked his weapon, making sure the pilot's machine pistol was also ready as he needed to concentrate on his flying.

"We're going down, Karl. Stand by."

Fischer called back to his men, "Brace! Brace! Brace!"

The glider's ski made contact with the ground, the pilot still keeping it steady through control of the ailerons and tail flaps, but eventually it was left to chance. The landing was perfect; the glider slewed to a stop some twenty metres from their target, the battery on the right side of the glider. Fischer and Engels quickly exited through the cockpit area, dropping to the ground, turning right and heading straight for the AA site, throwing a grenade as they did so, keeping the Belgian gunners' heads down.

Lanz, Halm and Braemer kicked their way out through the glider panel and went round behind the pilot and their assault troop commander as they had practised, while Sesson and Roon, with a light machine gun and supported by Wagner, went around the tail of the glider and immediately hit the deck to provide fire support for the section moving forward. The three paratroopers gave covering fire almost immediately, as an ever increasing swathe of metal found its way towards them, chipping bits of wood and cloth from the glider's wings. Fortunately, as the enemy slowly awoke from their preoccupation with the skies above and galvanised by the hell that had just descended upon them, they made the main focus of their fire the glider, little knowing that the paratroopers had already decamped.

One section opened up a crippling fire on the Belgian unit from one angle whilst being assaulted from the opposite side by a second group of screaming, angry Fallschirmjager, led by Fischer.

Fischer's section had opened fire on the rattled Belgian soldiers who had now switched their fire from the glider. Realising too late that it wasn't firing back, they shifted their fire to the MG 34 team that was ripping them apart with its devastating firepower. Some turned to face the other assault, hesitating, not knowing whether to fire at the glider still, the machine gun shooting at their left flank, or the screaming maniacs boldly charging straight at them. By the time three of the artillerymen decided to target Fischer's group, it was already too late.

A grenade thrown by Halm exploded just to their rear, shrapnel taking two of the soldiers in the hips and lower legs, their arms unconsciously raised in the air to counter their bodies' uncontrolled forward movement. The astonishment on their faces turned to panic as it dawned on them what had just transpired. Their knees crumpled, their other colleague collapsing beside them as Fischer pumped rounds into him from his machine pistol.

The remaining eleven Belgians still functioning out of the sixteen-man platoon turned to face this second onslaught but, with two more of their number being taken out by the MG, they started to panic. An NCO attempted to rally them, coaxing one section to keep the heads down of the machine gunners tearing into their left flank, and the second section to counter the assault that was almost on top of them. It failed. The young soldiers facing the MG were too frightened to raise themselves up for fear of being hit by the rounds zipping past them at a phenomenal rate. Sesson, firing short five-round bursts, conserving his ammunition and ensuring his aim held true, kept the enemy's heads down.

The second section, hit by a further grenade landing behind them, panicked, thinking they were being attacked from the rear, and delayed their response long enough for Fischer and his men to get amongst them. Halm struck one of the soldiers on the side of his face with the butt of his rifle, his Kar 98 having jammed during the attack. The young soldier hadn't even raised his weapon to defend himself, so shocked was he by the suddenness of the attack and the aggression clearly etched on the paratrooper's face. He just froze. Engel's machine pistol, fired within an arm's length of the NCO who was still bravely fighting back, etched a row of bloody holes across his abdomen, throwing the soldier backward.

Seeing their NCO struck down so violently, for the rest of flagging defenders it was the last straw. They quickly threw down their weapons and raised their hands in the air. The fight had gone out of them. The paratroopers quickly disarmed the Belgian soldiers and grouped them together in the centre of the battery, dragging the wounded over.

The grenades thrown by the attackers had damaged two of the machine guns, and Fischer had the remaining two disabled, making sure they couldn't be used again in anger. He quickly decided to leave Roon and the pilot with the prisoners. Two Fallschirmjager were more than enough; the Belgian troops were completely demoralised and had enough on their plate caring for their many wounded. Although he felt for the injured soldiers, Fischer had greater things to worry about. He gathered up the rest of his troop and they returned to the glider to get the explosives they would need for their next task: Cupola-120.

They carried two sets of the heavy hollow-charge weapons with them and two of the smaller ones. With a five-minute tab to their target, it was too far to run back if they needed to restock quickly. They were already running behind.

Fischer set off with Lanz, Braemer, Wagner, Halm and Sesson in tow, leaving a quarter of his assault team behind guarding the prisoners. There was a sudden explosion and a flash of light off to their left, north-west of their current position en route to their next target.

"That must be two-troop, so it looks like they've beaten Unterfeldwebel Grun to it," whispered Halm to his commander who was in front of him, clearly proud that his troop may yet beat troop-four commanded by Max.

"It could be Leutnant Brand. They're in roughly the same direction," added Lanz.

There was a drive to beat the sergeant's troop, and bets had been placed in the form of drinks after the operation. The rivalry in the assault force was fierce, as it was across Group Granite, spurred on by Hauptman Kaufmann's drive for perfection. But it was healthy competition and demonstrated the pride they had in each other for their respective abilities and those of their comrades.

"That's one down, we'll be next. They'll definitely be buying the drinks tonight then," said Braemer, close in behind.

"Quiet," hissed Fischer forcefully. They hadn't finished the job just yet. "I can see the cupola now."

They hit the deck. They had approached from the south-east and, apart from firefights and explosions from other areas of Eben Emael, it was quiet in their immediate vicinity. The guns were pointing towards the north, but weren't firing, which seemed strange to Fischer as the rest of *Sturmabteilung Kaufmann* had already started their attacks on the bridges. Surely by now they must know that an enemy has landed right in their backyard, but also that German forces were at this very minute attacking their key bridges on the canal.

"Look, the turret's turning," called Sesson.

Fischer could see the turret rotating slowly from side to side, but still no shells were being fired from the two guns that could be seen jutting from the slits in the armoured dome. It spurred him into action. His job was not complete until he had destroyed this last target, or had at least put it out of action. He was determined that this artillery emplacement would not fulfil its role of firing on an invading force attempting to cross the Albert Canal. He called Sesson and Lanz to him. "I want you to place one of the large charges on the turret, just above one of the gun barrels, OK?"

They both nodded their understanding and, without further hesitation, picked up one half of the charge each and dashed forward to Cupola-120. They scrambled up the sloped, large concrete platform, into which the armoured turret was embedded, moulding their bodies to it once alongside, ducking down as the turret swung in their direction. Once past, they quickly assembled the device and, both carrying it, tracked the rotating turret and placed it above the left-hand gun barrel, set the fuse and bolted back to their comrades.

They all buried their heads into the grassy top of the fort as deeply as possible. Although they had seen trial explosions of the device at Hildesheim, they had not seen it explode as it was meant to, attached to an armoured artillery turret. They were about to find out the results for real. Ten seconds after the fuse had been set, the charge exploded. The immense pressure generated by the detonation of the explosive, drumming through the heads of the Fallschirmjager as they hugged the ground ever more tightly, drove a high-velocity jet of metal into the armoured dome. A cloud of smoke billowed up. They felt the searing heat pass over where they lay, thankful that it was not them on the receiving end of the explosion. They were suddenly engulfed in a white cloud of smoke, dust mixed with it, finding its way into their nostrils and throats, making them gag as they breathed in more and more of the toxic fumes. Once the air had cleared enough, Sesson shot up and made his way back to the cupola. Although he could see where the blast had occurred, it had not penetrated the armour plate. He returned to pass the bad news to his troop commander.

"Nothing," he informed Fischer. "It's made a dent, even a small hole, but it hasn't penetrated all the way through."

There was indeed a dent about fifteen centimetres across and ten centimetres deep, but it hadn't blasted through the armour. The device had let them down.

"*Scheisse*, I thought these charges were meant to be good!" Fischer exclaimed. At least the turret has stopped moving. "We can't leave it like this," he concluded. "We mustn't assume that the turret and guns are no longer effective."

"What about the barrels?" asked Braemer. "We could stick something down them?"

"Excellent idea, my thoughts exactly, let's get it done."

"Two small charges should do it," suggested Halm.

Halm, who already had two of the small standard one-kilogram charges in his pack, was joined by Sesson and they both ran back to the turret. The cupola was still stationary and they quickly lit the fuse, dropping the explosives down the barrels. Four seconds later, the crump of the explosions could be clearly heard as they damaged them beyond repair.

Fischer called his men together and they returned to their grounded glider where his two paratroopers were guarding the air defence prisoners. Once he checked that all was well, they set out to find their platoon commander who was supposed to be at the group headquarters, at MiNord. They ran at speed. They had roughly a kilometre to cover, to rejoin their comrades and make themselves available for other tasks, or to back up any unit that was in trouble.

Halm almost somersaulted as the bullet passed through his leg, knocking it from under him, his momentum keeping him going until he tumbled to the ground. He ended up sprawled on the damp turf, feeling no pain, but unable to move his leg, not having a notion of what had happened. His first thoughts were that he had stumbled over a dip in the ground but, when he tried to move his foot, a stab of pain shot up his thigh making him gasp, feeling nauseous and close to passing out. "I'm hit," he shouted, hoping his comrades had heard him as he didn't want to shout a second time just in case he drew the wrong sort of attention. He sat up and looked down at his right leg. It felt numb and he couldn't move it, no matter how hard he tried. The blood was seeping through his trousers now and he could see the dark stain spreading out. Panic started to well up inside him as he lay back down, his head resting on the cool of the grass. Another spasm of pain ravaged his leg and he had to grit his teeth to prevent himself from crying out in agony. He was just about to call for help again when Sesson threw himself down by his side. He was soon joined by the rest of the troop as they immediately formed an all-round defence. The troop commander joined Sesson and Halm on the deck.

"Where are you hit?" demanded Sesson, looking at his comrade's pained expression.

Halm sat up on his elbows and looked back down at his useless leg. "It's my right leg; I can't move it."

"Lie back, let's get this wound exposed so we can see the damage." Sesson pushed him back down and started to cut away the uniform trousers with his gravity knife, ripping them right back exposing the upper leg to the cool air. In the meantime, Fischer had acquired a hypodermic of morphine and pushed it into the top of the wounded limb. Sesson scrutinised the injury: a black hole, no bigger than his fingertip, was welling up with blood, a steady pulsating flow that exuded out onto his thigh. He felt underneath, looking for the exit wound, where Halm was probably losing most of his blood, his fingers discovering a much larger hole where the bullet had exited. Pulling his hand back out, it was covered in a black sticky mess, congealing on his fingers.

He called to Fischer. "Uffz, get his belt off and strap it round the top of his leg. We need a tourniquet on this; he's losing blood fast."

Fischer complied. Sesson was in charge of the patient and knew exactly what he was doing. Sesson looked at Halm and could see his pale, translucent skin. If they didn't get the blood loss under control soon, they could lose him. While Fischer dragged the belt from around Halm's waist, Sesson was tearing the black rubberised wrapping off a first field dressing, placing the large absorbent pad over the exit wound, binding it tightly.

"Hurry, Uffz, we need to get that tourniquet on."

He then placed a second dressing on the entry wound. By the time he had finished, the troop commander had the tourniquet on which was now restricting the flow of blood. Fischer called Lanz over to take control of the tourniquet. He had a troop to lead.

"Grab this, but release it every two minutes. We don't want his leg dropping off, do we," he said, smiling at Halm, the humour for his benefit, trying to relax him.

Sesson continued to examine the injured paratrooper. The upper thigh looked straight and, judging by the angle of the path of the bullet, he surmised that the thighbone was not broken. He placed a second pad on the lower wound. He was extremely worried by the amount of blood being lost. It could only mean an artery had been hit. Without the belt around his upper thigh, he would bleed to death in minutes. Halm groaned, the pain starting to filter through intermittently, only partially blocked by the pain-relieving injection administered earlier. Sesson tore off the complete leg of Halm's uniform trousers and placed it under the thigh, binding that to the bandage already there.

Sesson rocked back and sighed. The tourniquet seemed to be working. He had done all he could, and believed that Halm would make it through this. Halm looked at Sesson through his bleary eyes, asking the unspoken question.

"You'll live," Sesson said, putting him out of his misery.

Halm relaxed, the confidence of his colleague putting him at ease. His thigh was throbbing now and he was starting to feel cold, shivering. He felt sick, but just wanted to fall asleep. Sesson saw what was happening and grabbed him by his chin, shaking his head from side to side. "Look at me. You stick with us, OK?"

Someone wrapped a tunic around Halm's shoulders in an effort to keep him warm, as he was slowly slipping into shock.

"Let me sleep," whispered Halm. "I just want to rest my eyes."

"No, you don't, you bugger." said Sesson with a smile. "You owe me a few beers. If you think you can welsh on that, you've got another think coming."

A kitbag was pushed underneath Halm's head and his leg was raised above his abdomen, to try and stem the blood loss from his leg.

"Keep releasing the tourniquet," instructed Fischer, having returned. "We're setting up one of the ladders as a makeshift stretcher and then we're going to move to MiNord, the Group HQ."

They lifted Halm onto the stretcher, an involuntary cry escaping his lips as his leg was jarred against the ladder.

"Sorry, mate," apologised Sesson. "We'll soon have you at the HQ and we can make you more comfortable."

"Are you ready?" demanded Fischer, keen to get moving, get back to the fold.

"It's the best we can do. We're ready."

"Sesson, I want you to take point, keep ahead about ten metres. Lanz, Braemer, take the stretcher. Wagner, tail end Charlie. Let's move."

A few minutes later Fischer caught up with Sesson. "All clear?"

"Yes, but we need to keep our eyes peeled. There aren't just our guys wandering around, I'm sure."

"Agreed, you watch front left, I'll cover the right."

They continued forwards, but about halfway to MiNord they stopped to change over the bearers for Halm; Sesson and Braemer now carrying their wounded comrade. They set off again. It was starting to get light and Fischer didn't want to get caught on the flat top of the fortress in full daylight, particularly with two of his troop guarding prisoners and two having to heave a stretcher.

He touched Lanz on the shoulder and they stopped and crouched down. "We must be close now. Keep the men here and I'll go ahead and try and make contact."

Fischer crept forward. He was more worried about getting shot by his own now than by the enemy. He knew that close to MiNord, there would be a high concentration of paratroopers. He saw something. He was certain he had seen movement ahead. He could just see the outline of what he took to be MiNord and was about to continue moving forward when a paratrooper raised his head above the grassy mound in front of him and said, "Good to see you, Uffz." He immediately recognised the dirty-looking Fallschirmjager in front of him as Pelz.

"It's good to see your ugly mug too, Pelz. Is all well back there?"

"Yes, MiNord has been taken along with MiSud."

"Is Leutnant Brand with you?"

"Yes, and Unterfeldwebel Grun."

"Wait here. I'll get the rest of the troop and you can lead us in."

Fischer shot back to give his team the good news. Pelz then led them all to the HQ complex and to meet his platoon commander. Paul and Max walked up to Fischer as he entered the area under Fallschirmjager control.

"Uffz Fischer, I thought you'd got yourself lost," said Max.

As soon as Max saw that the troop had a stretchered casualty, he called for two troopers to take the stretcher off the two labouring soldiers, and had them take Halm to their company aid post. If you could call it an aid post; it was just somewhere to secure the wounded and collectively keep an eye on them until they were relieved.

"He'll be in good hands," reassured Paul, referring to the wounded Halm. "Get your men over to the bunker. We'll have an O-group shortly. We still have work to do, I'm afraid."

"What's the score so far, sir?"

"We've got MiNord and Sud, Maastricht one and two so far. And Cupola-120?"

"The hollow-charge didn't pierce the turret, sir, but we've put paid to the barrels."

"Excellent, Fischer, another to add to our toll."

"Any more casualties, sir?"

"A few, but in our platoon we only have Weyer who unfortunately is hanging on by the skin of his teeth. It's not looking good, and Kienitz's got a minor wound. Now, of course, we have Halm. I see you're missing Roon and Engels."

"They're back at the AA site, sir, looking after some prisoners. Some are wounded."

"We'll talk it through in a minute but your troop could patrol back to that area and pick your two men along with the prisoners. Let's get over to the bunker and we can plan our next move."

Chapter Thirty

Leeb, in the fourth glider of Paul's group, sat directly behind the glider pilot, in line with the other six troopers, could see the outline of the fort in the distance. The tow plane had released them and the glider pilot was now coaxing his engineless plane to the ground and on to its target. From north to south, the fort was over nine hundred metres long and seven hundred metres wide, an area equivalent approximately to some one hundred football pitches. It would not be easy to pinpoint their target.

Leeb's troop had to destroy Cupola–Nord and its two seventy-five-millimetre guns. His glider was approaching from the east. The pilot, seeing he still had too much height, pulled on the ailerons and flew in a large circle at a speed of some one hundred kilometres per hour, slowly losing height. The glider gradually dipped round bringing it nearer to the target when suddenly unexpected wisps of light could be seen passing the cockpit. Leeb looked out of the front right of the Perspex and could see the anti-aircraft position that had opened fire on them, some two hundred metres ahead.

"Shit, Menzel, they're firing at us, and they're getting bloody close!" exclaimed Leeb, involuntarily ducking.

"I know!" replied the pilot as he immediately started to rock the glider from side to side trying to make it a difficult target for the gunners in this dim early morning light.

Leeb shouted back to his men to hang on and that Menzel would be throwing the glider about. The pilot continued to roll the aircraft to the left and to the right as they shot through the withering fire, the gunners trying to keep track of them using the tracer bullets as a guide.

The pilot also ducked involuntarily as tracer rounds whipped past his cockpit. "We'll be below the flak in a moment," he said, half to himself and half to his commander. "Stand by. One minute," he shouted back. He peered forward, getting his bearings in the gloom, ensuring he was on course, making minor adjustments to the joystick and pedals, easier to control now that the AA battery had sought out another target. By now, with eleven gliders descending on the fortress, they had a lot to keep them occupied. He wiped his forehead beneath his helmet to stop the sweat from running into his eyes. "We're going in!" he yelled.

"Brace! Brace! Brace!" shouted Leeb. "We're going in!"

Just as he had finished shouting the warning, the glider's left wing support, attached to the body near the front, struck a machine-gun post, tearing the machine gun out of position and flinging it to one side, the glider finally coming to a halt next to a second machine-gun post.

The pilot quickly pushed at the Perspex cockpit, shoving it up and out of the way and clambered onto the front edge of the glider, bravely jumping down onto the ground then straight into the machine-gun trench where the Belgian gunners seemed frozen in fear. He jarred his legs as he landed alongside them, the trench at just about shoulder height in depth. He almost lost his footing. Leeb quickly followed suit and, along with the rest of the troop, exited the plane. Leeb jumped down to join Menzel. They must have made a chilling impression on the Belgian troops trapped in the machine-gun trench. The soldiers manning the emplacement immediately threw their hands into the air in surrender. Leeb ordered Menzel to get them to climb up the metal ladder and out of the trench and then to secure them.

Menzel motioned them to move towards the ladder, talking to them in German, but using gestures indicating that he wanted them to ascend the ladder. They understood his gesticulations and did as they were told, moving towards the ladder, frequently looking over their shoulders nervously, still in shock at what had just happened. There were three of them; one appeared to be an NCO, probably a Korporal, thought Menzel.

Leeb had already climbed up the metal rungs and was watching over them as they clambered up and out. He pointed to the front of the glider, indicating they should move there, and then, moving his hand, palm down, signifying he wanted them to sit.

The rest of the troop had exited through the side of the glider, after discarding the side panel, and were in the process of gathering the necessary equipment they would need for their part of the mission. Two paratroopers had gone to secure the machine-gun post they had struck on landing, and they brought a further three prisoners to add to the three already on the floor at the front of the glider. The prisoners were mesmerised by the speed of events, watching these professional soldiers going about their business as if it was second nature to them. It was. With a quick look at the prisoners, the Fallschirmjager noticed that the gun crews were all very young-looking. They were probably a similar age to some of the paratroopers, but lacked the hardness of these tough soldiers who had just descended out of the sky.

The Belgians looked afraid and demoralised, and Leeb felt sure they were no longer a threat. He instructed Menzel to watch over them, promising to send help once they had completed their mission. His men had finished pulling their equipment out of the glider and were in the process of splitting it between them, allocating explosives to those that would need it. Once he could see that his troop were ready, he sent half of them forward, the ones with the lighter loads, the MG section consisting of Geister and Beiler and Fessman with the ladder and two small hollow-charges. Behind them would follow Petzel, Stumme and Jordan, the latter two carrying one of the larger hollow-charges between them. He turned to the pilot who was guarding the six prisoners. "Sure you'll be OK watching these on your own?"

"I'll be fine. They're in no fit state to do any fighting. Look at them; they're scared out of their wits."

Leeb looked at the prisoners huddled together, some sneaking a look at the mud-spattered faces of their captors. He could see they were too shocked and scared to start a fight. "OK. I could do with you with us, but I daren't leave them wandering around."

"Get off, Uffz, I'll be fine."

Leeb turned and left, catching up with the leading section which was waiting for him. They started running east towards the area where their target should be located. They stopped after a minute to regroup as their target loomed up in front of them. Leeb crouched down and they all followed suit. "The cupola is about fifty metres east of us. You know the score: Geister and Beiler, cover, Petzel, Fessman, Jordan, Stumme with me."

Leeb jumped up from the ground and led them forward to the cupola. Its turret had been raised and the two seventy-five-millimetre guns were looking northwards, sniffing out targets to prevent this German invasion. As practised many times, Leeb ran to the left of the armoured doors at the rear of the cupola, and Jordan moved to the right, with Fessman covering the rear, as the ladder and the two small charges would not be needed yet.

Petzel and Stumme ran forwards to the steel door, the concrete monolith extending at least twice their height above them. Petzel placed his hand against the thick, cold steel door, almost sensing the activity behind it as he heard the guns above rotating. He placed his ear up against the armoured door, listening to the thrumming of machinery transmitted from the encased confines of the battery. He moved away and, between them, they placed the fifty-kilogram charge against the steel door.

"God help them when this goes off," Petzel volunteered to his colleague.

"It's going to spoil their breakfast, that's for sure," responded Stumme.

After setting the ten-second fuse, they ran for cover round the side of the bunker, Fessman joining them from his exposed position at the rear. They flattened themselves against the bunker wall and, holding their hands over their ears, waited for the explosion they knew was to come. Even expecting it, the force of the blast still shook them to their very core, the ground trembling beneath their feet.

Whooomph – the remnants of the discharge, the element not eating its way into the protective layers of the door, shot out picking up the dust and detritus surrounding the rear of the bunker, projecting it at a velocity in excess of five thousand metres per second over the rest of the troop. They had buried their heads in their hands, grasping clumps of turf, pulling themselves down, but still it tore at them, trying to wrestle them from their place of safety.

The hot blast ripped through the steel door. The searing, molten slag splayed out killing many of the Belgian gunners hiding behind its perceived invulnerability. A young gunner, only having completed his training three months earlier, took its full impact; a slug of heated metal, scouring his upper face, the skin pared back exposing his cheekbone and the pale white of the frontal bone of the skull. Still alive, he was thrown back against the rear of the bunker wall screaming as he went, clutching the remnants of his face, his service with the Belgian army ended that morning.

A second gunner, having heard a clunking sound up against the door, was mimicking Petzel, his ear up against the door straining to interpret the activity outside. He was equally unlucky. The blast blew the door off its hinges, smashing it into his body, crushing him up against the concrete wall.

A third soldier, who had only eight weeks to go before his conscription was fulfilled and he would be demobbed, missed the direct force of the explosion. But the rapidly expanding gases were too much for his fragile brain which, acting like a sponge, absorbed the full force of the shock wave, rupturing the blood vessels, the blood immediately pooling inside his skull. He was dying as he fell. The rest of the battery crew were either dazed, wounded themselves or also dead. The battery would not function again; its role in helping to hold back the German invaders ceased at that moment in time.

Once the explosion had expired, Petzel and Stumme both rushed back to see the state of the damage, to see if it had indeed blown a hole in the door. Returning quickly, they passed on the good news to Leeb: the charge had done its work.

"It's not just blown a hole, it's shattered the door completely, taking it off its hinges!" exclaimed Petzel.

"Excellent, but we'll still take out the observation dome as well. Fessman," Leeb hissed, "bring up those small charges. Hurry, let's get this done." He was impatient to get their task completed.

"Stumme, Petzel, chuck some grenades through the entrance and spray it with machine-gun fire, quickly, before they come round." Fessman ran forwards, Beiler at his side with the ladder. He thumped the ladder up against the bunker side; noise no longer an issue, the enemy was well aware of their presence now. He scurried up the ladder, keen to get the job done, the weariness of his legs forgotten for the moment, the task his priority.

Once on top, he ran rapidly to the dome, placing both charges on top, setting the fuses, and counting down in his head as he sped back. He practically fell down the ladder in his haste to get away before the charges detonated, nearly crashing into his comrade looking up, watching out for him. In the meantime, Stumme and Petzel had thrown two grenades each through the opening of the doorway and, after firing off a full magazine in for good measure, they could hear no activity.

"Heads down," shouted Fessman. They all hit the deck, the charge erupting a few seconds afterwards.

They waited a few minutes for the dust to settle then shone their torches in to the darkened interior of the obliterated artillery battery. There was no sign of life, and it was obvious that the bunker could not be used to fulfil its purpose of firing on the bridges over the canal. Rejoining their troop, they held a quick conflab.

"Well done," Leeb praised them, pleased with their night's work. "We're done here. This is what we're going to do next. Stumme, Petzel, rejoin Menzel, get the prisoners and bring them over to MiNord. Got that?"

"And you, sir?" questioned Petzel.

"The rest of us will head over to MiNord ahead of you, in case there's a problem. I don't want you turning up with prisoners and walking into a trap."

"We'll be off then." With that, they both headed towards the glider, their pilot and the Belgian prisoners.

Leeb gathered the remaining four of his assault troop and they headed north-east towards MiNord. The route there was uneventful, but gunfire and explosions were still occurring around the perimeter of the fortress. They were met at the HQ by one of the sentries and quickly taken to Paul. Once there, he could see that Fischer, Kienitz and the Unterfeldwebel had already arrived. He received claps on his back from his two fellow Uffzs who were naturally pleased to see their comrade safe and well.

"Have you done it?" asked Paul and Max in unison, both having just joined the group and keen for an update.

"Yes, sir, those charges certainly do the trick, blew the steel door right off its hinges, made a right mess of the bunker inside. And the rest of you?"

Fischer jumped in first. "Not so hot on our target, didn't penetrate the turret, we had to blow the barrels in the end."

"But it's finished?"

"Definitely, they'll not be firing again."

"Sir," interposed Max. "We need to move."

"Quite right, Unterfeldwebel Grun. The bunker, we have plans to make."

They headed for the MiNord bunker for a council of war. They gathered around their platoon commander, Max and Oberfeldwebel Waechter.

Chapter Thirty-one

Oberst Wilhelm Meisters's infantry regiment, with a pioneer battalion attached commanded by Oberstleutnant Hans Metzger, was to spearhead the German advance to Eben Emael. Metzger's primary mission was to complete the capture of the fort and, as a consequence, relieve the hard-pressed Assault Group Granite.

The Oberstleutnant, responsible for the attached pioneer battalion, ran up to the command tent, pushing the tent flaps aside seeking out his regimental commander. The forty year-old commander was bent over the map table, studying the routes allocated to his units to get them to their objective. The roads would no doubt be severely congested, he thought. Various units would be given priority, his included, in order to pave the way for the bigger, heavier formations following close behind.

"They've managed to blow the bloody bridge over the Maas!" Metzger said as he stormed into the tent.

The Leipzig-born Oberst looked up. "What's being done about it?"

Metzger joined him by the map table. "An assault bridge is being put up now, sir."

"How long's that going to take?" he demanded, looking down at his watch frustrated by the destruction of the bridges in Maastricht, now slowing his advance. "We're behind schedule already."

"We hope to have it ready by midday, sir." Metzger, his broad face with a wide mouth and flattish nose, pointed to the map. "We're taking this route and, providing the bridge is ready on time, we could be starting to cross within the hour."

"We've got to get to the fort, Hans. Those paratroopers will be in the thick of it already and we don't know how long they can hold out for."

"Or even if they've succeeded, sir."

"I have every confidence in them." The Oberst moved round to the other side of the map table, pointing to the fort. "But if they don't succeed then we've got to secure it."

"If they don't knock out at least some of those guns, it'll cause mayhem at the crossing points."

"Don't remind me," Meister responded, reflecting on the immensity of the responsibility on his and the Fallschirmjager unit's shoulders. "What's your planned route after the Maas?"

"Still the Kanne Bridge, sir." Metzger pointed to the crossing at the southern point of the canal. "We can go down Canner weg, that way we can avoid the built-up areas," he said, tracking the route with his finger.

"OK, Hans, just do it." The frustration was clearly etched on the commander's face. "The entire bloody army is waiting on us."

"We'll get it done sir." Hans started to move towards the exit, itching to get back to his command.

"Get off with you then, Hans I'll move my HQ to the Kanne Bridge. You can update me when I get there."

Metzger flashed a quick salute then, brushing the tent flap aside, rushed out, jumping into the passenger seat of the Steiner Jeep, waiting for him outside, its engine still running.

"Let's go, Gunther," he commanded his adjutant.

"How's the old man, sir?"

"Frustrated as hell, but at least he didn't blast me out."

The major steered the Steiner expertly through the busy streets, all of the traffic military, the civilians still in a state of shock, staring at the invaders as they passed by. They cleared the built-up area travelling north along the edge of the Maas, a barrier they needed to cross quickly. They reentered the urban area, a mix of shops and commercial premises. Just as they were approaching the bridge, the one that was no longer available to them having been blown up by the Dutch engineers, they were stopped at a barrier manned by a section of Chain Dogs, military police.

The Oberstleutnant returned the Feldwebel's salute and impatiently handed over his orders. The policeman scrutinised the orders, seemingly not in any particular hurry.

"Damn you, man, let us through quickly. We have a bloody war to fight, not to sit here while you scratch your arse."

"We need to check all documents, sir," the policeman replied officiously.

"Listen, Feldwebel, it says on that docket that we are to be given priority over all other units. If you can't fucking read that then get an officer here who can." Metzger's anger was growing by the minute.

The Feldwebel knew he was on dodgy ground. The officer was an Oberstleutnant, so he shouted to the soldier who was manning the barrier to lift it and let them through.

Metzger flicked his hand in a mock salute and the Steiner roared through the barrier. The soldier had barely had time lift it up and was sure at one point that the Jeep was going to hit it.

"I know we need military police, but they don't half take their duties to the extreme at times," grumbled Metzger.

"They certainly pick their moments, sir," agreed Hoffmann, smiling. He knew that military police baiting was one of the Oberst's favourite pastimes.

They got to the site where the assault bridge was being assembled across the Maas, the pontoons and boats being floated out into the centre. When questioned how long they would be, the bridging unit informed them at least another hour.

By midday, the assault bridge was finally complete and the pioneer battalion was allowed to cross, their task being the most urgent. Once they had crossed over, the battalion took a narrow road that ran close alongside a smaller inland waterway that linked the Maas with the Albert Canal. This time they had a military police escort ensuring they had a fast passage to the Kanne Bridge. Parked either side of the road was the paraphernalia of war: tanks and armoured cars, and infantry sitting on the roadside, smoking cigarettes and passing the time waiting for the call to go forward and into action, small-arms fire and artillery pounding in the distance.

By late afternoon, the lead elements of the pioneer battalion had reached Kanne. Metzger looked out of the side window. A flight of Stukas droned by overhead, en route to inflict more pain on an enemy already in a state of shock after the day's events. His thoughts were brought sharply back to his immediate vicinity as the Jeep slid to a halt, a half-track blocking the road. He was out of the vehicle in double-quick time, recognising the Oberfeld as one of his advanced guard.

"What's the problem?" he demanded.

The Oberfeld saluted. "The bridge has been blown, sir."

"God, not another one!"

Hoffmann appeared at his side. "Problem, sir?"

"You might call it that. The Kanne Bridge is down as well."

They were again to be frustrated, this time by the demolition of their second crossing point. This was the designated route for the combat engineers, so Metzger had to come up with an alternative plan.

"Christ, this isn't going our way at all, is it. What about one of the other bridges, sir?" Asked Hoffman

"Even if they're open, it's too far to move there now. Anyway, we'd never get our lot through the traffic that's backing up."

"Bridging operation?" suggested Hoffmann.

"Take too long. Time's not on our side, Gunther, and we're running out of it."

"Excuse me, sir," interrupted the Oberfeld. "There's always the boats."

"Of course, the boats. How many men could we get over?"

"That's high risk, sir," challenged Hoffmann. "We only have the four and eight-man rubber boats."

"We've no option, Gunther. We've got to get across now. I want Oberleutnant Wolf's company down to the canal as quickly as possible."

He turned to Oberfeld Pfeifer. "Where are the boats?"

"They're with the Oberleutnant's company, sir. They were sharing transport."

"Excellent. Right, let's move it."

He turned to Pfeifer. "Rejoin your platoon, Oberfeld." He laid his hand on the man's arm. "And thank you." Then he turned and dashed back to the Steiner, Hoffmann already revving the engine.

They arrived at the company position, the company that had the unenvious task of crossing the exposed canal, probably under fire. Although by the time they were ready to cross it would be close to dusk, there would still be enough light to potentionally make their crossing difficult. Metzger quickly got down to briefing the young Oberleutnant, and he and his two senior commanders stood round the front of the Jeep, map spread out across the bonnet, peering at the canal and its approaches.

The Oberstleutnant straightened up. "Wolf, you've got twenty boats. Once we get into that water, we've got to row for our lives. We'll be even more exposed if we turn back and try to get the men back up the canal bank, so our best option is to just keep going."

"At least we'll be a moving target, sir," Wolf replied with a grin.

The adjutant broke in, "You sound like you're going with him, sir!"

"This is too important, Gunther. We've got to make it across."

"Then let me go instead, sir," he said, almost pleading.

The young Oberleutnant looked away, slightly embarrassed, feeling like an interloper.

"I need you to look after the battalion in my absence."

"But—" He didn't get to finish as Metzger raised his hand to silence him.

"I've made my decision. Wolf, get those boats moving."

They made two attempts at crossing the canal but were driven back on both occasions, receiving heavy fire from Canal Nord. Embedded in the sheer wall of the cutting, Canal Nord had two mutually supporting two-storey emplacements, each with a sixty-millimetre anti-tank gun and supporting machine gun to defend the canal and resist any enemy crossing.

It was now dawn, the early hours of the morning, and the Oberst was pushing his men to make yet another attempt. The increasing pressure to get across and relieve the paratroopers was adding to the battalion's woes. They approached the Albert Canal again. The water looked deep and unwelcoming. Above and to their left towered the cliff face with its gun emplacement embedded deep in its side. At the moment it lay quiet, like an omnipotent demon.

The company making the crossing on this occasion was lined up on the bank of the canal. It was Wolf's company again. They had made the first attempt earlier the previous day. But now, rested and reinforced by Three Company they were to try again. Alongside the men lay a mixture of four and eight-man black rubber inflatable boats, lined up and ready. Infantry threw rope ladders down the sheer concrete sides of the canal, looking nervously at the cliff face that dominated their view. The anti-aircraft guns, assigned to Metzger's unit, moved into position to their north, setting up on the eastern bank of the canal to provide fire support for the river crossing. Once the crossing attempt was spotted, which was inevitable, they would discharge their projectiles at the Belgian bunkers across the river. They would hold their fire until the last minute, not wanting to give the enemy prior warning of the impending third canal crossing. The hope was that the enemy, having thrown the German sappers back twice, would think they had given up.

They groped their way down the ladders to the bank, the heavy boats straining at their shoulders, crushing the men underneath, pulling at the soldiers lowering it from the top. Once the boats were grounded, they had a few moments to catch their breath. The last thing the commander wanted was his men totally exhausted before they had even started to make the crossing. Eight soldiers carried the larger assault boats, four either side. The boats were heavy and cumbersome, lighter once in the water, but would offer no protection should they be hit by enemy fire.

Metzger, along with his nine men and their eight-man dinghy, reached the water's edge and they eased the assault boat into the water. He had decided to squeeze two more soldiers in; they would be needed on the other side. Either side of them were a further eight to ten assault boats also being tentatively edged into the water with over one hundred assault troops quietly embarking. The commander looked across the eighty metres of the canal. It looked silent to the front but, in the distance, a firefight was undrway on top and beneath Fort Eben Emael. Once across, they needed to fight their way into the fort and meet up with Faust's force.

The water was relatively calm with a slow meandering flow making the going easy. The conditions were good but it would still be a strong pull for his men and, when on the other side, they would still need to find the reserves to fight the enemy waiting for them. They had to cross, they had to relieve the embattled paratroopers, isolated in hostile territory.

The commander stepped into the boat which was being held by one of the soldiers. It lurched beneath his weight and he had to shuffle his boots to maintain his balance. The soldier who had been holding the boat, boarded and they pushed off. The four oars, two either side, propelled them slowly across the canal with the water rippling around the oars as they thrust the boat forward. Ten men in the inflatable boat caused it to be overcrowded and unsteady; the slightest movement which placed excessive weight on any one side and the dingy was in danger of tipping over. The soldiers listened, not without some trepidation, at the noise created by the rowing. To them, the sound seemed magnified beyond all proportion. Those not occupied with the rowing, watched the puddles created by the oars, rippling out across the canal waters, willing the rowers to be quieter. In reality, they would not be heard by the Belgian soldiers on the opposite bank, the fighting on Eben Emael and at the bridges masking their approach. Their biggest risk was actually being seen, from reflections off their equipment or splashes from their oars in the water. The rest of the boats were in the water now, heading west to the opposite bank. Looking down on them, they looked like black beetles or water boatmen scurrying across the black water.

Halfway across, the commander looked left and right to check that the assault boats immediately adjacent were in line. The boats either side would line up on their leader, ensuring that they all hit the shore at the same time. The second wave, four or five boat-lengths behind the first, would land some twenty seconds later when, hopefully, if all went to plan, the first wave had disembarked and was making its way inland to secure the landing area. All seemed well; they were three quarters of the way across now. They could do this, thought Metzger.

Just as his optimism was growing, the sky lit up. The fort's defenders had launched a flare, the Commander, not tracking it as it arced across the sky. Although his night vision had been partially affected, he still closed one eye, safeguarding his night sight as best he could, and looking down into the boat to protect the other from the blinding light. It didn't matter, it was too late. Gunfire suddenly opened up and they were now under a continuous hail of fire from the opposite bank.

Thump, thump, thump, of the anti-aircraft guns could be heard, and the subsequent whine of the shells rebounding off the sheer rock face and the immense concrete bunker as the AA guns fired in support of Metzger and his men. Boat after boat frantically crossed the river, undeterred by the incessant bombardment of grenades, machine-gun fire and the occasional shell from the turrets still operating on Eben Emael. The rowers hacked at the water with their oars and the other soldiers joined in with their rifle butts; anything to get more speed out of the ponderous boats, get them to the bank. Not necessarily to safety, but at least to get their feet on terra firma.

The first pioneer assault wave reached the western bank, despite the hail of gunfire. The pioneers leapt out, guns facing towards the unseen enemy, firing their rifles from the hip, more for their own peace of mind than to hit anything. But, it would perhaps help to keep the enemy's heads down. Metzger charged forward, his machine pistol spluttering death ahead of him. He threw himself down on the ground, just behind a lip in the terrain. Wolf hurled himself down alongside him. "The second wave has landed, sir," he informed him, looking back.

"Right, let's keep moving then," and he was up and forward again.

They ran forward to meet with the lead platoon that had secured the enemy positions, now abandoned. The enemy had deserted their positions once the pioneers had landed, knowing there were too few of them to hold back the onslaught. Once landed and regrouped, the reinforced company advanced towards the northern tip of Eben Emael to relieve the paratroopers still in combat there. They grabbed whatever transport they could: local cars, merchant vehicles, bicycles, anything, loaded them up and travelled as fast as they could, taking out any enemy on the way. They had to root some of the enemy out of trenches, shell holes and buildings, those who stubbornly continued to put up a defence.

They were making steady progress, but had still not reached the embattled paratroopers. Metzger called a council of war with his senior staff, going through the options open to them. They huddled in a bomb crater, a result of the earlier bombing by the screaming Stukas.

"The options open to us, gentlemen, are pretty limited."

"When will we get more support, sir?" Wolf enquired.

Metzger shifted in the crater, trying to get more comfortable, ducking down when a bullet plucked a stone from the edge of the crater. "There's still some fight in them yet," he surmised. "We'll have another company joining us, but we need to do something now. We've got to get into the fort. I'm less worried about securing the surrounding area at the moment."

Oberfeldwebel Pfeifer spoke up. "My platoon could make it into the fort, sir."

Metzger looked round at him. "And how do you propose to do that?"

"With a reinforced platoon, sir, I could take them south along the edge of the canal, hit the moat, a cul-de-sac that leads to the fort, and attack them right under their noses."

Metzger looked at him, mulling it over in his mind. "Where's the map?"

The Oberfeld pulled a map from his tunic pocket, unfolded it in front of his commander and pointed to the canal tributary that he was referring to. It was still quite dark and Metzger could barely make out the detail but could just about extract enough information for him to agree with the sergeant's suggestion. He grasped the Oberfeld's left arm. "I think that just might work."

He turned to Wolf. "We could continue to probe west, keep them occupied."

"We've only got just over a hundred men across at the moment, but it could be done," Wolf responded enthusiastically.

Metzger turned to Pfeifer again. "Would fifty men be enough?"

"More than enough, sir, any more would be too noisy. Stealth will be our true weapon."

"We'll go with your suggestion. What weapons will you need?"

Pfeifer stroked his top lip unconsciously. "A flame-thrower for one. Probably best to take one of the new hollow-charge weapons as well. I've always wanted to see if they're worth all the fuss made about them."

"See to it, Wolf," commanded Metzger. "Oberfeld, get your platoon together, we'll get the equipment down to you on the canal bank. What boats do you want?"

"I'll go for the smaller ones, sir. We'll be harder to spot."

He then headed off to gather his men and prepare for this new escapade. The boats had been gathered alongside the canal's edge – ten four-man dinghies, but each would carry five men. They loaded the equipment they would need, in particular a fifty-kilogram hollow-charge and a flame-thrower. Once all were on board, they pushed off from the side and made their way south, sticking close to the canal shore. Pfeifer's platoon cautiously made its way along the canal until they arrived at the junction with the moat at the fort's northern tip. Then they followed the moat until they reached the area of block two. Dawn was starting to break through; it was the second day of the battle to relieve the paratroopers.

They grounded their boats on the bank, getting as close to the bunker as possible without being seen. Pfeifer called forward his flame-thrower team, Riemer and Broch, forward. "I've got a section covering you on your left and right. Once we throw the smoke grenades, it's over to you. Are you ready?"

"Yes, Oberfeldwebel," replied Broch, picking up the flame-thrower, the tank of fuel strapped to his back.

Pfeifer hissed the command to his men to throw the smoke grenades, at the same time indicating to the flame-thrower team to move forward. The grenades exploded, two in all, a fog of smoke immediately issuing from them obscuring the area directly in front of the bunker. The flame-thrower team ran forward, stopping at about twenty-five metres from the target, the maximum effective range of the weapon. Broch knelt down, the thirty-six kilogram weight heavy on his back. Riemer joined him, covering him while he focused on firing the deadly weapon at the bunker in front of them.

Broch aimed and squeezed the trigger. The flaming oil, a mixture of petrol and tar making it heavier and giving it better range, was ignited by a hydrogen torch. The fiery liquid shot out, a smoking flame of death hitting the bunker, feeling its way through the gaps and crevices. Thick, black smoke blew back onto the operator as the wind changed direction, but he still maintained the first blast for a full four seconds, the soldiers behind the bunker walls screaming as the flame found its way in and onto their skin.

The soldier that was struck the worst had been peering through an observation slit and the burning liquid fuel instantly stripped the skin from his face and then his hands as he used them to try and protect himself, but to no avail. He fell to the ground, face and hands blackened and charred, screaming, demented by the pain that a human being could not possibly imagine. The sickly smell of burning flesh, percolating through the bunker made some soldiers gag. Broch released the trigger for a split second before firing a second blast of death and destruction at block two, catching more soldiers in its blistering heat.

The soldier lying on the floor was no longer screaming, but blissfully unconscious; the skin had been stripped from his hands and wrists, pulled away from the bone as one of his comrades tried to drag him to safety. The rescuer got caught in Broch's second blast, the burning fuel blistering the man's face, his clothes smouldering. Desperately trying to get some non-existent oxygen into his tortured lungs, he flew from the site of his torment, screaming in agony as he fled down the bunker's steps, seeking safety and relief that was not forthcoming from the horrific pain. The harrowing scenes, smell and noise of screaming men were too much for the remaining occupants who pulled back to a place of safety down the steps. They could no longer defend block two.

Pfeifer still had work to do and, calling back the flame-thrower crew, ordered his men to place a hollow-charge weapon on the observation dome. This they quickly did with the force of the explosion shattering any likelihood of resistance inside the bunker and engulfing the Oberfeld's platoon in a cloud of smoke and debris. The noise, the smoke and the toxic fumes from the flame-thrower were too much for the Belgian sergeant commanding the detachment at the sandbagged barrier blocking the tunnel to block two, and he reported that the Germans had blown the steel doors and withdrew his men. This was not true; the sergeant had reported this to his superiors erroneously.

Pfeifer immediately tasked three of his men to follow the tunnel as far as MiSud. Once there, they threw explosives down the shaft which then blew the doors under the steel barrier off their supports. The Belgians soon abandoned the barricades in the tunnels to both positions, the two bunkers now belonging to the German pioneers. Now they needed to move south-east and meet up with the paratroopers.

Chapter Thirty-two

Paul, Max, Fischer, Kienitz and Leeb hunkered down just outside the bunker complex of MiNord. It was now nine in the morning, and daylight was well and truly with them. They needed to plan their next actions.

"Gentlemen, it appears we've taken out most of the targets set for us, although unfortunately some of the targets were actually dummies, so some of our strength has been wasted."

"So, our next steps, sir?"

"Well, Max, the way I see it, we haven't yet been hit by a counter-attack from the Belgians, and it must only be a matter of time before they do. Secondly, it seems that we probably won't be relieved on schedule."

"Have we an ETA for our relief, sir?" asked Leeb.

"I'm afraid not. Our relief is having problems getting across the Maas and the canal at the moment."

"We'll need some resupply, sir," added Fischer. "We're not too bad for ammo at the moment, but if we've more fighting ahead of us, we need it restocked."

"Water too, sir," joined in Kienitz. "We're all pretty low."

"It's true," supported Max. "We're all gagging for a drink."

"Can you organise a resupply, Max?"

"Sure, sir, shall I keep my troop here as a reserve?"

"Yes, that would make sense."

Paul pulled out his plan of the fort's defences. "Right, we have two missions. Mission one is to take a force down into the tunnels beneath the complex. We've got to keep them occupied. We've battened them down so far, so if they are not coming to us then we will have to go to them."

"The tunnels, sir?"

"That's the only way, Max. So, Leeb, I want you to take your troop down into Maastricht one, understood?"

"Yes, sir, will do."

"What charges have we left?"

"We have one hollow-charge left, sir and a couple of one-kilogram conventional explosives."

"Excellent, that will more than do the job of blasting through that steel door. Unterfeldwebel, I want you to organise resupply and defend MiNord. If it all goes to pot, this will be our fallback position. OK?"

"Understood, sir."

"Mission two: we've been getting sniper fire from the shrubbery north-west of here. It's quite possible they're forming up for a counter-attack, so I'll take my and Fischer's troop to flush them out. Any questions? Max?"

"I'm fine, sir. We'll get resupply organised." With that, Max headed off to organise his troop.

"Fischer?"

"I'll get the two troops together. Move out in five?"

"Kienitz, are you OK with that leg wound?"

"It's only pain, sir," he said, smiling. "I'll be fine."

"Right, let's get moving then."

Paul met up with Fischer who had pulled the two assault troops together. He called the two groups together to talk through their tactics. "Fischer, I want you to cover us while we advance. We'll sweep round to the north, but be ready. We'll be pretty exposed. But I want to take Lanz, Sesson, Braemer and Roon with me."

"We'll watch your back, sir, don't worry."

Fischer led his men north-west until they could see the shrubbery that his commander was going to check out. They got themselves into position, with the MG 34 on their left, ready to cover their *kameraden*.

Paul took his troop east of MiNord; they then advanced north-west moving towards the shrubbery where a possible enemy could be waiting. They didn't have to wait long: flashes lit up the bushes opposite and rounds started coming their way, kicking up lumps of earth in front of them. They hit the dirt.

"They're immediately to our front at about two hundred metres," called Kienitz. "It looks like a slit trench behind some sandbags."

"I see it too, sir," shouted Forster, returning fire. Just as he spoke, a grenade was launched from behind the sandbags. Fortunately they were too far away and the grenade exploded short.

To their left, Fischer's troop had opened up, trying to pin the enemy soldiers down, giving Paul's men a chance to retaliate from the opposite flank.

Kienitz called out to his men, "Straube, Hempel, throw smoke then cover me." They were manning the second MG 34 so would put a hail of fire down once they had thrown the smoke grenades. "The rest of you with me. OK, sir?"

"Yes, go for it, Kienitz. I'm with you," shouted Paul.

Kienitz began to move forward as the two smoke grenades exploded in front of the trench, Paul at his side followed by the rest of the troop. The machine gun manned by Straube and Hempel laid down a wall of bullets across the front and to the side of the trench, the MG 34 machine gun firing its belt at the rate of over six hundred rounds a minute.

Kienitz ran forward and, as he threw himself to the ground in front of the sandbagged slit trench, he threw a grenade over the top. Paul and Kempf joined in. Once prone on the deck, they proceeded to prime a second grenade which they lobbed over the top, immediately after the first one had exploded.

Their fire support had ceased in anticipation of their next move and, when the second grenade exploded, they were up on their feet and round to the side of the slit trench pouring in fire from rifles and machine pistols at the three soldiers writhing in agony from the devastating effects of the grenades exploding amongst them. The remaining Fallschirmjager, who had been providing covering fire, joined their colleagues.

Paul moved his team back slightly, ducking below the line of sandbags offering him protection against the whining and spinning fragments of bullets and shrapnel constantly making its way towards them. They had not finished yet. Now the smoke had cleared, Fischer's gun group again opened up, giving Paul and his men a moment's respite, the enemy ducking down to avoid the intense fire coming their way.

Paul ordered his men to start firing over the top of the sandbags. He wanted Fischer and his men to join them and provide cover again as they moved further forward. Paul felt sure the Belgians were planning something else. They put down a wall of fire and Paul saw Fischer and his men pack up and start to move towards them.

Fischer stood out easily from the rest of his section, being only five feet eight inches tall and wiry with it. But god help anyone who thought that was a weakness and took advantage of it. Fischer had quite a reputation for being able to take care of himself, and more than one infantry soldier had picked on this wiry paratrooper and regretted the day that they had met him.

Fischer threw himself down heavily by Paul and Kienitz. "My half section at your service," he said grinning like a Cheshire cat. He ducked as a bullet whined over his head.

"Even if you stood up, they would miss you, Karl," joked Kienitz.

"I thought he was standing up," interjected Forster.

"Alright, stow it for now," cut in Paul.

But all were smiling at Fischer's ribbing, including Paul. Paul knew he could and would take it from his fellow paratroopers, but it would be a different story if it were someone outside the family. "Now you're all here, this is what we're going to do."

While the rest of Paul's men snaked around to outflank the enemy, Fischer's team fulfilled their role again of providing cover, both through the use of smoke grenades and the MG 34, although they were rapidly running out of ammunition for the machine gun.

Paul took his men quickly north under cover of the smoke then west, he hoped, on the flank of an unsuspecting enemy. They were fifty metres away from the enemy when they came under fire. The red tracer, theirs was green, coming from the concealed enemy. Some of the Belgian soldiers had obviously been ordered outside to try to gain control of the nightmare that was occurring in and around them. Like a sleeping giant awoken by an army of ants, they were desperately trying to swipe them off as their bites dug painfully deep. Their fire was wild. Although good troops, they lacked the discipline and training of the German Fallschirmjager, the 'Green Devils'.

Keinitz's section quickly returned fire with their machine pistols and karbines and, within seconds, an MG 34 was brought into play which quickly forced the Belgian troops to go to ground and take cover from the blistering swathe of metal coming their way. From then on, the soldiers found it difficult to get their heads off the ground to return fire and take on the German shock troops. The paratroopers took advantage of this and, within moments, three grenades were lobbed in their direction, exploding as one. Forster's half section ran forward, covered by the remainder of the unit, to take advantage of the fire, smoke and the stunned Belgian troops. His half section's machine pistols tore into the area in front of them, the shocked and, in some cases, wounded soldiers dropping to the floor as the bullets did their work, scything down all who got in their way.

The area was quickly secured. Eight Belgian soldiers lay dead, some unrecognisable, torn apart by a mixture of grenade shrapnel, small-arms fire and the heavier calibre bullets of the fast-firing MG 34 machine gun.

Leeb and his men ran quickly to MiSud. The more they could do to keep the enemy on their toes, keep them trapped below, the greater their chance of survival and to continue to prevent the enemy from interfering with the main invasion. Their instruction was to secure some of the tunnels below, pre-empting any potential counter-attack, making the enemy think that the force on top of their fortress was greater than it actually was. Leeb had no idea what he and his men should expect; all he knew was that the fortress had four and a half kilometres of stairs, corridors and lifts. There were also five hundred men responsible for the gun batteries and five hundred men responsible for the immediate defence of the fort; quite a task for him and his seven men, he thought, smiling to himself. They skirmished forward to the entrance, finding the blast holes in the bunker that would take them to the steps leading them down into the bunker's depths. They didn't throw any grenades; they didn't want to alert the enemy if they were nearby.

Leeb crept through the gap in the bunker wall, catching his hand on a piece of jagged reinforcing metal. Holding back a yelp, he placed his hand against his mouth to stem the flow of blood. He crouched down, listening for any evidence that the bunker might be occupied. There was some daylight filtering through but, coming from outside, his night vision was non-existent; he would be blind and vulnerable for a few minutes. He didn't want to use his torch, again not wanting to advertise their presence. It seemed to be clear. He stood up and beckoned the next paratrooper to come through. Fessman, Petzel and Stumme, the remainder watching their backs outside, joined him. The time had come to use their torches, cupping their hands around the lenses, reducing the beams to a mere glow.

They now carried out what they had planned earlier. Lanz quickly descended the winding steps, returning after his reconnaissance to confirm that no one was there and that the two steel doors were closed. Petzel and Stumme now took a turn as they carried the fifty-kilogram hollow-charge between them, a half section each, down the steps. Their backs covered by their comrades above, they moved slowly down the steps, approaching the five-centimetre thick steel door at the bottom. Petzel took his section of the shaped charge from his pack and placed it on the centre of the steel door. Stumme followed suit with his.

Once ignited, the 'Monroe effect' of this hollow-charge explosive would do its job and blow a hole in the door, hopefully giving them access to the tunnels below. This operation on Fort Eben Emael, saw hollow-charge explosives being used for the first time as a weapon, since its discovery during the American Civil War. During the Civil War, slabs of explosives were embossed with the initials 'US', and, when detonated, these initials left a deep impression on the surface of the target. This had since been improved upon.

They placed them up against the doors, setting the fuse, running back up as fast as they could, diving through the breach they had just entered, hot on the heels of Fessman and the Uffz Leeb. They all threw themselves to the ground. They now knew what to expect from this wonder weapon. When the explosion occurred, it shook the ground beneath them and even made their teeth rattle. Smoke and debris were hurled up the steps, channelled by the narrow passageway leading up from the steel door.

They again entered the bunker, this time with the intention of exploring the tunnels below. Uffz Leeb, Fessman, Stumme and Petzel cautiously moved down, chunks missing from the concrete steps now as a result of the blast. Choking on the dust and fumes of the explosion, Petzel retched as he ran down the steps. On reaching the bottom, Leeb could see that not only had a hole the size of a fist been blown in the door but the door was hanging off its hinges and sagging to the side. Smoke and dust was still billowing out, and Leeb could see very little as he stepped through into the tunnel. The dust was grating on their throats and there was another smell that Leeb couldn't identify, but tasted toxic on his tongue. He ordered gas masks to be worn. After pulling his gas mask over his head and replacing his helmet, he continued cautiously down the narrow tunnel.

Fessman followed him carefully, covering Leeb's back. His foot caught on something and, staring down and playing his torch over the floor, he could see the shattered body of a Belgian soldier who had obviously been caught in the blast, blood oozing from his nose and mouth. "Uffz, look."

Leeb also shone his torch on the unfortunate soldier. He was, astoundingly so, still alive, although Leeb doubted it would be for much longer. They would do what they could for him on their return; he was no threat to them in his current state. Leeb could see no one else in the murky, dusty interior of the tunnel. He decided to move further down to the next junction where they would leave a couple of small explosives. He doubted they would do much damage, due to their size, but it would hopefully keep the enemy guessing and, as Leutnant Brand put it, battened down. They got to the junction and, if his memory served him right, the right-hand one led to block two. Continuing on would take them to Maastricht one and two and the key junction for the fort's tunnels. It was there that they wanted to cause confusion. They continued on, Fessman staying by the junction for block two, ensuring they weren't taken by surprise from behind.

They arrived at the junction with Maastricht one. Petzel quickly set the charges while they watched over him. "I've set them for ten seconds, so once I initiate we'll have to run like bloody hell."

Leeb passed the information back to Stumme and nodded to Petzel who triggered the fuse.

They ran like a bats out of hell, picking Fessman up on the way, charging through the hanging steel doorway, running up the steps, taking two at a time, until they were through and into the main bunker compartment. Not a moment too soon as the charges exploded, a hollow boom, followed by a pall of smoke and dust funnelled up the steps. They climbed outside, ripped off their gas masks and sucked in the welcome fresh air.

Max was thrown sideways by the shock wave of a one hundred and fifty-millimetre shell that exploded fifty metres away, knocking him to the ground, the earth lifting up around him, dirt, rocks and debris pattering on his helmet as it was strewn around him.

"Where the hell did that come from?" shouted Geib.

"They have some bloody big grenades," retorted Waldau, running over to see that the Unterfeldwebel was OK.

Max got up, shaking the dust off his huge frame. "I'm OK. Start digging in," he shouted to the section. "That was a one-fifty, probably from Forts Pontise or Barchon, and there will doubtless be more on the way. That was just a ranging shot."

The troop took out their small collapsible spades attached to their webbing and started to dig themselves in. "I'm a bloody paratrooper," groaned Rammelt. "We're supposed to plunge from the sky like descending heroes and kick arse, not dig bloody holes like a bloody gardener!"

Shells were landing on other areas of Fort Eben Emael now, a mixture of one hundred and five-millimetre from Barchon and a hundred and fifty-millimetre from Pontise. Another explosion landed close by, and Rammelt shut up and redoubled his efforts to dig deep. Within ten minutes, they all had some sort of shell scrape, enough to give them some protection, but not full protection from the red-hot splinters of shrapnel released by the deadly artillery shells. They were all sweating furiously from the energy they had just expended, their full battlegear making them hot, sweaty and uncomfortable. The Belgians were attempting to dislodge the paratroopers through artillery bombardments and counter-attacks, but so far all had failed.

Max's troop improved their shell scrapes, shallow recesses that gave them some protection from explosions landing close by, but not a direct hit; some protection from small-arms fire although it was not sufficient protection for a heavy, sustained attack. This was part of Max's responsibility: to give them a secure area to the north-east of the fort, close to the Albert Canal. Paul and Fischer's troop were securing the north-west, Leeb targeting the tunnels, and the rest of Group Granite focusing on the east. The shelling eased off and Leutnant Brand and his men, having completed the rout of their enemy, joined them.

"Well, Max, that was a bit hairy!"

"You're right there, sir, for us too."

"How are the lads holding up, do you think?"

Max as the senior NCO was the link between the paratroopers and their officer. Often he would see what Paul would miss. "They're on top form, sir. Their confidence hasn't been dented. In fact, they're even cockier now that they've seen off some Belgian troops."

Paul shifted into a more comfortable and safer position as the whine of a spent bullet passed close by. "They're good soldiers, Max. You've taught them well."

"They were great learners, sir, and they knew the consequences of getting it wrong."

Cruuump, cruuump, cruuump could be heard in the distance

indicating a battle was raging to their east, possibly the very troops who were fighting their way to relieve Granite Group.

In a more serious tone, Max asked, "What's next, sir?"

"The Belgian troops could still be trying to regroup somewhere, possibly for another counter-attack. We need to be ready for that."

Paul's men were weary from the long fight they had just been through. They were joined by a breathless Leeb returning from MiSud.

"How did it go?" asked Max.

"All sorted, Unterfeldwebel. We set off some explosives between MiSud and here; should make them think twice before they venture out this way."

Paul sat with Max and the section commanders of his platoon Uffz Leeb, Kienitz and Fischer. They all looked weary, but seemed in good spirits.

"How is your troop, Uffz Fischer?"

"Shattered, but in good spirits, sir, but Halm is not so good."

"How bad is it?"

"He's certainly got a hole right through his leg, although there are no bones broken. We've stopped the bleeding. I hope it doesn't prevent him from staying with the unit."

"We all do. He's a good paratrooper."

"What about Weyer?" asked Max.

"We're doing what we can for him, sir, but the prognosis is not good unless we can get help soon."

"We expected a lot more casualties, sir," interjected Max. "The boys all did well. Casualties seem pretty light across the company."

"The Belgians have lost a few though, sir," Kienitz joined in.

"They put up a good fight but were outclassed," contributed Leeb, smiling.

"Your men did a good job on Cupola Nord," Paul said.

"Thank you, sir, those explosives certainly did the trick. Those guns will never fire again. I wouldn't have liked to have been on the inside. Those screams were enough to give anyone nightmares for life."

"Any casualties?"

"None on my team."

"Your section did well too, Max. I saw the damage those charges caused."

"You bet, sir, I thought they were going to take out the troop as well as the casemate."

They all laughed quietly.

"How's Daecher from Troop Six doing, Max?"

"Just a scratch, sir, he'll be fine. He just wants to get some hospital time so he can court some nurses."

"Beiler has a minor wound to his hand, sir," said Leeb. "Other than that, they're tired but in good spirits. We did beat one and three section in destroying our primary objective though, sir, which means we don't pay for the drinks when we get back."

"You had the easy job," hissed Fischer.

"You had the easy target," responded Leeb.

An outsider might have taken these jibes seriously, but they were men who respected, trusted and depended on each other and had a collective sense of humour that went with it. Their short break over, they were back to business with the task of flushing out the enemy.

"Get the men ready, Feld. If the enemy won't come to us then we're going to have to take the fight to them again. We don't want them to rally just as we're being relieved or as our troops are passing the fort." Max took a quick look around him then set off in a running crouch towards his section who had also been taking a breather waiting for his return.

Paul too checked around him before setting off, conscious that they had not yet subdued the fort completely and they needed to be on the alert for a potential counter-attack.

Chapter Thirty-three

The greyness of the dawn that up until now they had been hiding behind was slowly ebbing away, the fort's shape and colour becoming increasingly distinguishable. This was the morning of their second day. During the last twenty-four hours, particularly during the hours of darkness when they were at their most vulnerable, they had fought off two further counter-attacks and probed more of the tunnels, letting off explosives to keep their enemy on the hop.

Now they needed to be relieved. They were slowly running out of ammunition, rations and water. And, to make matters worse, they were again being intermittently hit by artillery fire from an unknown quarter. Paul, Max and Kempf were in the process of checking the units' positions when the artillery barrage suddenly switched to their location.

Thump!

Paul bumped into Max.

"Sorry, Max," he said, but the words didn't seem to be forming on his lips; there was nothing coming out of his mouth. He tried to turn around, to see who had thumped him on his back. Not Helmut, surely? It was the sort of greeting he usually got from his friend, but he was probably fighting elsewhere, perhaps at one of the canal bridges. Or even in a dugout somewhere eating, thought Paul, smiling to himself. Max was saying something to him; well, at least his lips were moving, but he couldn't hear anything. Perhaps it was the ringing in his ears. He suddenly felt tired, had an urge to sleep. He couldn't sleep now, he had work to do. He put his hand out and rested it on Max's shoulder.

Why was Max covered in dust? Why was Max holding him? They needed to get the troops organised, just in case there was another counter-attack.

"Quick, get him down!" shouted Max. "Kempf, get his upper clothes off!"

Paul felt himself being lowered to the ground. He wished he

could hear what was being said, but the persistent ringing in his ears was muddying his thoughts. Why was he lying down? Why were they stripping off his webbing and uniform?

"Where is it?" shouted Max.

"It's at the back. Turn him over."

Max helped Kempf turn Paul onto his front. His face was now resting on its right side and he could see Max was kneeling down, leaning over him. Max leant back, resting his buttocks on his heels, as he looked at his wounded Leutnant. Paul could see his lips working again but, like a marionette, there was no sound.

Max leant forward over Paul, examining his wounds now his upper uniform had been stripped off. A large piece of shrapnel from an exploding shell had struck him just below his left shoulder blade. There were numerous other small nicks that peppered his upper shoulders and six small pieces about the size of a small coin to the right of the larger one. The unit had been taken by surprise, but no one else had been hit. It was too far away, and Paul had sheltered them from the extremities of the explosion and this one lethal strike.

Max checked him over. A small chunk of metal had gouged out a groove to the left side of his skull. Starting just above his left ear and finishing above his left eyebrow, it had left a bloody trail. It looked a mess, but Max felt sure it was not a major wound. He returned to Paul's back, blood oozing from the smaller wounds, but at a much faster rate from the larger one.

"Get his field dressing," instructed Max.

Kempf rifled through Paul's tunic, looking for the first-aid bandage. You always used theirs first, never your own; you never knew when you might need it. Kempf found it, ripped it open and passed it over to Max. "Here."

"That chunk has to come out," Max mouthed to himself. "I can't stop the bleeding with that still in there." But how deep was it? he thought. Has it pierced his lungs from behind? He surmised that it was not too deep as Paul's breathing, although shallow, seemed regular. All the same, he leant back, grabbed Paul's chin and checked his mouth for flecks of blood, a possible sign of a damaged or punctured lung. It looked clear. He looked into Paul's almost pleading eyes. "It'll be alright, sir. We'll get you sorted."

He lowered Paul's head back down and re-examined his back. Making the decision at that exact moment, he grasped the piece of warm, jagged metal and pulled it free, a sucking sound as the flesh suddenly released its hold. It was about the size of a baby's small fist, a third of it had been embedded in the Leutnant's back. He placed the bandage, a thick pad at the centre, and covered the wound, pressing down to stop the flow of blood that had increased now that the object had been removed. The bandage was absorbing the blood, but was quickly soaked; he needed more.

Leeb crouched down next to them. "What can I do to help?"

"Petzel has some extra dressings. Get him, and be quick!"

Leeb pushed himself up off the ground and darted off in search of Petzel, and for the extra wound dressings needed, calling out to him as he ran.

He found Petzel, quickly making his request for bandages.

"Who is it?" Petzel asked.

"It's the Leutnant."

"*Scheisse*, not him surely." He rummaged around in the bag, passing two dressings to Leeb.

Relieving Petzel of the two dressings, Leeb returned to where the Unterfeldwebel was still pressing down on the wound, the bandage now sodden with blood. Max pulled his helmet off so that he was better able to see what he was doing, leaving a smear of blood on his blackened face. Leeb sank down next to them, tore the black wrapping off one of the dressings, and placed this second dressing on top of the one already in place.

Max moved his hand to the top of the new one and continued pressing down. That helped. The absorption by the additional dressing, both Max and Leeb maintaining downwards pressure, seemed to be slowing the flow of blood down. Max examined the other wounds. The half a dozen fingertip-sized wounds were not so deep, and the splinters were quickly removed with his gravity knife. Paul cried out in pain, but Max held him down. He needed to get them out and clean the area. There were bits of clothing embedded in the wounds, dragged in by the shards as they penetrated his uniform. Once done, he got some alcohol from the medical kit which had now appeared and started to clean around the area of the injuries. "This is going to sting, sir," he muttered. He felt Paul pulling away underneath him but continued. He bandaged these last wounds, the smaller fragments that peppered Paul's upper shoulders would have to remain for now.

Leeb slipped his hand past Max and jabbed Paul's leg with an injection of morphine. "That will help," he concluded.

Max then checked Paul's head wound, now a mass of congealed blood. He didn't want to touch it, not knowing the extent of the injury, so decided to bandage it and leave any examination to an aid station, or a more qualified medic who should be available once they were relieved. He looked at Paul's eyes, now glazed over, his pupils dilated as a result of the drug just administered. He looked sleepy, and was drifting off. Max gently placed a folded tunic under Paul's head. "We've got you sorted now, sir, don't worry. But you have to stay awake, OK?"

The ringing in Paul's ears had settled down to a steady drone and he could now hear Max's voice, muffled though it was. He was in safe hands, he wanted to sleep, he needed to sleep. He felt the water bottle at his lips; although warm, the water was refreshing. He wasn't going to be allowed to sleep.

"We need to get him to the aid station, Unterfeldwebel," suggested Leeb.

If you could call it an aid station, a place where they just congregated the wounded so they could be watched over and administered by as few people as possible, leaving more paratroopers available for defence.

"Yes, find a ladder and we can get him there straightaway."

Leeb disappeared, returning a few moments later with one of their collapsible ladders, placing it down by Paul's side.

Petzel had now joined them and, with Max, Kempf and Leeb, lifted their commander onto the temporary stretcher, Paul's groans eating into Max's soul as they inflicted pain on his officer, his *kamerad*, and, yes, his friend.

They each took a corner, grunting in unison as they lifted up the casualty, Paul's legs dangling over the one and a half metre section of the foldable aluminium ladder. Max steadied Paul's head as they ran, or rather hobbled, to the aid station.

"We'll get you to somewhere nice and peaceful, sir. Just hang on." In between panting breaths, Max kept talking to him, keeping him informed, keeping him awake.

"I'm sure there will be a nurse there to take care of you," grunted Kempf, joining in.

"You've got to be kidding," added Leeb. "Sesson is as ugly as sin!"

Even though in a dream state, being badly shaken on the jolting jury-rigged stretcher, the humour of his men permeated through to his befuddled mind causing a spontaneous smile.

Max noticed the slight smirk on Paul's face. "God, Leeb, the Leutnant must be in a bad way; even he found your joke funny."

They arrived at the aid station, basically a piece of ground sheltered by MiNord. They lowered their commander to the floor, lifting him off the ladder onto the ground, alongside the other wounded. To his left was Halm, his thigh heavily bandaged, smoking a cigarette; to his right was the seriously wounded Weyer, unconscious again. Three bullet wounds and heavy blood loss, he was really in a bad way. There were three others from the other half of Group Granite, two with minor wounds and one, his face now covered, was dead, a rifle bullet straight through his heart.

"How's he doing?" asked Halm.

"Not good," responded Max. "But if we get relieved soon and get him some decent medical care, he should be OK. What about you?"

"Leg hurts like hell, but the bleeding is under control now."

"Keep an eye on the Leutnant, yes?"

"Will do, Unterfeldwebel. One cripple looking after another," Halm said, smiling.

Leeb grabbed the Unterfeldebel's shoulder as explosions could be heard to the north-west and shellfire had restarted again to the south.

"Something is happening near block two, Unterfeldwebel. I think we should investigate."

"We'll take your troop and mine. It's either another counter-attack building, or maybe our relief has finally got here."

"I'll get the men together," Leeb said as he ran off to gather the two troops together.

"I'll be with you in two," Max called after him.

He knelt down next to Paul, pulling the extra tunic provided to keep him warm over the officer's shoulders. "We have some more business to see to, sir. You're in good hands here; Halm will keep an eye on you."

He placed his hand on Paul's shoulder. "You just sit tight, everything's under control and our relief must be here soon."

Paul's eyes flickered open and he managed a grimace. "I'll come with you," he said as he struggled in vain to get up. "God, Max, my back's on fire."

"You're not going anywhere, sir. You just hang on here and we'll get some proper medical attention as soon as we can."

Max couldn't wait any longer; he had work to do. It was a wrench but he pulled himself away and ran after Leeb, seeking out the two troops who were going to investigate the sound of battle to the north. He met up with Leeb and the other thirteen paratroopers who were lying in the short grass awaiting his arrival.

"Right, Leeb, let's go."

They skirmished forward and reached the outskirts of block two after only a few minutes. There was clearly a battle raging, and the sound and smell of a flame-thrower was distinctive.

Max pulled Leeb to him. "That can only be the pioneers."

"I agree, we could end up in a crossfire if we're not careful."

"We've got quite a big perimeter to secure," Max pondered. "We'll pull back to our perimeter and await our relief. Let's move."

The unit pulled back to their original position and patiently waited for the pioneers to finish their fight and come to them.

Chapter Thirty-four

It was now relatively quiet, the artillery barrage had finished, and the explosions around them had stopped. The Belgian troops, although still in shock, must surely be gathering themselves together to counter-attack yet again and clear these paratroopers away from their fort. Their attacks so far had failed and their casualty count had been high, with minimal loss for the paratroopers. They would be determined to kill Paul and his men, along with the rest of the company. But they didn't come. Tired, demoralised, frightened and beaten, they stayed within their fortress.

The quiet now was almost eerie. The previous hour had been filled with deafening explosions, smoke, a debris of earth, stones and shrapnel flying all around them. They were fairly sure that the pioneer battalion that was fighting its way to relieve them was close by. Now, all they could do was wait. Keep alert, stay alive, but wait.

Jordan broke off a piece of dark German bread, bread made in Leipzig, Northern Germany, and the home of Obergefrieter Whilhelm Jordan. The *leberwurst* was spread thickly on it and a portion passed around.

"Is this the *leberwurst* that's sent by your mother?" Leeb asked.

"Yes, Uffz."

"You know its fame has spread throughout the company."

"I don't know about famous," replied Jordan. "There's always a demand for it." He grinned, his white teeth showing through the dark camouflage of his dirty face.

Leeb bit into the bread and *leberwurst*, the aroma as well as the taste making his mouth water and his stomach groan in anticipation.

Jordan, born in Leipzig, was popular with the men and was always seen to be sharing with the men of his unit the contents of the food parcels he received from his doting mother. At thirty-two, he was the eldest in the platoon and, apart from a few of the NCOs, was the oldest in the company.

Max too bit into a slice and grunted, "God, this is good.

Fighting always makes me hungry." He pulled out his water bottle and took a strong gulp of water, washing down the thick black bread and *leberwurst* pâté. Then he gently put the bottle to Leutnant Brand's lips.

"Drink, sir?"

"Thank you, Max," responded Paul, lifting his head up slightly, supported by Max's arm, taking an equally large drink of the now warm but refreshing water. But he tried to drink too quickly, choking on the water, coughing it up, pain racking through his body as he did so. They were all dry and thirsty after over twenty-four hours of combat. They had fortunately been resupplied from the air, dropped additional ammunition, they had been particularly short of MG34 belts, and water. The water had provided the biggest relief. All were suffering badly from a seemingly unquenchable thirst.

Max took the bottle away from Paul's mouth and passed it on to the rest of the assembled men.

"What happens now, Unterfeldwebel?" Forster piped up.

"We just wait, keep our eyes peeled. We mustn't lose focus yet. Although the Belgians seem to be defeated, it doesn't mean they won't make one last-ditch effort to get rid of us."

"Look!" Fischer called and pointed to two soldiers approaching them from the area of block two. He could tell from their uniforms and flashes that they were from a pioneer battalion, probably Battalion 51. Leeb was about to rise up to greet the troops that were on their way to relieve the battle-weary paratroopers from this hell-hole when Max placed a hand on his shoulder holding him back.

"Nice and easy, Leeb, they can't see us and will probably be a bit trigger-happy."

Leeb nodded in agreement and stood up slowly, hoping his familiar uniform and distinctive paratrooper helmet would identify him as a friendly.

"Group Granite!" he shouted.

The advancing soldiers immediately took cover, the officer in command shouting, "Identify yourselves."

"Uffz Leeb," he shouted in response. "Group Granite!"

"Advance towards me slowly," instructed the pioneer Oberfeld.

Leeb lowered his weapon to his side – he wasn't prepared to let go of it just yet – and slowly edged forwards.

"Keep your wits about you," hissed Max. "We're not out of the woods yet. We've got you covered."

As Leeb got closer, he became more and more assured that this was their relief, and they were here under their own steam and not the hidden control of their enemy. He was five paces away from the pioneer sergeant and could now see other sappers rising up in their familiar engineer's uniform, grins slowly spreading across their faces. They were as pleased to see the paratroopers as the Fallschirmjager were to see them. The engineers because their mission had been completed successfully, the Fallschirmjager because their isolation was over.

"Oberfeld Pfeifer, we've come to get you out of this mess."

"Uffz Leeb, and boy, are we glad to see you."

"Where's your commanding officer?"

"Back that way," said Leeb, pointing behind him. "But he's badly wounded."

Behind Leeb, the rest of the paratroopers, positioned along the perimeter they had formed, started to rise up from their battle positions.

"Let's go then. We have a medic with us. Braun, up front," called Pfeifer.

Leeb led them back to the command bunker and there was backslapping all around.

"Unterfeldwebel Grun," Max introduced himself. "This is Leutnant Brand."

Pfeifer crouched down by the side of Paul. "We'll have you out of here as soon as possible, sir. Hang in there."

"How's the fight going?" Paul asked.

"OK, sir. Sorry we got delayed though; they managed to blow some of the bridges."

"How many men have you got with you?"

"Just under fifty, sir, so I could do with some help from your men to keep the pressure on the garrison until the full battalion gets here."

"How far behind you are the reinforcements?" croaked Paul.

"In addition to the rest of the Pioneer Battalion, elements of the 151st Infantry Regiment and the 161st Artillery Regiment are moving up to support us. They're moving across the pontoon bridge as we speak. If that isn't enough, sir, the rest of the 61st Infantry Division is backing them up to ensure that the fortress was taken and you boys are relieved."

The medic threw himself down by Paul. "Let's have a look at your wound then, sir. See if we can't make you more comfortable."

Another pioneer came to a sliding halt amongst the group. "The fort's surrendered!"

"What happened?" they all shouted at once.

"The rest of the battalion arrived and they were able to position an anti-tank gun in the village and have been giving block one and six hell."

"Go on," ordered Paul, ignoring the medic peeling the bandages off his back to get to the wound.

"It seems that as soon as the lead companies of Infantry Regiment 151 arrived, they heard a bugle call and saw a white flag being waved outside the fort's entrance. One of our officers went to negotiate with the Belgian commander, a captain, I think, but, before he could speak to the Belgian captain and negotiate the surrender of the fort, hundreds of Belgian soldiers began filing out of the fort."

"My God, it's over," said Max. "We've done it, sir, and you've done it."

Chapter Thirty-five

The two orderlies dragged the stretcher out of the back of the ambulance, picked it up and quickly carried it into the German Aid Station. Paul, strapped to the stretcher, looked around him, his mind a whirl, his eyes as if looking through a goldfish bowl. He was carried through what appeared to be a casualty clearing area, a nurse looking down at him.

He felt her hand on his shoulder. "What's your name, Leutnant?"

After a few seconds, Paul managed to respond with a barely audible whisper, "Brand, Paul Brand."

"Well, Leutnant Brand, you're in good hands now and we'll have you fixed up in no time, so rest easy."

The gentle but confident voice made him feel easier, but the throbbing pain in his back remained and he still felt cold and nauseous. They transferred him to another room, the triage area, used for assessing new arrivals to the hospital. They laid him down on the floor, still on the stretcher, putting it in line with other German soldiers who had varying degrees of injuries. Intermittently, the soldiers were picked up and taken away. When it came to his turn, they moved him onto a table where a doctor, a Hauptman, examined him.

The two nurses with him helped to roll Paul on his side, one of them cutting the bandages away, peeling them off so the doctor could see the wound. She couldn't help but wince at the bloodied mess that was revealed. The doctor prodded and probed his back, Paul arching away, trying to escape the invasive pain.

"You're very lucky, Leutnant. Once we get these bits of shrapnel removed and the larger wound sewn up, you'll be as good as new. The gash on your face is not too deep, a few stitches will put that right. Might leave a bit of a scar though, I'm afraid."

Paul smiled weakly, which was all he was capable of doing.

"Take him to room five, Nurse, get these bits of metal removed, clean him up and I'll be along to stitch him up."

The orderlies picked him up again and transported him to

what appeared to be a small hospital ward. They lifted him up off the stretcher, it would no doubt be needed for the other wounded pouring in from the front, onto some form of table. He was still on his side, his wounded back covered by a light sterilised cloth to protect it from the environment. In his immediate vicinity, he could see another table opposite, and a soldier clearly being attended to by a nurse. If he looked across and down the room, he could see another table. There was obviously a person on the table but, whoever it was, they were unattended and had a blanket over them, covering their face as well as their body.

He wrinkled his nose; what could he smell? It seemed to be a mixture of disinfectant, vomit and bleach, making him heave and feel nauseous again. He felt a hand on his shoulder again and an upside-down face peered at him. It was the same nurse once more. Although she seemed to carry the same aroma as the rest of the room, it was interspersed with the faintest scent of coal tar soap, the fragrance like an island in a sea of storms.

"We're going to lie you on your front and then get these filthy clothes off you, OK? Give me a hand here," she called to an auxiliary.

The nurse indicated to a second auxiliary close by and they both managed to manoeuvre Paul onto his front after which they cut away the remnants of his paratrooper's uniform. "I believe you've come from the fortress across the canal, Leutnant Brand?"

He felt the cold scissors against his arm as they cut away his shirt. The auxiliary was slicing away at his tunic trousers. Paul nodded his head, briefly, as the effort brought bile to his throat making him gag.

"Rest easy, soldier," said the auxiliary who appeared to be dressed in the black and white robes of a sister or some other religious persuasion. She looked to be in her early thirties, the nurse tending to him seeming younger, maybe in her early twenties.

"Don't talk, you rest, let us do all the talking."

Paul sighed, wanting this nightmare to be over and to be back with his men, back in command. They had cut away his uniform completely; all he had covering the lower part of his body now was a thin grey army blanket.

The upside-down face peered into his eyes again. He looked into her brown eyes; they looked friendly and caring. He noticed a curl of auburn hair escaping from beneath her nurse's cap.

"We're going to clean your wounds now, Leutnant Brand, and take out some of the debris that has peppered your back. We'll wash it with a mild anaesthetic first before cleaning it with antiseptic wash, but you'll still feel some occasional pain. OK?"

The nurse wiped his brow, wiping away the thin film of sweat that not only covered his face but now his entire body. He tried to nod again, but the nausea returned making him close his eyes and breathe heavily, causing the sweat oozing from his pores to double.

"Anyway, we were forced to make a promise by some hulking Fallschirmjager Unterfeldwebel. He was threatening the orderlies with their lives if they didn't make sure you got here in one piece."

She laughed. "They had to stop him getting in the ambulance to come with you. It was only because of three Unteroffiziers holding him back that you're here on your own."

The smile was involuntary; he could just picture the orderlies' faces confronted by his bulky sergeant, face and clothes plastered in dust and blood. He would have made a fearsome sight. Paul felt something cold touch his back; at first it felt quite soothing, cooling his back down easing the throbbing pain that seemed to be his constant companion. It was short-lived; once whatever lotions and potions they were using seeped into his wounds, they stung like hell, and he issued a groan.

A hand was placed on his head. "It'll soon be over."

They spent half an hour plucking out bits of metal, uniform fabric and other bits of detritus the force of the explosion had embedded in his back. They had finished cleaning up the wounds when the doctor appeared. Paul didn't see the doctor; he just drifted in and out of consciousness as he was examined and the major wound was sewn up and smaller ones patched up. He remembered his face being cleaned and more stitches to repair the gash on the side of his face, and then he drifted off again.

He woke to the sound of curtains being swished back from the windows, the light bursting through, the low, early morning sun lighting up the small ward. He was lying on his back and was immediately attended by the nurse who treated him yesterday, or was it today.

"Leutnant Brand, you're finally awake then?"

"How long have I been asleep?" he croaked.

She moved to the small cabinet by the side of his bed out of the way. "Here, let me help you sit up. You've been asleep for nearly twenty-four hours."

She called over another nurse and they helped him sit up,

protecting his heavily bandaged back as they did so. Once he was leant forward, she placed some pillows behind him which he sank back into, suddenly feeling weak. She poured him a glass of water, placing it against his lips, allowing him to take a sip. After a couple of sips, he pulled away.

"That's better," he said, "but I feel really weak."

"You will for a few days, but every day you'll notice an improvement. I'm Nurse Keller, Christa Keller. I shall be looking after you during your stay with us."

"Paul, Paul Brand, where am I?"

"You're in a hospital in Maastricht. It was requisitioned by the army to take care of the wounded."

"Are there any other Fallschirmjager here?"

"Not in this ward. This is one of the wards for officers and there are none in here."

He was about to ask her to make enquiries for him when he was overcome by a desperate need to sleep.

"Right, Paul, you're going to feel a bit rough for the next few days, but we'll get you out of bed and sitting up by tomorrow. For now, we're going to change your bandages and then just relax. In fact, try and get some sleep again."

Paul awoke on his third day in the Maastricht hospital and was able to pull himself up into a sitting position on his own. It took him some time and he had to be careful about his back injury. In fact, he had slept most of the night on his front.

He looked about him. He was in the end bed of a line of four with the same number on the opposite side. There was a tall window between each bed and the ceilings were very high and ornamental. All the beds were full, the curtain drawn around the one immediately next to him. Across from him, the other patients were lying down, two of them with drips suspended alongside their beds. It looked like he was the healthiest of them all.

He saw the nurse. What was her name? he thought. Keller, Christa. She was adjusting the bedding for what appeared to be one of the more seriously injured patients. She looked nice in her blue and white uniform, the tunic riding up her thighs as she reached over to the other side of the hospital bed. She stood up, noticed him looking and smiled. He smiled back. She was slender, almost bordering on petite. Her auburn hair, just touching her shoulders, partly hidden by the trail from her cap, glistened in the sunlight shining through the windows.

She finished off adjusting the bedding and made her way over to Paul's bed. "Good morning, Leutnant Brand," she said very formally. "How are you feeling today?"

"Much better, thank you," he replied.

She came to the side of his bed, leaning over him tucking in the sheet of his bed. He was sure he could smell a scent of sorts. He breathed deeper absorbing the sweet perfume.

"I'm glad, because you have visitors today."

Paul's eyes immediately lit up, the nurse noticing how clear and bright they were. "Who is it?"

"Well, for one, there's that over-sized Unterfeldwebel of yours and three Uffzs. They came earlier but were sent away by the doctor, but not surprisingly they're back again."

"When can I see them?"

She could see the excitement in his face at the thought of seeing his *kameraden* again. It brought some welcome colour to his usually pale face, a pink tinge to his cheeks.

"We need to change your dressings first, Herr Leutnant, then you can have visitors."

"Call me, Paul, please."

She looked at him, their eyes locked for a few seconds. "Then you call me Christa."

The auxiliary nurse who came to help Nurse Keller change his dressings interrupted them and the moment was broken. They quickly changed his dressings and then gave him a bed bath to freshen him up. They joked with him, telling him that he would be out of bed tomorrow and there would be no more pampering or bed baths. Once they had finished, they left him to his own thoughts, to await the visit of his friends.

He heard them before he saw them. Max's voice could be heard above all the others. The ward sister was on to them immediately and Max received a berating and was warned to keep quiet or they would be thrown out.

They approached Paul's bed, four of them, Max, Fischer, Leeb and Kienitz, grins splitting all of their faces. Paul's face also broke into a broad smile from one side of his face to the other. They saluted and crowded round his bed. Max sat on the edge of the bed; the others pulled up chairs they found in the ward.

"Well, sir," started off Max, "you seem to have landed on your feet here." He glanced around the ward. "Living in luxury, you are."

"Three meals a day, sir?" added Leeb.

"Are the nurses Dutch or German?" asked Fischer.

"Does it matter," stepped in Kienitz. "They're all lookers."

"Seriously, sir, how are you feeling?"

Paul couldn't help but break into a smile. He had missed the banter.

"Back is as sore as hell but, apart from that, I'm on the mend. How is Halm?"

"He's on the mend, sir. He'll be back with the unit in a few weeks. His leg will need a couple of months before he can start training again, though."

"How's your arm, Kienitz?"

"Well on the mend, sir. It was just a scratch, nothing like yours."

"Where have they billeted you?"

"We've been given some accommodation in Maastricht, so we're not far away," replied Leeb.

"It's luxury, sir, after Poland and Hildesheim," Fischer informed him.

"The locals are a bit quiet, but the beer is great," added Max. He then took out a couple of bottles of Dutch beer, stuffing them under Paul's blankets. "For later, sir."

"You're going to get me thrown out, Unterfeldwebel."

"That's the general idea, sir. When will they let you out?"

"I'll be seeing the doctor this afternoon, but will be up and about tomorrow."

"Don't rush, sir," suggested Leeb. "We don't seem to be going anywhere soon."

"And we're all heroes at the moment," added Kienitz.

Fischer jumped in. "The minute they see our uniform, we immediately get our drinks paid for, whether by soldiers, airmen or sailors."

"I'm sure there are no complaints from you," said Paul.

"No way, sir," they all added.

"How's the war going?"

"Well," said Max, "we've already advanced well into Belgium. They're finished. Doesn't seem to be anything stopping us."

A white and blue uniform suddenly appeared at the end of the bed. "I'm sorry, gentlemen, but the Leutnant needs to rest, so you have two minutes."

Christa started to walk away and, after a few steps, stopped and turned round, looking directly at Max. "You might want to take those bottles of beer with you, Unterfeldwebel. You wouldn't want to see them wasted."

Max's face turned red, the first time Paul had ever seen him embarrassed.

"Maybe next time, eh, Max?"

"Well, we'd better leave you to your pampering then, sir." Max turned to the others, " could you give us a few minutes?"

The three Uffzs understood that Max wanted to speak to their commander alone for a few minutes. They stood up pushing their chairs back then moving them back to their original positions. They saluted, wished Paul a quick recovery and left the ward, chatting excitedly as they left.

Max grabbed one of the vacant chairs, dragged it to the side of the bed, sat down and shuffled it close to Paul. "Are you truly OK, sir?" There was an unmistakable look of worry on his face now that their subordinates had left.

"Yes, Max, truly I am. I'll find out more today, but I have every intention of getting out as soon as possible. What about the platoon?"

"They're all fine, sir. Halm will be with us before we know it and the rest are fine."

"Has someone written to Weyer's parents?"

"Yes, sir, Hauptman Volkman did it in your absence."

"Good, Max, good," Paul said sleepily.

"Right, Unterfeldwebel, he needs some peace and quiet now," whispered Christa who had silently appeared by Paul's bedside.

"OK, Nurse, I'm off now."

He turned to say goodbye to Paul, but his eyes had already closed and he was drifting off into a deep sleep, the effects of his wounds, the trauma of the last few days and the drugs taking over.

Christa handed Max the two bottles of beer, smiling. "I know soldiers will be soldiers, but these are not a good idea for him at the moment."

Max took the bottles. "You will look after him, won't you."

"You can be sure of that, Unterfeldwebel."

Max got up out of the chair, took one last look at his platoon commander and left.

Christa looked at the NCO as he left and then looked at the sleeping Fallschirmjager officer, recognising the strong bond between them. I'll look after him, she thought, I'll look after him.

Chapter Thirty-six

She trundled the wheelchair round to the side of his bed, two orderlies also stood by waiting to assist. Although his legs had not been injured, his back was very weak, the muscles damaged by the large chunk of shrapnel that had struck him from behind. Fortunately, the blow had not been too severe as he was hit at the periphery of the shell's blast zone. Had it been closer, it may even have punched a hole straight through his body, an event he probably wouldn't have survived. The two orderlies helped Paul manoeuvre his body so he was sitting on the edge of the bed, his legs dangling over the side.

Christa placed the wheelchair alongside him, the orderlies helping Paul to stand, being careful of the dressings on his back, turning him slightly, then helping lower him into the seat of the wheelchair.

"There, Leutnant Brand," said one of the orderlies, his accent indicating that he may even be Dutch. "We can get you outside into the fresh air now."

"Right," said Christa. "We need to get you on your feet one more time. You need this dressing gown on to keep you warm."

They raised Paul to his feet again, Nurse Keller gently placing his arms in the over-sized gown, ensuring it didn't catch his back, disturbing his healing wounds. They sat him down again and she fussed around him, placing slippers on his feet and a blanket on his knees, tucking it in around him.

"Shall I wheel the Leutnant outside?" asked one of the orderlies.

"No, I'll take him," responded Christa.

"But aren't you off duty soon?"

"That's OK," she replied, her face reddening slightly.

She proceeded to push the chair down the centre of the ward, past the three beds on Paul's side, through the double doors at the end, turning right which took them to some French doors. Christa left Paul in the chair and opened the framed glass doors then wheeled him out onto a slabbed patio. To the left was a row of cane easy chairs, some occupied by recuperating patients, fronted by a waist-high, white picket fence, interspersed with potted plants. To the right it was very similar, except for a few additional circular tables with parasols. She pushed Paul forwards along a path, lawn on either side, until they reached another squared patio area, covered by an ivy-blanketed arbour.

She positioned Paul next to a low, black cast-iron table, and then sat opposite him on a matching black bistro seat. On the table was a crystal jug of freshly squeezed orange juice and two crystal glasses.

"Would you like a drink, Herr Leutnant?"

"Yes please, and please call me Paul."

She poured them both a glass, pushed one over to him and raised her glass. Paul picked his up and she clinked them both together. "To your recovery," she said, smiling.

"Thank you," he responded. "What part of Germany are you from?"

"Charlottenburg, in Berlin, and you?"

"Ah, the 'new west'. I'm from Berlin too," gasped Paul.

"Where do you live then?"

"Brandenburg, that's only eighty kilometres from you. What are you doing here?"

"I'm with the DAK, the German Red Cross. They asked for volunteers, to support our soldiers and airmen."

"But how did you know you would be sent here? The war has only just started."

"They told us that we would be going to Poland, but at the last minute we were sent here."

"I'm glad about that," said Paul, looking into his lap, fiddling with his blanket.

"Me too, but you won't be here for much longer. I overheard the doctor. I shouldn't really be telling you this. He said you would be out in a few days, but would be sent home to recuperate then on light duties only."

Paul's face lit up. "It will be good to get out of here."

He saw the disappointment in Christa's face, and immediately regretted what he had said. "I-I didn't mean I wanted to get away from the hospital, or you. It's only that I want to be up and about and get back to my unit."

Before one of them could interrupt the embarrassing silence, there was a cough behind them.

"Leutnant Brand, I see life is looking up for you."

Christa stood up and Paul twisted round to see Hauptman Volkman, immaculate as ever, his cane tapping the side of his highly polished boots. Paul immediately tried to get up out of his chair.

"Stay put, Leutnant Brand, you're not ready to move just yet."

Paul stopped struggling, settling back into his wheelchair, frustration patently on his face.

"I'll be out in a few days, sir."

"Glad to hear it, Brand. Now, Nurse, I need a moment with the Leutnant, if you would excuse us."

"Certainly, Herr Hauptman, but the Leutnant isn't fully recovered and shouldn't be taxed too much," she said defiantly, feeling very protective of her charge.

"He is a Fallschirmjager officer, Nurse..." he peered at her name badge, "...Keller. He has experienced much worse, I can assure you. Now, please leave us."

Christa stormed past the Raven, stopping to warn him that he had no more than ten minutes. But before she could leave, the Raven added, "If you could get someone to organise a hot drink for the both of us, it would be appreciated."

She continued her vexed exit and went back to the ward, to finally book off-duty. Volkman took her vacated seat, crossed his legs and placed his crop on the iron table.

"She's a feisty one, Leutnant Brand. You'll need to handle her with care."

The bemused Paul responded, "I'm not sure what you mean, sir. I'm sure she was just doing her job."

"Yes, yes, of course," Volkman replied distinctly aware that his junior officer had no idea of Christa's attraction to him. "She is just concerned for your health."

He leant forward. "You have made quite a name for yourself, Brand. The attack on Eben Emael was a resounding success. Everyone is talking about the Fallschirmjager, the Green Devils."

"We lost some good men though, sir."

"I know, Brand, but the casualty count was nowhere near as high as was expected, and certainly not as high as it could have been had it not been executed so successfully."

"The troops did well, sir. To be honest, the Belgian defenders didn't really stand a chance. They didn't have the aggression or, more importantly, the motivation to defeat us, sir."

"Or the leadership. It's evident that they were badly led and made too many mistakes."

"At a high cost, sir, they lost a lot of men."

"Yes, they did. But one thing we have learnt from them, and from this particular action, is that the shock tactic worked, Brand. Suddenly hit out of nowhere by gliders full of well-trained troops with the appropriate equipment, we had an impact on the enemy that was disproportionate to the size of our force."

"I take it the powers that be are satisfied with the Fallschirmjager, sir. Maybe there will be a greater role for us in the future?"

Before Volkman could answer, an orderly arrived with a tray holding a pot of steaming coffee, milk, sugar and even a plate of biscuits. He placed the tray on the table and asked, "Do you want me to pour, sir?"

"Damn it, man, we're not invalids! Be off with you."

The orderly scooted away, pleased to get away from the frightening Fallschirmjager captain.

"Coffee, Brand?"

"Yes, sir, thank you."

He stood up, pouring both of them a cup. "Milk and sugar?"

"Please, sir."

"We need to get you out of here soon, Brand. You'll be getting soft with all of this pampering."

"I'm ready to return to the unit, sir, just as soon as I can get out of this chair."

"We'll get you back soon enough," Volkman said as he passed the coffee to Paul. "But, in the meantime, I have something for you."

Paul looked curiously at his Adjutant. "What's that, sir?"

The Raven stood up and walked over to Paul's chair, pulling out a small oblong box. On opening the lid, Paul could see the lining that looked velvet in texture. The Hauptman proceeded to pull out a medal, the Iron Cross, 1st Class.

"The other senior officers and NCOs are at this very moment receiving their awards from the Fuhrer himself. He sends you his congratulations and regrets that you cannot, through your injuries, be with the others at this moment in time."

The Raven lifted the Iron Cross, 1st Class out of the presentation box and proceeded to pin it to Paul's dressing gown.

"General Student himself was coming to the hospital to present this to you, but I requested that honour. I hope you don't mind?" He then straightened up and saluted Paul. "Congratulations, Leutnant Brand, I'm proud to have you in my battalion and the Fallschirmjager is all the better for having you in its ranks." He held out his hand and shook Paul's.

"I don't know what to say, sir. Everything has happened so fast. One minute we were landing on top of a fort in enemy territory, the next minute I'm here in a Maastricht hospital."

"A few more days' rest, Leutnant Brand, and you will be as right as rain. Speaking of rest, your guardian angel is on her way to chase me off. So, before she gets here, I just want to add that you have shown true courage and leadership, you are a credit to your unit, and I look forward to you rejoining the battalion."

He saluted and marched away, leaving Paul staring down in disbelief at the Iron Cross pinned to him.

"At least you can be left in peace now," huffed Nurse Keller as she came up behind him. "I'll wheel you back inside. The doctor wants to check you over and speak to you."

She moved around to the front to adjust his blanket and noticed the medal. She gasped. "Is that what I think it is?"

Paul looked down at it, embarrassed. "Yes, for some reason they think I deserve it." He thought back to the dead and wounded Belgian gunners and his own injured men and, in particular, Weyer. No medal would bring him back or diminish the hurt and deep sense of loss his parents and family would be experiencing now at his demise.

A tear ran down his face and he suddenly felt a deep sense of loss himself. He was desperate to get out of his wheelchair and return to his unit. Christa noticed his despair and crouched down in front of him instinctively placing her hands on his face.

"It'll be alright, Paul, you're getting better, you'll be out of here soon."

She moved in closer, pulling his head into her shoulder, placing her head on his and just held him while the tears flowed. After a few moments she pushed him back into the ward.

The doctor was standing at the end of Paul's bed, checking through his charts.

"Well, Leutnant, you've been with us for five days now and we think that's more than long enough," he said, smiling. "Your wounds are healing well but, when you leave here, you are to go home. You still need some rest and recuperation, and you won't find that in an army barracks."

"When will I be ready for active duty, Herr Hauptman?"

"Not so fast, soldier, your wounds are healing, but far from healed. You rip those stitches open and you'll be right back here with us, do you understand?"

Paul nodded.

"I'm not exaggerating, Herr Leutnant. Your wounds need time to heal properly. Anyway, from what I've heard, you and your men have more than done your bit. Nurse Keller, I've signed the release papers." He handed them to her. "Has it been organised to have the Leutnant picked up?"

"Yes, sir," she replied. "Unterfeldwebel Grun is bringing him a fresh uniform and will be taking him to the station."

"Excellent."

The doctor walked round to the side of the bed and shook Paul's hand. "I wish you the best of luck, Leutnant. As much as I like you, I have no wish to see you back here, OK? Right, I have other patients to see. I'll leave you in Nurse Keller's capable hands."

With that, he walked to the end of the bed, replaced the chart on the hook and walked across the ward to his next patient.

"That's it, Leutnant Brand, you are free to go." Nurse Keller sat down on his bed, halfway down, twiddling with the top sheet that was folded part way down the bed. "Your sergeant is waiting outside. I'll call him and we can get you dressed and ready to go."

"I can't thank you enough for taking care of me," said Paul, the tips of his fingers touching hers.

"That's what we're here for, Leutnant Brand," but her hand stayed where it was.

"Paul, remember?"

"Yes, Paul. Where will you be staying?"

"The Luftwaffe won't let me go back on duty just yet, so I shall go home. When will you return to Berlin?"

"I don't know. We're quite busy. Perhaps when it has quietened down here."

Paul looked straight into her eyes for a second, but quickly looked down, too shy to ask her to visit him.

"Well, Herr Leutnant, time to get you back into action, I think," boomed Max's voice, making both Christa and Paul jump.

"Keep your voice down, Unterfeldwebel," scolded Nurse Keller. "You're not on a parade ground now."

"Sorry," whispered Max, pulling a bundled uniform from under his arm. "I've got some decent clothes for you, sir."

Christa stood up from the bed. "I shall leave you two soldiers to it, then. Good luck, Herr Leutnant. I'm glad we could take care of you," she said with a trembling lip, not unnoticed by Max, and she left the bedside.

Max pulled the curtain around Paul's hospital bed so he could get dressed in peace and with some privacy. "Get these togs on, sir, and then you and I are going to get ourselves a beer and flash these bits of tin they've given us."

"And you can tell me about your trip to see the Fuhrer, Max," Paul added.

"Right, sir, I'll leave you to get dressed. I'll be back in five." Max pushed through the curtain and disappeared.

Paul started to pull on his uniform, finding it strange wearing such restrictive clothing after his loose hospital gown. He would need some help with his tunic jacket, he thought, but he could manage the rest. Max returned ten minutes later, helping him with his tunic jacket and lacing up his boots. Paul stood up, still feeling a bit woozy.

"Take it easy, sir, you'll feel better once we get you out in some fresh air." Max plucked the curtain aside and escorted Paul out of the ward. Paul looked around, hoping to get a last glimpse of Christa, but she was nowhere to be seen and his face dropped. They arrived at the exit door where he had come in, but that was on a stretcher, plastered in blood and delirious.

Max handed him a piece of folded paper. "You might be needing this, sir. You can hardly pay the young lady a visit if you haven't got her address, can you?"

Paul's face lit up. "You rogue, Max."

He was led outside where the entire platoon was waiting to greet him, a deafening cheer drawing the attention of all around them.

Christa looked through the glass in the exit door. You have clearly earned the loyalty of your men, Paul Brand. I hope one day I can share in it, she thought wistfully. She turned round and walked back into the hospital. She had patients to see to.

Chapter Thirty-seven

Paul stood on the platform of the Anhalter Bahnhof, looking up, the sun glinting on the glass-covered roof of the station. On this Monday morning in late June, the weather was not hot, but pleasant. He was on his way back to his unit, his convalescence now over. His father had driven him to the station, his mother remaining at the hotel where they had stayed overnight after enjoying an evening at the theatre, too upset to see her son going back into what she felt was surely more danger.

In some respects, Paul was glad to be going back to his unit. Although his mother had made sure he didn't go without, after a while it had started to become oppressive. He loved her dearly but, like many sons, he needed some space to himself. He had spent much of his convalescence strolling along the der Havel, probably contributing most to his recovery.

He had spent many hours walking along the water's edge, his thoughts running through the battle on Fort Eben Emael, testing alternative scenarios, considering the what ifs. If he had led his men better, would Weyer have survived? Would the other men that had been killed be alive today? He never found the answers and, as each day went by, he challenged himself less and less. He touched the scar above his left eye, a noteworthy reminder of just how close he had come to death.

Now he needed to get back to the familiar sights and sounds of a Fallschirmjager unit, be amongst his men, his *kameraden* and his friends. He had received many visits from his friends. His closest friend, Erich, had stayed overnight on a number of occasions. The boisterous and larger than life Helmut had also been to his home in Brandenburg.

Max had been twice, it being much harder as an NCO to get away. His visits had been the most welcome. Although his subordinate, the bond between him and his Unterfeldwebel, although strong from the very beginning, had been tempered by war.

But the battle for France, the German invasion of France and the

Low Countries, executed on the 10th of May, 1940, had now ended.

There were two main operations: *Fall Gelb*, Case Yellow, where German armoured units pushed through the Ardennes to cut off and surround the Allied units that had advanced into Belgium, and the second operation, *Fall Rot*, Case Red, executed from the 5th of June, German forces pushing deep into France, outflanking the Maginot Line. Paul's unit played a significant role in bringing off the success of the attack.

On the 22nd of June, an armistice was signed between France and Germany. The war in the West was over.

Paul was jolted back to the surroundings of the station, the Tannoy announcement informing him that his train for Rathenow, where he would change for Stendal, would be departing in thirty minutes. He brushed some lint off his uniform jacket. He was still getting used to his new uniform which Max had delivered on his last visit to the Brand home. He looked at his four-pocketed jacket, his preference to the *flieger* blouse, with his trousers and jump boots. Under it, he wore a white shirt and black tie.

The golden-yellow Fallschirmjager *waffenfarbe* denoted him to be in the now famous Green Devils. The exploits of the unit had been plastered across the media, and they were now famous.

Paul was aware of the glances of the other station occupants as they walked by, recognising his uniform. To the public, he was the archetypal soldier: young, fit, wearing his Luftwaffe ground assault badge, his Iron Cross 2nd class ribbon and Iron Cross 1st Class medal pinned to his left pocket, and now a hero of Fort Eben Emael.

He touched the two eagles on his collar, showing him now to be an Oberleutnant. He had received one more visitor during his convalescence: Hauptman Volkman. The Raven had informed Paul not only of his promotion but that he was to take command of One Company, the very company recently commanded by Volkman himself. Looking at his watch, Paul could see it was time to make his way to the platform and the train that would whisk him back to the arms of the military regime he had come to know and love. He hoisted his kitbag on his shoulder, still careful. Even though his back had fully healed, it was still sensitive in places. He made his way through the throng, soldiers saluting him as he passed them, finding his train and quickly boarding, finding a seat next to a window.

After ten minutes, the train shunted forward, the steam and smoke plying its way past his window. The steady shunting slowly changed to a more rhythmic sleep-inducing resonance. The conductor clipped his ticket and, laying his head against the window watching the city suburbs slowly changing into green countryside, Paul slowly drifted off to sleep. His last thoughts were of Christa and her failure to come and see him. Maybe Max had got it wrong; maybe she had just pitied a wounded soldier, or maybe her affections were now elsewhere.

He awoke to the conductor shaking him. "We're here, Oberleutnant, at Rathenow."

Paul yawned and stretched, thanked the railway official, grabbed his kitbag and changed trains, this next one taking him to Stendal.

Max, looking smart in his Fallschirmjager uniform, met him at the station, throwing him a parade-ground salute. It was good to see him again.

"Welcome to Stendal, Herr Oberleutnant," said Max beaming, enjoying calling Paul by his new rank. "Hauptman Volkman sent me to collect you, for some reason he said you needed to see me. Is all well, sir?"

Paul returned his salute. "No, Feldwebel Grun, it's not."

A frown formed on Max's brow and a look of concern clouded his joy at seeing his platoon commander again, although he was no longer responsible for just a platoon.

"What's the problem, sir?"

"You are improperly dressed, Feldwebel."

Max looked puzzled.

Paul's face broke into a smile as it slowly dawned on Max what this was all about.

"I can't be expected to run a company for the first time without a decent Company Feldwebel, can I?"

"I don't know what to say, sir."

"Say nothing, Max, it is well deserved, and I can't think of anyone better to help me command one of the best companies in one of our country's best units, can I."

Max was speechless.

"Right, Feldwebel, lead me to my transport. Then, as soon as we get back, you had better get that eagle sewn on. I want you properly dressed for when we meet our company for the first time."

He walked up to Max, grabbing him by both shoulders, looking down on his sturdy comrade. "Congratulations, Max. Now, let's go."

Silk Drop

"Come on Paul, you can finish your letter later. You know we daren't keep the Raven waiting," called Helmut, one of Paul's fellow Company Commanders.

"Yeah, yeah," responded Paul. He was frustrated at trying to correctly word his latest letter to Christa. They had met in a Maastricht hospital where Paul had ended up as a result of the injuries he received during the assault on the Belgium fortress, Fort Eben Emael. Christa, had been one of the nurses who had helped treat him and care for him during his time there. He was trying to get the tone of his letter just right, not wanting it to sound too pressing, but equally not wanting to sound too uninterested. In fact, he was desperate to see her again.

He touched the scar above his left eye, the consequence of a piece of shrapnel gouging a thin furrow from just above his left ear to his eyebrow, missing his eye by a hair's breadth. They had stitched it well and although not invisible, the scar wasn't unsightly. The injury to his back, although still slightly sensitive, had also fully healed.

"Oberleutnant Brand, get your arse in gear, we need to get going."

Helmut's shout pulled Paul out of his reverie and he jumped up out of his seat.

"Come on then, let's go," said Paul. He grabbed Helmut's arm and began dragging him to the exit door of the officer's canteen.

"Hang on," replied Helmut. "There are some cakes left over there. Do you think they will be missed?" Before Paul could answer, Helmut had grabbed two of the cakes and stuffed them into his tunic pocket.

"Food will be the death of you," scolded Paul. "Let's go, now."

They left the canteen, walking through the small hallway and stepping out of the door onto the road than ran in front of the brick built barracks. Opposite them sat a further building similar in design and build.

Turning left they headed for the parade ground, where a platoon of Fallschirmjager were being put through their paces. They passed two further red brick buildings either side of them. Keeping the parade ground on their left, they headed for the battalion headquarters opposite a similar three storey brick building, where the battalion briefing was to occur. As they walked, they heard the marching platoon being halted and dismissed; the young Leutnant in command was also destined to attend the briefing.

As they stepped through the door, they were met by a wave of heat. The room was stuffy and baking in the hot July summer weather. Its clinical white walls were unadorned apart from a portrait of The Fuhrer, which dominated the far left wall. Opposite, three tall sash windows overlooked the parade ground they had just passed.

The small room, , although ten metres at its widest point, was cosy to say the least. Set aside for battalion briefings, it was sufficient to accommodate the officers and senior NCOs of the Fourth Battalion, the first Fallschirmjager Regiment. The windows had been kept closed to deter inquisitive ears, which indicated the importance of the meeting.

The tall windows furnished shafts of light, in which dust particles glinted as they floated in the fetid air, having been disturbed by Paul and Helmut's entrance. They slowly settled back down on the surfaces of the room. Paul surveyed the briefing area. How times have changed, he thought. A matter of months ago he would have attended a company level briefing as a mere Platoon Commander, now he was a Company Commander in his own right.

To the left, below the portrait, was the ubiquitous six foot, wooden table, behind it, draped on the wall, a map of Great Britain, the focus of todays briefing. The initial war with England, the fight against the British Expeditionary Force in France was over. But the English were still courageously fighting a battle against the Luftwaffe. The Luftwaffe were currently bombing England, a prerequisite to a full German invasion of the solitary island, that was now standing alone against the might of the Third Reich. Most thought the invasion would be a simple matter that could start as soon as the Luftwaffe had finished off the Royal Air Force, the RAF. German troops could then land and England would succumb quietly. Paul was not so sure. He thought they would be a tough nut to crack, and in their own country they would fight even more aggressively to maintain their independence. There were also rumours that the Luftwaffe pilots were not getting it all their own way and were sustaining high casualties.

In front of the table were a row of chairs, usually reserved for the Company Commanders and the Adjutant, Oberleutnant Kurt Bach. Two chairs were already occupied by two of their fellow officers, Oberleutnant Bauer, Two Company and Oberleutnant Hoch, Three Company. Behind the first row of hard, wooden seats, were two further tiers, currently occupied by the Platoon Commanders. They were there ahead of schedule, clearly not wishing to be late for the Battalion Commander's briefing. Not wanting to incur the wrath of their Company Commanders, and definitely not of the Battalion Commander, the Raven.

On the left sat Leutnant's Nadel, Krause and Roth. They started to stand in acknowledgment of their Company Commander's entrance, but a quick nod from Paul allowed them to sit back down. Further to their left, the rest of the Battalion's Platoon officers were also settling back down in their seats. On the far left of the room, ensconced on the sill of one of the two tall windows, Paul could see Feldwebel Max Grun, his Company Sergeant.

A nod in his direction was all that Paul needed for a connection to be made between them. Max's nod said it all. The Company was ready for whatever was required of them. The Platoon Commanders would have thoroughly checked their respective unit's readiness, on the subtle suggestion from Max. It was not only the imposing size of the stocky, ex-Hamburg docker, that would have leant weight to his suggestions, but also his self assured presence, his knowledge and experience, honed by being involved in actions in Czechoslovakia, Poland and Belgium. Not to mention the Iron Cross Second Class ribbon and the Iron Cross First Class medal pinned to his tunic pocket. Sitting either side of Max were the other Company sergeants, and in front of them the platoon sergeants. It was a full house. To the right, the rest of the headquarters staff, from Clerks and Signals to Engineers and Medics.

Paul and Helmut made their way forward and took their places on the reserved seats, acknowledging their fellow officers.

The Adjutant, who until then had been stood behind the table, walked round the front to join them. He perched himself on the edge of the surface in front of the four officers.

"The Hauptman will be along shortly. He's had a last minute communiqué from Regimental HQ," Bach told them.

"Is this a follow up to the Op Sea lion briefing, sir?" asked Paul.

Although they were of the same rank, Bach was the Adjutant, effectively the battalion second in command. The day Hauptman Volkman was bumped up to Major, the slim, mousey haired officer, would follow suit and be appointed Hauptman.

"Yes, he wants to ensure we're ready."

"He's been riding us for weeks, sir," interjected Paul.

"You know the Raven, gentlemen. He'll not brook any mistakes." They all grinned.

"Will we get an update on the wider situation?"

"Yes, Paul, I'm sure he will update you all."

"Is my leave still on the cards?"

"As far as I know, he's not indicated otherwise."

"Where are you off to?" enquired Helmut.

"I was thinking of spending some time at home."

"Ah, going to see that nurse, I bet." Helmut grinned when he saw Paul blush.

The others joined in, laughing at Paul's embarrassment.

From across the room, Max looked up from his conversation with Steffen Fink, the second Company Feldwebel, Feld. He glanced towards the source of the laughter. He could see his young Company Commander blushing, and could hazard a guess he was being ribbed about Nurse Keller. Paul had invited Max back to Brandenburg, to stay with him and his parents on his next leave, but Max had tactfully declined. He knew that Paul would be obliged to entertain him, and he didn't want anything to distract his commander from a reunion with Nurse Keller.

Max's thoughts were interrupted by the crashing of the briefing room door opening and the entrance of Hauptman Volkman, the Battalion Commander, preceded by Oberfeld Schmidt, the battalion senior sergeant.

"Shun," called Oberfeld Schmidt.

The entire room rose up and brought themselves to attention, watching their Ccommander closely as he made his way to the end of the room where the table and map were situated. They were all trying to judge his mood. The tall, immaculately dressed officer, his dark hair and hooded, deep set eyes, his prominent, almost Roman like nose that had quickly given him the nickname, The Raven, stopped in front of the table, turned and surveyed his officers that were stood in front of him. He nodded to his Adjutant and acknowledged his four most senior officers, Oberleutnant's Brand,

Bauer, Hoch and Janke, his Company Commanders. These were the officers that would lead his men into battle.

"Gentlemen." His voice was quite soft, but penetrating, almost school master-like. "Please be seated."

The assembled men shuffled back into their seats, or the positions they had found to perch on earlier. They looked at their commander expectantly, knowing this was an important meeting. Paul and Helmut glanced at each other, sharing the close bond that had been formed during their Fallschirmjager training in Stendal and then in battle when their unit fought in Poland and later in Belgium.

The Raven perched on the edge of the table. He looked at each one of his Company Commanders, the intensity of his stare making them want to look down. Each of them resisted it, knowing he was testing their resolve. They held his gaze and he looked away from them satisfied.

"Feldwebel Grun," he called, "have our new recruits been allocated to their respective units?"

Max jumped down from the windowsill and brought his heels together in an ear splitting crack, arms rigid by his side.

"Jawohl, Herr Hauptman."

Max, his powerfully built frame almost bursting out of his Fallschirmjager tunic, had been tasked, in the absence of the battalion Feld, with settling in the twenty new recruits who had arrived straight from training.

"Excellent. You haven't corrupted their minds yet I hope, Feldwebel Grun?" The entire room laughed. This was one of the few times that the Raven cracked a joke with his troops.

"Their first task was to write home to their mothers, sir," responded Max, still stood ramrod straight.

Volkman smiled, even he struggled to get the better of this tough, fair-haired sergeant. In the Raven's mind, he had already identified Max as a potential Battalion Oberfeld. Max was not only respected by his men, but also by the officers and his fellow NCOs.

"Thank you, Feldwebel. I'm sure their mothers would thank you. Stand at ease."

Max relaxed and resumed his seat on the window sill, noticing Paul's raised eyebrows, a slight reprimand, as if saying, 'you'll say too much one day, Feldwebel Grun'. The frown didn't last for long as the Raven began to speak.

The Raven got up from the table and made his way behind it,

the map of Britain behind him and to his left. He took off his cap and placed it on the table, shortly followed by the swagger stick, a fall-back to his Prussian, aristocratic roots. In less than a minute it was back in his hand, tapping the side of his leg.

"Oberleutnant Bach, the map if you please."

The Adjutant unrolled a map that had been held in his hand and proceeded to pin it up on the board alongside its smaller scaled partner. While he was doing this the Hauptman continued. He turned to the map behind him and tapped the southern part of the country.

"Operation Sea Lion, gentlemen. We've had our warning order for this operation, the invasion of England. Well, it has now been confirmed that the invasion is to go ahead and we will play a full role in it."

Bach had finished pinning the second map to the board. It was a map of England, but a much larger scale than its cousin, showing just the south-eastern corner of the country.

"Continue with the briefing if you please, Oberleutnant."

Bach faced the first battalion officers and NCOs and picked up from where Volkman had left off. "The focus for the impending invasion is to be this stretch of the country along the southeast coast," he said, turning to the map and pointing to a sixty kilometre stretch of the English coast. "A force of one hundred and sixty thousand men will conduct the initial assault, and as inferred by the Battalion Commander, the Fallschirmjager Division has a key role to play."

For more information about Harvey and the *Devils with Wings* series, photos and maps visit www.harveyblackauthor.org.

as they turn yellow so that the seeds can be collected before dispersal. The
fruits are dried in a warm place and extracted by shaking, experience of
reasonably good crops suggests about five or six seeds will be obtained per
fruit. The seeds are small, light and winged.

The seeds require a period of chilling to overcome embryo dormancy
and this is almost satisfactorily achieved by sowing after collection, however
seed may necessarily have to be imported and this should be sown or
stratified to obtain three months chilling.

Viability of the seeds is not always good and can be as low as 50%.

At sowing these small, light, winged seeds should be pressed or rolled
into the soil thoroughly, so that contact for moisture uptake is achieved.

Seedling management is unexceptional and a population of about 300
per square metre is adequate.

Species	Seedcount ,000s/kg
L. styraciflua	200 ± 25%

ASSOCIATED READING

Wilcox, J.R. (1968) 'Sweetgum seed stratification requirements related to winter
climate at seed source' Forest Sci. *14*:16.

LIRIODENDRON

The 'Tulip Tree' *(L. tulipifera)* is the only species of this genus which is at all
commonly encountered in cultivation in the British Isles. It is a native of the
North American continent where it is known as the 'Yellow Poplar' and has
been extensively planted. It is much more widely grown in these islands than
is commonly supposed and proves to be considerably hardier once
established than is normally anticipated. Once established it grows with
reasonable vigour and has even succeeded as an avenue planting in such a
rigorous environment at Chatsworth in Derbyshire. The only other species,
L. chinense, has not succeeded here except in the milder conditions of the
south west, it is a native of central China and suffers from the effects of late
spring frost as it commonly flushes vigorously into growth once temperatures
rise in the spring.

The yellow magnolia like flowers of the Tulip tree are produced in June
and the fruit matures in the autumn. The fruit is cone like and breaks up to
shed the seeds in the early winter period. Fruiting in the British climate is very
spasmodic and usually only occurs in very hot summers. Seed production
when it occurs, is extraordinarily prolific but a very small proportion is
sound, often as low as one per cent. The seed is long and winged, and is not
unlike an Ash key in appearance. The seeds are in fact winged carpels,
orginally with two seeds of which one aborts. The food store is largely
endospermic and is very oily.

Commercial seed has very low viability generally, because of the
normally inherent proportion of unsound, void seed and because short term
storage prior to despatch is usually warm and dry and the oily nature of the

deteriorates rapidly. The seeds exhibit a conventional cold embryo dormancy which requires a period of chilling before will occur. Fresh seed, therefore, sown in the autumn will e following spring. However seed from commercial sources en dried and stored often shows a delayed dormancy due, it , to the marginal development of an impermeable seedcoat so of warm temperature stratification is needed to overcome this.

virtually no need to store *Liriodendron* seed as supplies are most commercial sources on a regular annual basis.

is broadcast onto the seedbed to achieve a population of 250 to per square metre. This implies a fairly thick layer of seed which must be rolled to ensure adequate contact with the soil for imbibition of water.

Seed size is variable but is usually about 30,000 seeds per kilogram.

ASSOCIATED READING

Boyce, S., C. and M. Kaieser, (1961) 'Why yellow — poplar seeds have low viability' Central Sta. For. Exp. Sta. U.S.D.A. Tech. Paper *186.*
Giersbach, J. (1929) 'The effect of stratification on seeds of *Liriodendron tulipifera'* Amer. Jour. Bot. *16:*835.
Guard, A.T. and R.E. Wean (1941) 'Seed production in Tulip Poplar', J. For. *39:*1032.
Hinson, E. (1935) 'The collection of Yellow Poplar seed', J. For. *33:*1007.
Wean, R.E. and A.T. Guard (1940) 'The Viability and collection of seed of *Liriodendron tulipifera* L.', J. For. *38:*815.

MAGNOLIA

The propagation of Magnolias from seed is limited to the production of rootstocks for grafting and for the development of new varieties and hybrids in a breeding programme. Most species can be propagated from seed but the length of time between germination and flowering is, in most cases, so extended that it is not a feasible commercial proposition, especially as the quality of flower production is not invariably satisfactory. Thus the number of species of Magnolia which are grown commercially from seed is normally limited to *M. acuminata, M. kobus,* occasionally *M. virginiana* and the evergreen *M. grandiflora.*

Mature seed bearing trees of these species can be found with reasonable frequency in the British Isles although they are usually only encountered in the larger private gardens and specialist parks, inevitably their occurrence is more frequent in the favoured climatic conditions of the South West. However mature specimens are nevertheless found in many sheltered gardens in other parts of the country.

The chief problem in obtaining seed from such sources is that by no means do all mature specimens set viable seeds and that as most mature magnolias are likely to be single and isolated specimens of their species it is probable that fertile seed will only be set if the plant self pollinates, *M. acuminata* is especially intriguing in this respect having several clones of differing pollination requirements.

The flowers of *Magnolia* are chiefly produced in the spring, although odd species *(M. sieboldii)* are summer flowering, but seeds of all types mature at the end of the season, are autumn maturing and dispersal is normally by wind. The seeds are produced in fleshy cones like fruits which are made up of one or two seeded coalescent follicles which split open to liberate the seed. The outer seed coat is easily recognised at dispersal as it is fleshy, oily and brightly coloured, orange, red or scarlet, the inner seed is hard stony and dark coloured.

The germination of Magnolia seeds, from imported samples or of seeds stored dry, has proved a difficult and erractic business. It would appear that drying causes several problems notably viability losses due to degeneration of the stored food reserve which is very oily, and the development of complex dormancy conditions. Thus successful and uncomplicated production is achieved only with freshly collected seed.

The cones split to expose the seed, the splitting being a fairly lengthy business, until such time as the seed is dispersed. It is usually most convenient to collect the cones just as this stage is starting and then open the cones by drying them in a sunny, warm glasshouse so that the seeds can be extracted as soon as they are ready. It is important not to collect cones until the splitting stage is reached as they may not open subsequently and seed viability is quickly lost.

As soon as the seeds are available they should be sown without delay on a conventional open ground seedbed, where exposure to a winter's cold has a sufficient after ripening effect to allow germination in the spring. The chief practical problem to overcome, before sowing is possible, is the extraction of the seed from the outer fleshy and sticky seed coat, which otherwise militates against even and efficient distribution. This pulp is relatively easily removed by fermentation in water for a week to ten days, by maceration in 'hot' water, or by mixing with damp peat and sand for about three weeks, in all cases the seed must not be allowed to dry before the sample is sown.

If seedbeds are not available for autumn sowing the uncleaned seed can be stratified in peat and sand either in tins or bins, or by sealing in a polythene bag with damp peat and placing in a cold store.

Imported seed had usually been cleaned and dried which produces the dormancy and viability problems, however, it would appear from various suggestions that seed dried in its outer pulp does not deteriorate nearly so badly or develop such intransigent dormancy conditions and if such is available should be purchased in preference to clean seed.

M. grandiflora is somewhat exceptional in its characters in that it is evergreen and has a more southerly distribution than its deciduous relatives, this also produces less stringent dormancy controls with a consequent ease of propagation. Dried and imported seed also seems to deteriorate less readily with a higher likely viability of the sample at sowing.

Seedlings of Magnolias do not germinate particularly early in the spring but should they appear before the danger of late frost is over then definite protection should be provided as they are particularly susceptible to frost damage.

The seeds should be broadcast on a conventional open ground seedbed in which a large amount of organic matter has been incorporated in order to encourage a fibrous root development on the seedlings. As plants are required for rootstock purposes the seedlings should be encouraged in developing a single, straight, upright stem which will be encouraged by a high density population, however, ultimate size is significant also and provided water and feeding are maintained at adequate levels, a population of 250 to 300 per square metre will be sufficient.

Magnolias do not normally experience any troubles in the seedbed although routine precautions to prevent damping off should be taken at emergence of the seedlings.

ASSOCIATED READING

Afanasiev, M.A. (1937) 'A physiological study of dormancy in seeds of *Magnolia acuminata*' N.Y. (Cornell) Agr. Exp. Sta. Mem. *208.*
Argles, G.K. (1969) 'Plant production 3: The propagation of Magnolias', Nurs. and Gdn. Centre. *148*:361.
Evans, C.R. (1933) 'Germination behaviour of *Magnolia grandiflora'*, Bot. Gaz. *94:*729.
Galle, F. (1953) 'The propagation of Magnolias by seed', Proc. Plant Prop. Soc. *3*:105.
McDaniel, J.C. (1970) 'Two cultivars for upgrading *Magnolia virginiana* seedling production', Proc. Int. Plant Prop. Soc. *20*:199.
Meahl, R.P. (1953) 'Recorded work on the propagation of magnolias — a review', Proc. Plant Prop. Soc. *3*:98.
Plumridge, A.J. (1957) 'Magnolias', J. Agric. Vict. *55*:535.

MAHONIA

This genus, of relatively few hardy plants, is closely allied to the Barberries. Although many species of doubtful hardiness are encountered in the more favoured gardens of the milder climatic areas, only *M. aquifolium, M. bealei, M. japonica* and occasionally *M. lomariifolia* are grown from seed. These species also exhibit much the same problems as many of the Barberries in relation to hydridity and 'trueness to type'. It is therefore essential not only to ensure that any proposed parent plants are not subject to cross pollination from any closely related species, but that the parent plants themselves are typical of the species and are not of hybrid origin. This requires in the first instance a simple progeny test to assess the degree of variation in the offspring.

M. aquifolium is liable to pollination from *M. pinnata* and it is this parentage which normally produces the taller, shrubbier less spreading hybrids of *M. aquifolium. M. japonica* and *M. bealei* are both notoriously prone to pollinate one another and all seed samples of these should be treated with suspicion unless the source has been verified. It is usually safer to propagate these two species vegetatively. *M. lomariifolia* can normally be propagated safely from seed but occasionally hybridisation does occur and it was such an occurrence which gave rise to the hybrids 'Charity' and 'Winter Sun'.

The propagation of this genus from seed does not present any real problems especially if one is able to collect ones' own material. As might be expected with a subject which flowers during the winter and early spring, the fruit ripens and is dispersed relatively early. In most years the fruits of all these species will be sufficiently ripe to be taken by birds during the early part of July: and it is therefore necessary to anticipate this and collect the fruits at an earlier date. The fruits should be checked early in the season to determine whether seeds are in fact developing, as the fruits will often develop and ripen while void of seed. If the berries are collected at this stage and are sown immediately then germination will be uniform and vigorous in the following spring. If seedbed is not immediately available it would be prudent to stratify the berries so that the seeds do not dry and the flesh rots away; this also allows a more even distribution of the seed.

Normally the berries of this genus will contain some 4 or 5 developed seeds.

The dormancy of the seeds of this genus is somewhat variable, certainly *M. lomariifolia* does not require chilling prior to germination occurring, while it is obligatory for a much hardier subject such as *M. aquifolium*. The requirements of *M. bealei* and *M. japonica* are marginal, but experience suggests that a limited period of chilling not only enhances the number of seedlings emerging but also improves the rate and uniformity of germination.

Seedbed conditions for this genus should be quite normal and generally the seedlings do not appear to suffer any particular problems or checks to growth.

Species	Seedcount in ,000s/kg
M. aquifolium	16.0

MALUS

The production of seedling Apples in the United Kingdom is virtually limited to the growing of small quantities for research purposes. The species of *Malus* are rarely propagated from seed in the nursery trade, as all the types commonly encountered in cultivation are compatible with available rootstocks and are more readily produced by budding or grafting to produce the required numbers and type of tree.

At present the vast majority of ornamental *Malus* are worked onto seedling Apple rootstocks, although a few are produced using the available clonal rootstocks. Of these seedling rootstocks virtually all are imported from the continent and are derived from seeds extracted during the various processing systems to which apples are subjected in the production of juice or canning. Provided that seed is available, circumstances suggest that there is no valid reason why the crop should not be produced in this country.

As the parent source from which the apple seed is obtained are highly bred commercial apple varieties then it would be expected that the mixed genetic complement would induce a very variable seedling population and, in general, this is the pattern. However certain sources have provided samples of seed in which the seedling population is considerably less variable, and seedlings of sufficiently uniform characteristics can be produced. The selections 'Bittenfelder' and 'Graham's Jubilee' which are currently offered by continental seedsmen are of this type. In North America the selection

'Antonovka' is gaining prominence in areas where rootstock hardiness is of importance, as this selection contains *M. baccata* in its parentage and this species is notably hardy.

The chief problem in connection with seed extraction is associated with the sheer bulk of pulp in relation to the size and number of seeds in each fruit. It is for this reason that seed is usually obtained from a commercial processing source but inevitably this means that a proportion of the seeds will be dead or damaged. Subsequently the seed will be cleaned and dried and this process may induce or enhance the development of hard seedcoats in a part of the sample as well as causing some deaths.

Should the propagator wish to extract his own seed from the fruit, then the fruit needs to be macerated and partially fermented, unless only small quantities are required when cutting and hand picking is effective but tedious.

Malus does not exhibit any complicated dormancy problems, the greater proportion of any sample germinating after a fairly extensive period of chilling. The viability of a sample is normally fairly good but it will inevitably be affected by the method of extraction, especially if this has involved maceration or cutting.

The most obvious limiting factor which appears to prevent a full germination is the hard seed coat development; however, less obviously, germination of a proportion of the sample will be limited by inadequate chilling during the winter. Most apples appear to need a good three months of exposure to cold temperature and this is not always provided by an average winter in the Midlands and Southern Counties. For this reason it is probably wise to provide artificial chilling in order to ensure germination. The degree of chilling required under these circumstances is not well researched, but an elegantly simple piece of work has recently been reported for this type of treatment on a sample of 'Antonovka' seeds. The seeds will, of course, need to be imbibed before exposure to cold, if the technique is to work satisfactorily. Thus if the seeds are stratified with damp peat, sealed in a polythene bag and then cold stored, a number of details must be clarified. This particular work indicated that the moisture/medium ratio was significant (probably by affecting the degree of aeration) and that most satisfactory results were achieved when 1½ to 2 times the weight of water was added to a quantity of air dried peat. The period of cold temperature storage also proved critical in relation to the quantity of seeds germinating and the rate at which they germinated. Storage at 1°C provided adequate chilling but no economic germination occurred until after 10 weeks exposure, germination rate then improved steadily both in terms of numbers and vigour until some 14 weeks of storage were complete.

There is no reason to suspect that other apple seeds will vary dramatically from this particular set of recommendations or at any rate require periods of chilling in excess of these requirements as the parentage of this selection is adapted for survival in the colder regions of the distribution of this genus. This work also demonstrated that this particular sample would withstand temperatures as low as −5°C without significant damage.

Because of this fairly extensive chilling requirement it is important to begin the treatment sufficiently early so that sowing can be carried out while soil temperatures are still cool or only warm, if the seed is sown late, when soil temperatures may be in excess of 15 to 20°C in the seedbed, then a secondary dormancy condition may be induced.

The seeds are broadcast onto the normal seedbed to produce a population of approximately 400 per square metre. As they are relatively small seeds they will need rolling or pressing to make contact with the soil and then covering.

In the seedbed apple seedlings are particularly susceptible to Mildew *(Podosphaera leucotricha)* which produces the typical white powdering of the leaves and may severely check growth. The seedlings are also susceptible to various Aphids and on occasions to Fruit Tree Red Spider Mite infestations, control of pests and diseases should be by reference to the current recommendations provided in the Advisory Leaflets.

If seedlings of a sufficient size for field lining as 1 year old rootstocks are to be produced attention must be paid to feeding and pest and disease control. Normally these are in the grade 4-6 mm and under reasonable growing conditions will make up for budding the following summer.

Species	Seedcount ,000s/kg
M. communis 'Bittenfelder'	27.5
M. 'Antonovka'	30.0

ASSOCIATED READING

Sladen, N.A. (1973) 'The effect of the moisture: medium ratio and the duration of stratification on the rate of germination of 'Antonovka' apple seed', Plant prop. *19* (1), 12-15.
M.A.F.F. Advisory Leaflets 205: 'Apple Powdery Mildew'
245: 'Apple and Pear Scab'
106: 'Apple Aphids'
532: 'Fruit Tree Tortrix Moths'
10: 'Fruit Tree Spider Mite'

MORUS

Only two species of Mulberry are commonly grown in the British Isles — *Morus alba* which was cultivated at one time for Silkworm feeding and *M. nigra* which has been planted as an ornamental-cum-fruiting tree for architectural value.

Seed of both species is readily available from european sources, although seed can be easily extracted from local fruiting specimens by maceration and floating off the pulp in water.

It is probable that the seeds exhibit some degree of embryo dormancy which requires a short period of chilling to break. Mulberries are subjects which appear to have only a marginal chilling requirement but in common with many such plants, germination rates are considerably enhanced by a period of chilling prior to germination.

Although the seeds are fairly small and membraneous coated they seem 129 to survive drying reasonably well and viability, at any rate in the short term is generally good. The seedlings grow vigorously and it is prudent to avoid sowing too thickly as it is necessary to thin if a poor and spindly crop is to be avoided. Populations of about 200 to 250 seedlings per square metre will be quite adequate.

Species	Seedcount in ,000s/kg
M. alba	420
M. nigra	460

NOTHOFAGUS

The 'Southern Beeches' are a group of fast growing timber trees of considerable ornamental value, which have come to prominence in the last few years as a result of large importations of the seed, of a couple of the more suitable species, from their native habitats.

The genus contains both deciduous and evergreen species, but it is really only the deciduous species of the South American continent which are likely to prove sufficiently hardy and prolific in this country.

The fruits, which closely resemble those of the 'Common Beech' contain three nutlets — the outer two, of which, are three angled while the centre one is more or less flat. These seeds are dispersed by the fruit splitting open and the nuts dropping: collection is therefore either by simply collecting fallen seed or by picking the nutlets just prior to splitting, gently drying them to open the fruits and then picking over to remove the shells.

Because of the fleshy nature of the seeds they are prone to lose viability with excessive drying and are therefore best stored without further drying, at low temperatures (1 - 3°C).

The seeds exhibit an ordinary cold temperature embryo dormancy which can be satisfied by late autumn/early winter sowing or by artificial chilling when mixed with damp peat for a period of six weeks prior to sowing. The seeds are big enough to handle individually and can very nearly be station sown although broadcasting would be more feasible: because of their size the seeds should be pressed firmly into the compost in order to ensure a good soil/seed contact for water uptake.

The seedlings grow vigorously and the seeds generally exhibit high levels of viability. They are grown to achieve a population of between 120 and 150 per square metre and will produce seedlings in an 18 to 24 inch grade at this population.

The seedlings are most susceptible to the effects of wind and it would be prudent to reduce water stress by adequate artificial wind breaking.

It was at one time suggested that the two different shapes of seed might have differing chilling requirements but observations have not supported this idea. Because of the considerable variations between the provenances of various species it is not deemed prudent to indicate seedcounts as they could well be misleading. As the major source of supply is the Forestry Commission it is more reasonable to purchase on the basis of the number of germinable seeds required.

OSTRYA

This genus of medium sized trees — the 'Hop Hornbeams' — are close relatives of the Hornbeams. Only two species, the european, *O. carpinifolia* and *O. virginiana* from the eastern United States are usually found at all commonly in cultivation although the former species is the more predominant.

These trees are rarely grown from seed and the few which are produced are usually worked onto rootstocks of *Carpinus betulus*. However they are readily grown from seed and deserve a wider planting: the chief drawback to their successful cultivation being their slow growth in the initial establishment period.

Mature, fruiting specimens of both species which will provide adequate seed can be found, although seed of *O. carpinifolia* — at least — is usually available from commercial sources.

The seeds (nutlets) are produced by September in loose strobiles (cones) which are similar to those of *Carpinus* but differ in that the involucre bracts enclose the seeds. The fruits should be collected by picking from the tree when the bracts are brown in colour but the nutlets are still green. At this stage the scales can be rubbed off the stalks in order to separate for sowing: it is simplest to sow all the material, as separating the seeds is not easy in this condition although detritus can be picked out.

If this 'green' seed is sown fresh and kept moist so that no drying occurs, then germination will take place in the spring following the winter's chilling. Dried, imported seed is probably best stratified as hard seedcoat conditions may develop and require a twelve month to overcome and it is this factor which accounts for the various failures reported.

Like the Hornbeams, these trees appear to be present no particular problems in the seedbed and if fresh seed is used good crops can be anticipated.

Seed counts are appended but are for dried seed.

Species	Seedcount in ,000/kg
O. carpinifolia	190
O. virginiana	65

PARTHENOCISSUS

This genus of climbing and clinging vines includes only four species which are at all widely grown — *P. quinquefolia* (the 'Virginia creeper'), *P. tricuspidata* (the 'Boston Ivy'), *P. henryana* and *P. inserta*. Although it is possible to grow all of these from seed in practice the latter two species are usually produced vegetatively: *P. henryana* — in order to maintain a good coloured form and *P. inserta* because being so similar to the Virginia Creeper demand for it is limited.

Although seedling plants of the first two species are generally acceptable for ornamental planting it is the usual practice to propagate all species vegetatively in order to perpetuate particular forms which have been selected 131 for vigour, leaf shape and size or autumn colouration. Seedlings of both *P. quinquefolia* and *P. tricuspidata* are required for use as rootstocks when vegetative propagation is by grafting. Various types of cutting propagation are successful but for the production of a saleable plant in one growing season, grafting is the only practicable system.

Seedling production is therefore chiefly geared to the production of rootstocks. Seed of both species is readily obtainable from the usual commercial seedhouses although home produced seed is normally available in all but the cooler summers. Established plants growing on a warm sunny site will yield large quantities of fruit which can be picked quite readily when the berries are turning colour.

The fruits are small fleshy grapes containing one to four seeds, but usually two or three. These are extracted either by a short period of warm stratification or by maceration and cleaning in water. In common with most other members of the Vine family the seeds are soft and fairly easily damaged by mechanical processing if it is at all rigorous. As seed is not always produced annually in most parts of the British Isles it may be prudent to extract sufficient seed in fruiting years for at least the subsequent years crop. Such seeds should be dried marginally and it can then be successfully stored in a sealed container at cool temperatures (3-5°C) for up to two years without any profound change in its viability.

When extracting seed from the fruits, it is simplest to macerate the fruits and leave to ferment in warm water for twenty-four hours; subsequently the mixture is rubbed and the pulp floated and decanted off. It is advisable to wear gloves for all the handling processes as at least one operator has contracted violent irritations from contact with the fleshy material of the fruit.

The seeds exhibit a simple embryo dormancy, at least when dried, which requires a fairly short period of chilling (about six weeks) in order to facilitate germination. This can be achieved by a period of stratification or by autumn sowing. Autumn sown seed extracted fresh and sown without drying may not develop an embryo dormancy. Most samples of seed exhibit good levels of viability and productivity is generally high. The seed is sown broadcast onto a prepared seedbed and then firmed in to achieve rapid imbibition and subsequent chilling. A population of about 250 per square metre will produce one year old seedlings of a suitable size for grafting.

Germination is not particularly early but the seedlings are susceptible to frost; as might be expected with a subject whose seedlings would normally be protected by the vegetation canopy in its natural surroundings; some protection against frost is therefore advisable. The seedlings are not usually subject to attack by any particular pest or disease and the normal problems will be contained by the routine spray programme.

Species	No. of seeds/kg
P. quinquefolia	36,000
P. tricuspidata	80,000

PETTERIA

This southern european leguminous genus is monotypic, the single species,

P. ramentacea, being surprisingly hardy, at least in the south of the British Isles.

It is not a commonly encountered plant in cultivation in this country, although it is more widely distributed than might be suspected. It normally flowers abundantly in early summer and copious quantities of seed are produced by August when the pods normally dehisce to disperse the seed. It is therefore necessary to collect the fruits prior to this stage, to a certain extent this early harvesting militates against hard seedcoat development and eases the necessity for severe seed treatment.

As the seed has no cold temperature dormancy controls the seed is usually spring sown, unless fresh seed is available when it may be autumn sown to prevent the development of a hard seedcoat by drying. Normally dry seed will germinate evenly if given a twenty four hour, warm water soak prior to germination although old or extensively dried seed may require sulphuric acid digestion before imbibition will occur.

The seeds are sown broadcast onto a conventional seedbed and covered with grit to give a population of 200 to 250 per square metre.

As the likelihood of demand for this plant is limited it may be more convenient to germinate the seed in a warm glasshouse and pot on the seedlings.

Viability of the seeds of this plant is normally good and the seeds store well in dry, warm conditions.

PICEA

The Spruces are a genus of Conifers which are closely related to the Silver Firs *(Abies)* and the Douglas Firs *(Pseudotsuga)* and there are close similarities between the structure, characteristics and treatment of their seeds.

There are approaching forty species of Spruces and virtually all of these are natives of the north temperate region of the world producing an almost continual spread in this geographic zone. A very high proportion of the Spruces are of ornamental and decorative value and indeed the genus contains two species *(P. breweriana* and *P. omorika)* which are among the rarest conifers of the north temperate regions because of their very limited geographical distribution. This tends to make their seed amongst the most expensive of those conifer seeds which are usually commercially available. Many species are of considerable significance in timber production and it is likely that two species at least are amongst the most important forest timber trees of the world's temperate regions (*P. abies* and *P. sitchensis).*

In their native habitats the Spruces are quick growing pyramidal, shapely and ornamental trees although in cultivation in the British Isles some species, especially those from China and the Himalaya, do not succeed in all parts because of their habit of flushing into growth early in the spring and their consequent susceptibility to late spring frosts.

The female cones, which are produced on the same tree as the male flowers, develop in the spring around the crown of the tree and are pendulous or leathery in appearance. They mature in the autumn of the same 133 year and the seeds are dispersed without any unusual delay. The cone scales open to liberate the seeds although the cones remain intact on the tree for some time (cf *Abies*). The cones should be collected just prior to opening, at this stage the seed is ripe and can be extracted by simply drying the cones in a sunny glasshouse until they open, and then shaking out the seed. This can be done without any detriment to the seed although any further drying, than is absolutely necessary, should be avoided, as the stored food in these seeds is predominantly oily and this type of food reserve deteriorates dramatically if dried beyond a critical point.

The seeds are small, thin coated and 'oily' to touch, but are not as fleshy as those of *Abies*. However, rigorous mechanical treatments such as removal of the wings should be avoided if undue damage is to be obviated.

Picea seed, in common with *Abies* and *Cedrus* which are of similar constitution, does not store well unless temperatures are maintained at a low level (1 to 3°C). Because of the thin seed coat and oily food reserve the seed is also subject to fungal attack.

Most species of Spruce are amongst the small group of conifers which appear to exhibit cold temperature dormancy controls in the embryo and require a period of chilling before germination will occur. This dormancy is not always present in all seeds of a particular sample and the degree of chilling needed may be quite small. As it is difficult to assess the amount of chilling needed by any particular sample, seeds of this genus should be sown early, that is soon after collection, so that the chilling requirement is catered for in the seedbed over the winter. This system also obviates the necessity for any short term storage and maintains good levels of viability by preventing any further drying of the seed.

The seeds are broadcast sown onto a conventional open ground seedbed at a rate designed to achieve a population of about 500 per square metre.

In the seedbed the seedlings are particularly susceptible to 'Damping Off' diseases and routine precautions to prevent such an infection are paramount to the successful production of this crop; spraying just prior to and after emergence will achieve control. Spruce seedlings are also attacked by adelgids which can be controlled by a suitable insecticide of the systemic type, however, probably the most successful pest of Spruce is the Red Spider Mite which can build up massive infestations quickly causing the cessation of growth and defoliation if not checked, thus routine spraying against this pest is a regular feature of Spruce seedling husbandry.

The seedlings emerge early in the spring from an autumn sowing and as the protection of the forest canopy is missing some form of protection must be provided to prevent damage. Cold stored seed can be sown later and so avoid the risks of frost but this technique depends on available facilities and the prevention of undue seed loss during storage.

In forestry practice Spruce seedlings usually occupy the seedbed for two years (2 + 0) but when produced for ornamental purposes under improved seedbed conditions they are usually less severely treated and are big enough to handle at the end of the first year.

The periodicity of seed production in *Picea* species is somewhat variable in the British Isles but most species would appear to produce crops of seed at least once every three years. The literature indicates that light crops are usually infested by Megastigmus flies but except perhaps in the forest situation they do not seem to be important in this country.

Storage of seed is generally more successful than in *Abies* or *Cedrus* which have seeds of broadly similar constitution, and good levels of viability can be maintained by sealing in an airtight container and keeping at 1 to 3°C. Most species can be kept for up to three years with reasonable success under this regime.

ASSOCIATED READING

Heit, C.E. (1968) 'Propagation from seed 13: Some western and exotic Spruce species', Amer. Nurs. *127*(8):12.

Species	Seedcount in 1,000s/kg		
	Source 1	Source 2	Source 3
P. bicolor	220	+	+
P. brachytyla	+	+	250
P. breweriana	125	137	155
P. engelmanii	315	297	392
P. glauca	230	520	270
P. glehnii	290	+	+
P. jezeonsis	440	+	+
P. koyamai	230	+	350
P. linkiangensis	+	+	180
P. mariana	900	888	+
P. morrisonicola	+	+	400
P. omorika	308	+	250
P. orientalis	175	+	200
P. polita	57	+	+
P. retroflexa	+	+	280
P. smithiana	+	75	+

A comparison of seedcounts from the average figures of two reliable sources with averages produced from limited data derived from samples in the seasons 1973 to 1975 by the author. The data compared is to indicate the extensive variations which can occur as well as giving the propagator an indication of the seed size in each species.

PINUS

The Pines are one of the largest, most diverse in habit and most extensive in distribution of all the conifers cultivated in the British Isles.

They are virtually exclusive to the Northern Hemisphere and have a distribution from the most notherly tree line to tropical regions. Some species have an extraordinarily extensive geographical distribution and for this reason it is of paramount importance that a source of seed is selected which will be suited to the area of proposed use, if successful production of seedlings is to be attained.

It is difficult to select those species which should receive consideration in   135 these notes as a wide variety of species could merit inclusion; however, many species, although very ornamental, have not proved sufficiently hardy for cultivation in the United Kingdom, except in the most favoured localities. Some species of the five needle group are also very susceptible to White Pine Blister Rust *(Cronartium spp.)* which severely limits their cultivation. Inevitably the selection of the species included has been coloured by personal observation and experience and they have been chosen for their ornamental value and interest rather than for their value in Forestry or as Shelterbelt subjects. As the Pines are relatively difficult to propagate from cuttings, vegetative propagation is usually by grafting and some of the timber species may require to be grown for rootstock purposes.

The seeds of Pines are extremely variable in size from species to species, being large and edible as in the case of *P. pinea* while those of *P. mugo* are quite small.

The seeds are produced in cones, which are familiar to most propagators. The female flowers are fertilised in the spring or summer but the cones do not ripen to the stage of liberating their seeds until the autumn or winter of the second year. In some species the cones do not open and the seeds are not shed until the flash heat of a fire induces dispersal *(P. nigra)* while in other species the cones are shed unopened *(P. cembra)* and are not dispersed until the cone disintegrates.

In the majority of species the cones should be collected just prior to opening so that a short period of drying opens the cones and the seeds can be shaken out. On a commercial scale this is usually achieved in a drying kiln. Those species which do not normally open have to be broken up or torn apart in order to extract the seeds. For the sort of scale of production which would normally be operating for ornamental purposes, it is not likely that the seeds will require dewinging.

The biggest problem for the collector is actually obtaining the cones — the very habit of growth of most species being single stemmed, and of medium tree size, means that the cones are produced at a fair height — and this involves tree climbing. A wide range of seeds can be obtained from commercial sources and as these normally retain good viability through their collection, extraction and storage treatments, no problems in obtaining stocks should be experienced — but attention must be paid to selecting a suitable source.

Most species do not exhibit any particular dormancy problems — one or two have hard seedcoats and a few have embryo dormancy: however, all the available evidence does indicate that a short period (about 6 weeks) of chilling prior to germination not only increases emergence but also speeds up the rate of appearance and uniformity.

Hard seedcoat conditions are rarely intractable and can usually be overcome by an autumn sowing (viz. *P. cembra* and *P. cembroides).* Chilling can best be provided by a February/March sowing.

Normally storage can be provided by air dry conditions at room temperature for short periods. Long term storage, should it be required, is most realistically provided in an air-tight jar at reasonably low temperatures (5-10°C).

136 The seeds are sown broadcast on a prepared seedbed, although the

larger seeds can be station sown. Populations will vary from about 300 per square metre for subjects such as *P. pinea* to some 600+ per square metre for dwarfer species such as *P. mugo,*

Pines do not normally suffer in the seedbed from any particular pests or diseases: however they are particularly prone to radiation frost damage both in the spring and the autumn, and protection for most subjects (and especially those from a more southerly distribution) is an essential. Shade is often recommended for Pine seedlings, but under the majority of circumstances achieves no particular benefit.

Provided that germination occurs reasonably early in the season the seedlings will reach a size, by the autumn, at which they can be adequately handled.

Species	Seedcount ,000s/kg	
	Average	Author
P. aristata	51.0	57.0
P. ayacahuite	+	
P. cembra	4.0	4.6
P. cembriodes	+	*1.8*
P. griffithii	20.0	
P. monophylla	2.6	2.0
P. mugo	130.0	190.0
P. palustris	9.2	11.4
P. pinea	+	1.0
P. thunbergii	74.0	78.0
P. sylvestris	170.0	

This table indicates the relative sizes of the various seeds and in most cases emphasises the relative uniformity of size in most samples — variations being greatest in small seeded subjects.

PIPTANTHUS

The only member of this genus which is hardy enough to survive in this country is *P. laburnifolius (P. nepalensis)* and in most parts of the country it needs the protection of a wall.

Seed of this particular plant is readily produced in all but very dull years, wherever a plant has become established and flowers satisfactorily. Sufficient seed can usually be procured locally from such stock and in our climate the pods tend to remain on the tree, undehisced, for some weeks after maturing.

The seeds are fairly typically leguminous in possessing a hard seedcoat but no other dormancy controls, because of this hard seedcoat the seed can be stored in dry and warm conditions with relative ease. An even and realistic germination will be obtained if the seed receives a soak in warm water for twenty four hours prior to sowing, even if freshly collected seed is to be used.

Provided that the hard seedcoat condition is treated so that an erratic germination is avoided, germination is virtually a function of temperature. As the germination of this subject requires a fairly high temperature for 137 quick and even emergence it may be worthwhile covering the open ground seedbed with some glass or polythene protection to encourage an early enough appearance of the seedlings.

Spring sowing is quite sufficient as no cold requirement is necessary. The seeds are broadcast and covered conventionally to achieved a population of about 250 per square metre.

In many instances the numbers of this subject required annually will be quite small so that sowing in boxes in a warm glasshouse may be an adequate system if the seedlings are to be potted off when big enough to handle.

The seedlings do not appear to be subject to any particular pests or diseases in the seedbed.

If this subject is grown as a one year old seedling it may develop a tap root habit which makes survival on lifting somewhat hazardous and it may be prudent to lift and containerise seedlings at a considerably earlier stage.

PLANTANUS

The 'London Plane' or 'Sycamore' of Scotland *(P. x acerifolia)* is of course, a hybrid and as such is necessarily propagated vegetatively. Seed is however often offered and F_2 generation plants can be obtained. Seed propagation is the normal method employed for the other species of the genus although none is widely cultivated in the British Isles. The 'American Sycamore' or 'Plane' *(P. occidentalis)* certainly does not succeed when grown in this country, while the 'Oriental Plane' *(P. orientalis)* although developing ultimately into a stately tree of massive dimensions does not establish easily and appears to be susceptible to the vagaries of our maritime climate in its early years.

Thus the demand for Planes is relatively low and seed propagation in these islands is not very significant. Although fruits of *P. orientalis* can sometimes be collected in a local situation the seed is often poor in quality or non-viable. Seed has therefore to be obtained from commercial sources and is usually readily available each year. In order to break up the seed balls or fruits the whole is dried and flailed but unfortunately these treatments often cause a considerable deterioration in the viability of the sample.

In nature the seed balls remain on the tree over winter and break up in the spring, so that although the seed dries continually it is rarely desiccated and so produces a good level of viable seeds and reasonable germination, if removed from the tree in the spring and sown without delay germination is rapid and uniform.

Commercial dried seed however should be stratified so that it receives at least six to eight weeks chilling prior to sowing. Viability should be assessed prior to sowing, and this is best achieved by a Tetrazolium test, so that accurate populations can be produced. As the seed is often so variable in its viability it is prudent to make these arrangements at this stage.

The seed is broadcast to achieve a population of about 300 seedlings per square metre: when covering with grit it is important not to bounce the seed out of contact from the soil.

The seedlings do not appear to suffer from any particular problems in the seedbed.

PRUNUS

A large genus of small trees and shrubs which are chiefly natives of the north temperate regions of the world, varying from the highly ornamental deciduous flowering cherries to the shrubby evergreen laurels. Despite the size and diversity of the group the behaviour of the seeds is remarkably similar.

The fruit is usually a fleshy drupe containing a single, fairly large nut seed. Most of the genus are early flowering and this in turn often produces early fruit maturation and dispersal.

The greater proportion of plants grown in the nursery trade from this genus are hybrids and varieties, and in consequence are propagated vegetatively, most of the tree type subjects are produced by working onto a rootstock and in many cases this is a seedling.

The following members of the genus are commonly produced from seed:—

> (i) for rootstock purposes; *P. armenaica, P. avium, P. cerasifera, P. dulcis (P. amygdalus), P. persica* and *P. padus.*
> (ii) for general hedge plant production as an alternative to propagation by cuttings; *P. laurocerasus* and *P. lusitanica.*
> (iii) for production in quantity for naturalised plantings; *P. avium, P. padus, P. sargentii* and *P. virginiana.*

Virtually all the subjects listed above, with the exception of Peaches and Apricots fruit regularly in most years in the British Isles although the Myrobalan, in common with most Plums is very much governed by the incidence of spring frosts.

The fruits should be picked when ripe and care should be taken to collect before the stage at which they are taken by birds, who will strip the fruit from a tree very quickly. The season of maturity of these subjects is variable, cherries becoming available as early as July while the Plum does not mature until into September.

When the fruits are collected, the seed is of course, contained in a considerable amount of flesh which must be removed prior to sowing. This is mostly, for ease, carried out by the immediate stratification of the entire fruits in peat and grit. This also has the advantage of providing a period of warm temperature, which if achieved prior to sowing appears to enhance germination the following spring.

The seed is best sown directly from stratification in the autumn when the flesh has rotted, the seed can readily be extracted from the stratifying medium by riddling so that the seed can be counted, assessed for viability and cleaned.

If autumn sowing is not feasible the seeds can be left in stratification for the winter as all species possess an embryo dormancy requiring a period of chilling before germination will occur. Seed bought in from commercial sources will usually be cleaned and dried, this does not cause too marked a deterioration in viability in the short term provided it is dealt with on receipt. Such dried seed should be stratified or soaked and sown depending on the availability of seedbed.

139

Species	Fruit Maturation	Period of Chilling
P. armenaica	—	3 - 4 wks
P. avium	Aug.	12 - 16 wks
P. cerasifera	July - Aug.	10 - 12 wks
P. dulcis	Sept. - Oct.	3 - 4 wks
P. laurocerasus	Sept.	8 - 10 wks
P. lusitanica	Oct.	8 - 10 wks
P. padus	Aug. - Sept.	12 - 16 wks
P. persica	—	12 - 16 wks
P. sargentii	Aug. - Sept.	10 - 12 wks
P. virginiana	Aug. - Sept.	10 - 12 wks

The seed is sown broadcast onto lightly prepared seedbeds and firmed in to achieve good soil contact so that water uptake is not limited.

The plant density of 250 per square metre will provide a high proportion of rootstocks suitable for lining and budding the following summer *(P. avium,* 6-10mm).

Summer and autumn planting provides problems of seedbed maintenance insofar as the seeds must be prevented from drying and wind blown weed seeds could arrive, but these are readily overcome. Over winter the seeds will be subject to losses from birds and rodents unless precautions are taken.

The seedlings of most species are fairly hardy but damage will be caused by exposure to late spring frosts. Aphids are certainly the most likely pest to infest the crop but these should be controlled by routine sprays. Particular diseases, such as Peach Leaf Curl may cause problems in odd years but these must be dealt with on an ad hoc basis.

The chief problem as far as the rootstock producer is concerned is the incidence of virus disease, which is a problem throughout the genus and is especially relevant with some subjects (e.g. *P. avium*) in which certain diseases can be seed transmitted. It is therefore very important that possible parent trees should be screened for virus infections prior to their use as a source of seed.

Species	Seedcount in ,000s/kg	Seasonal Variation
P. avium	5.5	± 15%
P. cerasifera	2.0	± 10%
P. padus	15.0	± 15%
P. virginiana	13.0	

ASSOCIATED READING

Giersbach, J. and W. Crocker (1932) 'Germination and Storage of Wild Plum seeds', Contrib. Boyce Thompson Inst. 4(1):39.
Stribling, I. (1972) 'Propagation of mazzard *(Prunus avium)* cherry rootstocks', Plant Prop. *18*(4).

PSEUDOLARIX

This monotypic genus is a native of eastern China, the 'Golden Larch' (P. amabilis) and introduced as long ago as 1852 by Robert Fortune. It is not a widely planted subject but its autumn colour, from which it derives its name, is worthy of greater recognition. It has a reputation for lack of hardiness and it is chiefly found in the south west, but it is basically a slow growing subject and the favoured climate of that area encourages it to grow at a more acceptable rate. It is in fact a thoroughly hardy subject.

The cones which resemble small globe artichokes in structure are produced in quantity along the branches during, apparently, alternate years. In Britain seeds have not been produced, although this may simply be a function of the maturity of the available specimens.

Seeds are produced readily in southern Europe and most supplies come from Italy. Supplies are available regularly each year so that the necessity for storage is not a problem.

The seeds are sown broadcast onto the conventional seedbed, firmed in and covered. Autumn sowing will enhance the rate of emergence in spring by providing a period of chilling during the winter, however, the seeds do not appear to exhibit an actual embryo dormancy and late spring sowing does produce germination, albeit more slowly.

As the seedlings are relatively vigorous a population of 500 per square metre will be quite sufficient.

It is probable that the seedlings will require protection against late spring frost as although they are quite hardy they can be severely checked which will affect their yearling size.

Species	Seedcount in ,000s/kg
P. amabilis	66.5

PSEUDOTSUGA

The Douglas Firs are a small genus of conifers closely allied to both *Abies* and *Picea*. In general they are broadly pyramidal in shape but not particularly decorative or ornamental. They are not particularly tolerant of chalky soils and thrive best in deep, moist, retentive soils. When established they do grow into tall and stately trees but in general are less successful in the British Isles than either the Silver Firs or the Spruces.

The cones of the Douglas Fir are produced in the spring with both sexes on the same tree, the female cones are produced around the crown of the tree and the seeds mature during the one season. The cones are leathery and pendulous and often fall without liberating the seeds. Normally, the seeds are dispersed by the wind which are shaken from the cones during the early autumn, the cones being shed soon after dispersal is complete.

Cones should be collected just prior to the stage at which they open and liberate the seed. This period is relatively early when compared with the habits of its closely related genera and collection could be expected as early as September. The seed is extracted by drying the cones in a warm house and 141 shaking out onto a receptacle. The seeds are somewhat similar to those of the Larch in appearance and have the same characteristic large wing.

Storage of Douglas Fir seed is less of a problem than is found with the Spruces and Silver Firs. They are considerably more tolerant of drying, but this does not imply that drying more than is necessary for extraction is advisable if good levels of viability are to be maintained. Douglas Fir seed can be stored dry at room temperatures for one or two years, albeit with a declining viability; but the most successful conditions for storage are achieved by low temperature (c. 3°C) in a sealed container and as such will maintain viability for as long as would normally be required. Periodicity in this genus is variable and good seed crops are rarely produced more frequently than one in three years.

As a general rule all the species exhibit an embryo dormancy which requires a period of chilling to overcome and all seed samples should be treated on this basis. Some seed samples of *P. menziesii* from the south west of its range are reputed to be free of dormancy status it is apparent that a period of chilling seeds up the rate of germination.

Autumn or winter sowing of the seed is therefore an essential feature for the production of good seedling stands. The seed is sown broadcast onto the seedbed, firmed in and covered in the traditional way to achieve a population of 500 or more per square metre.

The seedlings are susceptible to the various 'damping off' conditions just prior to and after emergence and spraying with a suitable fungicide is an essential feature of production of these particular conifers.

Various sources of information suggest that the seedlings should be shaded during this first year but under British conditions this does not appear to produce any benefits.

Species	Seedcounts in 1,000s/kg		
	Source 1	Source 2	Author
P. macrocarpa	+	11.0	+
P. menziesii	88.0	92.4	96.0

As a general rule only *P. menziesii* and its various forms produce seed in this country.

PTEROCARYA

The only species of 'Wing Nut' which is at all commonly encountered in cultivation is the 'Caucasian Wing Nut' *P. fraxinifolia,* the other species grown are chiefly from China and Japan and exhibit an early flushing habit which causes cut back of the early growth by radiation frosts in the spring — for this reason seed is rarely produced.

Seed of *P. fraxinifolia* is produced on mature trees in this country under the same general seasonal conditions which encourage the cropping of Walnut trees.

The long racemes of flowers are produced in early summer and each flower may develop into a small nut-like fruit and an unusual winged seed
which gives the tree its name.

The seeds deteriorate rapidly with drying but germinate well if sown soon after dispersal, this keeps them moist and provides any chilling requirement. Seeds bought in from commercial sources are inevitably dried to some degree and immediate soaking to arrest further deterioration is an essential in successful production. Sowing as soon as feasible also helps so that chilling is provided and further drying is prevented.

The seedlings are very susceptible to radiation frosts in the early stages and protection against this agency is essential to survival of the crop.

Species	Seedcount in ,000s/kg
P. fraxinifolia	14.0

PYRUS

Pear seedlings are rarely grown in this country except for research purposes, and virtually all the ornamental pears are produced by budding or gratfing on rootstocks of the 'Common Pear' *(Pyrus communis)*.

The rootstocks of the Common Pear are normally bought in from continental sources, which suggests that, providing seed is available, there should be no good reason why such seedlings could not be produced in this country.

Although it would be expected that pear seedlings would show considerable variation in the population, in practice selected varieties produce a remarkably uniform crop and although most seed is offered simply as 'Common Pear' selections such as 'Kirchensaller Mostbirne' are available from certain continental sources.

The treatment of Pear seed is very similar to the pattern which was suggested for Apple seed, the only significant difference would possibly be the length of time required for the chilling process needed to break dormancy and for this genus it is probable that a shorter period (8-10 weeks) would be sufficient.

With the increasing demand for such varieties as *P. calleryana* 'Chanticleer' 'Bradford' etc. in the United Kingdom, it might be prudent to consider producing a wider range of rootstocks to avoid the problems of incompatibility, which appears in a proportion of any sample of Common Pear seedlings when worked with these serai evergreen types.

Reference to the various seedsmens' catalogues indicates that *P. calleryana, P. ussuriensis,* and *P. pyrifolia* are fairly regularly offered especially from north american sources, *P. calleryana* which would be the most desirable however is the least regularly available.

In the seedbed Pears are susceptible to the usual problems which beset rosaceous subjects *viz.* scab, Mildew, Aphids, etc., but particularly they show symptoms very readily of Crown Gall *(Agrobacterium tumefasciens)* and seedbeds known to be infected should not be used for Pears.

Species	Seeds/kg
P. betulifolia	98,000
P. calleryana	20,000 ± 10%
P. communis	30,000
P. pyrifolia (serotina)	40,000

143

ASSOCIATED READING

Westwood, M.N. and H.O. Bjornstad (1948) 'Chilling requirements of dormant seeds of fourteen Pear Species as related to their climatic adaptation', Proc. Amer. Soc. Hort. Sci. *92*:141.

QUERCUS

The Oaks are an extremely large and diverse genus of woody plants varying in stature from that of the most majestic of trees to small, multistemmed scrubland subjects. Some species are evergreen but of the deciduous group considerable variation may occur in the period of leaf fall. Between 200 and 400 species are recognised, of which the majority are natives of Europe and Asia and all, more or less, are inhabitants of the north termperate regions of the world. A relatively small number of species are native to the north american continent and many of this group are significant and worthy of cultivation, because of their vivid autumnal colours. Although the greater part of the genus is not suitable for, or worthy of, cultivation in the British Isles, there are well over 50 species to be found in the larger collections. However, not more than a dozen alien species are of real significance in nursery practice and, together with our two native species, these provide the vast majority of seedling trees and rootstocks of the genus required under most circumstances.

Unfortunately, the alien Oaks are largely encountered as single specimens and often they are grown in company with other species of Oak. Both these factors militate against the use of these specimens as parent plants for the collection of reliable crops of seed. The very nature of their isolation encourages self pollination, which in this genus produces notoriously poor quality seeds and indifferent seedling stands; the admixture of species as single specimens in such collections encourages the likelihood of cross pollination and the production of hybrid seed, as the majority of species are naturally out-crossing.

Seed should therefore be collected only from trees in single species groups, avenues or boundary lines and even under these circumstances should only be collected from the contiguous parts of the trees where satisfactory, in species, cross pollination will have occurred. Collection from the peripheral parts of the group should be avoided, especially with european species as cross pollination by the native species is almost inevitable because of their ubiquitous distribution.

If suitable sources are not available then recourse must be made to the commercial seed houses, who however, do not normally offer a wide selection of species. It is also wise to negotiate delivery as soon after collection as is possible as many species lose viability dramatically with increasing dessication.

The seed of the Oak is generally termed an acorn and these are normally dispersed in the autumn after a period of frost which finally separates the acorn from its cup. As would be expected with subjects producing large fleshy seeds the storage life is limited and precarious because of the high lipid content. Storage recommendations for acorns should allow for high humidity and low temperature (0-2°C) and even so this is only successful in the short term (6-9 months), although the Red Oaks will store for longer.

From a practical standpoint Oaks are classified into two groups on the basis of the time taken by the acorns to mature and disperse. The 'White Oaks' produce acorns from pollination to dispersal in one growing season while the 'Black Oaks' require two seasons. This has some significance for the propagator as it effects the periodicity of crop production, is related to dormancy conditions and affects storage ability.

Generally the White Oaks have no dormancy controls and the acorns will germinate after shedding if conditions are right: they normally produce crops of seed regularly and frequently. At dispersal they usually have a relatively high moisture content (55-60%) and lose vitality quickly if allowed to dry appreciably. The Black Oaks have a conventional cold temperature embryo dormancy which is overcome by one winter's chilling: their production of crops is very much more erratic than the White Oaks and in many cases the acorns will often abort at the end of the first season. At dispersal the seeds have a relatively low moisture content (15-20%) and consequently store more successfully and survive commercial handling better.

The seeds of most Oaks are very susceptible to infestation by Weevils *(Curculio spp.)* which eat out the embryo and cotyledons. In general nursery practice it is usual to sort acorns for soundness by flotation in water, so that damaged, blighted and infested seed can be extracted and only sound, viable and useful material retained and a theoretical 100% stand on sowing should be achieved. All the relevant sources of information prescribe hot water treatment (30 minutes at 9°C) for Weevil control but the writer has not actually ever observed this in practice. Weevil infection is normally highest in years of light crops.

The acorns are usually collected by picking up from the ground under suitable trees, and unless the sample is to be screened and dealt with fairly quickly it should not be kept in bulk, as these seeds heat up very rapidly. Heating causes rapid deterioration of the seed and acorns damaged under such conditions will turn black. If even only for a few days storage, the acorns should be cooled to remove 'field heat' and then to prevent desiccation stored preferably in a jacketed cold store.

Ideally all acorns should be sown as soon after collection and screening as is feasible, so that even the most precocious White Oaks which produce their radicle very quickly are catered for; so that the remainder of the White Oak group will not lose viability; and so that the Black Oaks will receive adequate chilling to break dormancy.

Should the seeds have to be stored because the seedbed is not ready they are most successfully maintained by mixing with damp peat and keeping cool; however White Oak seeds will often develop the radicle in this type of storage but sowing in such a condition is not normally detrimental. The seed will withstand fairly severe damage to the radicle and still establish quite satisfactorily.

Autumn sowing provides the most desirable system for successful production, but it does leave the seed exposed to the predations of birds and rodents. Precautions, such as seed dressing with Red Lead or tainting with Oil, may well be necessary on some sites.

The acorns are most satisfactorily sown onto a fairly loose seedbed so 145 that they can be firmed in to their full depth thus achieving good contact for soil moisture uptake. The seed is often broadcast, but the particular size and shape of an acorn does lend itself to fairly precise machine drilling or with small lots accurate station sowing.

Germination generally tends to be fairly late despite the relatively early chitting of some species, but it is prudent to have frost protection available in an early season.

The chief check to seedling growth is provided by a Mildew caused by *Microsphaera quercina,* which once established on the seedling effectively stops growth for the season. The european species are particularly susceptible and the american species less so, indeed *Q. rubra (Q. borealis maxima)* appears to be resistant. Routine precautions should be taken to prevent infection.

The rates of growth for the various species during the seedling year is very variable, some such as the Red and Scarlet Oaks easily reaching 40-50 cm in height, but others barely 12-15 cm, especially the evergreen types.

These growth rates are achieved with populations of about 300 per square metre and assume two flushes of growth.

Seed of the two native species can be readily collected in most parts of the British Isles. *Q. cerris* is fairly widely planted and can often be found in groups or boundary lines. *Q. suber* is not widely planted and is chiefly limited to the southern half of the country where it is usually encountered as single specimens. *Q. ilex* is reasonably common throughout the South and Midlands but some progeny testing of parent trees should be undertaken as it is a very variable species: varying from multistemmed bushes to stately standard trees. *Q. rubra* is not widely planted but seed bearing specimens can be found among the perimeter plantings of some forest and woodland plots where they were established to provide protection for the main crop. Although *Q. phellos* and *Q. palustris* can be found growing very satisfactorily they rarely set seeds in these islands. Other north american species can be found, while of the european species *Q. canariensis* and *Q. lusitanica* are fairly frequent in the larger parks and gardens. Seed of these however cannot be relied upon to come true because of the ease with which all the european species hybridise. Most shed their seed in October but *Q. lusitanica* is exceptional in dispersing its seed later.

All the commoner american species in cultivation with the exception of *Q. agrifolia,* exhibit embryo dormancy. Simiarly the european species show no dormancy, with the exception of *Q. castanaefolia* and *Q. cerris;* while *Q. suber occidentalis* is unusual in taking two years to mature its acorns.

Species	Seeds/kg
Q. cerris	320-350
Q. petraea	280-300
Q. robur	240-260
Q. ilex	440-500
Q. suber	320-360
Q. rubra	300-320
Q. coccinea	
Q. palustris	c. 1,000
Q. phellos	

These figures are offered as averages to indicate the relative size of the acorns of each species; however, the range within species from season to season and source to source may be as much as $\pm$ 40%. In 1975 for example, the acorns of *Q. cerris* weighed 220 seeds/kg when a local sample as assessed.

ASSOCIATED READING

Anon. (1962) 'Collection and storage of acorns and beech mast', For. Comm. Lflt. *28*.

Bonner, F.T. (1968) 'Storing Red Oak acorns', Tree Plant. Notes *24*(3):12.

Farmer, R.E. (1975) 'Long term storage of Northern Red and Scarlet Oak Seed', Plant Prop. *21:*11.

Holmes, C.D. and G. Buszewicz (1966) 'The longevity of acorns with several storage methods', Rep. For. Res. 1955:88.

Stanley, J. (1975) 'On Oaks', Gard. Chron. *178:*30.

ROBINIA

The only species of this genus of 'Locust Trees' or 'False Acacias' which is at all commonly found in cultivation is *R. pseudacacia,* although both *R. hispida* and *R. kelseyi* are sometimes encountered. Most of this group except the False Acacia itself are propagated vegetatively by grafting onto a rootstock or occasionally by root cuttings or suckers. The only species, therefore, to be grown from seed is usually *R. pseudacacia* either for specimen purposes or as a rootstock.

The fruit of this genus is a typical leguminous pod containing up to ten seeds but seed production is not at all common in the United Kingdom although in occasional hot summers crops are sometimes set.

Seed is readily obtainable from most commercial seedhouses; in Europe it is chiefly collected from southern France and Italy. Various american references suggest that seed samples of *R. pseudacacia* develop a sufficiently hard seedcoat that a degree of sulphuric acid digestion is necessary if the entire sample is to be germinated satisfactorily. However samples of seed imported from Europe have germinated well without such a pre-treatment if sown during the late winter; it is possible that a limited hard seedcoat condition is developed in european samples but that the method of extraction scarifies the coats sufficiently well to allow almost immediate imbibition; and as the author has not had access to 'undamaged' home produced seed it is not possible to determine the natural condition at dispersal. Whatever state seeds are supplied in, the hardcoat is only thin and impermeable to water. The best results of germination are obtained if the seeds are given a warm water soak for forty-eight hour period prior to sowing, so that any seedcoat condition is reduced and the seed imbibes.

The seed is sown broadcast, after soaking, onto a prepared mineral soil seedbed to produce a population of 250 to 300 seedlings per square metre. This density will allow the development of plants in the 40-60 cm height grade.

There is little difficulty to be encountered in the cultivation of this species provided viability is assessed and the plant population correctly determined. Pests and diseases are rarely a problem. It is perhaps prudent to

147

ensure that the seedbed is adequately irrigated to prevent drying if previously soaked seed is sown.

Species	Seedcount ,000s/kg
R. pseudacacia	60.0 $\pm$ 30%

Although seed can be stored quite effectively if kept dry, it is not really necessary as supplies are readily available annually.

ASSOCIATED READING

Anon. (1962) 'Locust Seed Treatment', Amer. Nurs. **96**(4):31.

ROSA

The author has obtained only limited experience in the germination of Rose seeds, but because of the widespread interest in the production of certain species for use as understocks, the following account is derived from the work of Blundell during his period at the University of Wales at Bangor, limited personal involvement and the practical experience of a couple of propagators who have attempted to use this technique.

Traditionally the rose achenes has been warm stratified for one summer season in order to reduce the hard seedcoat condition, cold stratified for an entire winter and then spring sown. However only an emergence of 5% or so is obtained by this method and this consequently requires fairly massive seed rates — in the order of 200 kg/ha — and this makes seed costs a very key factor in the total production costs.

Blundell's work was concerned with achieving an emergence of 80 to 85% and seed rates of 10 to 12 kg/ha or less. It depends on acid digestion, a period of warm stratification followed by a conventional chilling.

The first problem the propagator has to overcome is the collection of the hips (fruits) and the extraction of the seeds from them. If the hips are left until they are deep red and soft, the flesh has to be separated by maceration, fermentation and decanting off the scum — this leaves the skins to be separated by picking over. The seeds are most easily separated by picking the hips when they are changing from green to orange and then 'squeezing' them so that the seeds are literally spat out — this produces a very clean and immediately usable sample. If large quantities of seed are required they can be extracted by passing the hips through a suitably adjusted, old fashioned, oat crusher or similar roller mill. Having extracted the sample it should then be counted and tested for viability so that the potential is known from the start.

Subsequently successful production depends on attention to detail and a precision approach: however a slavish adherence to the recommendations following should be avoided and the technique should be adapted for the various species and varieties, the time of harvest, the condition of the seed
and the degree of seedcoat maturation.

All roses have a hard seedcoat in some degree, although only *R. canina* and *R.* 'laxa' of the commonly encountered groups have a sufficiently developed condition that prevents germination in the first season: for this reason it is necessary to reduce the seedcoat with an acid digestion.

Because of the reticulate nature of the hard seedcoat conditions it is possible for concentrated acid to permeate through to the embryo and cause damage if the seedcoat is still damp. For this reason the seeds should be thoroughly dried before digestion so that the hard seedcoat is fully developed.

When the seed is digested with concentrated acid the seedcoat chars and it is necessary to keep the mixture stirred in order to keep the reaction going: otherwise the conventional technique of acid digestion is adopted (see page 58), the digestion should be concluded as soon as an odd seed imbibes.

The seedcoat reduction is completed by a short period of warm stratification, this also appears to mature or after ripen the embryo and finally it causes all the seeds to imbibe when the seedcoat has been reduced. The seeds are stratified using vermiculite or damp sifted peat (see page 62) and then keeping the mixture at a temperature between 81°F (27°C) and 90°F (32°C) the end stage, when all the seeds have imbibed, will probably be achieved after a period of about 14 to 21 days.

After this stage the mixture is subjected to a cold temperature so that the seed is chilled and germination can be induced. The seeds will require chilling at below 5°C (ideally 3°C) and once chilling is complete the seeds will generally chit; the commencement of chitting can be recognised by the pericarp splitting. Once 60% of the sample has chitted the seeds are sown, this will generally occur after a period of 14 to 16 weeks. In order to obtain a maximum emergence and speedy germination the seeds should be sown when soil temperatures are rising, and sufficiently late to avoid any great subjection to radiation frosts.

The object of his exercise is an attempt to induce all the seeds to germinate simultaneously so that all the seedlings have an equally competitive chance and an even grade out of seedling understocks is achieved — a feature which is of paramount importance in the economic production of rootstocks. From this detail it will be possible to assess the date of which the various treatments should begin.

Species	Seedcount ,000s/kg
R. canina	40.0
R. 'laxa'	66.6
R. rubrifolius	53.0
R. rugosa	65.0

If the seeds of such species as *R. rubrifolius* and *R. rugosa* are extracted early in the green/orange stage and are sown immediately in warm soil temperatures any limited seedcoat condition will be reduced during the autumn and adequate chill will be achieved over winter. Alternatively stratify in peat and keep warm for a month or so prior to chilling in a refrigerator.

One approach which has not yet been researched is the possibility of extracting seeds, when the hips are still green, and when the seedcoat has not hardened. This might offer a possible alternative to the acid digestion technique. It would however depend on an ability to separate the seeds readily from the hip while it is still in a very green and immature condition but may in the long run produce a safer and easier answer than the use of acid.

ASSOCIATED READING

Blundell, J.B. (1973) 'Rootstock seed growth improved' Gard. Chron. *174*(1):16.
Blundell, J.B. and G.A.D. Jackson (1971) 'Rose seed germination in relation to stock production' Rose Ann. 1970, Lond. : 129.

SCIADOPITYS

The 'Japanese Umbrella Pine' *(S. verticillata)* is the only representative of this genus. It is a fine, slow growing, dark green, well clothed, coniferous subject which is still relatively rare in the United Kingdom. Although seed is relatively easily obtained from the usual commercial sources and appears to be sown fairly regularly, few trees ever appear at a saleable size. The reasons for this are somewhat obscure but could be attributed to, i) very slow (relatively) seedling growth in its initial years, ii) low viability/field emergence and iii) failure to overcome dormancy conditions.

The plant is perfectly hardy, as might be expected for a subject emanating from the more severe climatic areas of Japan. It is also this factor which creates the dormancy problem. Normal advice for seed sowing of conifers has been to sow late and avoid frost damage after emergence; this depends for success on a minimal chilling requirement of the seed; this particular species however has a fairly hefty chilling requirement and should be sown early in the winter. If seed is bought in, it will be received too late to chill naturally and it is therefore stored until the next season; this in itself may cause deterioration of the sample and a dramatic decline in viability. Some germination will occur late in the season from late sown lots but these will do little more than produce the cotyledon leaves before the onset of winter.

The cones of this species, which are only occasionally encountered in the British Isles because of the lack of mature specimens, contain about 10 seeds. They are somewhat difficult to extract and it may also be this factor which reduces the vigour and reliability of the sample because of the system of processing: although if freshly collected cones which are beginning to open on the tree are taken and gently dried, good results can be obtained.

Mature specimens will cone in this country at fifteen to twenty feet and can sometimes be found in sheltered, established gardens.

The seedling growth of this subject, as has been intimated, is nevertheless fairly slow even under the best of conditions.

Seedbed conditions for this species are quite normal and rarely are the seedlings troubled by pests or diseases.

Species	Seedcount in ,000s/kg
S. verticillata	37.5

SORBUS

The genus *Sorbus* is a large group of small trees and shurbs of varied habit but remarkably constant in the production of their white or near white flowers and highly coloured ornamental berries. There are inevitably divisions taxonomically within the genus but from a horticultural aspect they are divided into the Whitebeams, the Service Trees, the Rowans and those early flowering types usually referred to as the *Micromeles* section.

The genus has an extensive geographical distribution although the vast majority of the species occur in the north temperate regions of the world and as might be expected with rosaceous subjects from these regions, dormancy is limited to an embryo condition requiring a period of chilling before germination can occur.

The greater portion of species are propagated, in the nursery trade by working onto a suitably related rootstock and the majority of seedlings are produced for this purpose. The use of other genera as rootstocks, such as the use of Thorns for some Whitebeams, cannot be condoned, as the resultant trees are almost always short lived. In practice the production of seedlings is limited to the following species:—

S. aucuparia — as a rootstock for all the species, varieties and hybrids of Rowan or Mountain Ash.

S. intermedia — as a rootstock for most of the species, varieties and hybrids of Whitebeams, it is not however compatible with all, *(viz.* 'Wilfrid Fox' and 'Mitchellii') although it is preferred for its ease of production and rapid growth: for natural plantings.

S. aria — as a rootstock for Whitebeams, although it is relatively slow growing in its seedling year and is not favoured because of this; however relatively short plants have adequate girth for budding.

S. latifolia — often offered as a substitute rootstock for Whitebeams although its growth rate of scions is very variable; also used in natural plantings.

S. domestica and *S. torminalis* — for use in natural plantings, small numbers of the various *Micromeles* types are also produced from seed but successful propagation is only achieved if fruit can be collected from reliable trees in a single species group so that the incidence of cross pollination is reduced to a minimum.

S. reducta — a dwarf species usually produced from seed for garden planting purposes.

The fruit is a pome containing 2 to 5 seeds depending on the species and number aborted. An annual check on the number of seeds per berry is essential for accurate collection procedure as fertilisation varies from year to year; seed abortion occurs usually for climatic reasons but infestation by various insect grubs, especially chalcid flies can reduce crops dramatically.

The berries are collected as soon as they are ripe and begin to be dispersed, however collection in advance of this period has several benefits, most noticeable being the reduction in the degree of embryo dormancy occurring in the sample. The fact that the fruits, especially of *S. aucuparia,* are attractive to birds also ensures the collection of a full crop. For this reason it is also important to determine collection periods for most species as the fruits can be stripped by birds very quickly.

Good crops of seeds are produced in most years. The seed is extracted from the fruits by maceration and either stratification or fermentation and flotation of the pulp. In the latter case it is important not to dry the seed too drastically or a hard seedcoat condition may be engendered, this is particularly true with *S. aucuparia.*

If the seed has been dry stored or obtained as dried berries from commercial sources then a hard seedcoat develops which may impair regular germination. Indeed in most seed samples of the European species some delayed dormancy occurs because of this factor, but with experience adequate crops can be harvested in the first year allowing for a certain proportion which fails to germinate. If the propagator is collecting his own seed, then early collection cleaning and direct sowing into a still warm seedbed will usually reduce failures to a very small minimum.

Although it has not apparently been tried, it would seem feasible to adopt the chilling procedure outlined on page 61 and with observation and experience the period of cold treatment required can be determined.

From experience it would appear that *S. aucaparia* is much more prone to develop a hard seedcoat of sufficient proportions to delay germination than either *S. aria* or *S. intermedia.*

The seeds are sown conventionally, i.e. broadcast onto a prepared seedbed to produce a population of about 300 per square metre; *S. aria* produced relatively little top growth but root development is comparable with other species and so should not be grown at an increased density. *S. reducta,* of course, can be grown at populations of 500 to 600 per square metre.

The seedlings of most species are hardy and rarely suffer from the predations of pests or diseases in the seedbed.

Species	Period of Fruit Maturation	Seedcount in ,000s/kg
S. aria	Sept. - Oct.	36 - 37
S. aucuparia	Aug.	275
S. intermedia	Sept. - Oct.	40 - 44
S. latifolia	Oct.	+
S. torminalis	Oct.	28

FURTHER READING

Flemion, F. (1931) 'After-ripening, Germination and vitality of seeds of *Sorbus aucuparia L.'* Contrib. Boyce Thompson Inst. *3*(3):413.

STEWARTIA

Seeds of the various species of this genus all appear to require a period of warm stratification to overcome seedcoat conditions followed by chilling before germination will occur. Under normal conditions this makes these seeds into 'two year' dormancy types, however artificial treatments can be carried out on freshly dispersed seed which will permit germination the following early summer. The author's experience being significantly limited, when concerned with this genus, refers readers to a reliable source for detail.

ASSOCIATED READING

Sponberg, S.A. and A.J. Fordham (1975) 'Stewartias — small trees and shrubs for all seasons' Arnoldia *35*(4):165

TAXUS

Although the majority of Yews grown in the nursery trade are propagated vegetatively because of the need to produce particular clonal forms, seedlings of the English Yew (*T. baccata*) are produced for hedging purposes and also, in limited quantities, as rootstocks for grafting.

This coniferous subject produces unusual fruits which consist of a single, hard stoney seed surrounded by an open ended, round, red fleshy pulp or 'aril'. These fruits mature in the late summer to early autumn. These can be readily collected by picking from the tree prior to dispersal or by sweeping up from the ground, although reputedly taken by birds there is usually more than sufficient falling to the ground.

Collection is the only easy aspect of propagating these subjects, as actually germinating them can prove somewhat difficult. The hard seedcoat prevents germination for at least one season and has proved intractable, insofar as sulphuric acid digestion has not been successful. The collection of immature seeds does not overcome the problem either as the impermeability of the seedcoat appears to develop early in the maturation process. The only alternative therefore is to pursue a traditional stratification process; if this is commenced straight away after collection, the seedcoat of the majority of the sample will have been reduced by the end of the following summer: however this is only effective if the stratifying medium has adequate peat, is kept sufficiently moist and warm temperatures are maintained; the introduction of some leaf mould to accelerate the decomposition is also advantageous. Theoretically this could be achieved with artificial warm storage immediately after collection, so that chilling could follow and germination would occur in the early summer following. In practice however this has not yet been carried out successfully. Artificial treatment would need to be practiced on an extracted seed, and this is readily achieved by maceration in water, a short term fermentation and the flotation of the scum including the void seed.

153

Stratified seed is therefore sown twelve months after collection so that embryo dormancy can be overcome by chilling in the seedbed over the winter period. This system does not produce a maximum response but it has so far produced the best results.

The whole essence of successful seedcoat reduction revolves around quick treatment and the avoidance of any period of drying.

It may be possible that hot water treatment prior to warm stratification may enhance the seedcoat reduction and so develop an improved response.

Stratified seed can reasonably easily be separated from the medium for sowing and should be broadcast to achieve a seedling density of some 400 - 500 per square metre. As the seed is relatively large it should be pressed into the seedbed to maintain its ability to take up water.

The seedlings do not generally suffer from any particular problems in the seedbed.

Species	Seedcount in ,000s/kg
T. baccata	17.5

TILIA

A relatively small genus of trees from the north temperate regions of the world, being distributed through the eastern half of North America, Europe and Central Asia. In Britain they are commonly called 'Limes' and traditionally 'Lindens' while in North America they are still called 'Lindens' and particular species, variously as 'Basswood' and 'Whitewood'.

This particular genus develops a seed and fruit which in combination has proved, to the producer of tree seedlings, to be notoriously difficult to germinate, with consistent results, at any reasonable level of productivity. These species must constitute, collectively, one of the most intractable of the more commonly grown subjects to understand and to determine the dormancy controls within the seed. Under natural conditions the seeds of all species do not normally germinate until the second spring after the seeds have been dispersed and even then germination is incomplete and further response occurs spasmodically over several years until all the remaining viable seeds have germinated. This may take up to eight years.

As a general rule the plants of this genus produce regular, frequent and abundant crops of fruits. In good years virtually all the fruits contain at least one viable seed and often two. 'Off' years do occur as a result of untoward climatic variations but no pattern would appear to exist and in this situation all the fruits, at the extreme, may be void but more usually a proportion of the fruits contain viable seeds. It is therefore very necessary to check each parent tree annually in order to assess productivity. This is easily accomplished by a simple cutting test.

The seedlings are generally required for natural plantings or as rootstocks for working the varieties, various hybrids and small quantities of the alien species. Thus the variety of species which are raised from seed is fairly limited.

Continental sources usually offer seed of *'T. vulgaris'* for rootstock

purposes and in practice this is often *T. platyphyllos,* regularly seedlings of
the hybrid *T. x europea* and sometimes *T. cordata.* The most suitable species
for rootstock production is probably *T. platyphyllos* for the limited range of
hybrids and varieties which are offered by the British nurseryman. Other
species can realistically be raised from seed with success and include *T.
cordata, T. japonica, T. mongolica, T. petiolaris* and *T. tomentosa*: it is
quite feasible to locate mature fruiting specimens of these fairly easily,
although the frequency of seed production in *T. mongolica* and *T.
tomentosa* is usually more spasmodic.

The problem of this genus then is not in the availability of seed, but that
otherwise good samples of seed fail to germinate successfully; often even
after sophisticated artificial methods of breaking dormancy. In consequence
seedling appearance is erractic.

The causes of dormancy are due to the presence of an impermeable seed
coat, and the occurrence of a conventional embryo dormancy requiring a
period of chilling to overcome it. The picture is further complicated by the
fact that the impermeability of the seedcoat is attributable to two different
conditions, the seed possesses a normal hard seedcoat but externally the
pericarp develops into a tough and resilient coat which is also impermeable.
It is this combination of seedcoat characteristics which causes the variations
in delay to germination, as both require extensive decomposition before
water will pass through successfully. In any particular sample the effect of
each component may not be standard and each has to be treated on its own
merits if an acid digestion is to be undertaken. Each parent tree may produce
a different pattern which itself may vary marginally from year to year.

Various techniques have been used to overcome this dormancy problem
and the following two have proved most successful:—

(i) Using seed which has previously been dry stored, the sample is
stratified at high temperatures for at least 16 to 20 weeks and this is followed
by a period of chilling for a similar period. High temperatures such as will
occur in a warm glasshouse or polythene house with diurnal fluctuations
between 10° and 30°C have proved most effective.

This technique will usually produce a minimum of 25% germination,
but often more.

(ii) Acid digestion is more successful if carried out correctly: but it
involves the use of Nitric Acid for decomposing the tough outer pericarp
followed by Sulphuric Acid for etching the conventional inner hard seedcoat.
The seed subsequently requires to be imbibed and is then chilled for 16 weeks
at 1°C.

It is suggested that seeds of *T. americana,* at least, have a partially
immature embryo (Barton 1934) and if this is a common characteristic it may
account for the greater success attributable to the warm stratification
treatment.

The most successful and least troublesome method of overcoming the
problem appears to be the simple expedient of avoiding it, by collecting the
fruits 'green' and sowing straight away to avoid further drying. This
superficially appears to be quite simple but real success is governed by the
ability to discern the correct stage at which embryo development and food

storage is complete and then allying this to a readily and visually observable condition of fruit development. It is impractical to suggest particular dates for collection as all the species mature at different times and that this stage is variable annually. However, the fruits do change colour from green to a buff or brown colour and this phase occurs relatively rapidly once it commences; fortunately this change makes a fairly useful reference point. Bailey (1961) suggests, on his evidence developed from North American conditions, that collection and sowing the fruits as they turn colour induces germination the following spring; but his subject, *T. americana,* may not develop such an intractable seedcoat and autumn soil temperatures may remain warmer for a longer period than in the British Isles: similar treatment practiced in the United Kingdom on necessarily different species has not produced the same success. British experience does however suggest that collection at a substantially earlier phase, while the fruits are still green, will prove much more successful. It would appear that by collecting the fruits some 3 to 4 weeks before they turn colour, useful results can be obtained. However, this period is not easy to anticipate without experience; as a rule of thumb, the fruits are not ready until one can only just cut into the seed with a pocket knife or tough thumb nail, but this in itself is a very personal and subjective judgement.

Perhaps one of the greater problems which causes such delayed germination in this genus is the degree to which the embryo desiccates during the process of ripening, to such an extent that imbibition does not occur readily without prolonged soaking and so even seeds in which the seedcoat barriers have been removed will not necessarily respond to the cold temperature treatment because the embryo has not sufficiently imbibed. This situation further reiterates the significance of the early collection of seed and the arresting of further drying of the seed and its embryo.

The fruits are sown without delay to prevent any further drying and are broadcast to achieve a population of some 200+ seedlings per square metre, although this density could be increased by 25 per cent for less vigorous subjects such as *T. mongolica.* The fruits should be firmed into the seedbed to ensure moisture availability and are then covered to maintain good aeration as the fruit still has to be decomposed. Accurate populations are difficult to achieve because of the uncertainity of germination percentages from otherwise sound seed. Experience will eventually bring some exactitude but should germination rates prove excessive then the crop may need to be thinned. Seedlings of all *Tilia* species appear to be remarkably healthy and vigorous in the seedbed but the soft rapid growth does prove prone to aphid infestation, however routine seedbed sprays should control the problem.

These notes merely reiterate the uncertainties of other writers and although the experience and indications outlined above do suggest various avenues of approach they should only be treated as guide lines. Each propagator must determine a suitable technique within his own experiences and under his own particular circumstances.

FURTHER READING

Baily, C.V. (1961) 'Early collection and immediate sowing increase germination of Basswood seeds' Tree Plant. Notes *46*:27.
Barton, L.V. (1934) 'Dormancy in Tilia Seeds', Contrib. Boyce Thompson Inst. *6*:69.

The hemlocks are a relatively small group of conifers allied to both the spruces *(Picea)* and the Silver Firs *(Abies)*. In general they are tall stately trees and succeed reasonably well in the climate of the British Isles. There are about ten species which are distributed virtually all across North America and into Asia as far as the Himalayas, and in general all are hardy.

The flowers are produced during the early spring just prior to the onset of growth and the male and female flowers are produced on separate branches. The cones mature in the one season and are small, leathery brown in colour, pendulous and remain attached to the tree for most of the winter after the seeds have been dispersed in the autumn.

The cones should be collected just prior to opening and with a little warmth will open so that the seeds can be shaken out. The seeds are very small and light, and are produced in abundance. The seeds are fairly tolerant of drying and can be stored dry, however, this should not imply drying any more than is necessary for extraction or levels of viability will decline rapidly. Best storage appears to be achieved by dry storage in a sealed jar at low temperatures (3°C) and under these conditions viability can be maintained for several years.

As is common in this group of conifers seed production is periodic and good seed crops only occur about once every three years. In general all the species of Hemlock exhibit some dormancy in the embryo of the seed. Some samples of seed however show no dormancy condition although most samples have a proportion of the seeds which possess an embryo dormancy requiring a period of cold temperature before germination can occur. A period of chilling is not, therefore, essential for the crop to be obtained, but if the samples are sown sufficiently early to receive chilling then both the level and rate of germination are markedly improved. Autumn or winter sowing of the seed is therefore an essential feature of a good seedling stand production system. The seed should be sown broadcast, firmed in and covered so that a population of about 500 per square metre is obtained. As the seed size is so small, the field factor should be assessed on the basis of a high loss rate prior to germination.

The seedlings are susceptible to various 'damping off' conditions and routine sprays just prior to and after crop emergence are an important aspect of the successful production of these species. Various authorities recommend that the seedlings should be shaded in their first growing season as high light intensity can be damaging, however, in Britain it is probable that on balance the crop is better left unshaded.

Species	Average	Seedcount ,000s/kg Author
T. canadensis	270	
T. chinensis		500
T. diversifolia		
T. heterophylla	600	600

ULMUS

The native English Elm; so common in the British hedgerow until the advent of the current, virulent epidemic of Dutch Elm disease; is characterised by its inability to produce fertile seed and its incredible propensity to spread by suckers. Seedling trees for use as rootstocks for the various hybrids and varieties are therefore normally derived by sowing seed of the Wych Elm — *U. glabra.* Although the continental relative of our own native does produce seed and is variously offered as *U. camperstris* or *U. carpinifolia,* it is not the most successful plant for rootstock use.

Most Elms are late winter/early spring flowering and mature their seeds in midsummer. Dispersal occurs at this season and germination is virtually immediate. A few north american Elms flower at more conventional seasons with an autumn dispersal and embryo dormancy.

It is therefore important with *U. glabra* to collect the seed prior to dispersal so that the seed is not lost and viability does not decline with drying, in addition to the necessity for obtaining early germination and the production of an adequately mature seedling by leaf-fall. For this reason it is also prudent to advance collection into the 'green' stage so that a longer growing season can be developed. Experience has shown that much improved stands, both in terms of numbers and vigour has been achieved with this technique.

Assuming that with experience it is possible to postulate the time of dispersal in a particular season then the time of collection can be advanced as much as three weeks prior to this stage.

It is important when sowing fresh seed at this season (early June) to ensure that germination is not delayed or prevented by drying of the seedbed, regular spraying over the seedbeds is an essential factor of production.

When dealing with seed in the 'green' condition it is relatively easy to determine viable seed as the central portion is firm and plump. The proportion of viable seeds varies markedly from year to year and appears to reflect particular climatic conditions in the late winter to spring period, i.e. after fertilisation.

VIBURNUM

The genus Viburnum consists of a large and diverse group of shrubs which are found over most areas of the north temperate regions of the world. An extensive and varied selection of species, hybrids and varieties are cultivated in the British Isles and the great majority of these are propagated vegetatively — some readily and some with difficulty. Seed propagation on a large scale is only practiced on a limited range, the native species *V. lantana* and *V. opulus,* and the evergreen *V. rhytidophyllum.* On the North American continent however, a very much wider range of species are commonly propagated by seed both for natural as well as horticultural purposes. Small quantities of these alien species are occasionally propagated by seed in Britain, but the difficulties and uncertainties of achieving success have often deterred would-be producers. It is also the normal practice in this country only to offer selected, vegetatively propagated forms of a species for garden purposes.

The fruit of all species of Viburnum is a one seeded drupe which is produced during a normal growing season and is usually dispersed in the autumn, however, the fruits of many winter and early flowering types are matured soon after midsummer.

The problems of seed propagation in this genus are chiefly associated with the varied types and combinations of dormancy controls which are encountered in many of the species. At the simplest extreme only an embryo dormancy requiring a period of chilling is developed as occurs in *V. nudumn, V. scabrellum* and *V. sieboldii.* In other species the process is complicated further by the development of a hard seedcoat condition which in nature delays germination until the second season after dispersal.

Perhaps the most unusual and complex condition found in the genus is the existence of epicotyl dormancy, which under natural circumstances delays germination until the second spring after dispersal. During the first growing season the radicle emerges, as it requires no chilling pre-treatment to permit its emergence, and the plumule (shoot) emerges in the second spring after it has been chilled: this condition is also often associated with the development of some degree of hard seedcoat.

If conventional, extracted and dried seed is bought in from commercial sources, the seedcoat condition will be fully developed and a period of warm stratification — albeit relatively short — is required to affect its elimination, alternatively summer sowing will achieve the same end: this approach also allows the emergence of the radicle subsequently in those species exhibiting epicotyl dormancy.

Should it be possible for the propagator to collect his own seed, then early collection will provide an opportunity to avoid these dormancy controls and allow germination in the first spring after sowing. If the berries are collected at a sufficiently immature stage so that the hardness of the seedcoat is only partially developed, then the soil temperatures of late summer and autumn will be sufficient for any decomposition which is necessary, together with the development and emergence of the radicle if embryo dormancy is the case. In both cases adequate chilling of the embryos will occur over winter and germination will be expected in the spring.

The advantage of applying this system is that not only do the seeds have to survive for a much shorter period but as less food reserve is consumed, the seedling has a greater food reserve on which to start at germination. Thus bigger and more vigorous seedlings are produced.

The only real problem then is determining at what stage the berries can be collected without detriment to the seed maturation, i.e. when embryo development and stored food reserves are complete. The only species which has been assessed by the author is *V. lantana*, in this subject the berries change colour from orange to red and then finally to black: collection during the red stage has proved suitable and in the southern half of England this can be done in August and early September. The berries must be extracted as soon as is possible to prevent any further maturation of the seed and subsequently they must be prevented from drying to prevent enhancing any hard seededness — this is easily achieved by maceration, marginal fermentation and the flotation of the detritus followed by immediate sowing.

When collecting berries it is important that the seeds are extracted at an 159 early stage, as keeping the berries in bulk causes rapid heating which may materially influence the viability of the sample.

It would appear thus, that the problems of germinating seeds of Viburnum are relatively easily overcome; however, success may very well depend on knowing which species develop which particular dormancy controls and this information at present appears to be lacking. However, local collection and late summer sowing would appear to work for most species regardless of their dormancy situation under normal conditions.

The treatment of the hard seedcoat condition with sulphuric acid digestion is not of value as the hard coat is usually thin and brittle and responds readily to warm stratification. Acid digestion may well do more harm than good.

If seed is only available from commercial sources then it would seem that summer sowing or stratification is the only feasible proposition for all species as a general rule.

The seeds should be sown quite conventionally to produce a population of about 300 seedlings per metre: they do not suffer from any particular problems in the seedbed provided routine operations are maintained.

Species	Seedcount ,000s/kg
V. acerifolium	13.0
V. alnifolium	12.0
V. dentatum	28.0
V. lantana	22.0
V. lentago	8.5
V. opulus	14.0
V. rhytidophyllum	43.8
V. trilobum	13.0

Variations from source to source and year to year may be as much as ± 30%.

REFERENCES AND ASSOCIATED READING

Barton, L.V. (1958) 'Germination and seedling production in species of Viburnum', Proc. Plant Prop. Soc. *8*:126.
Giersbach, J. (1937) 'Germination and seedling production of species of Viburnum', Contrib. Boyce Thompson Inst. *9*(2):79.
Hess, C.W.M. Jr. (1973) 'Seedling Propagation of difficult species' Proc. Int. Plant Prop. Soc. *20*:378.
Knowles, R.H. and S. Zalik (1958) 'Dormancy in *Vibrunum trilobum'*, Can. J. Bot. *36*:561.
McMillan Browse, P.D.A. (1970) 'Notes on the Propagation of Viburnums', Proc. Int. Plant Prop. Soc. *20*:378.

VITIS

This genus of non clinging vines are not widely grown in the British Isles
although several varieties, requiring vegetative propagation, of the Grape

Vine *(V. vinifera)* are offered in the nursery trade. A number of species are offered by those nurserymen growing the more unusual subjects but under these circumstances propagation is usually vegetative by cuttings because of the relatively small numbers required and the desire to propagate superior forms. The only subject produced in sufficient quantities to warrant seed production is *V. coignetiae* although the seedling population is often variable both in leaf shape and intensity of autumnal colouring.

Fruit is rarely produced by *V. coignetiae,* in the British Isles but occasionally in hot summers crops are produced and good samples of seed can be extracted. The fruit is a fleshy grape containing up to four seeds which are relatively small in relation to the bulk of the skin and flesh of the grape but because of this are relatively easy to extract by maceration, agitation in water followed by decanting off the waste sequentially.

Seed of *V. coignetiae* is usually available from most commercial seed houses, continental suppliers obtaining their seed from sources in southern Europe. Seed of *V. amurensis* and *V. riparia* are also offered, although less commonly, and come usually from sources in North America.

The seeds can be just dried and stored in sealed jars at cool temperatures (below 5°C) when viability can be maintained without undue loss for about two years.

The seeds have an embryo dormancy but some germination can be obtained from spring sowing albeit slowly. Good crops will only be achieved by winter chilling prior to germination. This will be produced either by autumn sowing or by stratification over winter followed by spring sowing.

Seed should be broadcast on a prepared seedbed and covered with grit in the conventional fashion. As the seed is fairly small and thin coated, seedbed losses may be fairly high so that the field factor must be modified in the light of this experience. A population of 300 to 350 seedlings per square metre will produce reasonable sized seedling for potting on, larger seedlings can be produced at lower densities but they may be too large to handle reasonably.

The seedlings of *V. coignetiae* especially tend to exhibit limited juvenile characters, in this species the leaves tend to be rounded, small and with a toothed edge.

Seeds of *V. coignetiae* are fairly small, about 35,000 per kg are thin coated and easily damaged and rough handling either at extraction or sowing should be avoided. The seed sample is usually reliable and of good quality, as unsound seed will usually have been floated off in the extraction process.

Seedlings of Vine species will inevitably be at risk to the various Mildews but routine sprays over the seedbed area should contain any outbreak. Pests are not normally a problem. Frost many cause damage although Vines tend to germinate and emerge fairly late in the season.

FURTHER READING

Flemion, F. (1937) 'After-ripening at 5°C favours germination of grape seeds', Contrib. Boyce Thompson Inst. *9*(1):7.

WISTERIA

Except in very hot seasons it is unusual for Wisteria to set seed in the United Kingdom. Under normal circumstances seed is readily available from the commercial seedhouses, who are able to collect abundant quantities in southern Europe.

Wisteria is not normally grown from seed to produce a specimen for garden planting as it take many years before flowers are produced and these are often of inferior quality.

Wisteria seedlings are required, however, for use as rootstocks for the desirable forms. Although seeds of most *Wisteria* species and varieties are offered, all of these are compatible with *Wisteria sinensis* and it is only necessary to produce seedlings of this one species for use as a rootstock.

A well grown one year old seedling provides the most suitable rootstock and will have a hypocotyl diameter of 6-10 mm. This will only be achieved if the seedbed is of high quality, the plant population is correct and a warm site is available for early germination so that a long growing season is developed.

The seed is sown in the spring after being received in the early part of the year. Prior to sowing the seed is soaked in warm water for twenty-four hours in order to encourage quicker germination, a few seeds do not swell and these are discarded, the remainder should produce 100 per cent germination. The seeds are space sown at a population of 400 per square metre by pushing into a lightly prepared seedbed. Although the seed can be sown broadcast it is easier to sow in rows across the seedbed at a spacing of 8 cm by 3 + cm.

Germination is normally even and rapid as soil temperatures increase in the spring. A good size is achieved if water is not limited and adequate top dressing or liquid feed is provided.

Pests and diseases are not usually of any significance although occasionally Red Spider Mite does develop to nuisance levels.

The storage of Wisteria seed is not a problem for a year or so if the seed is kept dry and in a cool airy place. However, as seed is available from seedhouses annually the necessity for storage should not be important.

Seed obtained from southern European sources of *W. sinensis* has proved reasonably consistent in size from year to year, providing a count of about 1600 seeds per kilogram with a less than a 5 per cent discard after soaking, although samples of up to 2,400 per kilogram have been recorded in occasional years.

As the seedling population is often variable in vigour it should be reckoned that only about 60 per cent will produce the required grade — possibly a further 10 per cent being larger.

The inexperienced grower should not be too perturbed by an apparent paucity of top growth as below ground development is nevertheless vigorous in this seedling year.

ZELKOVA

The current epidemic of Dutch Elm Disease has led to a considerable discussion of possible tree species for the replacement of Elms in the countryside. One of the genera which has been suggested as being a feasible substitute is this small genus of closely allied trees: of which two species — *Z. carpinifolia* from the Caucasus and *Z. serrata* from the Far East —have proved amenable and successful in cultivation in this country, although the latter has problems in relation to spring radiation frost damage during its early years.

Seeds of both species can normally be readily obtained from conventional commercial sources although *Z. serrata* is, strangely, more often offered. Because of the drying of the seed which is usually associated with the handling of commercial samples the viability of samples can be very varied and it is essential to monitor this factor for each sample in some detail.

The seed is dispersed during the autumn and the embryo requires only a relatively limited period of chilling to remove any germination controls.

Few problems are encountered in the seedbed provided sowing and husbandry are carried out in the standard manner.

Best germination results are achieved using freshly collected seed, this can be collected 'green' in September and sown immediately. The only problem is in actually collecting the seed, which can best be obtained by cutting the twiggy branchlets and stripping the seeds after a limited period of drying.

Species	Seedcount in ,000s/kg
Z. serrata	93.0

The main problem associated with seedling production is obtaining a sufficiently dense population (c. 250 per square metre) to prevent the forking of the stems low down, which appears to be a natural habit or the response to even limited frost damage.